SISTER WIFE

Also by John Gates

BRIGHAM'S DAY

SISTER WIFE

John Gates

Walker & Company New York

For Dave and Ginny

First published in the United States of America in 2001 by
Walker Publishing Company, Inc.

Published simultaneously in Canada by Fitzhenry and Whiteside,
Markham, Ontario L3R 4T8

Library of Congress Cataloging-in-Publication Data

Gates, John.
    Sister wife / John Gates.
        p. cm.
    ISBN 0-8027-3363-8 (hardcover)
    1. Mormon women--Fiction. 2. Mormons--Fiction. 3. Utah--Fiction.
    I. Title

PS3557.A875 S57 2001
813'.54--dc21

                                                          2001017872

Series design by M. J. DiMassi

Printed in the United States of America

2   4   6   8   10   9   7   5   3   1

Acknowledgments

As always, there are those scholars and researchers who blaze a trail for their fiction-writing counterparts. In this case, it has been Martha Sonntag Bradley, author of *Kidnapped from That Land: The Government Raids on the Short Creek Polygamists*; Richard N. and Joan K. Ostling's *Mormon America*, and Richard S. Van Wagoner for his book *Mormon Polygamy: A History*.

I also want to thank Michael Seidman, my editor, for his experience and guidance; the legal expertise of Ralph Dellapiana of the Salt Lake Public Defenders and Michael Wims of the Utah Attorney General's Office; the suggestions of Nanette Williams and Melissa Winblood and, of course, Gabe and Ana and Phil.

Despite existing scriptural authorization for it, polygamy has been officially outlawed by the Church of Jesus Christ of Latter-day Saints, and it forms no part of present-day Mormon beliefs or teaching.

Further, the town of New Ammon, Utah, and its fundamentalist religious sect, the United Order of the Christ Brethren, do not exist; however, the practice of plural marriage—the Principle—does flourish in many parts of this country.

Finally, with the exception of Poetry Bob and Spooky Floyd, all characters in this novel are fictitious.

Part I

The descent beckons,
As the ascent beckoned.
—WILLIAM CARLOS WILLIAMS

1

A FTER Brig Bybee bought the Piute Villa, the odd, decaying tepee motel on the outskirts of Kanab, Utah, he was solemnly informed by the previous owners, Odell and Sytha Watson, that a dog, a mascot of sorts, also came with the property. They smiled apologetically at Bybee, then at each other, and told him that the creature's name was Floyd—simply Floyd—a harmless mutt that had wandered into their lives six months before and stayed.

But as the two climbed into their car, mumbling their good-byes, Bybee thought he overheard Odell refer to the dog as "Spooky Floyd," and then they were gone, each of them cheerfully fluttering a hand out a side window as they drove off the graveled lot and onto the Long Valley Highway, disappearing into the canyon lands to the north.

It took Bybee just three days at the motel, a place he had lived in a year earlier during the Parks murder case, to discover how the dog had earned his adjective. Spooky Floyd did not look or act—or even smell—like an ordinary dog. He was a quiet yellow-eyed thing with a broken tail, who crept about the tow-

3

ering cement tepees like a cat, never barking or howling or digging holes or chasing cars, never displaying the usual, panting recklessness of other dogs. Instead, he had a quiet interest in things human, an unsettling absorption in human activities, their condition, their curious affairs. And so he always watched those goings-on, usually from the other side of the glass door of the office tepee, and although he had two good eyes, he kept the side of his face pressed against the glass so that only one eye watched it all, observing. . . .

It was in this way, near midnight, in the middle of August, that Spooky Floyd watched Bybee struggle with a computer in the office, the human cursing the machine, clumsily poking at the keyboard with one finger as he squinted into the monitor.

"God *damn*, I hate these things!"

Spooky Floyd did not move, but one yellow eye shifted, slightly, from Bybee's face to the keyboard, then back again, trying to understand it all, make sense of it, see what the man would do next.

"The hell with it!"

Bybee angrily punched one last key, then threw his hands up, palms outward, in surrender, and pushed back a tangle of black hair from his forehead. His dark eyes were tired, and he looked helplessly at the dog, then walked to the door and bent down and tapped on the thick glass.

"Enough, Floyd," he said. He pushed his wire-rimmed glasses up along his nose, then made a crossing movement with his hands, like an umpire at home plate. "You jinx me. Go to bed. All the other dogs in town are in bed."

But Spooky Floyd would not move; instead he kept the side of his face pressed against the glass, his eye twitching, rotating in its socket as it watched Bybee's hands, then scanned the rest of him: his loafers, the gray slacks, the maroon knit shirt that had a tiny tepee embroidered in white over the left breast and, under it, in script, the name *Brig.*

"Lord, Floyd."

Bybee slowly opened the door, forcing the dog backward, then walked outside, the tiny bell tied to the handle jingling as he went by. The tepee rooms—twelve in all, counting the office—sat tall and white in the weak moonlight, about half of them occupied, shiny rental cars parked alongside. Overhead a monstrous arrowhead, rimmed in red neon and with the words "Piute Villa" in the center, revolved in slow circles, creaking like an old windmill. Beyond that, the town was quiet, darkened, most of it asleep, and the air was cool and fresh and filled with the smell of sage.

"C'mon."

With the dog reluctantly following, Bybee walked across the motel lot toward a circle of plaster Indians—white, ghostly things, full-size and propped upright by steel rods, some with missing hands or arms or noses, one with its head gone, another with a blackened hole at its crotch. As he passed the Indians, he heard a noise behind the statues, a rustling somewhere in a darkened corner of the lot, near a gate in the rear, and he stopped. A rabbit suddenly darted out and sprinted across the gravel, and Spooky Floyd simply glanced at it.

Bybee continued on and finally stopped at the eastern edge of the lot, near Duffin Judd's Wampum Mart, where, in a stand of willow trees, sat another tepee, a smaller one, a dog tepee. It was something Brig had built for the animal, four feet high, made from wood and chicken wire and rich mortar, painted white and even decorated with some of the same nonsensical symbols that were found on the larger versions: six-pointed stars, half moons, a cow's skull, even the pi sign. After a moment the dog, its broken tail dragging along the gravel, slouched into his tiny tepee and lay down.

"Good night," Bybee said.

Bybee remained crouched there, half expecting the dog to growl *"g'night "* in return, faintly curious about where the animal had come from, what sort of strange, tormented life he had lived before settling in at the Piute Villa. The motel was a place that had become a refuge, he guessed, a sanctuary, safe from the nameless cruelty that had driven the poor creature here.

After a few minutes, Bybee finally got up, turned around, and yelled—almost screamed—when he saw her. She stood in the middle of the plaster Indians, unmoving, another statue, an apparition in a dirty white dress, long-sleeved and buttoned to her throat, the hem extending to her ankles. Her hair was long and white and dirty looking, and it dripped in twisted tendrils around her face and shoulders, halfway down to her waist. Draped over one shoulder was a purse, a large brown leather affair that hung against her hip.

Bybee could feel his heart thumping in his chest, and his right hand began to shake. He took a tentative step forward, and then bent down, stooping, as if he were peering through a low doorway. Behind him he heard Spooky Floyd rustling about, and he knew that the dog had crept to the triangular door of his tepee and was watching.

The woman remained still, her hands clutched together under her bosom, staring ahead. The giant arrowhead squealed as it slowly turned, casting a rhythmic red glow across her, and finally, as if the light warmed her, melted her, she moved her head slightly and, by degrees, lowered her hands.

"Are you Mr. Bybee?" she said. Her voice was weak and thin, barely audible.

"Yes," Bybee said. "I am."

He took another slow step forward, the gravel crunching loudly under his shoe, and then another, until he came to within ten feet of the woman, where he could finally see her in the pulsating red light.

"Oh, Lord Jesus!" he said.

One half of her face was bruised and swollen, the eye only a black slit, and dried blood was caked around her nose and mouth and splotched down her neck and across the front of her dress. The other eye, bleak and staring, closed slowly, then opened again, and she moved her dried lips.

"Are you Mr. Bybee?"

Bybee quickly walked up to the woman and took her by the arm, just above the elbow, holding her, steadying her, and bent closer to her face, feeling her breath as it came in frantic bursts, smelling the hot, scared stink of her.

"Yes, I'm Brig Bybee. Who are you?"

The woman tilted her head back, revealing deep, ugly welts on her neck, and then lowered it, as in prayer, and said nothing.

"What's your name?" Bybee said.

The woman kept her head down, her hair curtained across her face, and continued to stare at the ground.

「"Ma'am—"

"Chenoya," she finally said, and she raised her head.

Bybee blinked at her; the name was familiar—too familiar—and he stooped again and peered into that battered face.

"Chenoya what?" he said. "What is your last name?"

The woman coughed, suddenly, an explosive spray of mucus and spittle, some of it splattering Bybee's face, and he drew back and wiped it away.

"My name is Chenoya Whiting," she said, and the one open eye glared at Bybee, challenging him.

He felt the heat in his scalp begin anew, dripping down through his body, and he put his quaking right hand behind his back. He knew who she was; he had memorized their names, their real names and their "celestial" names. As if to verify it all, he leaned back and stared at her rustic pioneer dress, the heavy boots, the plain, nineteenth-century look of her, in sepia, a daguerreotype come to life.

"He calls you Mercy, doesn't he?"

The woman nodded slowly, and then the one open eye closed and she half collapsed against Bybee, falling into him, and he reflexively caught her with both hands and held her to him.

"Merciful Christs!" she whispered.

Quickly Bybee bent at the knees and lifted her, one arm under her back and the other under her legs, like a bride on her wedding night, in her bloodied wedding dress, and carried her toward the brightly lighted office, her big purse still dangling from her arm. She was of average height, bosomy and full-bodied, but she felt light in his arms, like something made of glue and gauze and shredded paper, a flimsy toy.

At the office he inched the glass door ajar with his fingers, then swung it wide open with his foot and clumsily bumped inside, the woman's weathered boots jangling the tiny bell as they passed. He maneuvered between the counter and a coffee table strewn with tourist fare—free maps and brochures and discount coupons—and struggled into the rear of the office, where there was a wooden desk and chair and a simple green sofa. Carefully he lowered the woman to the sofa, then straightened her legs and arms and, finding a plastic cushion on the chair, placed it gently under her head.

She lay unmoving, except for the trembling of her bruised lips and the rising and falling of her breasts, large and full, pushing against the torn dress. Bybee bent and tenderly pushed back a tangle of her hair—whitish blond, almost silvery—from her beaten face.

"Oh, Lord," Bybee said, and then he bent down close to her. "I'm going to get you a doctor."

She opened her eye, and one hand rose slowly, hovering, and then found his arm and gripped it tightly. "No," she said.

"But you're hurt . . . bad. You need help—medical help. I'll call Doc Lundquist." Bybee suddenly pictured the man: pale and thin, stumbling in his pajamas toward the bleating telephone, struggling to put on his thick glasses. "I'll wake him up. He'll come."

"No," the woman said again. Her voice, although still faint, was tinged with panic, and her hand gripped Bybee's arm even tighter. "Father will know."

Bybee looked at the woman's tiny white hand, scratched and bloodied, the fingernails bitten short, and then lightly covered it with his own. He knew who "Father" was—Father of the Faithful, the One Mighty and Strong, the Grand Seer and Revelator . . . the Big Plig. He knew who almost all of them were at New Ammon.

"You're Rampton Crowe's wife, aren't you?" Bybee said. "One of them, anyway."

"Yes."

"You're . . . " He hesitated, thinking. The prosecution team had numbered them, ranked all six of them by seniority, an inventory, one investigator even inventing a childish schoolyard ditty as a way of remembering the order. *"First came Amity, a cohab calamity . . ."*

"You're six," Bybee said. "The newest wife."

"Yes," she said again.

She slowly rotated her hand until her dirty fingers—strong and rough, like a workingman's—intertwined with his, and then she pulled, urging him closer.

"Father will know," she said. Her voice cracked, and she coughed. "He will find me."

"No," Bybee said, and he squeezed her hand. "He won't."

But he knew the woman had a right to be frightened. When Faith—Roma Ann McCallister, wife number two—had run several months ago, Crowe's Blood Disciples had been dispatched within hours, the police had discovered, with orders to track her down and to bring her back, maybe to kill her. Now, Bybee knew, here was a witness who could probably verify the cohabitation, the multiple marriages, all the ragged children of the "lambing ground," as it was called—but it was somehow too easy.

"How did you know my name?" Bybee said. He leaned forward so he could see all of her face. "How did you know to find me?"

Mercy slowly turned her head toward him. "Someone at New Am' told me."

Bybee stared hard at that poor face. Nearly thirty years of confronting clients and witnesses and opposing attorneys— even judges—had honed his ability to detect the play-acting, to sense the evasion, to know, simply, when another human being was lying. But it was always—and only—found in their eyes, the barely perceptible shifting, the quick glance aside, the sudden, vacant dimming. Here, however, there was nothing, only one gray orb sunken in a mound of brutalized flesh. But it was all so sudden and so violent, so real. He *did* believe her.

"I'll help you," Bybee said. "I will. But you need a doctor, a—"

"No!" Again the panic rose in her voice. "The doctor will call Father."

"Ma'am—"

"Father knows everyone."

Bybee exhaled slowly, then turned and walked to the front of the office to a water cooler. He filled a paper cone—the same type he once considered distributing as a promotional gimmick, inverted, with "Piute Villa" printed on the side—and walked back to the couch, offering it to her.

Slowly the woman swung her legs from the sofa and, by degrees, sat upright, self-consciously smoothing her torn dress and pushing her greasy hair back. She took the cone of water and sat still, as though she were at a drawing room party—prim and mannered, heavy boots flat on the floor, her purse beside them, her hands folded around the paper cup, her wretched, ravaged face slightly thrust forward. After a moment she took a sip of the water and, like any bored guest, looked idly about her, studying the strange sloping walls of the tepee, the painted cement floor, the Indian throw rugs, and in the rear, a cardboard box full of severed plaster arms and legs, one white hand jutting straight up, as though it were waving . . . or signaling for help.

Bybee walked to the side of the office, to a tiny bathroom that contained only a sink and a toilet, and looked in a cabinet for any first aid supplies. There were none, not even Band-Aids or a bottle of peroxide, so he took a white washcloth from its ring on the slanted wall, soaked it in warm water, and returned to the woman. He took her small chin in his hand, and while she tensed, flinching and, at times, jerking her head away, he dabbed at her wounds and cleaned the dried blood and dirt from her face, repairing it the best he could.

And all the while, as he closely examined the awful damage to her, he tried to imagine how any human being could have done such a thing to her, how the beating was inflicted, when and how, with what instruments, by whom.

"Crowe did this to you, didn't he?" Bybee finally said. He

quickly returned to the bathroom and rinsed out the cloth, and came back to her. "Your husband." He laughed, involuntarily, a short, derisive snort. *"Father."*

Mercy had her head slightly bent back, looking at the vortex of blackness above, the nonexistent tepee ceiling, and she slowly lowered her face and turned toward him, allowing him to continue to sponge her face.

"Yes." She looked past Bybee at the office door, where Spooky Floyd had now positioned himself again, the side of his yellow face pressed against the glass. "And he will come here. He and the Disciples will—"

"Why did he beat you?"

She watched the dog for a moment, worried, then faced Bybee.

"No," she said.

Bybee stopped cleaning her face. "I can help you, but you have to be honest with me."

Mercy raised her head, proudly, almost defiantly. "I slept with another man."

Bybee nodded; he had expected just that. The reports had indicated that Crowe had similarly punished Patience, the half-Indian fourth wife, when she had been found naked in a bathtub with a man named Koyle Fenton, a Blood Disciple. Fenton had never been seen again.

"And the man you slept with," Bybee said. "What happened to him?"

Mercy tilted her face at a different, more severe angle, and in the wash of light from the scattering of bright lamps in the office, Bybee suddenly saw that, under the welts and bruises, the face was young, maybe twenty-five years old, and probably pretty, with its small nose, full lips, its young, cherubic roundness, its beaten innocence.

She slowly turned her head and looked for several moments at the box of plaster body parts, at an Indian's white, eyeless head lying on its side next to the extended arm.

And then she told him, quickly, in just five words.

Bybee actually felt the thin hairs on his neck and the back

part of his scalp move, as though someone were behind him, a phantom blowing its icy breath, taunting him, and he involuntarily shook his head. He had been trying criminal cases for almost thirty years now, and had represented some of the most depraved monsters on this planet, heard their horrendous, sickening stories, seen their grisly handiwork. And he had stoically faced it all, withstood it, clenched his teeth and accepted it, never flinching.

But the five half-whispered words he had just heard from this runaway plural wife chilled him, froze his soul unlike anything he had ever heard.

"Who?" Bybee finally said. He put the cloth aside and bent closer to her. "What was his name?"

Mercy looked at the man, then Spooky Floyd, nodding at him as though the animal already knew the answer. "Franklin Pugh," she said.

Again the tiny hairs on Bybee's neck stirred, and his stomach tightened. He had read the name; it surfaced often in the later reports, the most recent investigation, and his heart began pounding again.

"Ma'am," he said. "Do you know who I am?"

The woman looked confused. "You are Mr. Bybee."

"No—well, yes," Bybee said, and he shook his head, sending a tuft of black hair across his eyes. "I mean *what* I am. What my job is."

She looked around her, one finger pointing. "This," she said.

Bybee lifted the hair out of his face, took one long stride across the room, and retrieved the old-style oak chair at the desk and wheeled it close to the sofa, the tiny casters screeching across the floor. He sat down, his long legs splayed in front of him, his knees high, and leaned toward the woman.

"Yes, I own this place. I run it. But I'm also a lawyer, a criminal defense lawyer. But a few months ago, I was hired by the other side, by the government, as a special assistant attorney general, a temporary prosecutor." He stopped. A "hired gun" is what others in the profession would call him—*did* call him, actually, even to his face—but he knew she would not understand the expression. "I'm the chief prosecutor," he went on, "in a case that the state of Utah is bringing against your husband, against T. Rampton Crowe. He is—"

The woman's head jerked to the side. "The Principle!" she said. "I know."

Bybee nodded, slowly, then held his hands out, as though he were proving he held no concealed weapons, no lawyer's tricks. "Yes, the Principle." His voice suddenly seemed to die, to be swallowed up in the blackness above him. It *was* the Principle that must be prosecuted, more so than Crowe himself; it *was* the Principle that had become too visible, too laughable to some, too dangerous to others. It *was* the Principle that sat, viscous and vile and overpowering, in the middle of this state like a monstrous swamp, reeking of human suffering, of madness.

Now, in a matter of just a few minutes, a few words, all of that might be changed, the course of the prosecution altered. He looked at the severed white hand in the box, its chipped fingers curled as though it were motioning, urging him on.

"I want you to tell me exactly what you saw," he said. "What happened."

The woman dropped her head, as if in prayer again, and touched the fingers of her right hand to her darkened forehead. For a moment Bybee thought she was going to make the sign of the cross, like a Catholic facing the altar, confronting the everlasting disappointment of the priest, but then she raised her head.

"Why?"

"Because I'm—"

He stopped; he was coiled, tense, leaning so far forward in the old chair that he looked spring-loaded and cocked, ready to be released. As he had several times in the last month or two, he paused, inwardly surprised at how, after nearly three decades of fighting the government and its bullheaded, myopic prosecutors, he had so easily shifted loyalties and changed gears. Like all of his old opponents, he had taken up the same feverish, rabid hunt for a conviction and lengthy prison term —the "big pop." He had taken on the job temporarily, simply for the money, but he was nevertheless a prosecutor, and he had to think and act like one, at least temporarily.

"Because I'm supposed to know," Bybee said.

She leaned back into the sofa, the indifferent party guest again, looking slowly around her, and then drank from her cup, slowly, pausing after each swallow. When she was finished, she stared across the office at Spooky Floyd, who had not moved, the side of his face still flattened against the glass, the yellow eye bulging.

"That dog scares me," she said.

Bybee did not turn around. "Yeah, he scares me sometimes too," he said. "But he's harmless; he doesn't bite. Hell, he doesn't even bark." He waved his hand in the air, dismissing talk of the dog, and leaned toward the woman again, squinting into her face. "Ma'am . . . *Mercy*. I want you to tell me what you saw, everything."

Mercy continued to look past Bybee at Spooky Floyd, and when the dog finally drew away, when she had stared him down, she shifted her gaze to the hard, handsome face in front of her. In a low voice she told Bybee all that she had seen that night, beginning with the sounds of Crowe, of the screaming, then the shouting . . . then Franklin Pugh dragged naked into the muddy New Ammon road, bawling, pleading for his life. . . .

Her voice caught in the back of her throat, and she stopped and stared at a section of the cornerless wall where the Watsons had hung plastic spears, a bow and arrow, and, for whatever reason, a pair of rusted cavalry swords, crossed, real and lethal looking.

She turned back to Bybee and told him the rest of the story, of the screams, of she and Pugh being taken to the old cement water tank, of the whooping of the Blood Disciples, of Brother Griffity, and then of the appearance of Crowe, the quiet that descended in that cement tank . . . and then the vengeance, the violence, and Griffity, his T-shirt and beard and long hair splattered with blood, shrieking and laughing, hefted to the shoulders of the others.

Then, she said, the blood yelps stopped, and New Ammon,

the home of the United Order of the Christ Brethren, returned to its sleep as though nothing had happened.

When she had finished, Bybee felt sick, his stomach tight and churning, and he swallowed hard, several times, fighting back the nausea. He had just heard a firsthand account of one of the most nightmarish acts he could imagine.

"Lord God," Bybee said. His voice shook, and he discovered that he had been holding the woman's hand, tightly squeezing it, and he suddenly dropped it to her lap as though it were dripping with blood and gore.

Mercy began to cry, and as she did, almost as if on cue, a vehicle—a dark-colored van—drove into the Piute Villa's parking lot and stopped, its headlights on full bright, flooding the office with a blazing brilliance, a frozen explosion of white.

"Oh, Merciful Christs," she said.

Quickly, his long legs covering the office floor in three strides, Bybee moved to the front counter and reached below to find a baseball bat that he kept there. Several friends had advised him to keep a gun, loaded and ready, but he despised the things, believing that if he possessed a gun, one day he would have to use it. He hefted the bat; it was old and heavily varnished, one he had been presented with decades ago—in the 1960s—in Logan, at Utah State, and in the light, he could see engraved on the fat barrel some of the names of his old teammates: Tone Burgoyne, Farris Pratt, Foscarini, Smithson, Denton— all good athletes, all good men . . . and half of them dead, now.

He felt the solid, reassuring weight of the bat, then hid it behind the counter as he waited, breathing fast, squinting into the glare of the van's headlights. He had never used the bat; he had never been confronted with anything other than a disgruntled guest and, now and then, an addled hitchhiker who wandered in. But this, he knew, was different, and he moved his body back so that he would be able to swing the bat up and around easily, freely, staving in the skull of the first plig goon that charged him, then cocking again for the second. . . .

Suddenly the driver—a black, bobbing silhouette inside the

van—shifted gears, and the vehicle roared backward and spun around. As it pulled away, Bybee saw the California license plates and the jumble of luggage strapped atop the roof. It was another set of tourists—probably foreign, Germans more than likely—straggling in from the canyon lands in their rented vehicle, lost, using the Piute Villa, the last business on the western edge of town, as a convenient turnaround, as so many did.

He returned to the rear, still clutching the bat, and found Mercy cowering in one side of the office behind the desk, her hands knotted together under her breasts, the way he had first seen her outside with the plaster Indians. She was still crying, and with each sob her whole body seemed to shake, as though she were fevered, in the grip of a violent seizure.

Bybee lay the bat on the sofa and came up to her, taking her arm the way he had before. "It's okay . . . nothing. Just tourists."

But she was not comforted, not reassured, and she continued to cry, loudly now, the small office filled with the sound of her wailing, until Bybee gathered her to him. He awkwardly pressed her head under his chin, smelling the sweat and dirt in her hair, and then brought her close to him, into him, until he could feel her breasts swell against his chest with each sob.

"It's okay . . . Mercy," he said again, testing the name, wondering for an instant why he used her celestial name, Crowe's spiritual pseudonym.

For a minute or so he gently stroked her hair and the back of her neck, holding her more tightly, like a child, the way he used to hold his daughter, Brileena. The anguish streamed out of her, years of torment—maybe an entire lifetime—flowing from her, her soul draining itself in front of this stranger, in this strangest of places.

After a moment she relaxed and the sobbing subsided, and Bybee gradually drew back from her. Mucus bubbled at her nostrils, and she tried to sniff it back, then brought her hand across her face, smearing it.

Bybee took the damp cloth and walked to the bathroom, rinsed it out and returned, and found her standing next to the cluttered oak desk. She stared, her neck bent, at a framed photograph of a red-haired woman with blue eyes, dressed in jeans and a sleeveless yellow blouse, with earrings dangling at the side of her face. The woman in the photograph smiled into the camera, and behind her stretched a line of cliffs that bisected the picture horizontally by color, the upper half a deep, molten blue, the bottom a reddish orange.

"That's Zolene," Bybee said, and he stupidly held the wash-cloth out to the picture. "Zolene Swapp. She's my—" He hesitated; he was never certain what to call her, how to identify her, how to convey what she was to him without sounding adolescent or silly . . . or foolishly love-struck.

"Your girlfriend," Mercy said. She took the washcloth from Bybee, cleaned her face, then bent toward the photograph as though she were trying to smell it. "She's pretty."

"Yes," Bybee said, and he nodded, agreeing. "She's very pretty."

She continued to study the photograph. "Father says that I am pretty."

Bybee looked at her, at her savaged face, the swollen eye, the horrible, dark welts, and nodded again. "I'm sure you—" He stopped, realizing how clumsy the statement would be.

"Do you . . . live with her?" Mercy said.

He shook his head. "No. I live here, in town"—he waved his hand, pointing—"a few blocks over. Four hundred South. Zolene lives outside of town, in Johnson Canyon, in a house that—"

He suddenly drew himself up to his full, rangy, first base-man's height, the idea stiffening him, the purity of it straight-ening him like a jolt of electricity.

"Mercy," he said, bending back toward her, "you can stay in Zolene's house." He waved his hand again, excitedly pointing vaguely toward the east. "It's in a canyon, an orchard. It's hidden—*real* hidden. No one will know you're there. It's—" He stopped, his mind picturing what Zolene and her family called Lamb's house, so smothered by trees and vines, so secreted in perpetual shadow, that the few occasional visitors to Johnson Canyon—to Hell's Bellows—did not know the old house even existed. And certainly few people knew that he and Zolene, over the past year, had been restoring it, bringing it back to life, a new life.

"It's perfect," he finished.

Mercy looked at Bybee, then at the photograph of Zolene, as though seeking confirmation from her, or permission.

"Don't worry," Bybee said. "She's out of town for the next few days, on business, loans for the ranch. Her kids are in California for the summer—" He was talking rapidly, his breath short, and he suddenly waved his hand, erasing it all. "She won't mind." He smiled, imagining how Zolene's white face would cloud, her blue eyes fill with tears, when she saw this poor woman, heard of her suffering. "Believe me, she won't."

"I—"

"C'mon," Bybee said.

Before Mercy could say anything more, he took one of her hands and coaxed her—almost pulled her—to her feet, and as he did, the dirty, foul smell of her stung his nose again. "You can take a bath there . . . and rest."

Mercy stood, helpless, looking at Spooky Floyd, the red neon rhythmically glinting off his coat, and then gazed behind him, out to Center Street and the darkened cliffs beyond, barely visible, an ominous ridge of black, something heavy and crouched and waiting.

"Father will know," she said.

"No, he won't. No one will know."

As though Crowe and the Blood Disciples were watching them at that very moment, Bybee quickly moved around the office, snapping off the lamps, until they were in darkness, the only light coming from the computer monitor—and that just a dull, purplish glow.

"No one will know," he said again, then stopped, frozen in the blackened office. There was someone who should know, who must know: Tom Kendall at the Attorney General's office. He had to be apprised—and quickly—of the existence of this witness and this horrific new evidence, this dizzying turn of events.

Bybee bent toward the glowing computer monitor and read

the time in the lower right-hand corner, the only practical thing he ever used the damned machine for—an expensive clock. It was 12:33 A.M., too late to call, and so he decided he would phone first thing in the morning.

"Let's go," Bybee said.

He walked to the couch and retrieved Mercy's heavy purse, then guided her toward the door, one hand behind her back while the other made a shooing motion at the dog, who reluctantly moved a few feet away. Bybee urged her through the door, locked the office, and then hurriedly marched her across the lot, their feet loudly shuffling through the gravel, until they arrived at a battered 1979 Volkswagen bus parked to one side. It was green, with a rounded beige top, and had a white tepee painted on either side and, next to it the words "Piute Villa" inside an arrowhead, identical to the sign overhead.

Like an old-fashioned man on a date, Bybee opened the passenger door for Mercy, helped her inside, then clanged the door shut, ran around the front, and climbed into the driver's side. Within seconds the old, air-cooled engine clattered to life, the gears ground and caught, and Bybee piloted the rattling thing out to Center Street.

Back at the lot, Spooky Floyd walked slowly to the curb and watched as the green bus drove by the church, then disappeared into the heart of Kanab, past Big Joe's Junction, and was swallowed by the gloom. Still uncertain about it all, he shambled back to his tepee and, with one last look at the empty office and the darkened street—at the moon-shadows left by yet another mysterious drama he did not understand—settled in for the night.

2

YEARS before the Sipes debacle and the Parks trial, Bybee had been hired to defend Colin Caldwell, a pale, bustling little man from Orem, Utah, whom the state alleged had bludgeoned a man named Stephen Fowler to death with a coal shovel. The murder case would have been routine—if indeed a murder case is ever routine—except for one fact: Caldwell was a sitting, three-term state representative.

As expected, the state's political and religious machine was poised, ready to grind up and spit out Caldwell the instant the expected verdict of guilty was returned. Riding that machine —hard—was Darvis Gant, an aspiring politico who had filed to run against Caldwell, relying on the incumbent's sure murder conviction as his ticket to elected office.

But Bybee marched into trial on a bright Monday morning in Provo and, over the next four days, went about single-handedly destroying the state's case, slicing up witnesses—sixteen in all—so badly that they were forced to remember events differently, to recast their stories and observations, to reverse or readjust their assessments, and in some cases, to recant their testimony altogether.

In the end the jury, contentious and argumentative, did agree on one thing: the state had failed to prove its case beyond a reasonable doubt, and Caldwell's surprise victory at trial led to his surprise victory at the polls.

And so a stunned and defeated Darvis Gant drifted away from the political landscape—wispy and transparent, a political non-person, a nearly invisible creature who blew about like a scrap of paper until the governor, Todd Purcell, finally rescued him. Gant was officially anointed as a "special assistant," a sycophant who spent half his time licking Purcell's boots and the other half licking his wounds—wounds he blamed, to those who would listen, on Brigham B. Bybee.

The call to Gant at his Salt Lake condominium in "The Avenues" had come from Tom Kendall around six-thirty A.M., when it was just turning light, driving him from his sleep, his bed, rattling him half awake with a torrent of words that he barely heard, except for one: "Bybee."

Now, in the elevator at the capitol building, Gant viciously jabbed at a button with his thumb as though he were trying to break it. "Strength!" he whispered, and then, louder, when the elevator door closed: "*Strength!*"

He leaned back against one mirrored wall and studied himself in the opposite glass, the new contact lenses making his eyes constantly blink, as though he were troubled, fighting back tears. He turned to see the cut of his new suit, to see if the jacket hung properly, if the pleated pants broke cleanly—one time—just above the small, polished shoes. Satisfied, he moved closer to the mirror and inspected his teeth and then his nostrils, flaring them to detect any smut, then carefully smoothed his hair—blond and thick, but cut in a military style, the sides short, the back blocked and shaved.

The elevator stopped, the door slid open with a pinging noise, and he strutted down the corridor, staring straight through a young female intern who mumbled a shy "good morning," and opened the door to the outer office. At a secretary who sat behind a monitor, he made a strange, fluttering motion with his fingers at his mouth—a gesture for coffee—and continued down a narrow hallway until he came to a dark wooden door with brass lettering:

Darvis Gant
Special Assistant to the Governor

With a large key he extracted from his pants pocket, he opened the door, walked inside, and stopped suddenly on the beige-and-maroon carpet. Tom Kendall was already there, sitting in a wing chair, one long leg cocked across the other, his bony fingers tapping at his shoe.

"Morning, Darvis," Kendall said, and he smiled—he always smiled, a broad, friendly, genuine grin—and continued to tap on his shoe.

Behind him, framed by the large window with its sheer curtains open, stretched the Wasatch and Oquirrh ranges, and nestled between them lay most of the Salt Lake City grid—the wide, tree-edged streets that were now cluttered with construction, the facelift for the Olympics, the city's and the state's—and the church's—extravagant coming-out party.

Gant angrily slammed the door shut behind him. "How the hell did you get in here, Tom?"

Kendall stopped his tapping and pointed toward the outer office where the secretary sat. "I asked," he said, his voice deep and loud, almost artificial, "and she obliged." He shrugged. "I have a way with women."

Gant stared, his eyes furiously blinking, at Kendall's gangly frame, the leathery skin, and at the wretched, godawful clothes, typical of the attorney general's office: khaki pants, a leather motorcycle jacket with zippers and snaps everywhere, and a white shirt with a bow tie, a big, hand-tied paisley thing, crooked, one side drooping.

"I'm sure," Gant said.

The two men did not shake hands, and Gant quickly

marched across the big office to his oversize desk, which, with almost nothing atop it except a telephone, a coaster, and a crystal pen rest, looked more like a small, raised stage. He slipped behind it, drew up a high-backed chair, and sat down before the other man could see the cushion that rested on the seat. Finally enthroned, his small body elevated above the vast slab of a desk, he wove his hands together.

"So what's so goddamned important, Tom?"

Kendall took a pair of dark-rimmed glasses from his jacket and put them on. "Brig Bybee called me this morning—bright and early."

Gant blinked at him. "So I gathered. You haven't fired that asshole yet?"

Kendall stared at the other man for a moment, and when he saw that Gant's last statement was not rhetorical, that he was truly expecting an answer, he held his hands out—brown and thin, almost desiccated looking.

"No," he said.

"Well, maybe you should. Maybe you guys in the AG's office should just flat, fucking clean house, fire everyone—"

Gant stopped and looked over Kendall's shoulder at the cream-colored wall, where ten-inch-high brass letters—a gift from a former secretary—spelled GANT. He knew that it *had* to have been Bybee, the consummate clown, in this office three weeks ago along with Kendall and several other lessers from the AG's office, who had surreptitiously rearranged the letters to read GNAT.

"—starting with Bybee," Gant finished. "He's a loose cannon, Tom. Always has been."

Kendall took a deep breath to calm himself, to keep from growling back at the half-size martinet in front of him. Gant— and presumably, by extension, the governor—had never approved of Bybee's appointment by Cynthia Hassert, the attorney general, to head up the polygamy team, and he never missed the opportunity to chastise the office for the decision. And Kendall, the section chief of the Special Prosecutions Unit—arguably the number-two person in the AG's office—always seemed to be held personally responsible for it.

"Brig's doing a good job," Kendall said, his old stage voice deep and sonorous.

"Job? What job? He's got one witness hiding out in Manti, and that's it."

"This trial's harder than you think, Darvis."

Gant blinked at the other man. "What's so damned hard about a trial? Prosecution puts its liars on the stand; the defense puts its liars on the stand; and then the twelve liars on the jury decide—"

Kendall angrily waved his hand, cutting Gant off. "This trial's different; everything depends on that one witness. Anyway, Brig's the best in the business."

"Oh, yeah?" Gant stared at Kendall's bow tie, and then at his face, trying, as he always did, to guess the ancestry of the odd-looking man—Slavic, Middle Eastern—something strange and foreign. "Then I'd hate to see the worst. Don't you guys have someone—anyone—in the AG's office who can prosecute this thing?"

"A few," Kendall said, "but they're LDS—and Bybee isn't. Not anymore, anyway. You told me the governor doesn't want this thing turned into some . . . religious persecution—good Mormons going after bad Mormons, the fundamentalists—"

He broke off as someone tapped, timidly, on the door.

"Come!" Gant yelled.

The door slowly opened, and the secretary from the outer office—a heavy, matronly woman in a loose-fitting dress—came in with a steaming mug of coffee, walked to the desk, and placed it before Gant on the coaster. She turned around, looked expectantly at Kendall, and smiled.

"Can I get you—"

"The AG's office apparently doesn't drink coffee," Gant said, and he looked at Kendall, staring at the man's ugly tie again, rather than his face. "It's chock-full of good Mormons."

"Actually, I do drink coffee," Kendall said, and he smiled at the woman, "but only when I'm hung over. And I'm not hung over . . . yet. Thanks, anyway."

The secretary nodded and then, with her back to Gant, winked at him and walked from the room.

Gant blinked at Kendall for several moments. "Tom, if you're not LDS, why the hell aren't *you* heading this thing up? You've been a prosecutor damn near your entire life. You don't need a hired gun."

Kendall shrugged; he had asked himself that every day since the project began, even lobbying Cynthia for the job, but her answer was simple, and maddening: Bybee, she insisted, had a certain courtroom presence, a way with jurors, especially female jurors.

"I don't know," Kendall finally said, and he inched his chair closer to the desk. "Anyway, Bybee says that he was at his motel last night when one of— "

"You know, that's another thing," Gant said. He held the mug of coffee in front of him. "Not only is he a hired gun, but he runs a fucking tepee motel? You ever seen that place?"

"Yes," Kendall said. "I even stayed there one night." He was lying; he had visited Bybee in Kanab several times, the last trip about a month ago, when he talked with Bybee as he was spreading a truckload of gravel around the lot, a strange yellow dog lurking nearby. But he had never actually slept at the motel. "It's . . . unusual. I like it."

"I'm sure," Gant said, and he waved his hand. "Go on."

"Anyway," Kendall said, "he was there last night when one . . . you ready for this?"

"Oh, strength, Tom."

"When one of Rampton Crowe's wives—" He stopped, watching Gant's face. "I'm serious as hell. The Big Plig, Rampton Crowe. One of his wives came running in, all beat to hell, bloodied up, dress torn—"

"Another Bybee first date?"

Kendall theatrically closed and opened his eyes, slowly. "Anyway, this runaway says Crowe caught her screwing some guy, another plig, boffing his brains out, and so his Blood Disciples dragged this guy to some old water tank or something, naked as all hell, and then while a couple of guys held him, Crowe cut off his balls with a hunting knife. Christ Jesus! You believe that? Cut his balls off!"

He paused and looked at Gant, expecting him to stop

breathing, to gape and mutter some profane oath the way he had just done, the way he had done when Bybee had gushed the story, the way he had been doing all morning.

Instead, Gant just blinked and calmly took a sip of his coffee. "Eye for an eye, I guess. Go on."

"Well, according to this little plig, after castrating this poor son of a bitch, they propped him up and Crowe took an old sword and . . . you ready for this?"

"Tom, for—"

"He decapitated the son of a bitch right there, right in front of everyone. I'm serious, Darvis. He cut his goddamned head off."

Gant stared at Kendall, who seemed to have stopped breathing for a moment, then suddenly brought the edge of his small hand down on the desk in a fierce, chopping motion.

"Whop!" He smiled. "Like that?"

Kendall looked confused, his eyes wide. "Yeah, I—"

Gant's hand descended again. "Whop!" He majestically waved the same hand. "Go on."

"Well, this bitch says that then one of the pligs took the head—Christ Jesus, a severed head—and held it up while he was paraded around on everyone's shoulders. Big trophy. Big fun."

Unconsciously, while he was talking, Kendall had placed one skinny hand just below the bow tie, and now he began slapping slowly at his chest, as though his heart had stopped and he was urging it to start again. His eyes behind the thick glasses were wide open, frightened, staring at the image that had been in his brain all morning: the old black-and-white World War II photograph that had haunted him as a child, an American GI, kneeling, blindfolded, surrounded by grinning Japanese soldiers, all jostling for a better view of a . . .

"A beheading," Gant said. He looked bored, and he began toying with the pen rest. "Happens every day."

"The hell it does," Kendall said, and he took a deep breath. "Anyway, this little cohab says that Crowe and the other pligs then, well, for good measure, I guess, they cut off his arms and legs."

Gant laughed and shrugged, and then made the sign of the cross. "Rest in pieces."

Kendall suddenly felt dizzy, the way he had on the phone with Bybee that morning, and he rested his arms on his thin legs and stared at the carpet, silent.

"Is that all?" Gant said.

Kendall slowly raised his head. "Isn't that enough?"

Gant smiled and slurped at his coffee. "No."

"Christ Jesus, Darvis, there's been a murder—a goddamned nasty one, at that."

Gant snorted. "Oh, get a grip. You believe that happy horseshit? You believe it really happened?" He sipped at his coffee and then kept his head down, blinking into the mug, as though he had found something interesting floating there—a fly, a hundred-dollar bill . . . a tiny, severed head. He finally looked up. "A weirded-out plig who's about to get popped on bigamy charges, all of a sudden, out in the open, where everyone can see, supposedly chops up some guy. Then, like a miracle, one of his wives comes bopping up to a prosecutor—a *prosecutor,* not some shit-stick farmer standing in a field with his thumb up his ass—and says, 'Guess what I just saw, Mr. Prosecutor?' Give me a fucking break, Tom! You *really* believe it?"

"If Brig Bybee believes it, then I do."

"Oh, strength! Bybee will believe anything that squats to pee. He's probably pumping the living bejesus out of her right now."

Kendall blew a stream of air through his lips as though expelling some noxious gas, old and long bottled up, decayed. He half turned, taking his eyes off Gant, and looked at the rest of the office, spare and sterile and almost empty, except for the walls. One, the east wall, was festooned with dozens of framed photographs of minor politicos, meaningless awards and commendations, a diploma from an unknown university, and in the middle of it all, a large photograph of Gant, alone, waving to a crowd, his election banner drooping sadly behind him, symbolic.

He turned back to Gant. "You know, Darvis, Bybee won the Caldwell trial fair and square."

"What the hell does that mean?"

"It means you can stop trying to blame him for ruining—"

Kendall stopped and shook his head, embarrassed. They had been discussing a nightmarish crime, a mutilation murder, and now it had degenerated into petty personal vendettas. "Forget it. Look, we have to check it out. We have to get some investigators down to New Ammon . . . now!"

"Like hell," Gant said. "You're not sending shit down there."

"What are you talking about?"

Gant raised his voice. "I'm not *talking* about anything, Tom. I'm *telling* you. You're not sending the AG's office down there. No AG lawyers, no AG investigators poking around, no—" He stopped; he had been leaning forward, glaring at Kendall, and now he straightened and relaxed atop his cushion. "Tom, don't you see what's going on?"

Kendall didn't hear the question. "With this runaway's affidavit, we can get a search warrant and bust in there and turn the place upside down, looking for bodies—or parts of them. And while we're doing that, we can see just who's shacked up with who."

Gant actually leaned back and hooted at the ceiling. "A . . . raid? Are you talking about a *raid* on a polygamist colony?"

Kendall's face hardened, and he leaned forward. "Yeah, Darvis, I am. I hate those sons of bitches. It's about time we—"

"A *raid*? Jesus, I—" Gant lowered his head and fixed Kendall's face with his blinking eyes, then studied the weathered motorcycle jacket. "You know, it's feast or famine with you AG guys. You either pussy out and try to pop these pligs on adultery or incest or kidnapping or some wimpy bullshit, or go the other way and want to"— Gant stopped and laughed—"raid the place. Kick ass, gangbusters, Waco and Green Berets . . . balls to the wall."

"Yeah—"

"With you leading the pack? Riding in there on your motorcycle?"

"This isn't a joke."

"You're right; it isn't," Gant said, and he was suddenly sober, his grin gone. "Look, I hate pligs too, but for your information, the state of Arizona tried that gung-ho, Rambo-raid bullshit fifty years ago, at a place called Short Creek. They grabbed all the kids, browbeat the women, and all the men just hid out, vanished. And their governor ended up as political . . . dead meat."

"Oh, I see," Kendall said. "We're talking politics, not criminal conduct, not a violation—"

"Oh, strength! Earth to Tom! Of course we're talking politics." He waved his pale hand around his head, indicating the entire building, the city. "Where the living hell do you think you are?"

Kendall glared past him out the window, at a distant, silvery ribbon of highway that ran up the mountain toward the ski resorts—the "Olympic venues," as they were now called. "Sometimes I wonder, Darvis."

"Well, get a grip," Gant said again, and he put both his hands on the desk, palms toward one another, as if he were measuring an invisible object. "Look, Tom, there's a hell of a lot of state money and . . . political futures, political reputations, invested in all of this."

He lifted one hand and vaguely indicated the other decorated wall in the room, the west wall, one covered with framed posters of airborne, goggled skiers and whirling skaters; of a dreamlike world of snow sprites and crystal fairies, of icy magic. And the five-ringed Olympic logo was vividly splashed across them, the same logo that could be found in every filling station and store in the state, on about any item one could imagine: hats, cups, tea towels, pillows, headbands, socks, underwear . . . everything.

"PR is everything," Gant said.

Kendall took a slow, deep breath. He had heard this before, repeatedly, time and time again from Gant, from others, and it was draining, physically exhausting. "I know that, Darvis. Everyone knows that. But there's been a murder."

Gant sadly shook his head. "Tom, most everyone in the country—hell, the world—thinks that Utah is just one big polygamist colony, a bunch of *Book of Mormon* thumpers who sleep with their own daughters and sell off their sons and just do whatever the hell they want because the law can't touch 'em. Well, the governor and . . . others want to try and change that perception. How many times do I have to tell you that?"

"Once is enough, Darvis," Kendall said, his voice low, almost a false bass.

"Apparently not, so I'm going to say it over and over, Tom, until it sinks into your head, into Cynthia's head, into Bybee's head, into every fucking tiny pointed head over at the AG's office. The governor wants Crowe to go down hard for polygamy. Period. He wants a pure, straight polygamy trial, nothing fancy, a—"

"A *show* trial?" Kendall said.

Gant blinked at him. "Call it what you want, but Purcell wants a polygamy conviction, period, with no political fallout. And he sure as hell doesn't want a bunch of AG assholes running around screaming bloody murder."

"Even if there was a bloody murder?"

"There wasn't, Tom. Get real. Your hotshot hired gun Bybee is getting sidetracked the way you guys always get sidetracked. He's chasing some plig whore down a rabbit trail, one that supposedly leads to a murder." He shook his head. "It's pure bullshit, Tom."

"People don't lie about things like that."

"Oh, the hell they don't. Besides, these are pligs, not people. Look, it's a diversion, a way to shift attention. Get everyone poking around looking for a headless body, and when there's none, everyone looks like a bunch of government assholes. The same government assholes that used to raid all the pligs." He blinked and smiled. "Trust me. It's bullshit. She's a decoy."

Kendall looked at his watch, then got to his feet and stood in front of Gant, tall and bony, awkwardly dangling there like a puppet with half its strings cut, his leather jacket draped over him. "Maybe not," he said.

Instinctively, when Gant saw the man's height made obvious, he quickly swiveled his leather chair around. "So this is what I—what I'm sure the governor wants." He was facing the window now, his head unseen below the high back of the chair, but he continued to speak, one hand making grand gestures, as though he were addressing the hoi polloi below, his grimy, plodding subjects. "Keep the AG's office away from New Ammon, and also from this Kanab, or whatever the hell you call that shit-stick place where Bybee lives. The only thing I want you to do is to continue to march. Order Bybee to take this runaway back to New Ammon—A-sap—and forget any ideas that he, or your office, Tom, is going after Crowe for murder. Don't Rambo this. And make damn sure she doesn't end up at Manti. If your one witness is so damned critical, then don't screw it up. That's the number-one priority. I don't give a rat's ass about phony murder or bullshit stories about guys with their balls cut off and their heads rolling around." He hesitated. "It's polygamy, Tom, and that's all. Polygamy, polygamy, poly—"

He stopped, frozen in his chair, and did not finish the word. The room became unnaturally quiet; the only sounds were the faint murmuring of the air-conditioning and the thin, wavelike, to-and-fro wash of traffic floating up from outside, the hollow thrum of urban existence. And then there was the distant pinging of the elevator door down the hall.

He swiveled around, a schoolboy's grin on his face, obviously satisfied with a glowing thought, the perfect slogan . . . pilfered, but perfect.

"*It's the polygamy, stupid!*" he said.

But Kendall was gone, the door ajar, and on the wall next to it, the big brass letters read GNAT.

The grounds of the Utah state capitol building are, as one would expect in any state, a showpiece, a tourist attraction with flowers in tight clusters, grass green and trimmed, and a few statues of old Great Basin heroes overseeing it all.

But just to the east, across a street and down a slope choked with brambles and dying trees, some with broken branches that droop to the ground, lies a different piece of land, something utterly abandoned and ignored, diseased looking, a place receding into oblivion—despite its name.

It is called Memory Grove, a dry, weedy place given over to an odd assemblage of private memorials to some of the city's war dead: a rusted howitzer, a marble mausoleum, crumbling benches, dung-encrusted busts, and fountains layered with purplish fuzz, forever dry, forever forgotten.

Now Darvis Gant sat on one of the cracked and muddy

benches of Memory Grove, a copy of the *Salt Lake Tribune* tucked under his arm, idly staring at an illegible plaque in front of him. He heard the snap of dried twigs, and he looked up and saw a man named Vanoy Atherton walking—or rather sidling—toward him, his body twisted in one direction but moving in another, a crab-walk, like a truck with a bent frame. He labored up a small slope, almost stumbling at one point, and finally came up to where Gant sat.

"Mornin', Darv'," he said.

Atherton was a tall, heavy man, dressed in cowboy boots and pinstriped suit pants that were held around his swollen stomach with red suspenders. He wore a light blue dress shirt, with no tie, and to top everything off—quite literally—he sported a grand white cowboy hat, one that even bona fide cowboys would be embarrassed to wear. It was the same outfit that he always wore, even the first time that Gant had met him, in this very park, when he had hired the big, drawling slob to follow Royal Tanner, the effeminate ankle-biter who had loudly called for extending the investigation of the Olympics scandal into the governor's office. And Atherton had done his job, magnificently so, somehow securing compromising photographs of Tanner and a high school boy that finally silenced the man, in fact ruined him.

Atherton stood waiting, breathing heavily, and then he stuck out a big, raw-looking hand, each finger on it—as well as the other—glittering with rings.

"Ah said, 'Mornin', Darv.' "

Still sitting, Gant quickly shook his hand. "Morning, Vanoy," he said. He sniffed at the other man, at the dizzying smell of sweat and cologne and bacon . . . and booze. He looked dramatically at his watch; it was ten-fifteen. "Little early to be drinking, isn't it?"

Atherton sat on the other end of the bench, lowering his big frame with a tired groan, and then hawked and spit on the ground. "Early? Hell, it's August, damn near September." He smiled, and his lips looked wet and greasy, as though he had just tucked into a slab of pork fat—and maybe he had; his shirt was sprinkled with dark spots, like oily drool.

"Look, Vanoy, I don't want to waste time here," Gant said.

"You still doing some work down in New Ammon?"

"Yeah. Drav down about ever' other week."

"Well, what's going on there?"

Atherton laughed. "Ah dunno. Same ol' same ol'." His accent, like the clothes he wore, was faux Texan, comically exaggerated, something he had adopted when he worked for an insurance defense law firm in Fort Worth years before. He looked out at the clanking bustle of construction equipment on the city streets, men in hard hats and orange vests, the noise and hot energy everywhere. "No Olympics goin' on down there. That's a fact."

"Oh, yeah? Lots more going on, I hear."

"Lak what?'

"Like Crowe cutting off some plig's head, that's what."

Atherton looked down at the governor's assistant, a smile slowly spreading, his brown-stained teeth showing.

"Ah don't know what you're talkin' 'bout, Darv'."

"I'm sure," Gant said. "Vanoy, I'm not going to pussy around with this. Brig Bybee—you know him?"

"Bah-bee. Yeah, heard of him. Lawyer."

"Yeah, well, he says he's got one of Crowe's wives who ran—"

"Mercy," Atherton said, as a name, not an exclamation. "Chenoya. Real nas; the besta the bunch." He spit. "Yeah, she ran. Rampton called me."

"Why?"

"Whah he called?"

"Why'd she run?"

Atherton shrugged and then slapped at his stomach, as if he might instantly dislodge about thirty pounds of fat and send it quivering to the ground. "Ah dunno. Sometams they run. She ran."

"Bybee said she had the living bejesus beat out of her."

Atherton hesitated, then slowly shook his big head. "Don't know nothin' 'bout that."

Gant blinked several times and then blew out a gust of air from his lungs. "Well, just what the shit *do* you know, Vanoy?" Before letting Atherton answer, he made an odd half-turn, as though an invisible hand had grabbed him by the shoulder.

"Look, did Crowe or any other cohab whack someone? Was there a murder down there, Vanoy?"

"No," Atherton said, and he smiled and pointed at the capitol building, the solid, massive heart of the government brooding atop the hill. "Any murders up there?"

Gant ignored the remark. "So why would she run?"

"You a'ready ask me that. Sometams they just up and run." He grinned. "Tarred of waitin' in lan for the ol' man, ah suppose."

Gant made a face, looked straight ahead at an old army tank—blackened and scarred, covered with graffiti—and then shook his head. He could feel it in his gut; it was all an act, an elaborate charade, one carefully choreographed and planned, even to the point of actually beating the woman, all designed to lead everyone astray. It was Machiavellian, diabolical . . . pure Crowe.

Gant turned to Atherton and handed him the folded newspaper. "You like sports, Vanoy?"

"Jes.' football." He spit. "Cowboys."

"Well, read the sports section. You'll find it interesting."

Atherton nodded, took the paper, and, like Gant, pushed it under his arm. "All rat." He knew what was there; they had done this before—just like this—in the Tanner case and others.

"I want you to find out just what in the hell really is going on, Vanoy. What Crowe's up to."

"Rampton's mah client. You know that."

"Yeah. I'm your client too, remember. You got a problem with that?"

Atherton shrugged. He was Crowe's part-time investigator, a man who, in addition to any in-house sleuthing necessary, poked around the state trying to find information on any New Ammon defectors—like Faith—which he would then relay to the Blood Disciples. But the private investigator was not sworn just to Crowe; he was not sworn to anyone, really, or anything, just some private belief he called the Big Boomerang.

"Guess not," Atherton said.

"Good. Here's what I want. If there was no murder, as you claim, then find out why this bitch ran. Tell me their game plan, Vanoy. Something's not copacetic. You understand?"

Atherton looked at Gant, at his starched white shirt, the so-called power tie, the gleaming shoes—the governor's immaculate little field general in a seedy park full of war relics talking about murder.

"There's not much ah un'erstand any more."

Gant waved his hand. "Fine. Whatever. And here's the second thing. If there *was* someone murdered, there was no murder. You understand *that?*"

It was obvious that, for several moments, Atherton did not comprehend, for he sat staring at Gant, his green eyes dull, lost, waiting for something to register, to make sense . . . and then it slowly materialized in his brain.

"Yeah," he said.

"Good. If it happened, it didn't happen. Keep thinking that. And find the little bitch that ran. Bybee says he's got her tucked away, safe and sound. Find her; talk to her; get her back to New Ammon. That's priority. Understand?"

"Yeah."

"One last thing. You remember how we handled the Eggerton thing? Judge Pyle? All the criminal shit? The printout from the clerk's office?"

"Yeah."

"I want the same thing. This time, check out LeVar Eaton in Judge Rukamann's court. Two years back."

Atherton laughed, a phlegmy burbling that ended up as a cough. "Rocket Man?"

"Yeah. I need the printout A-sap. Shit, I need everything A-sap. You know that."

"Ah know, Darv'."

Gant began to say something, then stopped and smiled, his eyelids fluttering. "You said these plig bitches wait in line for the old man."

"Yeah."

"Well, that's something I've always wondered, Vanoy. How do they decide who's to get the sausage next? Draw straws? Arm wrestle?"

Atherton shrugged; he had answered this question before,

several times. "They all keep a little chart, a calendar. That's a fact."

"Strength," Gant said, and he waved his hand. "Have a nice day, Vanoy."

"Hey, you have a nas day, too." Atherton said.

With a groan, the big private investigator got to his feet, hawked and spit on the ground, and slowly walked away, teetering in the boots. The newspaper was awkwardly jammed under his arm, and his whole body was cocked to one side as though a howling wind was trying to blow him off course, steer him another way.

He left Memory Grove and slowly and painfully clumped down a wide, shady street that sloped toward the center of the city, along ruptured sidewalks that wound past old, tilting houses layered in vines and hidden by trees. Eventually he struggled out of the gloomy neighborhoods and came upon another park, but this one—Brigham Young Park, just east of the temple itself—was bright and clean and well tended, and had three-quarter-size statues of pioneer men and women bent to their chores, with clear water gurgling nearby, running over wooden mill wheels and through artificial vegetable gardens, the place like an odd movie set.

Atherton found a metal bench, sat, and then twisted his big body to each side to assure that he was alone in the park. He was; only he and the dozen or so miniature people—the bronze statues—were there, and they seemed to be deliberately looking down or the other way, embarrassed perhaps. Satisfied, he withdrew the newspaper, opened it to the sports section, and found, just above an off-season picture of Karl Malone, an envelope stapled to the page. With his thick, ringed fingers, he tore the envelope open and counted the money there: fifty one-hundred-dollar bills.

"Mercy!" he said, but this time as an exclamation, not a name, and then he bent down with a grunt and pulled off his cheap cowboy boots.

3

N his freshman year at Utah State, Bybee, certainly not a student of politics or history or international diplomacy, nevertheless had a chilling hunch about the ordeal in South Vietnam: it was not going to end soon.

So, knowing he would be drafted the instant he graduated, and despite his aversion to the military, and especially to guns, he had enrolled in the ROTC. But thankfully, by some cosmic chance, he had not been issued a rifle; instead he was assigned to a bass drum—a big wooden washtub of an instrument that he toted across campus every Thursday afternoon to the formation drills, his green uniform sagging over him like an old army blanket. There, unable to read music—as if any drummer ever really *could* read music—he thumped spastically and happily away with the band, off-tempo, keeping the entire cadet corps out of march step, forcing them to skip and shuffle like men walking over a bed of hot coals.

But he grew to love it, for he never had to disassemble and assemble an M-1 rifle; never marched anywhere other than around the football field; and never had to spit-shine his shoes or polish his brass or cut his hair. He was not a soldier; he was a baseball player first, and then a drummer, by God—and a bass drummer, at that—a special breed, shunned by the regular cadets, even by the other band members. He was a phony, jack-leg musician who could not read music, but earned his officer's commission in the United States Army by simply pounding on a drum . . . just pounding and pounding.

And then, as now, he was always a half-count off beat.

Bybee awoke to the same irregular thumping, a hollow, rhythmic sound that filled the room. With his head unnaturally cocked against an armrest, his long legs twisted everywhere, he lay on a couch, eyes closed, listening.

It was someone clumping in heavy shoes across the old wood floors, to and fro, the thin oak slats reverberating like a giant drumhead. He struggled upright on the couch, found his glasses on the end table, and got to his feet, swaying, still sleepy. He stood in the middle of Zolene's small living room, which the two of them, over the last year, had nearly restored to its original condition, the way it was when Nephi Lamb had built it almost a hundred years before: polished wood floors, antique furniture, Tiffany lamps, bevel-edged mirrors, wall sconces, even the old black, push-button light switches. It was a cool, quiet place that looked and felt—even smelled—of the past.

But now it smelled of something sugary and pungent—baked apples. He pushed his hair out of his face and then shook his head, trying to clear it. It had been nearly one o'clock the night before last when he and Mercy had bumped along the back road into the tomblike canyon and arrived at Lamb's house, Mercy already in a heavy sleep, her head lolling against the door. He had carried her from the VW van and into Zolene's daughters' bedroom, laying her fully clothed atop the counterpane of one bed, and then carefully covered her with a quilt.

Then he himself, rather than sleep in Zolene's bedroom, surrendering to some vague, incomprehensible need to distance himself from Mercy, if only twenty more feet, had stretched out in the living room—at least, as much as the old couch would allow. And he had slept wretchedly, awaking at every stray sound out in Hell's Bellows: the keening of a coyote, the moaning of one of Heber Batt's cows—and Mercy screaming out in her sleep, once, a sharp, terrified yelp.

Early the next morning, just as the sun glinted over the eastern cliffs, the blackness of the canyon turning to purple before it would give way, later, to the smoldering orange and red, he had gotten up, checked that Mercy was safe and still asleep, and driven the ten miles back to Kanab. There he made sure that Vesta Frost, Zolene's moody cousin and his part-time clerk, had arrived; he fed Spooky Floyd and saw that the Piute Villa was up and running for another day; and then he called Tom Kendall.

The remainder of the day, he had driven repeatedly back and forth between the Piute Villa and Lamb's house, each time finding Mercy in a heavy, unmoving, comalike sleep, and each time bending close to her to watch her face, to see the faint twitch of her eyes, to assure himself that she was indeed still breathing.

Finally, in the evening of that second day, with Mercy still asleep, he had collapsed on the couch again, wholly exhausted, this time finally and completely falling asleep himself, dreaming of Zolene, as he always did, and then, strangely, of Darvis Gant in the old ROTC band . . . and then of Mercy.

"Good morning, Mr. Bybee."

He turned around and saw her standing at the doorway to the dining room, her blond hair twisting down over the same dirty, bloodstained dress, still in her boots. She held a dish towel in her hand, her head was cocked, and although her face was still terribly bruised, it looked less swollen, and the one eye that had been hammered closed by Crowe's fist was partially open now, as though she were squinting.

Bybee stood stupidly, embarrassed about how he was dressed, which was to say, hardly at all—only his wrinkled gray slacks hanging on his hips. But he was vaguely grateful for all of the work he had done around this house and his motel in the last few months, all the bending and lifting, for the middle-aged ridge of fat around his middle was gone now, his stomach flat, even his chest and arms a bit larger, more defined.

"Morning," he said, and he walked across the wood floor and stood before her. "How are you feeling?"

"I'm fine," she said, but she did not look at his face; instead she stared at his chest, at the valley of dark hair that trickled down along his breastbone, his hard stomach, and disappeared into his pants. "I feel better."

"Good," Bybee said, and he sniffed theatrically and pointed at the dish towel in her hands, smiling. "Been cooking?"

"I . . . found some things," she said. "Flour and sugar and—" She pointed across the room to where half a dozen crates of apples lay against the wall, where Bybee and Zolene had placed them several days ago after an afternoon session in the orchard, the house now filling up with the things everywhere, the atmosphere redolent with the fresh, fruity smell of them.

"I made a pie," she said, and she straightened, proud.

"Apple?" Bybee said, and then felt foolish; what else would it be? Coconut? Lemon meringue? "Smells good."

Mercy took a step forward, proudly, as if she were accepting an award, and stood in front of an antique china cabinet—a light oak piece with brass pulls and a curved glass front, one Zolene had rescued from the basement of Lamb's house and painstakingly restored. Behind it, hanging from the dark ceiling molding, was an oval-framed picture of Nephi Lamb himself, typical of the era—long-bearded, resolute, unsmiling, his dead, soulless eyes surveying everything from a century away.

In her long, old-fashioned dress and outdated boots, Mercy looked as if she too were a period piece, as though she truly belonged here in this house, in this hazy, distant era that he and Zolene had so carefully re-created. But now the furniture and the pictures and the knickknacks were no longer antiques, no longer collectibles, quaint memorabilia from a period long dead and half forgotten. Now everything was real and alive, the present subsumed by the past, and it was teasing him, beckoning him.

"Come," Mercy said, and she held out her hand to him.

Clumsily, as though he were half blind, Bybee took the woman's chapped hand, and Mercy, like the lady of the house, led him to the cherry wood dining table that had once been in Doug Farnsworth's old house, just east, on the other side of the orchard. She made him sit, and while he waited—bizarrely out of place, half naked, numbed by how quickly, how naturally, the woman had adopted the place as her own—Mercy retreated to the kitchen. A moment later she reemerged, carrying a plate, a fork, and a spatula, and carefully laid them out on the table. She smiled and hurried back into the kitchen, came back with the pièce de résistance—her pie—and placed it before Bybee on a thick, folded towel.

"Wow," Bybee said, "this looks great."

Pleased, Mercy took the spatula, cut a wedge of the pie, and placed it on his plate. She sat down next to him, and he hefted a forkful of the pie and smiled at her, at her wretched but hopeful face, and then put it into his mouth—and nearly gagged. It was underdone, almost uncooked, and tasted like a kitchen experiment gone terribly wrong—glutinous and sugary, almost grainy.

"Great," he said, and he laid the plate aside and theatrically looked at his watchless wrist—he guessed it was eight-thirty, maybe nine o'clock. "A little too early for pie, though."

Mercy looked disappointed; leaning toward him, she picked up his plate, loaded up the fork again, and held it before his face. "It's good for you," she said, and she inched the half-raw chunks of apple toward his mouth like a mother feeding her child, coaxing him. "C'mon. Just one more bite."

"No, really."

"C'mon," she said, and she leaned closer still, so that they were face to face now, her nose only inches from his.

Bybee relented and opened his mouth and watched her beaten face, her lips wet and pursed together, the tip of her tongue peeking out, as she slid the apples into his mouth. He gently bit down, but she kept the fork between his teeth, grinning at him, then slowly pulled it out, deliberately dragging the tines across and down his lips.

"Good boy," she said, and she laughed and shook her dirty hair.

A strange but pleasant feeling surged through his body, and for one horrifying moment, Bybee considered eating all of the apple pie, just to please her, just to have her feed him again. But he pushed the plate aside, signaling that the gooey repast, this playhouse domesticity, was over. By all rights this poor woman should be in a hospital—at least in a bed—with others bringing *her* food, not her, in her booted feet, bustling about and preparing it. In that way, he had been thinking about her, almost continually, for the last twenty-four hours, and he was growing intensely curious about her, even considering, while she had slept, of pawing through her big leather purse, looking for any information, any clues.

"Where are you from, Mercy?"

The woman looked confused, and she nodded her head toward the southwest, precisely toward the colony, and Bybee, forever disoriented, forever half a beat off and ninety degrees awry, was impressed with her sense of direction.

"New Am'," she said. "I told you—"

"No." Bybee shook his head. "I mean . . . before. Before New Ammon, where did you live?"

Mercy turned her head and stared out the west window, at the wall of apple trees that insulated Lamb's house from the bright red sandstone blaze of Johnson Canyon, from the outside world.

"Idaho," she said. "A place called Packston."

"Packston," Bybee slowly repeated, as if trying out the word, testing it. "You still have family there?"

"I have a brother . . . somewhere," she said, and then she shrugged. "My parents are dead."

"I'm sorry," Bybee said. He thought, from the reports, that he knew the answer to the next question, but he wanted to be sure. "You have children?"

She looked down. "No. I . . . can't."

"I'm sorry," Bybee said again.

"Father says it is the way of the world," she said.

"Well, I'm sure *Father*—" He suddenly pursed his lips, stopping the next few angry words he wanted to spit out. "I suppose it is," he said. "Did you go to school in Idaho? I mean, high school?" He shook his head again, embarrassed. "What I'm trying to say is, were you like all the—" He did not finish; he realized he had blundered, and he began groping for a way out.

But it was too late. "All the what?" Mercy said. She had been absently toying with the fork, and now she suspended it in mid-air, aiming it at him, her eyes narrowed, hard. "Was I like all the what, Mr. Bybee?"

"Nothing."

"Was I like all the *other* kids? Is that what you want to know? Was I . . . *normal?* Did I have boyfriends; did—"

"Look, Mercy—"

"—I always want to be a plural wife? Is that the real question? Was I always messed up, or—"

"Mercy—"

She leaned toward him, staring hard, and with one bruised eye half-closed, the other red and raw and tired, she looked addled, demented. "—or did I just go *crazy* one day?"

Bybee lowered his head and said nothing.

"You know," she said, "I used to wear lipstick. I was in the pep squad and the drama club. I watched MTV. I"—she suddenly brought her hand up and grasped her left breast under the dress, the nipple erect and clearly visible beneath the cloth— "even have a tattoo, a roadrunner." She continued to clutch her breast. "It's right here. Wanna see?"

For a thrilling, electric instant, Bybee *did* want to see, but she released her breast, and he slowly shook his head. "No, and I apologize, Mercy. I truly do."

The woman said nothing, and in the uncomfortable silence she and Bybee stared out the window, watching a squirrel slowly spiral up one of the apple trees.

Over the last few months Bybee had read everything he could find on the subject until he felt reasonably knowledgeable and conversant about polygamy: its fuzzy biblical antecedent, the crazed embrace of it by the early Mormons, the struggles within the church, the U.S. Army's march toward Utah to stamp out the Principle, and finally, with the Saints' political and economic survival genuinely at stake, their ballyhooed renunciation of it all in 1890, in the so-called Manifesto—the great surrender, the grand defeat of the madness . . . and an outrageous sham.

For the Principle and its practice continued, stronger and more virulent than before, but now with reckless impunity, daring and arrogant and cavalier, a sizeable chunk of the state becoming overrun with polygamists, like a mutant breed, swarming, unstoppable, immune to anything that could or should control them: the law, decency, even the LDS church, which simply turned its back while some of the presidents and prophets, in the years after the Manifesto, took on more and more plural wives.

And they all thrived, not just in the hidden high-desert enclaves like New Ammon but everywhere, in the open, in Big Water, in Hildale, in Kanab, Circleville, Cedar City, Ogden, even in the Salt Lake suburbs, perhaps in the shadow of the state capitol itself, near Memory Grove, near Brigham Young Park . . . everywhere.

But the New Ammon colony, with its forced "missions" and required pioneer dress, was different—hideously different.

"What is your mission at New Ammon, Mercy?"

She did not seem surprised that he knew the vernacular, probably believing, he thought, that her prisonlike society was commonplace, part of the general world order.

"The Deseret alphabet," she said. "Father calls it 'New Deseret.' He taught me; now I teach others."

Bybee nodded; he knew what Deseret was—or had been: the name given to the old Mormon republic, the desperate attempt by the early church to break from the United States and establish its own country, with its own laws, its own flag and currency . . . and its own alphabet. But the Deseret experiment in secret orthography had failed—along with the republic itself—and now the queer alphabet was simply an arcane bit of history, something rarely discussed. The few extant volumes of works in Deseret—a first and second primer and the *Book of Mormon*—were all hidden away in the musty rare-editions sections of the state's libraries, usually on college campuses.

"You actually can read and write in Deseret?" Bybee said.

Mercy smiled. "Got some paper? A pencil?"

Obediently, Bybee got up and walked back to the living room; there, next to the old-style black telephone, one with modern electronics concealed inside, he found a ballpoint pen and a small pad of paper. He returned to the dining room and handed the items to Mercy.

"Thanks," she said.

Like a schoolgirl beginning her lessons, Mercy immediately bent over the paper, the pen lightly clasped in her fingers, and quickly and expertly scribbled something. When she was finished, she looked up and pushed the pad over to Bybee, twisting it around so he could see the unusual, Cyrillic-like scratchings, strange symbols that looked like they might belong on the tepees at the Piute Villa:

$$\text{1}\text{+}\text{Γ}\text{8}\text{7} \quad \text{Ɔ}\text{ə}$$

"What does it say?" Bybee said.

Mercy smiled. "That's for you to figure out."

Bybee studied the paper for a moment, then reached into his rear pocket, withdrew his wallet and inserted the paper into it, and returned the wallet to his pocket.

"You say you teach it," he said. "To whom?"

"Everyone at New Am'," she said. "Mostly the kids. Father makes them learn it. He wants everyone reading and writing New Deseret in a few years."

Bybee stared at her and unconsciously shook his head. A century and a half before, Brigham Young—himself, the possessor of twenty-seven wives—had made the identical effort, but had given up when he realized that a secret written language was only creating more difficulty, more ridicule . . . and more persecution.

He turned to her, his hands on the table, palms up, as

though he were surrendering. "Mercy, you have to realize that this New Deseret alphabet is just another example of why people on the outside think all sorts of strange things about plig—about New Ammon. Why they . . . ." He trailed off.

"Why they want to put Father in prison?"

Bybee bit his lip, his mouth working. "Well, yes, Mercy. But not because of a weird alphabet; not just because you're . . . different; it's because there are—"

"It's because Father is married to me and five other women."

Bybee looked surprised. "Frankly, yes," he said, and he paused and stared steadily at her. "It's against the law."

"Whose law?"

"The law of the land."

"Mr. Bybee, have you ever been married before?"

"Yes." He looked confused, and he pushed his glasses up along his nose. "I'm divorced."

"You going to marry Miss Swapp?"

He shrugged. "Maybe. We've talked about it. What does—"

"And then, after you marry her, something might happen, and you might get married again."

Bybee finally realized what she was driving at, and he shook his head in a patient, patronizing way, the way he would if he were trying to reason with a child. He had heard this particular argument before—usually in taverns—some wags even referring to a succession of marriages and divorces as "serial polygamy."

"That's different, Mercy."

She shook her head so hard that her dirty hair whipped in front of her face. "No, it's not! It's not different at all." She leaned toward him, pulling a tangle of hair from her eyes. "You tell me what the difference is? Three wives all at once, or three wives, one after the other?"

Again Bybee tiredly shook his head and smiled at her, and she immediately raised her hand and pointed a finger at his face.

"And don't treat me like I'm an idiot, 'cause I'm not!"

Bybee felt a faint wash of anger seeping down from his scalp, heating his face, but he looked away, allowing the feeling to drain away, to cool, and then decided that he would abandon the topic altogether. He had to admit to himself, the way he had in all those barroom debates, that he could not find a sound, logical response to her question other than the pathetic, "It's against the law."

"I know what you mean," Bybee said. "And you're not an idiot, Mercy. I didn't mean to imply that."

"Well, I'm not," she said, and she drew back, softening. "Anyway, if you go after us, after fundamentalists, than you should go after all the others, too. The main church. Read their D and C."

The D and C was the Doctrine and Covenants. It was standard-issue scripture from "the main church," revelations transmitted from God to several Mormon prophets—principally Joseph Smith and Brigham Young—all written down and codified as a handbook of moral principles, a manual of spiritualism found in every LDS home.

But this book, this basic part of mainstream Mormon culture, of *Utah* culture, also explicitly encouraged the practice of celestial marriage—polygamy—and further allowed for the outright murder of any plural wife who slept with another man.

"I know what you mean," Bybee said again. "It's Section One-thirty-two. But even if you believe that the Principle is right, Mercy, you have to believe—you have to *know*—that this awful thing that Crowe did to Franklin Pugh and"—he pointed a finger at her blackened eye, the welts and bruises on her face—"what he did to *you* is wrong. Terribly wrong."

She folded her hands in her lap and looked at him, at his face—his dark, hooded eyes, the straight nose—and then dropped her gaze to his naked chest again. There, caught up in the tangle of black hair, lay a tiny piece of burned pie crust, and, like a blond ape, a cavewoman, grooming her mate, Mercy reached out and plucked the food from his hair and deposited it on the table.

"I know," she said, and she smiled at him.

Unnerved, Bybee quickly got up and padded into the living room, found his knit shirt wadded in a ball, slipped it on, returned to the dining room, and sat down again. The emotional maelstrom that had swept around the tiny room just a few minutes before had subsided, had been sucked out the window and dissipated in the clear air above the canyon. Now, in the calm aftermath, they both stared out the window again, this time at the dappling of shade and sunlight in the orchard and, beyond that, working in a bright green field of alfalfa, two young men, Cloyd and LeMoin Batt—the Batt boys, as he liked to call them—two good-natured, oafish guys who had never read a book between them, and were probably better off for it.

Bybee turned to her. "Mercy, you have to talk about what you told me the other night, about what you know. You need to tell everything to me first, then some others, some investigators. They will want to talk—"

"Police?"

"No—well, sort of," Bybee said. "They're specialists, experts I guess you would say. They know what they're doing. They're pros."

Bybee, like most in his ego-driven profession, rarely praised other lawyers, even sage, senior graybeards who had rightfully earned acclaim. But he did honor his investigators, the drunken, grizzled veterans, the men and women who were in the trenches, slogging along, always searching for the truth, always trustworthy and loyal, never betraying him.

"They will call Father," Mercy said, and she began shaking her head, mechanically, back and forth, like a windup toy. "They will. They will call—"

"No!" Bybee yelled, and he pictured Crowe sitting on a jeweled throne, magically hovering in the dark clouds over New Ammon, his eyes shooting fire, his demonic spell burning down upon the bleak colony beneath the cliffs, upon her. . . . He suddenly slapped his hand down on the table, making the plate and fork jump. "Just *fuck* Father!"

At the word, Mercy drew back, and she put her hand to her face, covering her nose, as though Bybee had suddenly turned to rotted flesh, the stench overpowering.

"I'm sorry," he said, and he reflexively reached for her hand to reassure her. "Old army habit."

She did not understand, but she reversed her hand so that their fingers were briefly intertwined before he quickly withdrew.

"Anyway," Bybee said. "Crowe—Father—will not know. At least, not for now. Eventually you will have to testify in front of a jury."

Again, she began shaking her head, back and forth, her eyes closed.

"Mercy—"

"No," she said.

Bybee turned away from her. The prosecution team had been sworn—actually sworn under oath—not to reveal what they had been so carefully guarding at the "safehouse," as Gant insisted on calling it, the same thing that Crowe and his Blood Disciples had been so frantically seeking. But it was more than just a safehouse, Bybee knew; it was, in effect, the command post, the center of the pending strike against Crowe, and like any military base of operations, its location was secret.

But he also knew that Mercy *must* testify about the murder, about all of it: the castration, the beheading, the dismemberment, the monstrous, unspeakable violence that was inflicted in the name of God, in the names of Crowe's bizarre two Christs, and in the name of the Principle. And there was only one way to convince her to cooperate and that he and the others in the AG's office were her allies. He must violate his oath and reveal what was so zealously shielded and protected in Manti, what lay at the heart of the operation: another runaway, another scared, savaged defector from the New Ammon hellhole, someone Mercy knew . . . someone she loved.

"Faith is alive," Bybee said. "Roma Ann McCallister is alive, in our custody. She's—"

"Faith," Mercy blurted, and then her eyes clouded and she put both hands to her face, together, over her mouth, muffling a soft, choking sob. She looked at Bybee, and a tear began to trickle down her bruised face. "Faith?"

"Yes. She got away; she hid from the Disciples . . . somehow. She slept in barns and ditches and walked along roads at night.

She finally found a runaway shelter in, well, a shelter. She was sick; she had been beaten . . . like you. She almost died, Mercy. But she recovered, and then the shelter contacted us. We—our people—set up an office, a safe place. They're with her now, and she's fine."

Mercy lowered her head and began crying, but then she stopped and looked up and tried to smile. "Oh, Faith, merciful Christs." She closed her eyes and began moving her lips, soundlessly, as though she were praying.

Bybee gently took her hand. "She's safe, Mercy; she's healthy, now, and strong . . . and she's been talking; she's helping us; she's going to testify against your husband, about the marriages, all of the ceremonies . . . all the wives." He bent toward her. "She misses all of her sister wives, Mercy. She misses you."

"I—"

"I'm sure she would want to see you."

Mercy sniffed and then ran her hand over her face, smearing the tears and mucus across it, her lips trembling. "Yes, I—"

Bybee waited, and then moved closer to her. "You what, Mercy?"

"I want to see her, too."

Bybee suddenly felt relieved, and he visibly relaxed and exhaled. "Then you will," he said. "We'll go there in a couple of days."

"But Father . . ."

"Father doesn't know about this, where Faith is," Bybee said. "And he won't. You have to trust me."

Mercy looked at him for several moments, then nodded her head. "I do, Mr. Bybee. I trust you."

"Good. What we need—"

Bybee never finished; Mercy suddenly leaned across the table and kissed him quickly and girlishly, a dry, feathery brush of her lips against his, and then sat down again, smiling.

"What do we need?" she said.

Nonplussed, off balance, Bybee pushed his glasses up along his nose and folded his hands together on the table. In that brief kiss, just as he had the other night at the Piute Villa, and then yesterday as he continually leaned over her bed during the day, he could smell her unwashed hair, her dirty body, the dank stench from her underarms.

"We need to clean up," he said. "Take a shower. You can go first." He pointed at her dress—bloodied, torn, the bottom caked in mud. "And get rid of that. Zolene has some clothes you can wear."

For the first time, Mercy seemed aware of how she looked and smelled, and she nodded, embarrassed. "Okay," she said.

"And then you just need to rest some more, get stronger, eat something"—he glanced at the godawful apple mush on the plate—"I'll do the cooking. Then I'll work things out with my people, about seeing Faith, about getting you up to . . . up there."

"Okay," she said again.

"C'mon," Bybee said.

He took Mercy by the elbow and led her back to the living room and down a short hall to Zolene's bedroom, filled with old furniture: a brass bed, a bird's-eye maple dresser, a love seat, and a large, standing oval mirror in an oak frame. Bybee walked to the dresser and opened several of Zolene's drawers—one was reserved for him, his socks and underwear—fumbling, pulling clothes out here and there, dropping some, and then poked through a small closet again, a section of it set aside for his pants and shirts.

Finally he returned to Mercy and held out the armload of clothes, which she inspected, holding each piece up as though she were a shopper at a department store: an olive-drab tank top, white capri pants, tennis shoes, and a pair of skimpy yellow panties and a bra.

Mercy giggled and picked up the bra—a white, average-size, simple thing—and dangled it in front of Bybee's face. "I don't wear these," she said, and she smiled when she saw his eyes reflexively drop to her breasts. "It's too small, anyway."

With an embarrassed laugh, Bybee pointed down the hall. "There's a bathroom there, and—"

"I know," she said.

"—a shower, towels. Soap and shampoo in the tub."

"Thank you," Mercy said, and she reached out and gently touched his hand with one finger.

She turned around, and Bybee watched her clump down the hall to the bathroom, and then he walked back to the living room, glancing briefly into Zolene's daughters' bedroom, where Mercy had been sleeping, the only room in the house that was not restored, not steeped in the past. The walls were covered in silly posters and photographs, a CD player sat to one side, a computer on the other, and speakers were mounted high in the corners—the whole place oozing of modern adolescence. The girls were gone, visiting their paternal grandparents in California, but would be back soon, in about ten days, ready to begin school in Kanab.

He heard the water begin running in the shower, and he slipped on his loafers and went outside and stood on the small porch, made of cement and massive, circular chunks of petrified wood. Smaller pieces of the strange stone had been cemented into all the window ledges and lintels, making the whole yellow-bricked house look half ossified, primitive.

He remained on the shaded porch, looking out through the trees at the Batt boys in the south field, and then surveyed the rest of the place. When Zolene had inherited the ranch after the murder of her grandfather—a case that had brought Bybee to Kanab and into Zolene's life—the property was in ruins: the barn and stables half collapsed, the fences down and smothered in red sand, machines rusted and broken and lying everywhere, and all of the fields dead, overgrown with weeds.

But Zolene had found a tenant farmer, Heber Batt, a sturdy, broad-faced man who was more at home in the sun and green fields than he was at his actual home—a cramped house on the eastern outskirts of Kanab, near the Cliff Corral, an RV park. So the entire Batt family, Heber and his wife, DeVonna, and his two sons, drove out every day from town and worked the ranch. Within six months they had cleared the junk from the yard, repaired the juniper wood fences, leveled and harrowed the dry fields, irrigated with what little water there was, and finally brought a horse or two into the once leaking stalls and purchased a few head of cattle, which now, as Bybee could see, trudged along nearly somnambulant under the red cliffs, a half mile away, their hides glowing in the morning sun.

He took a deep, long breath, sucking in the delicious air of the canyon, holding it in his lungs for a moment like a dope smoker, almost becoming high from it. Like Zolene, he had come to love the canyon and the ranch, the quiet, restorative solitude of it, its calm. It was a place where, when Zolene's daughters were away, he spent almost all of the days—and nights—with her, the two of them content and happy, growing closer.

And it was this peace, this love, that had finally saved him, had kept him away from the bottle, away from the river of Scotch that had flowed through his life for so long, drowning his first marriage and flooding his career, nearly ruining it. Now, his life had been restored, resurrected, set aright—"made whole," as lawyers liked to say.

Aimlessly, he began to walk around the orchard, eventually stopping at a tiny stone grave marker at one corner of the house. It was there, about a year ago, on his first date with Zolene, that he had buried her grandfather's dog, Max, found cruelly hanged by its neck in the orchard. Along with her grandfather's homicide, it was a harbinger of the murderous violence that was to descend on Kanab in the weeks that followed: his cocounsel Ronnie Watters floating dead in the bottomless lake outside of town; Bybee falsely accused of the crime; and Bellard Sipes, who would have been the next prophet and president of the Mormon church, hanging like Max—like a dog—from a wooden gallows, his neck broken.

He shook his head to dispel the images of that horror, and then looked up. He was standing next to the bathroom window, built low, like the other windows, listening to the running water and, along with it, almost muffled, the sound of Mercy humming a song, something slow but cheerful, hopeful—a hymn, perhaps. He looked at the window; the old-style roller shade was up, the light on, and he could see the upper half of the shower curtain, the steam lazily drifting up and over it, and behind the thin cloth, the faint, shadowy outline of Mercy's body.

The sound of the water stopped, and the shower curtain was slowly pulled back.

Bybee stood, transfixed, only a few feet from the window, staring at her white breasts, at the water dripping from them, the dark, purplish tattoo just above the left nipple, and lower, the blond thicket of pubic hair . . . and then she saw him, but she did not move, did not fling the curtain closed, did not try to cover herself, but only continued to stand, her arms at her side, letting him stare, letting him drink her in.

Bybee turned his head and quickly walked away, out of the shadows of the orchard, out of the dense, tall grass and the layers of broken twigs, until he reached the road and the bright sunlight. His right hand was shaking, and he thrust it in his pocket and continued to walk down the road, straight into the warm morning sun—pure and true, undeceiving—and away from Lamb's house, away from the sounds of Mercy, who was singing again, her voice high and sweet . . . calling.

.

It had always been a fact of life in Mormon country—or at least a strong rumor—that non-Mormon businessmen, and especially businesswomen, received rather indifferent treatment from their LDS counterparts in the community. Zolene, a lapsed Saint who had resisted the repeated efforts of the stake missionaries—the hometown proselytizers—to tug her back into the fold, understood this. She knew that, although borrowing money from Zions Bank, just across the street from the LDS church, could be done easily enough, it might involve an inordinately high interest rate. So it was worth it to her to pack a suitcase, drive the three hundred miles to Tucson—just beyond the church's "jurisdiction," as Bybee called it—and talk to bankers there.

And it had been a success. Besides buying a new truck, she had emerged an hour ago from the First State Bank of Arizona, victorious, the papers signed, the loan for the water wells sealed—and a whole two days early, at that. But she decided she would not call and tell him the good news; instead she would check out of her hotel, spend the night with an old sorority chum in Flagstaff, and then, tomorrow, drive straight to Kanab in her new truck and surprise him.

Now she limped through the lobby of the posh Sunset Inn on East Broadway—an extravagance she felt she owed herself—carrying a purse and rolling her small suitcase behind her, every male head suddenly turning to gaze at this striking woman, at the brilliant red hair that flowed to her shoulders, the blue eyes, the body that, even encased in a conservative suit, looked perfectly sculpted. The only flaw, if one were looking closely—which many men were—was the outline of a thick scar on her left leg, one that twisted up and around, a spiraled cord of dead flesh that could be seen through the heavy white stockings, the kind nuns and nurses wear.

Whether over concern for her limp, or involuntarily moved by the beauty of this woman, a man in a coat and tie quickly marched to the door and held it open for her, smiling, and Zolene returned the smile and then struggled outside, and back into the ungodly, heat-island furnace.

"Jeez," she said, and she looked at the glowing red numerals on an electronic marquee across the street: 106°.

Turning away from two ogling, yellow-vested valets, she limped across the parking lot, her left leg skimming across asphalt that, in the ferocious heat, was soft, almost like black dough. She came to her new pickup—a Ford, red and shiny and powerful, one that, unlike her old Mustang, befit her new status as a rancher—tossed her suitcase into the tiny rear seat, and climbed in. Quickly, the trapped heat inside nearly suffocating her, she started the engine and switched on the air conditioner.

She waited, and when the cab finally cooled down, she opened her purse and withdrew the photograph she always kept there, one of Bybee and herself. It had been taken last spring when they were camping at Canyonlands National Park in Utah, the two of them standing together on a high cliff, seemingly half the state stretched out behind them, deserted and desolate, as if they were the last two people left on Earth.

"Brig," she said, and like a schoolgirl, she kissed her fingers and then touched them to the photograph.

4

THOMAS Kendall's ill-starred stage career had its prophetic beginning when, in the third grade at Alma School in Mesa, Arizona, he was cast as one of the three wise men in the school's Christmas play.

There, in the "cafetorium," as it was called, he waited nervously onstage, the curtain down, dressed in his mother's pink chenille bathrobe and clutching an oatmeal box wrapped in gold foil. He and the others—Mary and Joseph, the two other wise men, and a few peasants—stood around a straw-filled wooden crib in which, a minute earlier, the janitor had placed a naked lightbulb to create a bright, heavenly radiance.

But it was too radiant, really, for just as the curtain rose and the choir started to croak out "Away in the Manger," the straw in the crib began to smolder, and a thin finger of smoke arose from the bed of the newborn savior. Mary looked desperately offstage and Joseph peered, concerned and fatherly, into the crib, while Kendall and the other kings stood firm, stiffly holding out their gifts to baby Jesus, who by now, halfway through the song, was on fire, the play ruined.

From that night on, every production with which Kendall

was ever associated was equally disastrous. During a high school production of *Harvey*, his costar, Marsha Coy, simply blacked out in the middle of a scene, ending the play in mid-act. In college, in *Desire under the Elms*, a structural support on the set, a two-story cutaway farmhouse, snapped, suddenly canting the whole thing twenty degrees stage left, sending all of the props and actors—including Kendall—tumbling into a heap. And finally, in graduate school, he wrote and directed a play called *The Lower Rung*, which closed after two performances, the second attracting only nine people.

It was then, amid the ruins of *The Lower Rung*—appropriately named, he had always thought—that Kendall decided to leave the theater and, with only a backpack full of clothes and his motorcycle, entered one of society's refugee camps, a place that every year collected the country's misfits and malcontents and many of its failures: a law school.

On another motorcycle, a twelve-year-old Yamaha Virago, Tom Kendall drove fast—perhaps too fast, as he always did—down the Long Valley Highway, roaring south through towns like Ephraim and Orderville and Mount Carmel, his jutting knees and elbows and his bulbous green helmet with its dark face shield making him look like an oversize insect plopped atop the machine.

As though it were on a giant reel, the scenery unraveled around him: white cliffs rising from the spread of sage and juniper, yellow ridges and green meadows, then narrow, sandstone corridors of red—dark, deep, unyielding red: the Vermilion Cliffs. He raced down through it all, past something called the Moqui Cave, past the mysterious Three Lakes, and past a lone billboard proclaiming that Kane County had "The Greatest Earth on Show!" Finally, he rounded a curve and saw, towering above a few buildings and lesser signs, a ten-foot red arrowhead revolving against the blue sky, alone, almost defiant.

"Crazy-ass Brig," Kendall said, laughing, but the words were blown away, lost.

He throttled back, downshifted and slowed, and then guided the motorcycle toward the sign, eventually turning into the lot of the Piute Villa and coming to a stop at the office tepee. He shut off the engine, and as he sat pulling off his gloves, Spooky Floyd appeared and stared at this odd, balloon-headed creature, and did not retreat until Kendall removed his helmet and stared back.

Still straddling the bike, Kendall looked around him at the slow shuffle of Kanab life: tourists in gaudy shorts and T-shirts dawdling in front of souvenir shops, RVs and tour buses hissing along Center Street, a gray-haired rancher in his muddy hay truck moving through it all, oblivious, the entire scene framed by the red cliffs that surrounded the town, compressing it, sealing it off.

He heard the tinkling of a bell and, at the same time, a familiar voice.

"Tom."

Kendall turned and saw Bybee step out of the office tepee and walk toward him, dressed in his customary slacks and knit shirt with the Piute Villa logo, a uniform of sorts. Bybee had been expecting him; Kendall had called that morning and said he had urgent business—personal business—that could not wait. Kendall dismounted, laying his gloves and helmet on the seat. "Brig Bybee," he said. "As I live and breathe."

The two lawyers had known each other almost twenty years, originally as courtroom rivals, Kendall routinely representing the state of Utah while Bybee defended some murderous wretch. But, by degrees, case by case, they had become friends —true friends—each man developing a genuine respect for the other's legal skills and intellect . . . and candor.

"Won't be breathing long, you keep riding that," Bybee said, nodding at the motorcycle. "How fast on this trip?"

"Got it up to a hundred five on a stretch out of Panguitch."

"You're nuts," Bybee said, and then he warmly shook his friend's hand and inspected him—the leather jacket, the jeans, the old army jump boots. He smiled and nodded toward the machine again. "Arlene hasn't put her foot down?"

For an instant, they both seemed to envision that possibility in its literal sense: Kendall's big, overweight wife—skewed Jack Spratt domesticity straight out of a nursery rhyme—slamming her anvil of a foot into the bike and smashing it.

"Not yet," Kendall said.

"Well, give her time," Bybee said, and he nodded toward a pool of shade under the stand of willow trees, next to Spooky Floyd's dog tepee. "Let's get out of this sun."

The two men walked over to the trees and into a tiny clearing where Bybee had, several months ago, installed a red-wood picnic table and benches, a barbecue grill, and a stone-enclosed fire pit—a place used almost nightly by his guests. Kendall took off his jacket, and the two sat down at the table, on opposite sides, and placed their elbows on the wood, appraising one another.

"You look good," Bybee finally said. "World must be treating you right."

"It's *never* treated me right," Kendall said. He pointed at Bybee, at the tanned, rested face and the way his shirt hung crisply down from his chest, the stomach invisible. "You're looking pretty good yourself."

"Thanks," Bybee said.

"And Zolene?"

"She's fine; she's in Tucson right now."

Kendall pursed his lips and made a hollow, appreciative whistle, the way he always did when he raved about Zolene, about Bybee's life. "She is *so* fine, Brig. You are one lucky son of a bitch."

Bybee nodded and allowed a smile to remain on his angular face for a moment, then let it fade, signaling that the perfunctory pleasantries were over. "Let me guess why you're here, Tom," he said. "The little general told you what an out-of-control asshole I am."

"Yeah, he did, but I already knew that," Kendall said. He winked and, as Bybee had just done, let the kindness in his odd face suddenly vanish. "This is hard to believe, Brig."

"I know," Bybee said. "It's pretty damn ugly."

"But that's our business, buddy: dealing with ugly."

Bybee nodded, still not fully accustomed to the word "our," of being included in the prosecution's camp.

"So where is she, Brig? I want to talk to her."

"Sorry. She's hidden away, safe and sound."

"C'mon, man," Kendall said. "You're not talking to Gant. Remember, we're on the same side now."

"I know, but this woman is scared shitless. She thinks everyone's gunning for her."

"Well, hell, everyone probably is. Look, if she witnessed a goddamned castration-slash-beheading-slash-dismemberment, then I want her statement—signed and certified, notarized by Christ himself."

"Which Christ?" Bybee said.

Kendall looked puzzled, then smiled, remembering. "Right. Maybe both of them; cover all the bases."

Bybee laughed, then his face grew serious again. "Yeah, I want her testimony, too, Tom, but she won't talk until"—he paused, peering at the other man, gauging him—"until she sees Faith . . . in Manti."

Kendall's eyes widened. "Oh, shit! You told her?"

"I told her that Faith was alive, but not where she was, not about Manti. I had to, Tom. I'm telling you, this woman's for real. She's the real deal."

"That's not what Gant thinks."

"Oh, yeah? Well, what does that little turd—"

He broke off as two tall, young women in shorts and halter tops walked by on the sidewalk, cameras dangling from their hands. One of them smiled and waved at the two men, and both waved back—eager and boyish—and then continued to stare at the women until they were out of view.

"Nice," Bybee said, and then he turned back to Kendall. "So what does Gant think?"

"He thinks she's a plant, a fake, something to throw you off, get you barking up the wrong—" He stopped, suddenly, and looked almost apologetically at Spooky Floyd, who was now sitting near them, watching. "Anyway, he and Governor Purcell— God knows who else—want us to do what they've been telling us for months: stage their little antipolygamy morality play, and make it look good. And—" Kendall stopped and smiled. "I'm not sure what else he said; I walked out on him before he finished."

Bybee smiled. "Good for you." He leaned closer to Kendall

as if someone were listening. "But what do *you* want, Tom? Where does the AG's office want to go with this?"

Bybee waited, staring at Kendall's face, at the dark skin, like a hide, that seemed to have been inexpertly stretched over the skull—too tight here, an extra fold there, the whole affair clumsily pasted down. After several moments, when Kendall did not answer, he impatiently held out his hands.

"Having a prosecutor's moment, Tom?"

Kendall didn't smile; he looked uncomfortable, and he began nervously drumming his long fingers on the table, as if he were typing on an invisible keyboard. He finally stopped and looked above Bybee at a lone, white cloud that was drifting overhead in a sky that was so hard and blue that it looked like porcelain, a painted shell.

"Brig, the media's been on Cynthia's case ever since she was elected. They think she's soft on crime, a pushover . . . easy. I guess because she's a woman."

"Or maybe," Bybee said, smiling, "because she's the only Democrat in the whole damned state government."

"Could be, but it's no secret that Purcell wants her out, shit-canned. She doesn't embrace"—Kendall clawed at the air with two fingers on each hand—" 'Utah values.' "

"Whatever those are," Bybee said. "Anyway, I know she's in a dogfight; I read the papers."

"So then you know that her reelection next year is going to be a bitch—a real bitch. She needs something big to help her. She needs some—" Kendall paused and bit his lip, afraid of the next words. "Good PR."

Bybee's dark eyes narrowed and he leaned closer. "Good PR? What does—"

"Brig," Kendall suddenly said, cutting him off. "Let me ask you: what do *you* want for Crowe?"

Bybee looked confused, and continued to squint at the other man, uncertain about just where the conversation was going—or where it had even been. "Well, since I'm a prosecutor—at least, for now—I want to put him in prison for a long time," he said. "With this . . . new stuff, the murder, maybe for the rest of his life."

Kendall shook his head and tried to smile, but he looked worried, in pain. "Well, you're not thinking big, Brig." He winced at the unintended rhyme.

"What do you mean?"

"You're not thinking *beyond* murder."

Bybee shook his head and closed his eyes. "Sorry, I'm not—"

"Look," Kendall said. He took a deep breath, held it for a moment, then expelled it out the side of his mouth. "Have you ever thought about Crowe being tied to an old wooden chair while a firing squad puts a shitload of bullets through his heart, or—"

"What the hell are you—"

"—having him strapped to a gurney and so much Marvel Mystery Oil pumped into him that he just sort of . . . *oozes* away into hell?"

Bybee realized now what the man was saying, and he drew back, incredulous, his mouth partly open. "Death penalty?"

"Damn right!" Kendall said. He was rigid, now, excited, and he stabbed the air with his finger. "Aggravated murder, Brig. Death penalty, pure and *righteous!*"

Bybee immediately felt his scalp burning, the familiar, feverlike heat percolating down through his face and throat, and he turned away, panicked. He did not like this—he loathed it, in fact—and he immediately shifted gears, transformed himself into his old defense attorney persona, frantically searching for the flaws, the government's typical errors in thinking, its over-zealous rush toward punishment, toward an execution, official murder.

"It won't work," he said, and he turned back to face the other man, his voice loud, almost frightened. "You need murder in the course of committing rape or robbery, something like that. There's no scheme, no serial murder, no mass murder—"

Kendall impatiently waved his hand, cutting him off. "No, no. I know that. I'm not talking about that." He waved the same hand at the tepees, at the sleepy, sluggish town that was miles—years—away from Salt Lake City. "You've been out in the sticks too long, buddy. The death penalty statute's been toughened up for a long time. Here—"

Kendall reached across the table, snatched his coat, and from an interior, zippered pocket, withdrew a folded piece of paper. "Sub two-oh-two, the agg' murder statute; at the very end." He opened the paper, cleared his throat, and unconsciously raised one hand, almost as if he were administering an oath. " 'Criminal homicide constitutes aggravated murder if . . . the homicide was committed in an especially heinous, atrocious, cruel, or exceptionally depraved manner, any of which must be demonstrated by physical torture, serious physical abuse, or serious bodily injury of the victim before death.' "

He lowered his hand and looked up at Bybee, then leaned closer, almost whispering. "Brig, I think cutting someone's balls off before cutting his head off is"—he bent his head to the paper again—" 'exceptionally depraved.' " He handed the paper to Bybee. "Don't you?"

Bybee took the creased copy of the statute, and as he read it, absorbing the printed ghoulishness of it, his hand began to shake, and he quickly tossed the paper back to Kendall and thrust his fingers into his pocket. He narrowed his eyes while his mind desperately dredged up any relevant jurisprudence—statutes, case law, procedure, the Constitution—anything that could slow and then stop Kendall. But he could think of nothing to guide him, no precedent—that very heart of the common law—upon which he could fashion a contravening theory. So, like the semiliterate lawyers who never opened a book or set foot in a law library, all he had was bare, barroom argument.

"You're wrong, Tom."

"The hell I am. Why make—"

"You're crazy!"

"—the state of Utah pay to keep that asshole in food and toilet paper the rest of his life? Let's go agg' murder!"

"No!"

Kendall rose halfway from the bench, bent over, his skeletal frame awkwardly poised above the table, and he held one hand in the air again, the old stage actor now playing the Reaper in civilian clothes, aroused, disclaiming.

"We can kill 'im, Brig!"

Bybee clumsily swung his legs clear of the bench, hurriedly

got to his feet, and walked over to the fire pit, his back to Kendall, his hand violently trembling in his pocket. As he fought to compose himself, he heard the sound of laughter—thin, distant, almost like the chittering of animals—and he turned and saw, across the street at the park next to the church, at a pleasant place called the Gazebo, several children running and playing in the grass.

Children. A child. Nearly twenty years ago, in the first capital murder case he tried, Bybee had represented a child—or what he considered to be a child—a nineteen-year-old boy who, after they lost the trial, leaned on Bybee and sobbed, his mother screaming in the rear of the courtroom, as the formal sentence of death was pronounced by the judge.

An hour later, stunned and sickened, Bybee found his favorite Salt Lake City bar, D. B. Coopers, where he sat alone in a darkened corner—the world outside even darker, bleaker—trying to drown out the horror of what had just happened with one Scotch after another, the liquor trickling into him, filling him. . . .

Then, through the door, came the prosecution team—its lawyers and paralegals and investigators, even a few secretaries—laughing, whooping, buying drinks for the house, celebrating, turning the tavern into a delirious and chanting carnival of death.

"We killed him! We killed him! We killed . . . "

And Bybee, drunk and angry, barely able to stand, had waded into the middle of it all, damning them, screeching at them for gleefully murdering a child, until he broke down and bawled like a child himself, and was finally helped outside and driven to his home by one of their investigators.

Bybee turned away from the children and looked at Kendall sitting alone at the table, no different from all the others now, still nervously tapping his fingers, ready to pull the trigger.

Bybee walked back to the picnic table and stood over him. "I didn't sign on with the AG for a death penalty case, Tom."

Kendall nodded. "True, but you didn't sign on for a plain vanilla murder, either. But you just said that you're ready to prosecute that."

"It's different. I don't believe in the death penalty, and you know that—you've always known that."

"True," Kendall said again.

Years before, when he was a full-fledged, active drunk, Bybee had expounded at length to Kendall, in several of their posttrial drinking sessions, about the death penalty, the immorality of it, the government's seething hypocrisy. It was the only time the two friends had ever truly squared off, each shouting at the other, fingers jabbing.

"But whether you like it or not," Kendall went on, "you're a prosecutor, even if you are a hired gun. You can't have it both ways, Brig: prosecute but not fully prosecute. It's like being pregnant—either you are or you aren't."

"Oh, Lord, Tom. Give me a break."

"I am, believe it or not. Every prosecutor in this state, career or just a temp, wants a chance just like this—especially with someone like Crowe. Christ, he's the worst of the worst." Kendall hesitated and then smiled. "C'mon, a death penalty pop'll be a feather in your cap."

"Jesus!"

Bybee began to walk away again, but Kendall stretched one long, sticklike arm out and grabbed him by his knit shirt, stretching the thing, halting him.

"Sit down, Brig."

He gently tugged Bybee back to the table and, assured that the man would not escape, released his shirt. Bybee reluctantly seated himself again and stared at the tabletop.

Kendall cleared his throat. "When I told Cynthia about this," he said, his voice low, conspiratorial, "she damn near had an orgasm, man." He paused, knowing Bybee, like himself, was picturing the attorney general, a petite, attractive blond with short hair, in the grip of a shuddering climax, her eyes rolled back into her head. "She thinks this is it. This will show everyone—voters—that she's got guts, a pair of . . . balls. She needs this."

"*She* needs this, Tom? Or you?"

Kendall shrugged. "Okay. I won't try to bullshit you. If Cynthia goes down the toilet, I go with her."

"Oh, c'mon," Bybee said. "You're a smart guy, experienced. You can get another job. There's dozens of them out there."

Kendall shook his head. "Not for me. I've never been in private practice, like you. I've never tried a civil case in my life—hell, I've never even drawn up a will or done an uncontested divorce. I've been a criminal prosecutor from the day I passed the bar, Brig, and this is the last stop. I'm serious." He held his arms straight out to the side, putting his sad, scarecrow body on display. "Who would want me? Hell, Brig, even the army wouldn't take me." He dropped his arms to his side so that they made a hollow *thwop* and then pointed at his combat boots. "Got these at a surplus store—used. I get everything—"

He stopped and grinned, embarrassed, realizing that Bybee knew that Arlene had gone through two husbands before thumping down the aisle with him.

"I suppose," Bybee said.

"Anyway," Kendall said, "if Cynthia's out on her ass, so am I. The AG needs a death penalty pop—*bad*—and we're going to get it." .

"Well, not with me," Bybee said. He pushed his wire-rimmed glasses back along his nose. "Find yourself another boy, another executioner."

"But Cynthia wants you." Kendall stopped, the double entendre too obvious, and looked at Bybee, at the raw, athletic good looks of the man, a man many women in the AG's office—including the attorney general herself—constantly speculated about. "I told her," Kendall went on, "about your feelings about the death penalty. She understands, but she still wants you on this case. And so do I. That's why I drove all the way down here, rather than call." He tried to smile. "I wanted to hassle you personally."

"Well, you have. Look, Tom—"

Kendall held up his hand. "She wants you to think about it for a few days. That's all. Just think about it. If you really want out, then you're out. Simple. So just think about it. Okay?"

Bybee breathed deeply and tiredly, then slowly nodded his head. "Okay. I'll think about it, but you know what the answer will be. If the AG's office is going agg' murder—death penalty—you'd better start lining up a new prosecutor."

As Bybee had done several minutes earlier, Kendall awkwardly untangled his legs from underneath the table, his combat boots clattering against the wood, and stood up.

"We will, Brig, if it comes to that. By the way, we filed a motion for continuance with the Rocket Man this morning. I figured you wouldn't mind. Regardless of what happens—agg' murder, vanilla murder, bigamy, even"—he smiled—"if we lose you, we need some time to check everything out."

"I don't mind," Bybee said. "That's what I wanted to do, anyway."

"Good," Kendall said. He picked up his jacket, rakishly threw it over his narrow, sloped shoulders—where it instantly slid off—and then looked at his watch. "I've got to get back."

Bybee, seeing that the conversation was over, got to his feet as well, reflexively looking around for Spooky Floyd, who had disappeared. "What about Gant?" he said.

"The hell with Gant," Kendall said, and the two men began walking back toward the motorcycle, out of the shade and into the brilliant sunshine. "He doesn't know his ass from his elbow."

"Actually, I get that mixed up, now and then," Bybee said.

Kendall didn't seem to hear. "We're fighting for political survival just like they are, but"—he turned and winked—"God's on our side."

"I don't think he's on anybody's side in this mess," Bybee said.

They continued across the lot until they came up to the motorcycle, and Kendall slipped into his jacket and began pulling his leather gloves over his bony fingers. When he was finished, he swung his leg over the machine, sat down, holding the green helmet in one hand, and stared steadily at the motel, at the cluster of white tepees, their doors closed, the windowshades down, as if they all possessed a dark secret within—or maybe just one of them.

Bybee watched him for several moments, then lightly clapped him on his back. "Forget it, Tom. She's not here."

Kendall slipped on his helmet, his thin face wholly enveloped by it. "I didn't think she would be; you're not that stupid. Actually, I was just thinking that Piutes never lived in tepees—especially goofy ones with stars on them."

"I know," Bybee said. "It's just for tourists. The foreigners love it."

And, as if to underscore that contention, an Asian woman, flat-faced and heavy-legged, walked out of tepee number seven and crunched across the gravel toward Duffin's Wampum Mart. From nowhere, Spooky Floyd reappeared and gloomily began to follow her, his tail dragging. Kendall watched the animal for a moment, then swept his eyes over the lot, nodding, and turned back to Bybee.

"You got a sweet gig, Brig," he said, shaking his head at another unintended rhyme.

"Well, it's seasonal . . . tourists. It doesn't make—"

"No," Kendall said. "I mean all of it: the motel, your law practice, your woman. You've got a good life."

Bybee shrugged and smiled. "Yeah, I guess I do; I'm happy."

"I wish—" Kendall stopped and then waved his hand, his face growing serious. "Anyway, you know Crowe and his boys are probably turning the state upside down looking for this runaway. Keep your head on a swivel."

"Don't worry; I will."

Satisfied, Kendall lowered the mirrored face shield and started the engine, revving it, and then tilted his big helmet toward Bybee, yelling over the engine's roar. "I wish you were still drinking. I hear there's a bar just across the state line."

"I know—the Buckskin Tavern," Bybee yelled back. "Last time I got drunk, it was there, a year ago, and I ended up in jail accused of murder. No thanks."

Kendall kicked back the side stand and toed the old Yamaha into gear. "Strange days back then, Brig."

"Strange days *now*," Bybee shouted.

Kendall looked at Spooky Floyd, who was now slouching back to his dog tepee, and then yelled something about the dog as the motorcycle leapt away, gravel spraying. He turned out of the lot and sped back the way he came, along Center Street, his rail-thin body—not a mutant insect now, but Jack Spratt in leather—hunched over the machine, his elbows and knees pointing in all directions, everywhere . . . nowhere.

5

ON June 9, 1983, a date all New Ammonites were required to remember—and revere—Theodore Rampton Crowe, then simply a twenty-four-year-old high school dropout from La Verkin, Utah, and a fledgling polygamist, was hiking atop the Vermilion Cliffs, near Kanab. There, tired and resting amid a stand of juniper trees, he claimed to have come face to face with Adam and Jesus—the two sons of God.

In that "New Vision," as Crowe styled it, the two Christs directed him to abandon his earthly pursuits and, surrendering to the will of the Heavenly Father, create a new church—the true church: the United Order of the Christ Brethren.

And so he did—proclaiming himself to be the "Grand Seer and Revelator," the "Father of the Faithful," and the "One Mighty and Strong," inheriting several titles claimed by a succession of fundamentalist despots—and brought together the sluggish hodge-podge of polygamists in New Ammon to create his spiritual kingdom.

But that kingdom quickly became nothing more than a homophobic, patriarchal religious commune where all his followers were required to dress in nineteenth-century clothing and were assigned to work, with no or little pay, at a variety of tasks Crowe called "missions"—most of them in the leather factory—all under the constant and often brutal control of the Blood Disciples. It was, as one *Salt Lake Tribune* reporter had written, "certainly a New Vision, a new vision of white slavery."

And it all had its grand, epiphanous beginnings atop the cliffs just west of Kanab.

Later in the afternoon, when the sun just seemed to loiter above those cliffs, reluctant to leave, the day on hold, Bybee was coming out of Duke's Mercantile when he spotted what he knew was one of them. The man stood across the street from Duke's in front of the Stagecoach Bed and Breakfast, several blocks from the Piute Villa, his hands on his hips. He was of average height, maybe smaller, but tough and wiry looking, dressed like many of the older, gray-haired ranchers around Kanab—a straw hat, long-sleeved shirt, overalls, and heavy work boots. This man was young, though, maybe in his thirties, with a thick beard—dark blond, almost brown—that formed a ragged point just below his neck. It was the way all of the New Ammon men looked or dressed, fundamentalist farmers on a rare foray outside the commune, perhaps looking to buy those things unavailable in the colony . . . or simply just looking.

Bybee immediately stopped, turned around, walked back into Duke's, and stood behind the big display window, watching, hidden behind a mannequin outfitted in tight jeans and a multi-colored cowboy shirt. The man across the street did not move, but simply stared up and down Center Street, watching everything that walked or drove by. After several minutes he reached into his shirt pocket, withdrew a small plastic object—a cell phone—and flipped it open, punched several buttons, then spoke into the device.

About one minute later, a battered blue pickup truck with a white camper shell pulled up, and Bybee could see that the driver was also young, perhaps no more than twenty-five years old, with the same old-fashioned clothes and a bright blond beard that seemed to hide the entire lower half of his face. The man who had been standing on the street climbed into the passenger side, and the truck slowly pulled away and was gone.

They were Blood Disciples, Bybee knew; they had to be. The AG's reports had indicated that they were generally young, and had considerable freedom to roam about, even to possess modern, electronic gadgetry—and they were constantly vigilant.

As if the two Blood Disciples controlled it—or at least influenced it in some way—the sun finally dipped behind the cliffs, and a long shadow began to creep across the town. Bybee still stood behind the mannequin, paralyzed, almost like a second mannequin himself, while his mind raced in frantic, dizzying circles, trying to decide what to do next—what *they* would do next. He considered calling the new sheriff, DeRalph Seegmiller, a good, honest man who had, last November, to everyone's surprise, defeated LeGrand Little, the heir apparent to the office. But Mercy's sobbing, panicked words—*"they will tell Father"*—kept endlessly playing through his head, and he decided against involving Seegmiller—or anyone.

He continued to peer out through the window, thoughts foaming and fizzing through his mind. There were dozens of towns near New Ammon, hundreds of places that Mercy could be hiding, so why were they here? What did they know? As he had just witnessed, they were in instant and constant communication with one another, meaning that at this very moment, if they *did* know or suspect something, an entire squad of the Blood Disciples might be roaring out of New Ammon in a convoy of rattling, muddy trucks, armed and vengeful, stoked up with Crowe's pious, murderous fervor, and heading for Kanab . . . or Johnson Canyon.

As though, in his mannequin-like state, he had been magically brought to life, Bybee jerked upright. "Lord God," he said.

Quickly, he walked outside and, after carefully looking up and down the street for any sign of the odd, bearded men, jogged back to the Piute Villa, his hard leather shoes slapping loudly against the cement. Pushing Spooky Floyd out of the way, he unlocked the office door and, once inside, flipped a series of wall switches, turning on the outside lights, including the revolving sign. It was still about an hour before Vesta would relieve him, but the Piute Villa was not a concern now, and Bybee left the office, locked the door again, and ran across the lot to the old VW bus.

As he bumped out onto Center Street, he looked desperately in either direction, searching for the blue pickup with the white camper shell, expecting it to suddenly appear behind him or screech out from where it sat, waiting, in the side-street shadows. But he saw nothing—only the sluggish early-evening crawl of tourists and ranchers, the children still playing at the Gazebo, and the hordes of sandal-clad foreigners clambering in and out of the tour buses at the Pow-Wow, the big souvenir shop. The two Blood Disciples—or anyone that even resembled them—were not in sight.

At the other end of town, around a gentle curve, he drove south through the intersection next to Lloyd Honey's Texaco where he should have turned east, toward Johnson Canyon. But he continued driving south, loudly cursing the old VW bus —humped and ungainly, a giant lime green, oil-leaking thing that was the most noticeable vehicle on the road. He constantly checked his rearview mirrors and, finally satisfied that he was not being followed, slowed and turned around near the Arizona state line, at the Red Land Roost—a ramshackle, cluttered trailer park where Old Jay still lived. It had been Old Jay—the silver-haired Navajo man—who, a year before, had revealed a simple fact about the Parks murder investigation that had eventually led to the stunning dismissal of the case the day of trial.

But that dismissal, that victory for Bybee, followed several nightmarish days of horror and cruelty and more murder. And it had all been here, in Kanab, in this sleepy little Mormon village that had always harbored strange and frightening secrets, secrets that were all too real . . . and deadly.

It was growing dark, and Bybee switched on his headlights and sped back to the intersection at Lloyd Honey's Texaco, turned right, and drove as fast as the clanking breadbox of a bus would allow, the tiny engine whining. Ten miles down the highway, he peered again into his mirrors to assure himself that no long-bearded thugs had pursued him, then veered off the highway onto the narrow, rutted back road to Lamb's house.

Like a ship on a rough sea, the old bus rose and fell as Bybee frantically pushed the machine along the road, its headlights crazily sweeping over the sage and the dark sandstone wall of a lone butte called Dishpan, causing jackrabbits to sprint and dart everywhere.

At last he passed the black gummy pond by the Farnsworth house and a stretch of new corral fencing and roared down the road by the orchard until he came to Lamb's house. He stopped, the bus actually skidding a few feet, switched off the engine and lights, and waited.

The house was dark and quiet, shrouded by trees and an unearthly silence, and other than the Batt boys' old Farm-All tractor, sitting alone and ghostly at the far end of the orchard, there were no other vehicles parked there, no convoy from New Ammon, not even a blue pickup truck.

Bybee jumped out of the van and hurried—almost ran—up the flagstone walkway, tripping and nearly falling in the dark, and then pounded up the steps to the petrified wood porch and opened the door.

"Mercy!" he yelled.

He waited, the door half open, his heart hammering in his chest . . . and then his hand began to tremble as the awful, empty silence of the house reared up, like something alive and evil, and descended upon him.

"Mercy!"

And then he heard the crying; it was like a child crying, a thin, muffled sound, the way his daughter used to cry in the middle of the night, in the middle of a nightmare. For a dizzying instant Bybee thought that there *was* a child inside this house, alone, abandoned, perhaps little Cassie Lee Lewis, lost for over forty years, still roaming the canyons at night.

He crept quietly into the living room, the old wood floors loudly squeaking as he walked through the darkness, stopped at the door to Zolene's daughters' bedroom, and listened. The crying had stopped, and he slowly pushed the door open, walked softly into the room, and stood over the bed. The darkness was thick, almost palpable, but he could see that Mercy lay atop one bed, the quilt coiled around her body, one arm flung to the side, halfway off the bed. He bent closer and heard her breathing —deep and heavy—and knew that she had only been dreaming, suffering through another nightmare, and then he lightly touched her cheek with his hand. She did not wake, did not even stir, and he straightened the quilt and spread it over her, then walked silently back out to the living room. He began to fumble with a floor lamp, trying to turn it on, but realized that, in the blackness of the canyon, the light would shine like a beacon. Instead, he walked out to the cement-and-petrified-wood porch, sat on the first step, his knees high, and stared out over the dark fields toward the gulch, Johnson Wash.

He knew that, along the line of Russian olive trees near the Lewis house, there ran an old road to a decayed, wooden bridge at the wash, condemned by the county years ago but still intact and serviceable, connecting the property to the asphalted highway that ran up and out of the canyon. Years before, Zolene had once explained, it had been the only route into the ranch, but now it was never used . . . except in an emergency.

Bybee turned and looked to the south, toward Dishpan, the flat-topped butte's outline barely visible against the dark sky, and the road he had just traveled. He would be able to see any vehicle—day or night—that approached, and it would afford him just enough time to hustle Mercy into his battered Volkswagen bus and spirit her away down the old road, hidden from view by the olive trees, across the bridge, and away from the canyon unseen.

He relaxed somewhat; it was a good plan—the only plan, really—and he mentally rehearsed it over and over, gauging distances and speeds and reaction times, until his eyes burned from staring into the darkness. But he remained on the porch, afraid to abandon his post—one of the few things he *had* learned in the army—letting the night thicken around him as the sheeting of stars pressed down, the sky lowering, the whole of existence contracting, gathering.

He knew Zolene kept, on the back porch in a locked, wooden cabinet, an old .22 rifle, one she had hunted rabbits with as a kid in this canyon, one she kept now, she said, for her own protection . . . or his. But he hated the rifle; he hated all guns; he hated the look and feel and heavy horror of them, and he drove away any thought of arming himself.

At last he stood and walked back into the living room and, as he had the two nights before, stripped off his shirt and shoes and stretched out on the uncomfortable couch and lay there, surrendering, allowing the darkness to finally surround and suffocate him, sinking him into sleep.

The light seemed to seep into the room, illuminating objects by degrees, causing him to believe that what he saw was like film in a darkroom, slowly developing, a blurred, nascent image forming itself into a photograph, but one taken out of time, out of context . . . but maybe not a photograph at all, but something real.

And then he heard the music, loud and insistent, pounding, rap or hip-hop or whatever rhymed nonsense Zolene's kids called it, filling the house, violating the sanctity of the place, something obscene.

Mercy stood in the girls' room amid the teenage, modern-day clutter, slowly gyrating to the music, standing before a mirror, dressed in the tank top and capri pants Bybee had given her that morning, both pieces of clothing too small, both exquisitely molded to her body. She was barefooted, and she made a half turn in her dance as if to display her hair, pulled back from her face now into a long, girlish ponytail, and then she leaned toward the mirror again and squinted, her body still pulsing to the music, and then drew back, a gold lipstick raised and poised in one hand, and moved her lips—now bright red—as if she were speaking to someone.

She turned then and smiled at him, at his barely visible face in the other room, and then she walked toward him, gliding soundlessly across the wooden floors, still in time to the music . . . and she was there, bent over him, smelling of soap and shampoo and perfume, and beyond that, something else, something sweet and musky that filled the room, something that conjured up images and illusions of women, of womanhood, of dark, intoxicating secrets never fully revealed, never fully understood, but demanding to be probed, insistent . . .

She kissed him, her mouth grinding against his own.

"No," he said.

"Let me take care of you." Her voice was soft, a husky whisper, rhythmic, a part of the music.

She bent and kissed him again, and he resisted, pushing against her shoulders, and she finally relented, but she bent again and moved down his body and began to unzip his wrinkled pants, grinning at him in the half-light.

"No," Bybee said again, but he did not fend her off this time but only lay back, allowing her to peel back his pants and then almost rip at his underwear, finally pulling it aside.

Her mouth descended on him, taking him in, all of him.

"Lord . . . Mercy . . ."

"Let me."

With one hand she reached across his body and covered his mouth while, with the other, she cupped him, lightly squeezing him, expertly working at him. He was stiffening now, and throbbing, and she plunged more viciously at him, deep, rhythmic, relentless, in time to the music, sucking him into her throat, swallowing him into the very center of her, her very soul, it seemed, making at first a soft, humming sound, then, as he grew harder, thrusting back at her, a growling noise from deep within her.

And he did nothing but lie back, one arm stretched out, dipping toward the floor, and the other resting on the top of the couch, his legs slightly parted, his pants and underwear halfway down his thighs in a tangle of cloth as her head bobbed, like a part of a machine, never stopping . . .

When he came, he screamed like a man suddenly run

through by a sword, a wild, anguished howl of pure and intense and explosive pleasure, a jolt of electricity that spread from his thighs and up his spinal column until it burst into his brain, blinding him, convulsing him, his back arched, emptying himself into her, groaning.

And then he fell, it seemed, for miles, tumbling into clouds and warm air as she finally released him and moved her mouth up along his stomach, licking at the hair on his chest, and then covering his mouth with her own, again, finding his tongue and plunging her own into him, silencing him as he drank in the sweetness of her.

"Mercy."

6

S HE hated this part of the trip; she always had. The highway
north out of Flagstaff seemed to leave the earth and to un-
wind into the air for several miles before it dropped
straight down into the reservation, a hellish land of wooden
shacks and burned cars and naked children standing in the sun,
black hair dripping down their heads. And worst of all, she hated
the hogans—those horrible, humped mud homes she had always believed, as a child, were the surface openings for underground colonies, subterranean human hives where the Indians
lived, unseen and waiting, waiting for one of the cars to break
down, waiting for a small white girl with red hair and blue eyes
to wander near. . . .

But the trip today was different. Zolene was going home with a
new truck and the loan papers signed and sealed, the promise
and prospect of water—abundant, gushing well water, not the
sad trickle from Johnson Wash—a reality, now. But more importantly, she was going home to Brig.

Eventually—gratefully—she began the grinding climb out of the valley, away from the hot desert floor and the huts and hogans and the dirty children, and at the top of the plateau she slowed and took off her sunglasses so she could look out over the broad sweep of House Rock Valley and the Colorado River and the first scratchings of the Grand Canyon, all of it spread before her, almost arcing at the horizon, the dark canyon looking like a crack in the shell of creation, a fissure that, according to local legend, had screamed open the day Christ was crucified.

She put her sunglasses back on and continued, through Page, Arizona, and across the dam at the tourist-choked Lake Powell, a beautifully queer place where Hollywood crews had once landed fake spaceships and set loose talking apes to make a movie, a silly science fiction thing about the curvature of time, of the future becoming the past . . . or maybe the past swallowing the present.

Away from the dam and the tourists, Zolene began to speed now, excited, swerving around the slower trucks and RVs, smiling as she thought of Brig, the surprise on his dark, handsome face, the shock of seeing her bouncing in a day early in a new truck—and a big, shiny, gaudy red one, at that. She sped past the polygamist colony at Big Water, through miniature cliffs and leached-out ravines and crusted yellow rock, and then the soil began to redden, the scattering of scrub pinyon and juniper thickened, and at last the first of the Vermilion Cliffs came into view . . . and finally Dishpan.

She turned off the highway and drove down the back road toward the ranch, toward Lamb's house, and when she was close enough, just past the smaller, twin-rutted road to the cistern, she began honking the truck's horn, its deep, irritating blare echoing up the quiet canyon, causing Heber Batt, who was raking hay into windrows under the cliffs, to stop and stand up on his tractor, and then slowly shake his head.

With pink dust billowing around her, she drove down the road by the orchard, still sounding the horn, and actually squealed like a schoolgirl when she saw Bybee's wretched green motel bus parked at the house. He was here.

She stopped the truck next to a small brick garage and lowered both windows. "Brig!" she yelled, and she kept honking the horn, insistent. "Look what I've got."

She turned off the engine and climbed down from the truck, her left leg sore, numb—"humming," as it often did—and as though she had been asked to pose for a photograph, she stopped and shook out her hair into a brilliant cascade of red that tumbled across her white face and down to her shoulders, shimmering there, shining, even in the dappled shade of the orchard.

"Brig!" she yelled again.

She limped away from the truck and stopped at the painted wooden gate near the walkway to the porch. She was dressed in jeans, a tight yellow T-shirt, and tennis shoes, and as always, a pair of silver-and-turquoise earrings dangled down the sides of her neck, framing her sunglassed face.

"Hey, babe," she yelled. "It's me. Come look."

There was no sound or movement from inside her house, and for a moment Zolene thought that Bybee was back at the barn, puttering, or maybe had hiked over to Wester Lewis's place to chat with the old man, the two men regular ranching chums, now.

The front door opened slowly, its old hinges squeaking, and Bybee tentatively walked out to the porch and down the steps. He was dressed in jeans and an old dress shirt and loafers with no socks, and he raised his hand, almost as if he were casually greeting a passerby, perhaps hailing old man Lewis across the fields.

"Zolene," he said.

He moved down the flagstone walkway, trying to smile, raking his hair out of his face, and came up to her at the wooden gate. He looked tired, worried, and he leaned across the gate and awkwardly kissed her, then drew back.

"What the hell are you doing here?" he said.

Zolene laughed and shook out her hair again, and then removed her sunglasses and hooked them on her shirt. "Jeez, babe, last time I checked, I lived here." She smiled, and her eyes—a deep, liquid blue—stared at his own, at the fatigue behind them. "You okay? You look tired."

"Actually—"

But she kissed him again, quickly, swiveled around, and pointed at the truck. "Look what I got. Neat, huh? Brand-new. Eight cylinders." She motioned toward Bybee's dented, rusted bus, the lime green paint coated with a layer of red dust. "Won't have to haul hay in that thing anymore." She turned back to him. "But I've got a bigger surprise—"

"Zolene. I need—"

"—for you, babe." She drew herself up straight, her small breasts straining against the T-shirt. "I got the money. I really did, Brig. Everything I wanted." She excitedly pointed west, toward several fields near Johnson Wash that were still dry and weedy, acreage that the tiny rivulet of irrigation could never reach. "Heber'll have alfalfa there next year, all along the gulch, and we can even get a stock pond over by Dishpan and get the highway fields going." She shook her head, her hair spilling everywhere. "Water, Brig. Do you believe it? I never, *ever* thought I'd see it out here." She laughed and leaned toward him. "Jeez, we can even put in a swimming pool if—"

She stopped suddenly, peering into Bybee's dark face. Something was wrong; she could sense it, feel it; it was almost emanating from him like a stench. She knew Bybee better, more intensely, than she had ever known any other man, even better than Drew, her late husband, or Doug, her grandfather, the man who had virtually raised her out here on the ranch. But unlike them, unlike every other man in her life, Bybee did not hide behind the veneer of manhood, did not conceal his feelings, brazen his way through a problem, stone-faced. He simply was not capable of it, and that was one of the reasons she loved him; he was vulnerable . . . and honest.

"What's wrong, Brig?"

Bybee took a slow breath and swallowed, the torment now overtaking his entire face. "Zolene, a couple of nights ago—"

Zolene put her hand out, touching his arm, stopping him. "Let's go inside, babe. Let's sit down."

"No," he said, and he shook his head. "We shouldn't go inside."

Her head jerked, and she stared anxiously at the house, panicked, squinting, looking for the collapsed roof or the burned-out kitchen, but it looked whole, untouched, unspoiled.

"What the hell are you talking about?" she said. "Let's go into the house."

"There's a woman in there," Bybee said.

Zolene froze, her hand moved slowly to her throat, and she stared at him, her eyes narrowing. "Did I just hear that right? A *woman?*"

"Yes," Bybee said, "but this woman—"

Zolene suddenly pushed the gate with her hand, knocking it against Bybee's knees, and then turned her back to him and limped away. It was what she always did when she was angry or upset, he had discovered; it was what she had done that night, over a year ago, when Bybee had confronted her at the Gazebo dance with Ronnie Watters's—and perhaps his own—frightening suspicions of her, suspicions that proved to be utterly and damnably false.

Neither one of them spoke as they stood, Zolene's back still to him, and listened to the faint popping sounds of Heber Batt's tractor against the cliffs, the echo giving it an uneven, staccato sound, like a ticking clock terribly out of balance.

"Just listen to me," Bybee finally said.

Zolene spun around; her eyes were wet, and her lips, always in a natural pout, had begun to tremble. It was clear to her now; it was like a revelation, a parting of the clouds, but instead of light bursting through, it was a greater darkness that rushed in, more clouds.

"Oh, I am, Brig. I have been—maybe for too long. God, you're so fucking . . . *middle aged!* A big middle-aged prick! Jesus, why can't you have your midlife crisis like everyone else? Grow a ponytail. Buy a motorcycle. God!"

She limped back to the fence and viciously hit the gate again, then straightened, balled her hand, and began striking Bybee on his chest with the bottom of her fist, as though she held an imaginary knife and were plunging it deep into his heart. She finally stopped, drew back, and made a choking, strangled sound as she violently shook her head, back and forth, tears running down her face.

"I knew it!" she screamed. "I just knew it would happen!" She slapped her hand against her left leg. "You finally got tired of sleeping with a gimp, didn't you? Got sick of screwing a cripple—"

"Shut up, Zolene! I didn't—" He stopped and stared at her and then closed his eyes, trying to dredge up what had happened last night, trying to separate hazy dream from cold, brutal fact.

"Didn't *what?*" Zolene yelled. "Finish your sentence, Brig! You didn't . . . sleep with her? Didn't wash up afterward?" She suddenly balled her hands and began to come at him again. "Or didn't think I was going to come home a *fucking* day early?"

Bybee batted away her fists, then grabbed both her forearms and pinned them to his chest, pulling her close to him across the fence. Zolene fought, trying to wrench free, but Bybee only tightened his grip, squeezing her arms until he knew it was hurting her, until she finally stopped struggling.

"Just listen to me, Zolene," he said. "Just shut up and let me tell you everything that's happened. All right?"

Zolene did not answer; her arms were now held by Bybee in an X in front of her, as if she were blocking him, protecting herself, or making a strange hand signal to someone watching from the red hills. She turned her head away at a severe angle, causing her hair to fall to one side, nearly to her waist.

"Will you listen, Zolene?"

She relaxed, her body sagging, and Bybee released her arms but kept his hands near her, to hold her if she fell, or seize her if she flew at him again. But she was spent, beaten; they were still separated by the low wooden fence and the partially opened gate, and she placed both her hands on the pointed tops of the wood slats, steadying herself, the marks from Bybee's fingers still red and visible on her arms.

"Okay," she said, almost in a whisper. She did not look at him, but only stared at her hands.

Bybee nodded; as if to gather his thoughts or to seek last-second solace, he bent his head back to peer up through the patchwork of sun and shade and blue sky, then looked into her eyes and began speaking. He told her about the runaway stumbling—beaten and frantic—into the Piute Villa, about the soul-searing horror she had witnessed, Mercy's fear and paranoia, Faith, the politics now raging about the new direction of the prosecution, and of the Blood Disciples and their maniacal, deadly hunt for the woman, a hunt that was ongoing and real, only a few miles away.

He told her all of it, everything—everything except what was absolutely privileged and confidential: the location of the safe-house . . . and what had happened, or what he thought had happened, last night.

When he was finished, Zolene removed her hands from the fence and pushed them into the rear pockets of her jeans. Her face was still wet, and her eyes were red and wild looking, but she had stopped crying, and she stared out at the eastern hills, at Heber still crawling through the sunlight on his tractor.

"Where has she been sleeping, Brig? What bed?"

Bybee hesitated, his mind beginning to tumble. "In one of the girls'; in their room. She—"

"Jesus." Zolene closed her eyes, her head slightly twitching, as if she were afflicted with a tremor. "And you? Where have you been—"

"On the couch," Bybee said, perhaps too quickly. "In the living room. I could have slept in your bed, but I wanted to stay, I don't know . . . apart."

Zolene kept her eyes closed. " 'Apart,' " she repeated. "And I suppose she didn't arrive fresh and clean off a tour bus, with a camera and a couple of suitcases?"

For a moment Bybee did not understand; then he nodded slowly; pushed his glasses along his nose and cleared his throat. "Zolene, she was beaten—badly—and her dress was torn up . . . bloody, and she stank. Jesus, she reeked. She had been—"

"In other words," Zolene said, "she's been sleeping in my house, been using my bathroom, and just for good measure, has been wearing my clothes." She hesitated, looking at the house, then glared at Bybee again. "My own fucking *clothes*, Brig! Did you help pick them out, huh? Show her everything?"

"Zolene, this woman needs help—bad. She's been through a helluva—"

"Oh, how noble, Brig. How noble of the good, kind Bishop Bybee."

Bybee turned his head and ran his hand across his face. The only instance she had ever called him Bishop Bybee, had ever taunted him that way, was the first time they had made love, both drunk, both wallowing and rutting and screaming in the freezing mud of Three Lakes, just outside of town.

Zolene suddenly jerked her thumb over her shoulder. "Why don't you just put a sign out on the highway, huh? *Bishop Bybee's Bed and Breakfast. Plig Runaways Welcome.*"

Bybee smiled, relieved at the humor that was seeping back into the conversation, and he reached out and gently took her by the shoulder.

She twisted away. "You big macho shit!"

"Zolene, please. It's just temporary. As soon—"

"You're goddamned right, it's just temporary." She leaned toward him, her face afire, her eyes full of hate. "I want that little cohab bitch out of my house now, Brig. Right now!"

"She will be; it's just that I need time."

"Time to do what? Time to experiment, try different positions? Time to invite all the sister wives over?"

"Oh, Christ, Zolene, get—"

"I want your little plig whore out. *Now!*"

"She's not my plig whore, Zolene. And I can't get her out . . . *now*," Bybee said.

Her eyes burned into his. "Then I'm going to find someone who *can* get her out."

She spun around and limped back to the driver's side of her new truck, climbed in, and slammed the door just as Bybee came up.

"Zolene—"

She wouldn't look at him; instead she started the engine and fought the shift lever, struggling, cursing, until she found the gear. The truck shot backward in a tight circle, the right rear fender scraping the corner of the garage, leaving a deep white scar on the new paint. She spun the steering wheel, lurched forward and turned, and then raced back down the road in a storm of roiling red dust, away from the orchard and her violated house, away from her lover, who stood paralyzed in the blackness of the shade, nearly invisible.

One of DeRalph Seegmiller's first official acts after being elected sheriff last November was to improve the appearance of the storefront, as it were. Under the old, corrupt father-son regime of Lamar and LeGrand Little, the sheriff's office on 100 South had been wholly denuded, so stripped of its trees and vegetation that it looked burned, radiated, something left behind from a military test.

But under the hand of Seegmiller—called simply "Seegy" by everyone in town, including his wife, Nora—a new lawn had been laid, a half dozen saplings planted, and the empty flower beds filled again with friendly color, almost inviting the citizenry to stop by, to have a chat or, if they really must, talk business.

Zolene's truck screeched to a stop outside the office, and she hurriedly climbed down and limped up the walkway to a small porch. She pushed open the door and walked inside, instantly smelling what everyone always smelled: dust and old paper and furniture oil, the inside of the office, despite the improvements outside, never changing—even the hired help. Marla Hamblin, the indifferent, big-bosomed secretary, had survived every administration, and despite her loyalty to the Littles, had been kept on in this one. In fact, since Seegmiller's deputy, Garth Haycock, had quit and moved to Montana last month, Marla had become a de facto deputy, often handling petty law-related matters herself.

She sat behind two computer monitors, and when she heard Zolene come in, she looked up and smiled.

"Hey, Zoley, how you—"

"Where's Seegy?" Zolene said. "I need to talk to him . . . now."

In the old totalitarian days of the Littles, Marla had been instructed always to inform the desperate public that the sheriff was "over to Hare-i-kin," a standing joke in the community. But under Seegmiller she had been advised—and was now properly conditioned—to tell the truth.

"He's har," Marla said, "but maybe I can help—"

Zolene shook her head. "I want to talk to Seegy."

"Okay," Marla said, and she nodded toward someone else sitting in the office, someone Zolene had not even noticed when she burst in, despite his size. He was a big, heavy man with a swollen stomach, wearing slacks and bright red suspenders, cowboy boots, and a ridiculous cowboy hat. "But this man's farst."

Vanoy Atherton, as though he had formally been introduced, struggled out of the plastic chair, grunting, and tipped his ugly hat, the rings on his fingers flashing.

"Ma'am," he said.

Zolene nodded, dumbly. Atherton suddenly hawked, and the two women waited, eyes wide, expecting him to spit on the waxed wood floor, but he swallowed and sat back down, groaning again, the molded plastic chair nearly collapsing.

"Well, this is kind of an emergency," Zolene said, and she tried to smile at Atherton. "Do you think—?"

Atherton nodded his head. "That's fan. Y'all go rat ahead."

Zolene blinked stupidly at him, not sure if the big man was making fun of Marla and her cow-town Mormon accent—an accent that Zolene's grandmother, Myrna, had studiously purged from her as a child—or if he truly talked with such a sloppy drawl.

"Thank you," she finally said.

"You bet."

Marla got up, walked to a closed door at one side of the office, and, without knocking, walked in. A few moments later, she reemerged with the sheriff in tow.

Seegmiller, dressed in the county's new uniform of dark

brown pants and a beige shirt with a scattering of patches and a name tag, was short and plain and egg-shaped, an unremarkable man, really, except for his earlobes. They were two large flaps of skin that jutted out from his face at forty-five-degree angles like tiny wings, airfoils that normally helped elevate his head and guide it steadfastly through his dreary life. But with Zolene they never worked; instead, Seegmiller kept his head half bowed and slightly cocked, as though he had an injured neck.

"Zoley," he said.

"Hi, Seegy. I'm sorry to bother you."

" 'S'okay," he said, and he shyly smiled at her, the way he always did, the way he always had.

Back in the late 1970s, when they were classmates at Kanab High School, Zolene had been the reigning, teenage royalty: Homecoming Queen, Hay Day Duchess, princess of this, lady of that. But despite that lofty celebrity, Zolene, whenever she saw Seegmiller shuffling lumpishly and anonymously down the hallways, always had a cheerful word for him, even stopping sometimes to talk. And because of that, Seegmiller, like every male who had ever been near Zolene, had been struck with a hopeless, lifelong crush on her despite, years after graduation, the grinding automobile accident that had left Zolene crippled and her husband dead.

"It's nice to see you," Seegmiller said. "What's going on?"

Zolene quickly shook her head. "I don't know, Seegy. It's—"

She stopped, and Seegmiller could see that she was upset. Her eyes, normally a brilliant blue, looked gray and watery, and her white face—a face he always believed should be on the cover of glossy women's magazines—was drawn, making her look ten years older.

"My office?" Seegmiller said, and he looked apprehensively at Atherton, who was wholly absorbed in examining one of his fingernails, oblivious.

"No," Zolene said. "I've . . . Seegy, I've got a . . . trespasser living in my house. Lamb's house, out at Johnson Canyon. She's a—"

"Trespasser?" Seegmiller said.

"Yeah. A damned plig run—"

She looked helplessly at Marla, a woman Zolene knew had descended from a polygamist family and, in fact, was rumored, years before, to have been involved in a plural marriage herself. She was angry, but she would be discreet, for Marla's sake, not Brig's.

"A runaway kid," Zolene said. "As damned crazy as that sounds. She's living in my house, Seegy. She won't leave. She's been there—"

"Wol, how—"

"—a couple of days."

"—she get thar? She break in?"

Zolene stared at her old classmate and then looked over at the strange man in the plastic chair, who was still indifferent to it all, now bent over and wrestling with one of his boots, breathing heavily. As angry as she was, she was too embarrassed, too proud, to admit that her boyfriend, her lover, had simply taken the woman there.

"I don't know," Zolene said. "She's just *there*."

"Wol, how do you know she's a runaway and all?"

"I just do. She . . . looks like one. Seegy, I want her out. Tell me what I have to do. File a report? Sign something?" She looked desperately at his belt, where he carried everything but a gun. "I just want her the hell out of my damned house!"

Seegmiller looked genuinely confused, and he shifted from one foot to the other and ran his hand over his half-bald head. He had been sworn into office in January, and in the eight months or so he had been on the job, he had presided over minor automobile collisions, a burglary or two, even had to arrest two French tourists who got drunk and demolished a room at the Red Hills Motel. But to dislodge a trespasser—and a runaway child, at that—was something new.

"Wol," he said, "I guess I'll just drive over to thar after lunch and see what's going on."

"Oh, I know what's—" Zolene shook her head. "Well, thanks, Seegy. I really appreciate it." She gently touched his upper arm, her fingers resting on the red cloth patch that read KANE COUNTY. "I really do."

Seegmiller ducked his head, cocking it the way it had been when he first came out of his office. " 'S'okay."

"I'm going over to my aunt Orm's," Zolene said. "You can call me there when . . . well, when you're through."

Seegmiller nodded, vaguely disturbed that Zolene did not seem concerned about the safety of her household possessions, in fact, the house itself, but had focused only on ridding herself of the runaway.

As Zolene turned and walked back toward the door, Atherton hauled himself to his feet, making a strained, painful sound as he did. Like a floor salesman or an attentive waiter, Seegmiller turned to him, his head erect now, stabilized.

"Yes, sar? May I help you?"

Atherton slowly shook his head and then waved his hand, as though he were swatting at flies. "Ah had somethin' missing, maybe stolen, but ah just remembered where it maht be." He nodded at the door closing behind Zolene. "Anyway, looks lak you got a pot full of problems, as it is."

"Wol—"

With another dismissive wave of the hand, Atherton clumped across the floor and walked out the door and onto the porch, just as Zolene was limping along the walkway toward her truck.

"Ma'am," Atherton said.

Zolene stopped, turned around, and stared at the big man who stood, almost swaying, his booted feet too close together, as if he were balancing on a rail.

"Yes?" she said.

Slowly Atherton eased down the steps as though he might fall, and then crookedly walked up to her, smiling, and touched his fingers to his hat. Zolene tensed; in the clownish cowboy outfit, the man looked demented, unstable—like the crazies that staggered around big-city parks or rode their buses, always proclaiming the end, the damnation of man—and she unconsciously drew back, hoping that Seegmiller was still in the front office, maybe watching all of this.

Atherton leaned toward her, so close that she could smell

the alcohol on his breath, and he grinned, showing yellowed teeth.

"That's a real nas truck you got. That's a fact." He pointed a pale, fat finger at the rear fender. "All scratched up, though . . . Zoley."

Without replying, Zolene turned around and limped to the vehicle, climbed in, and then slammed the door shut and quickly started the engine. Atherton stayed on the walk and raised one meaty hand, waving and grinning as Zolene pulled out into the street and drove away, racing through a stop sign at the end of the block.

Atherton kept his hand in the air for several moments, and then lowered it, hawked, and spit a gob of phlegm into the grass. His own truck was parked nearby, but with his body canted to one side, he walked slowly up the street along the sidewalk and, several blocks away, turned and hobbled north over to Center Street, the heart of Kanab. He painfully moved up the sidewalk, passing trinket shops and crowded, old-fashioned cafés, and finally stopped in front of the Pow-Wow, the souvenir store with a wooden Indian standing in front.

He was looking for someone—anyone—who could give him simple directions, orient him, get him properly pointed, but all he saw were tourists, droves of them, people dawdling along and looking half lost, as unfamiliar with this area as he. Suddenly he looked across the street, and there, its needle-like spire thrust into the sky like an antenna, sat the LDS church—solid and clean and deserted, the austere redbrick place seeming to scare away all the tourists, inviting only the true believers, those informed.

Which was perfect for Atherton. After waiting for the traffic to clear, he sidled across the street to the front steps of the church and stood waiting, idly inspecting a ring of glassed, inspirational posters. The sightseers in their shorts and sunglasses bustled by, almost afraid to look at *this* sight until, at last, a middle-aged man in leather shoes and slacks and a white shirt— a local—came up the steps, smiling eagerly at the freakish cowboy, a prospect who had actually come, unsolicited, to the church, rather than it to him.

"Mornin'," Atherton said, and he touched his fingers to his hat. "Ah'm lookin' for a place called Johnson Canyon."

The man stopped, disappointed, and he frowned and looked the cowboy over, staring at the scuffed boots, the pants that fit too tightly, the garish suspenders.

"Oh," Atherton said, and he smiled and held out his hands. "Don't worry. Ah'm just lookin' to surpraz my cousin. You probably know her. Ol' Zoley." Atherton laughed and waggled his jeweled fingers down and around his head, to his neck. "Red hair and all. Real purdy."

With that, the man seemed to relax, and although Atherton was not the mark he had expected, he smiled nevertheless and gave the big, friendly cowboy precise directions—not to a life of hope and salvation, but to Johnson Canyon . . . and Lamb's house.

7

ANYONE traveling through Utah, whether by air or rail or along the highways, is constantly reminded, at almost every stop, of the state's new legislative codification of the Saints' simple Word of Wisdom: smoking is bad for you. And although many states—most, probably—similarly condemn the public use of tobacco, none trumpet that victory as loudly, and as incessantly, as those in Utah do.

Everywhere, in airports and bus stations and trade centers—even in restrooms—a taped, priggish, female voice reminds the debauched visitors that here, in the Beehive State, home of the Winter Olympics, smoking in public buildings is punishable by fine—and, worse, the ghostly voice seems to suggest, those who light up might be struck down by the Heavenly Father himself.

But it has all had little effect. The smell of cigarette smoke hangs almost defiantly over the whole of Salt Lake City, and at night, near-phosphorescent clouds of it can be seen boiling out of the bars and video parlors and all-night cafés along State Street, where drunken revelers—cigarettes jutting from their mouths, their eyes squinting—whoop and sing, drowning out the recorded message that, when the music finally dies and the world ends, will still be heard, somewhere, droning away in the ruins.

Judge Ray Rukamann was among those who had not received the message, or if he had, he didn't care, or maybe didn't understand it. In his cramped chambers on the third floor of the Scott M. Matheson Courthouse, he had disabled the smoke detector so he could sit in peace in his torn leather chair, the lights out, the blinds closed, and happily puff away in the gloom—which somehow in his mind made the smoking acceptable, maybe even legal. Besides, he was a judge—not a very witty or active or energetic judge, but a judge nevertheless, a robed potentate—so who would be foolish enough to barge in here and speak out?

The place was made darker by an oppressive jumble of Spanish furniture, outdated law books, and old rugs on the wall, and his desk was cluttered with paper cups and newspapers. In the middle of the mess, a telephone buzzed, and a voice—another female voice, this one with a faint rasp to it—asked if he was in.

"Maybe," Rukamann said. He held his cigarette daintily between the tips of his thumb and forefinger, as though he were going to insert it in a slot. "Who's out there?"

There was a pause, and then the voice said, "A man named Gault from—" The connection was broken for a moment, and then the voice returned. "A man named *Gant* from the governor's office. He's a special assistant."

Rukamann slowly brought the cigarette to his lips, as if he were kissing it. "Don't need assistance," he said, and he smiled in the darkness, pleased with his dull humor, and took a puff.

"He says it's important," the voice said. There was another pause, the phone's silence disconcerting, and then: "He's from the governor's office, Judge."

Rukamann waved the cigarette in the air and whispered to himself, "Well, whoop-de-*friggin'*-do."

He sighed and shook his head, causing his thinning hair—a classic heavily sprayed combover—to fall forward a few inches, exposing the baldness on the top of his head. He readjusted it, almost as if it were a toupee, and then unconsciously smoothed his robe, a garment he did not have to wear while off the bench, but which he used as a smoking jacket, of sorts, something to keep from burning holes in his cheap dress shirts.

"All right," he said, his voice loud now. "Send him."

Almost instantly the door to his office opened, and a wave of fluorescent light from the outer office washed into the darkness, immediately followed by Darvis Gant, his eyes blinking, as though the little man were riding that wave, bobbing along in it like a human cork.

"Judge Rukamann," Gant said, and he stuck out his small hand. As always, he was in a dark business suit and a red tie, and he smelled faintly of talcum powder. "I'm Darvis Gant. Special assistant to Governor Purcell."

Before Rukamann could answer, his secretary's disembodied arm closed the door, and the office was immersed in the half darkness again, causing Gant to blink even faster and look apprehensively behind him.

Without rising, Rukamann shifted his cigarette from his right hand to his left, then leaned across and shook Gant's hand, the sleeve of his robe gaping open.

"Ray Rukamann," the judge said. He pointed to a chair and then held the cigarette out between his thumb and forefinger, as though he were offering it to Gant. "This bother you?"

Gant hated cigarettes. His ex-wife, Loretta, had been a chain smoker, their house on Pheasant Way always reeking of the things, but he smiled and waved his hand in the semidarkness, more concerned at this point with the fact that the window blinds were closed and there were no lights on.

"No, go ahead," he said, and he sat down in a padded, wooden chair with a broken armrest and then peered, disturbed, through the grayness at the judge, wondering if the man had some spooky physical aversion to light, an albino maybe, a red-eyed creature who had never seen the sun but just sat in the dark and smoked, wrapped in a pleated black robe, his skin slowly rotting, his brain drying out.

"What's on your mind?" Rukamann said.

"Quite a bit," Gant said, and he hesitated, knowing that if the same question were addressed to the judge, Rukamann would have to respond, if he were truly honest, "Well, not a hell of a lot. Never is." But Gant only stared at the man, measuring him, until he won the struggle and Rukamann looked to the side. "A lot's on the governor's mind, really. Politics, elections, voters . . . money. Things like that; things you understand yourself."

But the judge did not understand; instead, he kissed the cigarette again and shook his head. "Don't follow."

Gant edged his chair closer and placed his arms on the desk, exposing his cuff-linked shirtsleeves—so white that they seemed to glow in the dim office. "Judge, this is probably not too copacetic, but the governor's sent me here to talk about . . . well, a couple of things. One of them's a case." He hesitated. "A case in your court."

Normally, a magistrate might flinch at these words and become instantaneously apprehensive, the canons of judicial ethics suddenly clicking and whirring to life, an alarm sounding —maybe weak and muted, but triggered, nevertheless—in the recesses of the brain somewhere. But nothing like that happened in the brain of Ray "Rocket Man" Rukamann.

"Which one?" the judge said.

"The Crowe case," Gant said. He seemed relieved. "State versus T. Rampton Crowe. The plig. You know, the Big Plig."

Rukamann nodded and sucked on his cigarette before stubbing it out in a glass ashtray, already heaped with butts. "Yeah, Crowe. What's up?"

Gant slowly shook his head and tried to look worried. "Well, that's just the hell of it, Judge. I'm not sure what *is* up."

"Okay," Rukamann said. He looked as though he were drifting, losing interest, his eyes squinting across the room at a plastic clock on the wall.

"Look," Gant said, raising his hands a few inches off the

desk, "I don't want to pussy around with this, Judge. I understand that the Crowe trial is set in about two weeks."

Rukamann nodded, thinking. "Yeah," he said.

"Well, it's come to the governor's attention that the AG's office has filed a motion to postpone that trial."

The judge nodded at a plastic tray at the edge of his desk heaped with paper—motions, pleadings, proposed orders, even a legal brief or two, thick, spiral-bound documents that he would never read. "Yeah," he said. "Filed the other day. Hearing coming up."

Gant nodded, wondering for a moment why this judge—white and plain and undeniably suburban—talked as though he were an Indian chief in a bad western, his sentences chopped and clumsily pieced back together.

"Well, the governor's concerned," Gant said. "He really wants this thing to go to trial."

Rukamann squinted in the half darkness and then began fumbling inside his robe, finally bringing out a pack of cigarettes and tapping one out. "Why?" he finally said.

Gant waited until the judge had lit his cigarette, and then leaned forward again. "Judge, as you know, Governor Purcell likes to run a clean state: clean roads, clean water"—he pointed at the cigarette that Rukamann was pinching, and forced a smile— "clean air. But more than anything, he wants a clean . . . society, I guess you could say. Clean people."

For an instant, Rukamann envisioned a soap-and-toothpaste campaign, a push for communal bathing maybe, free haircuts, even a return to the blacklight lice inspections in Utah elementary schools, the kind he had always been subjected to growing up in Cedar City—the kind he routinely, along with the Indian kids, failed.

"Don't follow," he said.

"Polygamy!" Gant nearly shouted, and he slapped his hand on the desk. "He wants the goddamned pligs gone—or at least so far underground that we'll never see them again."

"Don't follow."

Gant could feel the veins in his neck begin to pulse. "Look,

Judge. The AG's got evidence that Crowe's an out-and-out polygamist, and they're ready to put him away. This trial's very important. There's a lot of people on the outside watching, waiting to see what we're going to do." He stopped, but his neck was throbbing now, actually aching. "Do you follow *that?*"

Rukamann nodded and pulled on his cigarette, aiming the exhaust of smoke just above Gant's head. "Yeah," he said.

"So we don't want a continuance of this thing. It needs to go to trial . . . now."

Slowly, with his cigarette held above him, Rukamann fumbled with one hand in the plastic tray, finally withdrawing a creased document, one several pages long and stapled at the top. He lay it on his desk and turned to the second page, slowly reading, and finally looked up at Gant.

"Says here the state's got newly discovered evidence. Doesn't say what the evidence is. Needs time to investigate." He puffed on the cigarette and dipped his head toward the document. "Might amend the charge." He took the motion and tossed it back into the plastic tray. "Good grounds to continue. I usually continue."

Gant glared at the judge. He knew that the nickname "Rocket Man," besides being an easy play on the last name, was true sarcasm, a bit of guffawing, head-shaking derision among all the Salt Lake lawyers. Ray Rukamann had the slowest docket in Utah—the "rocket docket," it was laughingly called—the cases in his court piling up like judicial sludge, thick and glutinous, barely moving through the system, all the lawyers and their clients angry and frustrated and completely helpless. All but one, it seemed: LeVar Eaton.

"Like hell!" Gant said.

He twisted suddenly in his chair as though gripped by a violent muscle spasm, and then reached inside his coat and withdrew a document of his own. It was several pages thick, folded lengthwise, and he began tapping it on the edge of the cluttered desk, his eyes blinking.

"Know what this is?" Gant said.

"No."

"It's a bit of *encouragement*."

"Don't follow."

"You will now," Gant said. "It's a printout we got from the clerk's office." Gant raised the document like a prosecutor at trial, as though it were a detailed confession, a bloodstained glove, searing, damning evidence. "It shows the final disposition of all the criminal cases in your court for the last two years, complete with the name of the defendant, the offense charged . . . and the name of the defense attorney involved."

Rukamann began to bring his cigarette to his lips, but instead he held it out in front of him and stared beyond Gant at the far wall.

"You don't move very fast," Gant went on, waving the sheaf of paper, "but when the cases in your court finally *do* get taken care of, maybe years later, you're a damned tough judge—prison sentences out the ass for everyone." He smiled. "Well, almost everyone. LeVar Eaton seems to be doing better—far better—than any other lawyer in town." He took the document and, just as the judge had done a few minutes before, slowly read the first page, pointing. "Let's see . . . Eaton, Eaton. Oh, yeah, here's one: 'Ruben Salazar, aggravated assault . . . dismissed, lack of evidence.'" He moved his finger down the page. "Here's another: 'Darren Holt, robbery . . . dismissed, want of prosecution.'"

He looked up at Rukamann, who sat frozen, unmoving, still staring at the opposite wall. Gant quickly turned the page. "Oh, here's a whole shitpot full of Eaton cases: 'Allred, rape of a child, reduced to public indecency; Cobb, aggravated kidnapping, dismissed; Montoya, murder'"—he looked up, his eyes blinking, and lowered his head again—"'confession suppressed . . . dismissed.'"

He folded the papers together again, slowly, deliberately, and then suddenly threw them at the judge, aiming at his stunned face, but the pages opened in mid-flight, and the document fluttered into his robed lap like a bird.

"And there's a hell of a lot more. Read it, you crooked *shit!*"

Rukamann slowly lowered his head and stared at the papers,

his eyes wide, the flap of comb-over hair edging down over his forehead. He was not accustomed to anyone—lawyers, laypersons, secretaries—yelling at him in his own chambers, and he was having difficulty absorbing it all, sorting it out. LeVar Eaton had paid him strictly in cash—the two of them were not *that* clumsy—but it had been a lot of cash, and he knew it would probably be an easy matter for Gant or his investigator to find the money trail.

The judge still held the cigarette out before him, and when the ash fell to the desk, he finally looked up, his eyes watering, as though he might cry.

"What do you want?" Rukamann said.

Gant smiled and relaxed and sat back into the broken chair. "A little, a lot. For now, just a little. I want the Crowe case to go to trial, as scheduled. Simple. You turn down the motion for continuance, and you get Crowe tried, and on the charge as filed: bigamy."

Gant paused; he knew that the AG's motion for continuance had not mentioned anything about murder, about this fantastic, make-believe beheading that had so enthralled Bybee and the AG's office, and so he would not apprise the judge of it and further confound him, bog him down. The case—and this bit of "encouragement"—was indeed simple.

"Bigamy," Gant repeated, "polygamy, plural marriage, plural . . . bullshit—whatever you want to call it. Crowe goes down on that and that alone. If the prosecution tries to change things around, you know, chase Crowe on other shit like incest or kidnapping, like they always do, you slap it down. You keep their feet to the fire, the bigamy fire." He blinked for several moments and then smiled. "You got any problems with that . . . Your Honor?"

Rukamann shrugged. "Guess not."

"Good." Gant stood up, straightened his tie, and shot his cuffs. "Everything's copacetic, then."

Rukamann nodded slowly, not sure what the word *copacetic* meant, and dropped his cigarette into the ashtray. Although all judicial robes were oversize, tentlike things, the one draped over

Rukamann seemed now like a black shroud that had enveloped him, his head and body shrinking, being absorbed into the giant folds of cloth, disappearing.

"Those robes don't have pockets, do they?" Gant said.

"No."

"Well, see, you're just the opposite of me. I wear shirts and coats that have plenty of pockets. I like to keep things in my pockets."

Rukamann said nothing, and only continued to gaze at the far wall.

Gant pointed at the cigarette smoldering in the ashtray. "Smoking in a public building is illegal, Judge. You could get in trouble." He walked to the door, stopped, and turned around. "So long, Rocket Man. Have a nice day."

He opened the door; again, the torrent of light rushed into the room, and this time Gant had to struggle upstream, blinking furiously, until he was safely ashore in the outer office.

As before, the disembodied arm appeared and closed the door to the chambers, leaving the judge alone in the dark.

Years before, on an airless, itchy day in a physics class in Moab High School, Vanoy Atherton slouched in the rear of the classroom, bored, half-listening, and then suddenly sat up, erect, hearing the only thing that had ever made sense to him. Nothing in nature, his teacher, Siler Mott, revealed, ever traveled in a straight line, for the universal laws of the heavens bent all progression into an arc back toward its origin.

It stirred Atherton, literally and figuratively, and he arose and walked, dazed, from class that day with a new cynicism, but a better, clearer view of the world. If even light and gravity strained along a curved path, as Mr. Mott had explained, then *everything* in the world followed an arcing, unavoidable route where it always fell back on itself. In other words, nothing ever really went anywhere, and so to try and seek out meaning, or purpose, or truth—or even love—would only bring the searcher boomeranging back to his starting point.

And that was what he called it—the Big Boomerang—his guiding tenet, a faith, really, since everyone had to have one, but a faith he occasionally questioned, wondering if it might not always be true . . . at least in certain instances.

Atherton shook his big, shaggy head, driving these troubling thoughts from it, and concentrated on the pitted road in front of him, the one the white-shirted man at the church had told him to take. In his old pickup he navigated around holes and half-rotted cattle guards and finally saw a house, a small, sandstone affair with a cement porch. He stopped and, heaving himself up to the porch, pounded on the door. When there was no answer, he tried the latch, but it was locked. Wheezing, he got off the porch, walked to the side, and cupping his hands to his big face, peered in the window. The place—the old Farnsworth place—was empty, only a scattering of furniture, the walls bare.

Then he remembered what the kind man at the church had said: there was another house, a hidden house just west. He struggled back to his truck and drove in that direction, down a shaded road, along an orchard, until he saw the massive chunks of petrified wood that he knew, from the description, was Lamb's house.

There were no cars or trucks anywhere near the house, and he stopped turned off his engine. When it ceased burbling, he reached across the cab and, in the glove compartment, next to his cell phone, found his pistol—a small five-shot revolver. He checked that it was loaded and, satisfied, fitted his cowboy hat on his head and slowly climbed down, groaned, and then spit into the red dirt. He paused, holding the gun, listening, but could only hear the chirping and complaining of the birds, seemingly thousands of them, fluttering around the house and orchard, the only creatures alive.

In front of his truck he saw a dark, damp spot in the dirt. He hobbled to it, tapped it with the toe of his cowboy boot, and then bent down and touched it, rubbing the greasy wetness between his ringed fingers. It was obviously oil leaked from an engine, and recently too, and on either side of the spot, he saw two parallel tire tracks, those fresh and newly made as well. Painfully, one hand clutching his swollen stomach as though to steady it, he walked along the tire tracks to the edge of the yard, where just beyond a wooden gate they turned and disappeared through a dead field, toward a line of Russian olive trees to the south.

He considered climbing back into his truck and following the tracks, but he could see that they would take him to the gulch, to the west, and probably across a bridge to the other side and to the highway, and then to anywhere.

She was gone; he had arrived too late. Slowly he struggled back to the front of the house, opened the small wooden gate, and walked up to the front porch, the pistol dangling at his side. He stopped and tilted back his cowboy hat, admiring the solid, century-old design of the place, the craftsmanship, the cleverness with the petrified wood, and then nodded his head, silently approving of the new dark green shingles, the fresh coat of paint on the fascia, the spurts of flowers and shrubbery here and there. He liked it; it was the kind of house that he would want to buy someday, the kind of home he would want to share with someone.

Suddenly he raised his fist and pounded on the heavy door, the loud, booming sound sending a flock of birds fluttering and wheeling overhead, screeching. He waited, and when he heard nothing—no faint cry or call from within, no demanding male voice, no frenzied rustling and skittering about—he opened the door, gun ready, and walked into the living room.

He stopped and looked at the antiques—the furniture, the lamps, the old odds and ends scattered about—and wondered, as he had about so many things since that day in physics class, at what point did mere junk become what folks called a collectible, and then a collectible become an antique . . . and then that antique become junk again? The Big Boomerang.

He dismissed the thought and, with the pistol thrust before him, quickly inspected the rest of the house—the rear bedrooms, the bathroom, the dining room—and then hobbled into the kitchen, his cowboy boots loudly clumping across the wood floors. There, on the tiled counter, loosely covered with a scrap of aluminum foil, was a pie, only one slice cut away. He smiled and, with two fingers of his left hand, scooped out a chunk of the glutinous stuff and jammed it into his mouth. He quickly chewed it and swallowed . . . and then smiled again, wiping his lips with the back of his hand.

"Mercy," he said.

He turned to leave, but as he did, he saw, near a rear door, next to a trash can, a pile of clothes, wadded, thrown against the wall. He walked to it, grunted, and bent down, and then his big hand involuntarily leaped to his throat, and he made a strange, hoarse cry. It was a dress—ripped and dirty and bloodstained— and he gently picked it up and unfolded it, and then pressed it against his face.

"Mercy," he said again.

He stuffed the pistol into his front pocket and, cradling the dress as though it were a child, a baby, walked back through the living room and out to the porch. He stopped; steadying himself with one hand against the petrified wood, he sat heavily on the top step and placed the dress in his big lap. He gently unfolded it, caressing it, smoothing it out, and then his thick fingers touched the purplish smear of blood near the collar.

And then this big, ponderous, greasy, cowboy-hatted man with a gun in his pocket—a man who some believed was once a professional wrestler, or a member of the Dallas Cowboys, others claimed, or probably, most insisted, just a cheap bounty hunter and arm-breaker—sat in the cool shade on the steps and cried, clutching the bloodied dress, his entire body heaving, his sobs filling the quiet orchard, causing the birds overhead to stop their cawing and chattering so they could listen to this new, sad sound.

8

THERE are only two prominent features in Manti, Utah, both of which are equally discussed or ignored by townspeople and visitors alike. One is an LDS temple—a gleaming white limestone structure sitting atop a hill, surrounded by tall trees—and the other is Poetry Bob.

Every day, rain or shine, weekdays or weekends, Poetry Bob—a thin, average-looking man in white shoes, white pants, and a white shirt—stands on the corner of 200 North and Main, not far from the temple, unmoving, a big leather bag slung over one shoulder, holding out a square of paper that reads, "ORIGINAL POETRY . . . $1.00." And indeed, to those curious souls who actually tender a dollar to the silent man, the poetry is uniquely original: rhymed and metered doggerel about Earth's three moons, or invisible airplanes, or secret societies where everyone wears a tinfoil hat.

To be sure, Poetry Bob is a half bubble out of plumb, and at least once a year there is an effort, by a church leader or a city councilman or some agitated citizen, to have the Manti police remove the man, arguing that he peddles wares without a license, or violates zoning restrictions or nuisance laws, or that he is just simply a communal embarrassment.

But Poetry Bob and his verse have withstood it all, and he remains as much a clean, white fixture as the temple itself, a bad poet dressed like an ice-cream man, holding out his sign, never saying a word. Like Spooky Floyd, he just watches.

Mercy stared at Poetry Bob as she and Bybee drove by him in the green VW van, and then she twisted back around, smiling, and gently put her hand on Bybee's arm.

"Let's buy a poem," she said. She was still dressed in Zolene's clothes—the tank top and capri pants—but she had arranged her hair in two ponytails now, one slightly larger than the other, and her leather purse lay in her lap. "I like poems."

"No," Bybee said, and he shook his head. "No time."

Two hours before, standing like a sentinel on the front porch of Lamb's house, he had seen a truck rumbling down the dirt road in Johnson Canyon, aiming for them, and he had instantly grabbed Mercy, physically seizing her by the arm and hustling her out of the house and into the van. They had driven out the back route—the one he had envisioned the night before—the VW bucking wildly through the dry fields, along the line of olive trees, and then had slowly inched their way across the wooden bridge at the gulch, the old, weathered timbers creaking, the whole affair groaning as if it would collapse at any second.

But the bridge had held, and they had climbed up and out, unseen by whomever was in the truck at the ranch, and then sped north along the narrow asphalt road into the heart of Johnson Canyon, winding out of the Vermilion Cliffs and into the Whites, as they were called. They had crawled upward, into Skutumpah Terrace, and then the road had withered into gravel and then dirt as they crossed Sink Valley and Kanab Creek and finally reached the Pink Cliffs and Highway 89, at Alton.

There, at a service station in the small town, after buying Mercy a soda and potato chips, Bybee had called Kendall from a phone booth and asked his friend to meet him, and to come alone. Later, once Mercy got settled in and was comfortable, the investigators—Sorenson and Ordoñez—could come and begin the task of recording her statement.

With Mercy eating potato chips and constantly searching for music on the van's old radio, they had driven on, now simply following the half-deserted highway, paralleling the interstate farther west, and finally, at Centerfield (called "Centerfold" by many, because of a pornography scandal there years before), they had turned off onto another highway and, five minutes later, drove into Manti.

It was in Manti, in the twin-towered temple, that he had been sealed to Helena nearly thirty years before, suffering through the voodoolike ceremony, his body aching for a slug of Scotch. But despite the wretched end to the marriage twenty-seven years later, Bybee still liked Manti, enjoying on each trip the quiet peacefulness of the place, the whole community drifting along, placid, unconcerned, perhaps because of the altitude, or the shade of its many tall trees . . . or maybe because of the temple, squarely in the heart of the town, creating a spiritual force field, something mellow and pacifying, soothing.

At the temple, Bybee turned off the main street and drove several blocks back into a residential neighborhood, climbing uphill into an old area of tidy brick houses and well-kept lawns and vegetable gardens, the air seeming to grow cooler, the sun dimming.

On East 200 North, in the middle of the sloped street, sat a large two-story house constructed of dark, purplish brick, with white shutters and white trim, fronted by a lawn and shrubbery and surrounded by a wrought-iron fence. It looked ordinary, unimposing, and there was nothing—no sign in front or lettering on a window—to indicate that this was anything other than another house on another street in another pleasant backwater of Utah.

Bybee slowed, pulled over to the curb, and stopped just behind a motorcycle parked perpendicular to the street, leaning on its side stand, the big, bulbous helmet propped on top.

"Good," Bybee said. "Tom's here."

Mercy, who had been surprisingly cheerful and upbeat the entire drive, now stiffened, her face worried, and her eyes darted from the bike to the house and back to Bybee. "Who's Tom?" she said.

"The guy I told you about," Bybee said. "He's on our side." He pointed to the house. "Everyone in there is on our side. On *your* side."

She looked down at the floor, at the childlike spray of potato chips she had left there, and clasped her hands under her breasts. "I'm scared," she said.

"There's no reason to be, Mercy. Faith is there, and La-Wanda Fae, the lady I told you about." He leaned forward so he could look into her troubled face. He had not told her of his decision; in fact, he had not told anyone. "Everything will be okay."

She turned and smiled, her poor, bruised face softening. "If you say so."

The entire day, from the moment they had both awakened—she back in Zolene's daughters' bedroom and he on the couch—and then in the van the last two hours, they had not discussed the night's frantic, moaning tussle on the couch. Instead, this morning Mercy had bustled around the kitchen, humming, content, finally presenting Bybee a grand breakfast of corn flakes and burned toast, which he dutifully ate while making stiff conversation.

Now she suddenly stretched across the gap between them, and as she had done over the apple pie days before, gave him a quick, sisterly kiss. "I like you, Mr. Bybee." She then grinned, the impish, playful look giving way to something darker, more sinister, almost demonic, and she deliberately poked the tip of her tongue out of her mouth and licked her lips. "I proved that last night."

Quickly Bybee unhooked his seat belt, climbed down from the van, and walked to the other side and opened her door. Without saying anything more, Mercy allowed herself to be helped down, dragging her purse with her, and then the two of them walked slowly and solemnly up the sidewalk to the wrought-iron gate. It opened with a loud squealing, and Bybee, when he sensed Mercy's hesitation, took her hand in his and led her up the flower-bordered walkway to the front porch. Before they were halfway across the painted boards, a voice—soft and quavering—came from behind the screen door.

"Oh, my poor child."

The door suddenly opened, and a large, matronly woman filled the doorway. She looked to be in her sixties and was dressed in heavy black shoes, a simple skirt, and a short-sleeved white blouse, and her gray hair was pulled back in a tight bun. Behind a pair of thick glasses, her eyes were deeply set and looked tired, and she slowly closed them, as though she could not bear to look, and then they opened again, filled with tears now.

"Oh, child. What they do."

The woman extended her arms—plump and pale, covered with a light fuzz of hair—and gathered Mercy to her, pressing the battered face to her big bosom, hugging her until Mercy tentatively put her arms around the woman, feeling her strength, her kindness, and then began crying the way she had the first night at the Piute Villa—loud, pain-filled sobs—while the woman continued to hold her, gently rocking back and forth, her rough white hand stroking Mercy's hair, softly murmuring to her.

"What they do. What they do."

At last the woman slowly released Mercy and looked over at Bybee, who had been standing on the stairs, watching it all, his own eyes wet with tears.

"Brigham," she said. She moved slightly away from Mercy, but still held her elbow with one hand, as if the younger woman might suddenly bolt—or collapse—and extended the other hand to him.

Bybee took the woman's hand and held it with both his own. "LaWanda Fae," he said, and then he released it and pointed at Mercy, who stood miserably next to the larger woman, tears trickling down her face. "This is Mercy—Chenoya Whiting." He looked at Mercy. "And this is Mrs. Covington. She—"

"LaWanda Fae," the woman corrected, and she turned, smiled at Mercy, and took both her hands in her own. "You call me LaWanda Fae. Not LaWanda or Fae, but LaWanda Fae." She hugged Mercy again and drew back and kissed her on her bruised forehead. "And I'll call you Chenoya. That's your real name." Her face seemed to harden, and she looked over at Bybee. "We don't use the . . . other names, here, Brigham."

"I know," Bybee said, and he smiled. LaWanda Fae Covington, a woman known by many descriptions—a universal mother, a godsend, a feminist champion, a saint (with a small "s")—insisted on a queer brand of formality in her home, eschewing shortened names or nicknames . . . or celestial names.

"Well, Chenoya, let's get you settled in," LaWanda Fae said, and she opened the door and ushered Mercy inside. "Are you hungry? Would you like something to eat?"

As she went through the doorway, Mercy dismally shook her head, and LaWanda Fae turned back to Bybee. "Something to drink, Brigham?" And before he could politely demur and be as politic as possible with this woman, who, he knew, enjoyed an occasional gin and tonic, she winked at him. "Like iced tea, maybe."

"Sounds good," Bybee said, and he followed the two women inside.

The house, as LaWanda Fae had once told Bybee, was about one hundred years old—as old as Lamb's house—with high ceilings, a staircase, and dark wood wainscoting and threadbare carpeting throughout. It had been part of the estate the woman had inherited from her father, and LaWanda Fae, herself once a plural wife for several years before she had run, had devoted the house—and her life—to the sheltering of other runaways. There were dozens of such shelters around the state, all of them secret and anonymous, generally receiving their "tenants," as LaWanda Fae liked to call them, through social service agencies. And although her home had never been used in such a dramatic way by state prosecutors, she understood the gravity of the AG's operation, and she easily overcame her early suspicion of the lawyers and investigators—the men—who routinely came to the house.

"Thomas is here," LaWanda Fae said, and she nodded her head toward the rear.

"Good," Bybee said.

Mercy had stopped just inside the door, her head down, her shoulders hunched, and LaWanda Fae gently took her by the hand and pulled her toward the center of the room, laying her purse on a couch.

"Don't be afraid, Chenoya. This is your home now."

But Mercy pulled her hand back, moved several steps, and stood beside Bybee, half hiding behind him like a child on the first day of school, her breasts pressed against his arm, her face brushing his shoulder.

LaWanda Fae smiled; she had seen this countless times. "Brigham," she said, "why don't you go and talk to Thomas?"

As he was told, Bybee stepped away from Mercy, leaving her standing alone and swaying on the dark carpet, and walked from the living room. In the rear of the house, next to the kitchen, he pushed through a flimsy aluminum screen door and emerged into a bright screened-in porch with a slanted ceiling. Wide wicker chairs were scattered about, and in one of them, in one corner of the porch, sat Kendall, his back to Bybee, staring out at the backyard.

"Tom."

Kendall twisted his thin body around, his neck straining and wrinkling, and looked at Bybee over one shoulder. "Brig." He didn't get up; instead he turned back around and motioned toward another chair near him.

Bybee walked to the chair and sat down, and as he did, the high, wide armrests elevated his shoulders, making him look as though he were about to levitate. "She's here," he said.

Kendall nodded his approval and then pointed a bony finger toward the backyard. "And Faith's going to have a fucking heart attack."

Bybee looked to where Kendall was pointing, outside the porch. A cool, grassy yard sloped away toward a stone wall in the rear, and in the middle of the lawn, in a circle of empty chairs beneath an elm tree, sat a woman, alone, her head bent over a book in her lap. She was thin, with long, weedy black hair, and was dressed like LaWanda Fae: a white blouse and a pleated skirt—an unofficial house uniform.

Bybee watched her for a few moments, seeing even from that distance the woman's dark eyes—round and staring, always staring, even when she read, never squinting or softening, never betraying some sort of emotion, a stirring of life within . . . only staring.

"Typical plig," Kendall said.

Bybee said nothing, but continued to peer through the screening. From the high vantage point, he could see the rest of the pleasant neighborhood—the other backyards filled with tall trees and shade, like LaWanda Fae's—all of it gently sloping toward the main street, where through a gap in the leaves and shrubs, Bybee could barely see Poetry Bob standing on the corner, tiny from the distance, stiff, unmoving, still holding out his sign.

After a moment Bybee shifted back around so that he faced Kendall again. The man was still in his leather riding jacket, but under it, Bybee could see part of a white dress shirt and half of a purple bow tie. And instead of jeans and the old army boots, he wore dress pants and leather loafers.

Kendall saw Bybee's puzzled look. "Your call caught me off guard," he said, and he swept one bony hand at his clothes, like a magician. "Didn't have time to go home and change."

"Sorry," Bybee said. "I didn't have a hell of a lot of time myself. One of Crowe's goons was on his way to Zolene's house. I had—"

"Zolene's house?" Kendall's eyes widened. About four months ago, on one of his visits to Kanab and the Piute Villa, Bybee had taken him out to Johnson Canyon and introduced him to Zolene and shown him around the ranch. From that day on, whenever he saw Bybee, all he could do was rave about the beauty of the canyon—and of Zolene. "Is that where you stashed her?"

"Yes."

"I should have guessed it," Kendall said, and then he began

tapping his fingers on the armrests as the two men fell silent, looking out at the quiet yard, watching Faith read, each trying to imagine how she would react when she saw Mercy.

"When can I talk to her?" Kendall finally said, and he nodded toward the house.

"Not for a while, Tom. She's still scared. LaWanda Fae's trying to get her relaxed. I just want you to meet her today. That's all. Just wait a day or two until she's comfortable, then talk to her. But go easy, will you?"

"Christ Jesus, Brig, she's not a kid."

"She might as well be. And tell Sorenson and Ordoñez to take it easy, too."

Kendall blew a stream of air out his mouth. "All right, but we need her affidavit quick. If she knows where the body is buried —literally—then it's the only way we're going to get a search warrant from the Rocket Man."

Bybee raked a tuft of hair from his eyes. "You going to tell Gant?" ·

"Oh, hell, no. Once we have the warrant, we'll send a whole crew to New Ammon, find the dead guy—or what's left of him—and, while we're at it, see who's shacked up with who. It's a whole new ball game, Brig."

"Well, good luck," Bybee said.

Kendall stopped drumming his fingers and looked away for a moment, and then faced Bybee. "So you're out?"

"Yeah, Tom, I am. If you're going agg' murder—death penalty—then I'm out. I'm sorry."

Kendall made a theatrical shrug and spread out his thin hands. "Well, that's that, then."

"Yeah. Who's going to—"

"I will. Cynthia's already approved it."

Bybee smiled at his old friend. "Well, good. As you say, it'll be a feather—"

The screen door suddenly opened with a screeching sound, and LaWanda Fae and Mercy slowly walked out on the porch. Instinctively, chivalrously, both men stood, and Kendall walked around the chairs and stood in front of Mercy like a shy high-school kid on his first date. He dipped his head—a silly bow—and then held his brown hand out.

"Mercy, I'm very glad—"

LaWanda Fae held up her hand. "Chenoya."

Kendall looked embarrassed, and he shook his head and smiled at Mercy, and then took her hand. "I'm sorry. *Chenoya*, I'm glad to meet you. I'm Tom—Thomas." He released her hand and twisted his body and pointed at Bybee. "I'm Brigham's friend."

Mercy smiled and, equally embarrassed, looked away. Suddenly her eyes widened; her face changed, almost as though gripped by a spasm, and her hand slowly rose and covered her mouth.

"Merciful Christs," she said.

She stepped away from LaWanda Fae and Kendall, walked slowly to the edge of the porch, and stopped at the screening, staring out at the woman on the lawn who was still reading, her head bent.

"Faith," Mercy whispered, and she turned around, her eyes filled with tears, and looked at Bybee. "You told me the truth."

Bybee began to say something, but LaWanda Fae walked to her, took her hand, and led her to another aluminum door at the side and opened it.

"Go to her, Chenoya," the older woman said. "She's been alone." She smiled and touched her rough hand to Mercy's face. "Like you."

Tentatively, as though she were feeling her way, Mercy stepped down from the porch and slowly began walking across the sloped lawn toward Faith, almost slipping once. When she was only a few feet from the big elm tree, swallowed by its shade, she stopped, and Faith slowly raised her head. For a moment it seemed as if the black-haired woman would simply stare, as she always did, and then return to her reading, but she made a sharp cry and stood up, letting the book tumble to the ground. The two women embraced instantly, fiercely, their arms flung around the other, pulling their bodies together as they both cried.

From the porch the others watched, LaWanda Fae crying

softly along with the two women on the lawn, and then she dried her eyes with her sleeve.

"Sister wives," she said, and she began walking back toward the house. "I'll get that tea."

She reentered the house, leaving the two men on the porch, still standing, still watching Faith and Mercy, who had now separated but still held one another by the arms, murmuring. Finally Faith turned around and positioned another chair across from hers, and the two of them sat facing each other, their knees touching, holding hands.

" 'Sister wives,' " Kendall mimicked, his voice low, almost hushed. "Plig bullshit."

The remark irritated Bybee, but before he could respond, there was a sudden eruption of noise in the house—a door banging open, a scuffling of shoes on the wooden floors—and then of LaWanda Fae's loud, panicked voice.

"Brigham!"

Bybee began hurrying across the porch floor, but stopped when the screen door was violently thrown open, banging against the wall, and Darvis Gant marched onto the porch, followed by LaWanda Fae.

"He just walked in," the woman said. She was frightened, and she looked desperately at Bybee and then at Kendall. "Shall I call the—"

"Shut up!" Gant said.

He was dressed in suit pants with suspenders, a white shirt, and his face was red and faintly wet with perspiration. He stood poised in the middle of the porch like a fighter, his feet apart, his arms out to his side, staring and blinking at Bybee.

"You ignorant fucking clown!" Gant said. "Where is she?"

Bybee bent low, as if he were expecting Gant to charge, and pushed his hair from his eyes. "What are you doing here, Gant?" He glanced briefly at LaWanda Fae and then at Kendall. "Who told you to come here?"

"Who told *you*?" Gant said, and he made a sudden half turn and then fixed Bybee with his blinking eyes. "I ordered you—the governor ordered you—to keep her away from here. Now, where the hell—"

"Brigham," LaWanda Fae said, "shall I call the police?"

Gant spun around. "I told you to shut the fuck up!"

"Don't you talk to that woman like that," Bybee said.

"Fuck you!"

"Get the hell out," Bybee said. He advanced toward Gant and stopped in front of him, towering over the other man. "Walk back out of this house—now—or I'll throw you out."

Gant tensed and looked away, and when he did, he saw the two women in the yard, both staring back up at the house, their eyes wide. He looked at them, then at Kendall, who was still standing near the chairs, frozen, one hand extended in midair, as though he were keeping the scene at a distance.

Gant glared at Bybee, his eyes angry, blinking. "So, there's the little cohab cunt."

"Watch your mouth," Bybee said.

Gant shifted his eyes to Kendall, then Bybee, and back out to the two women in the yard. "Isn't that a touching scene? Two plig whores sitting by a tree." He laughed, suddenly. "K-I-S-S-l—"

"Shut your mouth!" Bybee said. His scalp and face had begun to burn with anger, and his hand was shaking. He stepped closer to Gant. "I mean it! Now get the hell out of here!"

LaWanda Fae had backed up several steps so that she stood at the door to the house, and Kendall finally moved away from the chairs and positioned himself behind Gant, facing Bybee. The governor's assistant was now surrounded, as if they had cornered a wild animal.

Gant made a jerking motion, turned around to face Kendall, and then spun back around to Bybee. "I'm going to have your fucking head, you asshole!"

The heat in Bybee's head now gushed through the rest of his body, and his gut burned hot as he stared at Gant. Suddenly his entire body—his soul—seemed to reach a kindling point, to catch fire, and only one thing mattered now: to ruin the vile little man who stood, sweating and panting, in front of him.

"Good," Bybee said. "You can put it next to Franklin Pugh's head . . . when we find it. And we *are* going to find it."

Gant looked as if he was going to explode; his face seemed to swell, and the upper part of his body began to tremble.

"God damn it, Bybee, you even *think* about going after Crowe for murder, and I'll personally—*personally*—see that you never practice law in this state again. I mean it!"

Bybee snorted and put his quavering hand behind his back. "Oh, don't worry, Gant. I'm not going after Crowe for murder." He looked over Gant's head at Kendall, the fire inside him white-hot. "Am I, Tom?"

Kendall looked confused and helpless, and only stared back at Bybee, while Gant stood, his chest—his whole body— heaving, sweat now running down his face.

"No, I'm going after Crowe for *aggravated* murder," Bybee said, and he leaned toward Gant, his eyes narrowed. "And I'm asking for the death penalty, you little piece of shit!" He looked at Kendall and then back at Gant. "We're going to kill Crowe, so you and the governor can take your little polygamy dog-and-pony show and stick it up your ass—if you can even find it."

Gant stood, breathing so heavily that for a few moments it was the only sound that could be heard on the porch, and then he suddenly laughed and stepped back, shaking his head.

"That's all it takes for you, isn't it, Bybee?"

Bybee did not understand what the man was saying; he said nothing and continued to stare at him, the heat in his body now raging, searing him inside and out.

"That's all it takes," Gant said again, and he nodded toward the two women on the lawn. "Some little bitch just has to open her legs, and Brig Bybee will come sniffing—"

Bybee's right fist struck Gant just over his left ear, glancing off his skull so that it looked as though he had simply slapped him, but the blow was still fierce and powerful, snapping the man's head back. LaWanda Fae screamed as Gant staggered into Kendall, who pushed the smaller man aside and immedi- ately ran toward Bybee, holding out his arms as if he were going to embrace him.

"Christ Jesus!" Kendall said.

Bybee stood, his fist still cocked and raised, and for an instant it looked as if he would strike Kendall as well. But his friend seized both his arms, then wrapped his own around him and began to half drag and half push him toward the door, where LaWanda Fae stood, her eyes bulging behind the thick glasses.

"Christ Jesus!" Kendall said again.

Gant remained on the other side of the patio, his head cocked, one hand clasped over his ear as though he were trying to hear the turmoil more clearly.

"You're dead meat, Bybee," he said, his voice weak, childlike. "You are dead fucking meat!"

Bybee struggled in Kendall's grasp, trying to break free, but his friend pushed him through the door that LaWanda Fae held open.

"C'mon, Brig," Kendall said. "Get out."

Inside the house Kendall released Bybee but kept one hand on his back, steering him through the rooms, Bybee stiff, his head unnaturally elevated, until they reached the front door, which was still wide open from Gant's intrusion.

Behind them, Gant had come halfway into the living room, trailing after them, his hand still covering his ear.

"You know, Bybee," he said, "the only thing the state bar has ever done right—*ever* done right—is try to take away your law license a few years back. This time, they will."

"Fuck you," Bybee said. "Just—"

"I guarantee it. You're out of the business for good. I'll personally see to it!"

Bybee suddenly pulled away from Kendall, but his friend grabbed him again and pushed him out the door on to the front porch.

"Just get the hell out of here, Brig . . . *now!*"

"That little . . . shit," Bybee said. His breath and words came in short gasps. "Little piece . . . shit."

Kendall guided him down the steps and hurriedly pushed him along the walkway, through the wrought-iron gate, and up the sidewalk until they were at the VW bus. Without stopping, Kendall escorted Bybee to the driver's side and even opened the door.

"Get the hell out of here," Kendall said. "Don't fuck with this guy anymore. Jesus, you slugged the governor's assistant—"

"Tom, he—"

"Just leave; go home and lay low—real low. I'll try to smooth things out."

Awkwardly, Bybee climbed into the seat of the bus, wincing when he gripped the steering wheel with his right hand. He looked at it, holding it palm outward as though he were admiring a ring or a watch, and saw that the fingers were red and swollen. He slowly reached inside his pants, withdrew his keys, and started the engine.

"Tom—"

"Just go, Brig."

"Get back into the house. Make sure that little shit doesn't do anything to Mercy. I mean it."

"Don't worry," Kendall said. He hesitated, and then put his hand on Bybee's arm. "Were you serious back there, Brig?"

"What?"

"About staying on the case. About going after the Big Plig for agg' murder? Death penalty?"

Bybee looked out the windshield at the houses around them, quaint and peaceful, the people who lived in them—all of them—probably enveloped in secure worlds, decent worlds, none of them ever imagining the secret horrors that bubbled around them, unseen, but always there, lurking.

"Yes," Bybee said. "I am serious. I'm still in."

Kendall looked worried, and he slowly shook his head and took a step back from the bus. "Okay, Brig. It's your call, but . . . after this"—he nodded at the house—"all hell's going to bust loose in Salt Lake."

"We'll deal with it," Bybee said. Painfully, with his right hand, he jammed the old machine into gear and nodded at Kendall through the side window. "Take care of Mercy."

Kendall said nothing, and as Bybee pulled away, he slapped

the side of the bus the way a cowboy would a horse, making a loud, hollow sound.

By the time he rattled back into Kanab, Bybee's hand was throbbing so badly that all he could think of was jamming it deep into the bin of ice in the big, gray machine at the Piute Villa—and jamming it again—sometime, any time—into the face of Darvis Gant. The anger that erupted in Manti was now bubbling over, and he had driven down the Long Valley Highway like a maniac, barely watching the road.

As he turned on to Center Street, the first thing he saw was a bright red pickup truck pulling slowly out of Duffin Judd's Wampum Mart next to the Piute Villa. He accelerated and caught up with the truck as it passed Duke's Mercantile. With his left hand he pressed the horn button—making only a thin, bleating sound, like a sheep—and then violently swung the VW in front of the red truck, cutting it off and bringing it to a sudden halt. .

With his bus at an angle across half of Center Street, blocking traffic, and several tourists and townsfolk on the sidewalk watching, Bybee climbed down from the vehicle and strode furiously around to the truck. Zolene was halfway out of the cab, her red hair hiding half of her face, one silver earring tangled in several strands.

"You almost got a woman killed, Zolene! Do you realize that? Do you?"

Bybee stood so closely to her door that Zolene could not open it wide enough to exit, so she remained, suspended, bent, one white hand gripping the top of the window. She took her sunglasses off and looked up at him, her eyes as angry as his.

"You were shacked up with a plig in my house, Brig? What the hell was I supposed to do? Run and fetch doughnuts and coffee? Make sure you two were—"

"Go to hell, Zolene! Straight to hell. I asked for a simple favor—a simple favor—and you were too goddamned *selfish* to—"

Zolene's mouth gaped open. "Selfish? *I* was too selfish?"

"Goddamned right."

Zolene said nothing, then slowly put her sunglasses back on, adjusting them. "Fine, Brig. Why don't you just come out and pick up your things at *my* house. Today, preferably."

"Good. I'll send Vesta out to help you. That way, you won't have to bother—I mean, seeing how everything is such an imposition—"

"She won't even have to come in, Brig. Everything will be on the porch." Zolene gestured, violently, toward the green bus. "Now get your *fucking* stupid-looking bus out of my way!"

She sat back in the seat, slammed the door, and stared straight ahead, glaring at the tourists who were still standing motionless on the sidewalk, watching. Bybee slapped his right hand on the roof of the truck, instantly wincing at the pain in his swollen hand, then turned and marched back to his bus, got in, and made a squealing U-turn in the middle of Center Street, heading back toward the Piute Villa.

"Lord *God!*" he shouted inside the bus.

9

THE way the Kanab old-timers tell it, just after World War II, a new football coach arrived in town, a large, hairy man named Joe Holland, fresh from the Army Air Corps, where he had flown P-38s in Europe. On his first night in Kanab he was found drunk out of his non-Mormon mind at the intersection of Main and Center, directing the dribble of traffic with his engraved coach's whistle—a gift presented earlier that day by the Kanab school board.

The scandal mushroomed overnight, and Bishop Douglas Farnsworth, Zolene's grandfather, had lobbied for his immediate dismissal, for his banishment back to the Gentile hinterlands.

But Holland stayed, and the following year Big Joe, as he was soon called, took the Kanab Cowboys to the state playoffs, where he lost, but still won a measure of redemption, finally smothering the whispers—whispers that often swirled like a storm around outsiders in Kanab.

Like most coaches, Big Joe and his family moved on several years later, but the intersection of Main and Center became known as Big Joe's Junction, the bellowing coach and his whistle—and the whispers—forever a part of Kanab history.

About half a block up the street from Big Joe's Junction, at the Trail's End café, Bybee sat alone in one of the vinyl booths in the rear, the same booth where he had first met Ronnie Watters more than a year before. The place was filled with the sounds of clinking silverware, the clatter of plates in the kitchen, and a steady, murmuring babble of foreign voices—German, Japanese, Italian, even a British accent in the booth behind him.

From the teenage waitress dressed in boots, jeans, a six-gun, and a hat, he had ordered the "Rancher's DeLuxe," a heaping plateful of eggs and sausage and hash browns and toast—Doc Lundquist's low-cholesterol diet be damned—and now he sat with a mug of coffee, waiting, the *Salt Lake Tribune* spread out before him.

But he wasn't reading. Instead he sat and stared out the front window at Center Street, at the early-morning shuffle of tourists, sorting out his strategies and options almost like a football coach would do—like Big Joe would have done—assessing the strengths and weaknesses that had suddenly arisen in his life.

Zolene? In the cyclone of emotions and images that had roared through his brain all night, keeping him awake, the caustic breakup in front of Duke's kept reappearing, replaying itself over and over again. And somehow by dawn he had rationalized it all, neutralized it, convincing himself that Zolene, fifteen years his junior, subject to deep and disturbing mood swings, and saddled with two troubled—and troublesome—teenagers, perhaps wasn't something he needed in his life at this time . . . maybe at any time.

And Gant? Certainly, if the little martinet went to the police and reported the assault, or if he and the governor attempted to block the investigation into a horrifying polygamist murder, Cynthia, to save herself, would expose the entire sordid political game, and the media just might devour the governor's office whole. Besides, Kendall had said he would do something to smooth the mess over.

And himself? Kendall was probably right: If he was a prosecutor, then he should behave like one—not some mincing, delicate prima donna who sidestepped his responsibilities because of outdated moral and philosophical principles, principles the rest of the state—and surely his profession—almost wholly ignored. He would prosecute Crowe for aggravated murder, and more than likely, with a conviction and a sentence of death, his reputation in the state bar would be finally and firmly reestablished, his complete honor restored. And with that, wealthy clients and lucrative assignments would once again be his for the choosing —and the Piute Villa would continue to hum along, as well.

No, his life was not in turmoil, as he had feared twelve hours ago; it had taken on a different but steadier, more stable tack, and he was actually sailing—despite a sore, throbbing right hand—into calmer waters.

At almost the same time that the gun-toting waitress arrived with his sizzling Rancher's DeLuxe, Sheriff Seegmiller walked in the front door and, when he spotted Bybee, walked over to the booth and stood back until the waitress left.

Bybee, holding a fork awkwardly in his left hand, looked up at the man. "Seegy," he said, and he nodded at the other side of the booth. "Sit down."

Seegmiller was dressed in his uniform of brown pants and beige shirt, with a panoply of equipment—flashlight, handcuffs, a cluster of keys, everything but a gun—attached to his belt, and he simply shook his head and looked away. He reached inside his shirt pocket and withdrew a folded piece of paper.

"Brig, I—" He hesitated, his eyes worried, his face drawn, and held out the piece of paper. "I'm afraid I have some bad news."

A cold chill coursed through Bybee, and he suddenly felt weak, nauseous. His daughter, six months pregnant, was having difficulty carrying the baby, and had even been hospitalized once in Beaver.

"Oh, Lord," Bybee said. "Is it Brileena?"

Seegmiller shook his head and squinted at the paper. "No. I got a call from a man named . . . Kendall. He said he had been trying to reach you for the last hour or so."

"Kendall, sure. Tom. I've been out walking—"

"He told me to tell you . . ."

The sheriff bent toward the paper in his hand and cleared his throat. Behind and above him, one of the wagon wheel chandeliers seemed to encircle his head like a giant wooden halo, the flame-shaped bulbs glowing around him, one of them burned out.

" 'Faith has been murdered,' " Seegmiller read from the paper. " 'Shot. Mercy is gone. Disappeared. Call me.' "

Bybee did not move; he stared at Seegmiller's face, and then, unconsciously, focused on his badge, how bright it was, gleaming, how carefully the man must polish it every day, buffing it with a cloth, probably, then holding it up to the light, turning it. . . .

He then looked at the wagon-wheel chandelier, and it seemed to move, to spin, the lights blurring together in a stream of fire, whirling . . .

"That's all, Brig," Seegmiller said. He swallowed and cocked his head, a true look of concern on his face. "I shore hope it's not family, not . . ."

Bybee continued to stare at the lights. "No," he said.

Seegmiller hung there a few moments longer, then lay the scrap of paper on the table and cleared his throat again. "Well, I've got to go. If you need . . . anything, I'll be over at the office."

"Thanks."

The sheriff turned and walked out of the restaurant, and Bybee watched him leave and then stared out at the street, at the parade of passersby, at the endless stream of customers thumping in and out of the café, at the way the waitresses shepherded them about, their guns bouncing on their hips. . . . Guns.

She had carried a gun in that big, ugly purse.

He watched it all now without really seeing; he watched the

way the world continued to bustle along, blissful, unaware . . . wholly deceived.

The chandeliers were spinning now, shrieking, a roar of light blinding him.

Thirty minutes later, with his eggs and sausage cold and congealed on the plate, untouched, and Bybee still sitting, staring, the waitress with the six-gun approached him.

"Sar?" she said.

Bybee slowly moved his head and looked at her, not sure who she was, why she was standing over him. "What?" he said.

"Are you done?"

Part II

And then a Plank in Reason, broke,
And I dropped down, and down—
And hit a World, at every plunge,
And Finished knowing—then—

—EMILY DICKINSON

10

TWO days after he returned from Vietnam; two days after the family crowded into the small home on 600 North Street in Beaver, Utah, slapping him on the back and pumping his hand, talking endlessly about Beaver High football and fly-fishing and Dick Nixon—all of it loudly, with artificial smiles, as though he were an invalid—Bybee quietly slipped away.

He borrowed a friend's pickup truck, tossed in a tent and a sleeping bag, a camp stove, a box of food, and several jugs of water, and set out for Navajo Lake, near Cedar Breaks, only about an hour and a half away. There, at a small trailer overlooking the deserted lake, high atop the Markagunt Plateau and closed in by tall pines, he met the "lake master," an old man named Jack Yetter who, in addition to charging him a one-dollar camping fee, also sold him a heaping pile of firewood, white gas, and then, once he was sure Bybee was not a state agent, two cases of Schlitz beer.

For the next three days and nights Bybee sat beside a fire alone, staring, drinking beer, listening to the sounds of the forest, the wind soughing in the pines, the birds, the rustling of animals . . . but really hearing only one thing: the sounds of war, the incessant clattering of rotor blades, the whining of turbine engines, the radio's static—and the gunfire, always the sounds of guns, the ceaseless popping, spitting sound of guns, of death.

And then he heard the awful, deafening sound of his own desolation.

Now, thirty years later, Bybee once again heard the same sound as he ground up the mountain, up Highway 14, the back of the VW bus loaded with a tent and sleeping bag, some food and water, and, rather than a case of beer, a sackful of dog food for Spooky Floyd, who sat, sliding and skittering on the vinyl middle seat, his yellow eyes staring out the window, confused.

At the top of the mountain, the air now cool, almost cold, they drove through a watery meadow, past Duck Creek, where he and Helena and Brileena—and half the Boy Scouts in Beaver —used to fish, and finally came to Navajo Lake. There, in the same place, and what looked like the same rusted trailer, was the lake master, but he was now a younger man, dressed in overalls and work boots with a heavy black beard and long hair.

The man held up his hand and then walked around to the driver's side of the bus. " 'Lo," he said, and he bent and peered inside the vehicle at Spooky Floyd. "Going fishing?"

"No," Bybee said. "Just camping, just . . . " He shrugged. "Just nothing."

The lake master laughed. "Wol, still gotta charge you, even for doin' nothing. Five dollars—per day."

Bybee slowly nodded, staring at the man's woolly beard, his scarred, pitted nose, then dug his wallet out of his rear pocket and withdrew a ten-dollar bill.

"Two days," Bybee said, and he held the bill, not releasing it. "Used to be a dollar a day."

The lake master gently pulled the bill from Bybee's hand. "Yeah, wol . . . " He stuffed the bill into one of his pockets. "Need anything else? Farwood? Propane?" He studied Bybee for a moment, the same way old man Yetter used to inspect potential customers, the lake master tradition intact. "Fact, I got anything you need."

"Like Scotch?" Bybee said.

Again the man studied Bybee's face, then drew back and looked·at the Piute Villa logo, and finally returned his head into the window, glancing at Spooky Floyd.

"Yeah. Like Scotch. Beer, bourbon . . . you name it."

"How much for the Scotch?"

"Forty dollars a fifth."

"That's a helluva lot of money," Bybee said.

The bearded man smiled, and then waved his hand around him at the endless acres of pines, the vast emptiness of the mountain. "Not a helluva lot of competition."

Bybee took a long, slow breath—held it—then blew it out toward the floor. Since the very moment Seegmiller had stood over him at the Trail's End and dribbled out those horrifying words, he had thought constantly of a bottle of Scotch, of holding it, hefting it, then pouring several fingers' worth into a clean, heavy glass and letting it slowly seep into him, letting it numb him the way Seegmiller's words had numbed him.

"Just firewood," Bybee finally said. "A lot of it."

The lake master shrugged, disappointed. "Wol, okay." He grinned. "But you know whar to come."

Bybee nodded, then got out and opened the rear door of the bus, and within minutes the two of them had loaded a sizable stack of pine logs, dry and sweet smelling, into the cargo area. After paying him for the wood, Bybee climbed back into the bus, and he and Spooky Floyd drove away down a narrow, muddy road.

They crawled downward through a long, green tunnel of trees and then skirted the edge of the lake, which, through the infrequent gaps in the foliage, shone like a mirror, flat and placid and undisturbed, not a single boat or canoe upon it, the whole place even more remote, more secluded, than Bybee remembered. At one point he stopped the bus, turned off the engine, and, in the deep shade, he listened, straining to hear any sounds that did not belong in the forest—another car, a radio, a child shouting—but there were none. He and Spooky Floyd were alone, removed from the world . . . and that was just what he wanted.

Eventually Bybee found a clearing, about fifty yards up the slope from the water's edge, with a flat area for a tent and, off to the side, a fire ring of blackened rocks. He parked and, over the next half-hour, set up his tent—an outdated, triangular thing that sagged in the middle—laid out an air mattress and sleeping bag inside, and then gathered up several armloads of pine boughs and, next to the tent, made a bed for the dog.

By the time he had finished, the sun had dropped below the pines, and the forest was fast becoming dark and cold. He was dressed in jeans and a long-sleeved flannel shirt, and he struggled into his old flight jacket, sage green and shiny with a fluorescent orange lining, with the barely legible words US ARMY on the front, on one side, and BYBEE on the other, all of the letters faded, nearly gone . . . like himself, he thought.

He had been seduced; he had been cleverly duped by someone who was far more and far worse than a simple decoy or a tactical diversion . . . or a cohab whore. She was an agent, an assassin, a devious actress who sat at the Piute Villa and, surrounded by the raw material, the props, she needed—the decapitated head of the plaster Indian, the box full of severed arms and legs, the crossed swords on the wall—created a horrific improvised story of unimaginable violence, a story he had, in his stupidity, his raging ignorance, swallowed—completely, bodily . . . murderously.

And he had taken her straight into the heart of the prosecution; he had led her right to the doorstep of the key witness, the only witness, right up to the face of her victim, where she smiled and cried and embraced her sister wife . . . and then shot her.

Sister wife. Sister murderess.

With some of the wood, he started a fire, and for the next several hours he sat huddled before it, wrapped in a ragged, filthy quilt, with Spooky Floyd lying nearby. He hardly moved, but only sat and peered into the flames until they died, and then he continued to stare at the red embers until they, too, died and turned to ash. And then there was nothing, only the icy darkness around him, the same oblivion that he had seen at Lamb's house several nights before, the same empty fear that gnawed at him, the same fear—always—that needed to be drowned.

He looked up and, across the lake, he saw a tiny pinpoint of light: the lake master's trailer. It glowed at him, signaling to him like a faint beacon, winking, then seeming to flash, insistent, like a desperate SOS.

He stood up, walked to the bus, and opened the door, allowing the weak overhead dome light to turn on, then pulled his wallet out of his pocket and tipped it toward the light. He counted the cash there—twenty, thirty, finally a full forty dollars—and had begun to fish it out when he saw a scrap of paper. It was the note, in Deseret, that Mercy had written for him when they were at Lamb's house several days ago—several centuries ago. He carefully pulled it out and held it to the light:

$$\text{𐐄𐐻𐐸𐑌 𐐓𐐹}$$

He remained there in the cold, the door of the bus open, and held the paper, feeling its texture, squinting at the queer symbols as though he could divine what they meant, what they were trying to say. It was the only thing left of her; it was the only message she had given to him—or would ever give.

Carefully he replaced the paper in his wallet and then returned the wallet to his pocket. He closed the door of the bus and slowly felt his way through the darkness to his tent, made sure Spooky Floyd was settled on his pallet of pine boughs, then crawled inside. As he reached up to close the flap-door of the tent, he saw the pinpoint of light across the lake, but he released the flap, letting it fall, and then burrowed deep into his sleeping bag and closed his eyes.

Beneath the surface grid of wide, regular streets in Kanab there lies a dense web work of dirt paths, thin and twisting like a tangle of twine, rimmed by weeds and decades old, running behind and between houses, along the irrigation ditches and then over crude bridges, snaking in and out and around the lives of everyone in town.

During the day, in the stark stare of the Utah sun, it is only the children who are seen on these paths, running or walking or laughing, usually on their way to or from school, often in groups, dawdling along in single file, chatting, at times stopping in the shade of the tall old trees that are everywhere.

But at dusk, with the children home, these paths become an arterial system where flows the dark blood of rumor and revelation, the older townspeople silently coursing out and along these trails, crossing alleys and opening wooden gates and knocking on back doors, and then sitting at plastic-covered kitchen tables or in stuffy living rooms where they gush out the latest speculation and damnation, whispering, their eyes wide, excited. . . .

In the last few days, all the path-walkers could talk about was Brig Bybee, the owner of the Piute Villa, an ex-Mormon, an ex-husband, an ex-helicopter pilot in Vietnam, a man everyone knew was—or had been—sleeping with Zolene Swapp, a man who some say could have played pro baseball, a tall, trim, likable lawyer who often helped folks, for free, with minor legal problems, a man who was, if not one of Kanab's own, a permanent, friendly fixture.

But Brig Bybee, they hissed, leaning forward and drawing the listener closer, was somehow implicated in a plig murder upstate, in Manti, right behind the temple.

And there was also talk about the odd scarecrow of a fellow on the motorcycle, a man many along the Kanab pathways had seen several times in town, roaring around with his bulbous green helmet and dark face shield, some claiming they had seen him only as a blur, screaming down the Long Valley Highway at well over a hundred miles an hour.

And they saw him again, today, spluttering down Center

Street to the Piute Villa and, after talking to Vesta Frost at the desk, on to Bybee's house.

Bybee was unloading the camping equipment from the VW, stacking it on one side of the front porch, when Kendall swept down the street on his Yamaha, the engine abnormally loud in the quiet neighborhood, and pulled up at the curb. He quickly yanked off his helmet, dismounted, and came up the walkway, admiring as he did the tidy yard, the trimmed shrubbery, all of it surrounded by a white picket fence.

"Brig," he said. He was dressed in his usual riding gear of boots and jeans and a leather jacket, and he clumped up the wooden steps, a forced grin on his face. "Where the hell have you been?"

Bybee put aside the folded tent with which he was wrestling and stood, squinting through smudged glasses, still in his dirty jeans and the flannel shirt, his boots caked with mud, reeking of wood smoke and bacon and wet canvas. In one corner of the porch, Spooky Floyd, his paws and half his body splotched with mud, sat wretchedly, his broken tail angled out behind him.

"Lost in the woods," Bybee said, and he nodded toward the dog. "Lassie, there, found me and brought me home." His voice was nearly inaudible, and his unshaven face was drawn, with dark circles under his eyes.

"Well, Christ Jesus," Kendall said. He looked apprehensively at the dog, then forced another smile. "I thought maybe you were . . . I dunno . . ."

"Dead?" Bybee said. "Sorry, no such luck."

"C'mon, Brig. Don't talk like that."

Bybee limply took his friend's proffered hand and then walked to the front door, held it open, and stepped to one side, nearly stumbling. "Come in."

Like most homes in Kanab, Bybee's house was small and old, probably built in the 1930s, but he had not attempted to re-create the past as he had helped do at Lamb's house. Instead, the place—darkened and cooled by wooden shutters—was pleasantly furnished with a leather couch and matching chairs, oriental rugs, a few tasteful paintings on the walls, and a bookcase jammed full of novels and framed photographs. One of the pictures was of Zolene, when she was a high school cheerleader, the letters KHS splashed across her bosom, her red hair scattered everywhere, and the tiny, pleated skirt showing long, white, unscarred legs.

Bybee motioned toward one of the chairs. "Sit down." He looked helplessly at the man, his hands held out. "I'd get you something to drink, but I—"

"That's okay."

"—don't even keep beer around." He shrugged, and then remained there, helpless, a man lost in an unfamiliar world."

That's okay," Kendall said again, and he stripped off his jacket, throwing it across the arm of the chair, and then sat down. "I've got to get back on the road in a few minutes, anyway."

Bybee nodded absently, and the two men said nothing for several moments, each staring around the room, Kendall nervously drumming his fingers on the oversize armrests while Bybee continued to stand, his flannel shirt half out, his hands jammed awkwardly in his muddy jeans pockets, his whole body —his whole soul—slouched and sagging, the room now smelling of wood smoke.

Kendall finally cleared his throat. "How are you holding up, Brig?"

"Not . . . " Bybee paused and shook his head, and for an instant Kendall thought the man might begin to cry. Bybee took a sudden, deep breath and clinched his jaw muscles, but then exhaled, moved to the couch, and sat down, leaning toward a low coffee table, resting his elbows on his thighs.

"Not so good," Bybee finished. He pushed a tangle of hair out of his face and left his hand atop his forehead, as though he were feeling it, ensuring that it was still there, and then dropped his hand and stared at the floor. "I really fucked up, didn't I?"

Kendall held out both hands, the same way he had done at the shelter. "Look, man, we *all* did. We all believed that we—"

Bybee suddenly brought his dirty fist down on the coffee

table, slamming it so hard that a piece of the thin veneer on the top split. "Goddammit, Tom! Don't you realize what happened? She walked in; just walked right in and flat-ass told me the biggest crock of shit you could imagine—anyone could imagine —and I fell for it!" He slammed his fist down on the table again. "Hook, line, and . . . *fucking* sinker!" He suddenly stood up, banging his legs on the coffee table, and wildly began to gesture with his arms, waving them in all directions and shouting. "Hey, listen everyone! Listen up! You wanna have some fun? Huh? You got some bullshit story, some wild-ass fairy tale about headless pligs and swords and—"

"Brig!"

Bybee turned toward his friend, his eyes wild. "She had a fucking gun in her purse, Tom! Don't you understand that? She traipsed around Zolene's house in front of me for two days with a goddamned *gun* in her purse. Jesus, how can—"

"Shut up, Brig!"

Bybee stopped, his arms suspended in the air, and stared at the other man, his eyes red and watery behind his glasses, his mouth open.

"Just shut up," Kendall said again. "You're making an ass of yourself."

Bybee bent his head back and released a short, barking laugh, then looked unsteadily at Kendall. "Yeah, well, I sure wouldn't want to do that, would I?"

"Sit down."

Bybee blinked stupidly at the man for a moment and then, spent, deflated, he obeyed and plopped violently back on the couch as though he himself had been shot by Mercy, his head tilted toward the ceiling.

"Oh, Lord God, Tom. I—"

And then he did begin to cry. He made a soft, hiccuping sound and his eyes filled with tears, but then he violently shook his head and quickly took off his glasses and dragged one hand across his face. He put the glasses back on, adjusted them, and then looked at Kendall.

"Sorry, it's just that I've . . ." He shook his head. "God," he almost whispered, "she had a gun all the time, and I just chauffeured her right up. . . ."

"It's okay," Kendall said. He seemed stunned by the extremes of emotion that had so quickly fizzed up in the room, and he simply sat in his chair and watched Bybee writhe, mesmerized, unsure what to say.

"It's okay," he said again.

Bybee looked at him, embarrassed, and he finally collected himself somewhat and sat up straight on the couch. "No, it's not, Tom. What's going to happen to me?" He pointed at Kendall. "To you? To Cynthia . . . to everyone? What's going on up in Salt Lake? I've been gone, out of it."

Kendall took a slow breath. "Look, Brig, I'll be honest: all hell has broken loose up there, and you're right square in the middle of it."

He paused, waiting for a reaction, but Bybee only closed his eyes, nodding. "Go on," Bybee said.

"The little piss-ant political war between Purcell and Cynthia has gone . . . nuclear. When Cynthia got the news about Faith, she launched first, a preemptive strike, I guess you'd call it. She immediately filed a motion to dismiss the bigamy prosecution against Crowe, saying it was just one of the governor's bullshit political ploys in the first place, but Rukamann's sitting on it, won't dismiss it."

"Surprise."

"Then she went to Judge Lazenbee, you know him, crazy old fart that—"

"Yeah, I know him."

"Well, she went to him—Cynthia did, personally—and got an information signed against Mercy, Chenoya, for . . . agg' murder." He paused, leaning closer. "Murder of a witness in a felony case, Brig. Cynthia still wants it all."

Bybee's mouth slowly opened, and he seemed to deflate, to shrink. "Death penalty?"

"Yeah. Every other—"

"Oh, Lord—"

"—cop in the state's looking for her ass—even our office.

Lazenbee signed search warrants, and Sorenson and Ordoñez have been all over New Ammon. She's not there."

Bybee leaned back in the couch, absently took one of the pillows, and held it against his stomach, tight, as though compressing a wound. He knew there were scores of hiding places in New Ammon—coal cellars and attics and, the reports had said, even tunnels and old 1950s-era bomb shelters.

"She might be there," Bybee said.

The room grew silent again, and from the rear of the house, the bedroom, a clock softly began playing the Westminster chime, a tinny, hollow sound, and the two of them waited in the darkened room, listening, until the last bar was played and the clock tinkled out the hour.

"Anyway," Bybee said, "what else?"

Kendall cleared his throat. "Cynthia fired you—*instanter*. She's been telling reporters that you specifically disobeyed her orders, that you went . . . nuts, went off on some crazy-ass wild-goose chase, that you're a maverick, a hip-shooter, some hired gun who went way over the top."

"That's bullshit, Tom. You told me she wanted Mercy up there."

Kendall held out his hands again. "She did, man, but I told you, this is all-out political war now. She's fighting for her life, and you're expendable. She's thrown you to the wolves."

"Shit," Bybee said, and he reached out and absently began trying to repair the split veneer on the tabletop, smoothing it with his ash-blackened finger. "And Gant? Purcell? If it's all-out war, what have they done?"

Kendall began drumming his fingers again on the armrest. "They fired back. They called a press conference and brought down the wrath of God on the AG's office, especially you and Cynthia. Gant conducted it, cameras everywhere; claimed you specifically disobeyed an executive order, that you violated the ethical canons, that you even—" He hesitated, his eyes looking away.

"That I what?"

"That you should be criminally prosecuted."

"Oh, Lord God." Bybee said. His voice, still low and tired, now had a hint of fear in it. "Prosecuted for what?"

Kendall shrugged. "I don't know. Some kind of obstruction, I guess. Maybe as an—"

"Maybe for criminal stupidity."

"Anyway, Brig, that's not all of it." Kendall clasped his hands together, then released them. "The governor has demanded a full investigation into all of this—Manti, Mercy, you, everything—and the Rocket Man's complying. Purcell's got him in his pocket, somehow, and so the judge has set a show-cause hearing for the thirty-first at three o'clock." He glanced at his watch—a big, black rubbery-looking thing. "Two days from now, on Friday."

" 'Show cause'?" Bybee said. "Show cause for what?"

"The AG's office is to explain, on the record in open court, and probably with every goddamned reporter in Salt Lake there, the reasons—the cause—for wanting to dismiss the bigamy charge . . . just how all this happened, who's to blame. It's all pretextual crap, just an excuse to go after you—us. And only the Rocket Man is doing the questioning, if you can imagine that."

"I can't. I've never heard of any show-cause hearing being used like that."

"Neither have I, but the Rocket Man's going to do it."

"Show cause," Bybee said, and he angrily threw the pillow he was holding across the room, where it hit the wall with a soft thud. "So the governor gets his little dog-and-pony show after all? Show-cause, show-and-tell . . . show trial."

"Yeah, but this time it's not about polygamy, it's about Cynthia—and you, Brig." Kendall cocked his head and gave Bybee an exaggerated look of sympathy. "What Gant said in Manti is true. He wants your head—bad. And not just for punching him out. For everything; for all of it. He and the governor are going to crucify you."

"Christ," Bybee said, but he didn't return Kendall's tentative grin at the word; he hadn't meant to be clever. "Well, wake me when it's over; I won't be there."

"Sorry, buddy, but you *will* be there. Subpoenas are being

served today—got mine this morning. I imagine a constable or some process server is heading toward Kanab right now, as we speak."

"This is crazy, Tom, all of it. Just pure, crazy shit."

"Strange times," Kendall said, and he began bobbing his head, his eyes unfocused, seemingly distracted by other thoughts. "Strange, strange times."

Bybee stared at him, puzzled by the man's nonchalance. "You seem to be taking this pretty well."

"Not really," Kendall said, and he laughed. "Hell, you should have seen me when I heard the news; I was a basket case." He suddenly got to his feet, his lanky body seeming to creak open one bone at a time, and snatched up his jacket. "I've got to get back, buddy."

Bybee also stood, and he was escorting his friend to the front door when Kendall spotted the photograph of Zolene in the bookcase, walked over to it, and bent close to the frame. He studied the picture for a moment—the teenager's bright red hair, the blue eyes, her incredible white face.

Kendall straightened and looked approvingly at Bybee. "That is one beautiful creature, Brig. You are a lucky son of a bitch."

Bybee made a hollow laugh. "Oh, yeah. I'm lucky as hell."

"How's she taking all this?"

"I don't know," Bybee said, and he hurriedly walked to the door, dredging up some of the soap-opera clichés that had been playing through his mind. "We don't see each other anymore. It's over."

Kendall blew a gust of breath toward the ceiling. "Man, I am sorry. I really am."

"It's okay," Bybee said, and he opened the door. "It just didn't work out."

"Well . . . " Kendall shrugged and then walked outside.

After the darkened house, Kanab and the cliffs and the sky seemed to explode around them in a blast of bright sunshine and color, all of it rimmed along the horizon by a bubbling mass of white clouds—"movie clouds," some of the Kanab old-timers still called them. Across the street, two boys on bicycles with playing cards clothespinned to the spokes of their wheels sped by, sounding like cheap motorbikes.

Bybee watched the boys, then looked at Kendall. "I just can't believe Mercy actually did this, Tom. To Faith . . . to me."

Kendall struggled into his jacket. "She did, Brig. Sorry. People are already calling her a plig . . . Mata Hari. Is that how you pronounce it?"

Bybee didn't answer. "Have they found the gun yet?"

"No. I'm sure it's long gone, or back in New Ammon."

"How did she do it? Where did she—"

Kendall made a mock gun out of his thumb and forefinger and pointed it at his ear. "Right here, buddy. Right in her ear. LaWanda Fae last saw the two of them around nine o'clock. She showed Mercy to her bedroom, then left for about a half-hour, she says, to buy some things—food, clothes for Mercy. She got back, went to bed herself, and in the morning found Faith dead, her brains spread across the pillow, and Mercy gone." He shrugged. "Just like that."

Bybee stood, absorbing it, trying to imagine Mercy stealing into Faith's room, drawing the pistol from her purse, putting it to the ear of her sister wife . . . and then pulling the trigger. He closed his eyes for a moment, then opened them and looked at Spooky Floyd, still sitting in the corner of the porch, watching.

He finally turned to Kendall. "Tom, how did Gant know to come to Manti when I showed up with Mercy?"

"I don't know," Kendall said. "I've been trying to figure that out for days, now. When you called from Alton, I let Cynthia know what was happening—I had to—then called Sorenson and Ordoñez and told them to stand by. Those were the only people I told."

"Then one of them told Gant," Bybee said.

The two men remained silent for several moments, each thinking, sorting everything out, staring at the street. Kendall, despite the warmth of the day, slowly zipped up his leather jacket and then shook his head.

"Cynthia? No, I'm not going to believe that." His voice, as always, had the odd, theatrical resonance to it. "I'm just not. It's too—"

"Crazy?" Bybee finished for him. "Maybe it's not *that* crazy. Like you've been saying, these are strange days. You know as well as I, when people are pissed off, they'll take everything and everyone down with them."

Kendall simply nodded, and the two fell quiet again as Bybee began tapping his boots on the top step, knocking dried mud from them.

"I've got to get back," Kendall finally said. He turned and firmly shook Bybee's hand. "So long, Brig. I guess I'll see you at the hearing. Hang in there."

He turned and walked back to his motorcycle, mounted and started it, pulled on his helmet, and with a wave of his hand drove away, the sound of the big engine reverberating through the streets, causing the boys on their make-believe motorcycles to stop and gape at the real thing as it boomed by.

Bybee stood on the porch, watching, as Kendall sped north along the grid. Just as he approached Center Street, Kendall passed a car coming in the other direction, almost like a tag team, almost as though the two men should slap palms as they drove by one another. The car—a dented, dusty sedan—crept slowly along the street, the driver ducking and squinting through the window, and then he pulled up to the curb, exactly where Kendall had been parked.

The driver was a balding, simple-faced man, and he got out and walked around the front of his car. He had the look that Bybee had often seen, the look of the professional *poseur* finally gone to seed, like an insurance agent or a store manager or an aging missionary . . . or a process server. He wore a short-sleeved white shirt, a thin tie, slacks, and godawful shoes, the kind mailmen or referees wear—heavy and black and rubber-soled, the footwear counterpart of Kendall's watch.

The man glanced at a manila folder he carried in his hands. "You . . . Brigham Bybee?"

"Sometimes I am," Bybee said, and he walked toward the

man, his filthy hand out to accept the subpoena. "And sometimes I wish the hell I weren't."

After he had showered and shaved and changed clothes, Bybee
drove down Center Street to the Kanab Public Library—a small,
low-roofed building that was more like the local LDS genealogical center than a repository of books. The librarian, the quivering, hoary-headed Arcola Cox, twin sister of Arletha Cox, did
not have what he needed; in fact, she had never heard of it . . . or
pretended that she hadn't.

So he gassed up the VW at Lloyd Honey's Texaco and drove
south, across the Arizona state line, past the Buckskin Tavern—
the last place he had ever touched a drop of alcohol— and into
the Arizona Strip. He rattled past the old Mormon fort of Pipe
Springs, past Mad Rabbit, Cottonwood Point, and finally, he
drove by Colorado City, the polygamist stronghold once called
Short Creek.

The highway angled back into Utah, and a few miles later,
where a dirt road intersected with the highway, he saw the bent
green sign, pockmarked by .22 rounds and bird shot, screaming
at him, taunting him: NEW AMMON, 12 Mi.

It was the main road to the colony, angling northeastward
through Washington County and back to Kane County, and
Bybee reflexively turned his head to the side, his face beginning
to burn with humiliation, a deep, rumbling rage seething
through him. She was probably there, in a cellar or an old bomb
shelter, deep underground, in one of the scores of hiding places
in the colony, sitting at a table with the rest of them, with Crowe
and the sister wives and the Blood Disciples . . . and Franklin
Pugh, his head and arms and genitals intact, all of them laughing, celebrating, congratulating her on the successful comple-
tion of her mission—her real mission—her daring drop behind
the lines, the impersonation, the deception . . . then the inser-
tion into the enemy camp . . . the kill.

"Lord God," Bybee said aloud in the bus, and he accelerated, hurrying away from the place.

Thirty minutes later he entered St. George, a hot, barren place built amid another set of cliffs, but these colorless and uninspiring, the whole city dominated, like Manti, by a white-spired temple. It had once been Brigham Young's winter home, a place in the southwest corner of Utah known as "Dixie," the capital, a century and a half before, of the prophet's failed "cotton mission."

After stopping to ask directions, Bybee finally wound his way through the St. George streets until he was on the campus of Dixie State College, a small four-year school that was one of several that had offered him a baseball scholarship years ago. It was a pleasant place, once a private, church-supported Mormon academy—and now a public, state-supported Mormon academy —and after wandering a bit, he finally found the low, red-bricked library with odd columns in front, and he parked the VW and walked inside.

The fall semester had not yet begun, so the library was nearly deserted, only a few hangers-on dawdling in the front and a skeleton crew manning the rear stacks. An elderly woman behind a desk directed him to an alcove on one side, and there, after struggling with the computer and failing, softly cursing it, retreated to the old, wood-encased card catalog, which was still maintained. He quickly pawed through the file, then, coming upon the proper card, scribbled a quick notation and, in a rear recess, found what he came for.

It was a thin, small, hardbound book, not more than four inches by six inches, its faded brown cover decorated with ornate drawings—a beehive at the top and the Salt Lake temple on the bottom. In the middle, between old woodcuts of young children, were several undecipherable words, a jumble of strange, quirky symbols in Deseret, and the year, in Arabic numerals: 1868.

Quickly, Bybee found a deserted table, sat, opened the book, and just past the coded title page, found the translation guide, a listing of all symbols and their English phonetic equivalent. Grabbing a note card and a tiny pencil from a plastic tray on the table, he withdrew his wallet and brought out the scrap of paper that Mercy had written upon and looked at it, stared at it the way he had done over and over in the mountains, trying to feel what it meant, what she was saying:

ግቦᴚ ᴐᴚ

His tall body bent, his head only inches from the book, he began to compare the symbols on the scrap of paper to those in the book, then, finding the one that matched, wrote out the English letter on the card.

After a few minutes, he slowly lay the pencil down and stared at the two words that he had formed on the card, two words that seemed to glow in the dim library, two words that he knew were the only hope he had, the only voice, the only sound, in this swirling darkness around him:

TRUST ME

He carefully replaced Mercy's scrap of paper in his wallet, then walked to the librarian, borrowed two sheets of stationery, and returned to the table. There, with the same stubby pencil, he wrote a letter to Zolene, confessing, without blurring or hiding the facts, what had happened that night in Lamb's house with Mercy, beseeching her understanding, her forgiveness . . . a restoration of her trust.

11

I n his pre-sheriff days, DeRalph Seegmiller, for want of a better term, was a failed businessman. All of his previous Kanab ventures—a feed store, a souvenir shop, a laundry and dry cleaners, even a Mexican food café that featured Navajo tacos—foundered, and for one simple reason: he was the quintessential nice guy, a plain, trusting soul who always extended credit, forgave debts, and at times flatly gave his goods or services away.

Today, Seegmiller was the same sort of lawman as he had been an entrepreneur—never quite understanding his authority, usually, as he had done in retail sales, undervaluing it, and always willing to be coaxed or cajoled into doing just about anything that anyone asked.

It was only three blocks from Bybee's house on 400 South to the sheriff's office on 100 South, so he walked there, trying to enjoy the early-afternoon breeze, the warm sun, the air that smelled of mown alfalfa and watered grass—but it couldn't be done. His head remained bent, his eyes on the old sidewalks, his teeth gnawing at his lips as he tried, as he had done all morning, to rehearse mentally what he was about to do.

After he had translated Mercy's message, he had sat in the Dixie State College library for more than an hour, scribbling notes on the tiny cards, outlining, drawing a flow chart, then wadding them all up and beginning again. Eventually, his stomach growling, his neck and shoulders sore from hunching over the table, he left the library and drove back to Kanab, his plan now imprinted in his mind.

If anyone could truly call it a plan . . . or a mind. It was, at best, an ill-conceived, desperate ploy that, were Bybee an oddsmaker, a bookie, he would have to give only a five-to-one chance of actually succeeding. At worst, it was a suicide mission, a hopeless, anonymous, self-styled kamikaze attack, but without the martyr's glory, without an explosive flash of heroism. No, it would simply be part of his shameless slide toward . . . what? Toward further humiliation? Toward outright ruin? Toward eternity?

He paused only briefly at the front of Seegmiller's office, then pushed his hair from his face and walked up the front, past the bright flowers and freshly painted porch, opened the door, and entered the gloomy waiting room.

Marla Hamblin sat behind the desk—she always sat there; she would probably take sick, die, and be entombed there. She looked up from behind her computer monitor, her eyes widening.

"Hello," she said. "How you doing?"

"Fine, Marla," Bybee said, and then he hesitated. It was evident that he was not "fine"—his face was lined, his eyes red and tired, and his entire body felt feverish, his bones aching. "I'm fine," he said again. "Is Seegy in?"

Marla did not answer but only remained seated, continuing to stare at Bybee, half puzzled, as though she dimly remembered the man but could not place him, could not quite remember his name. Bybee remained in front of her, enduring it the way he had endured it with others in town, looking to the side of her face, avoiding her eyes.

Marla's fingers toyed with the name badge that rode atop

her enormous bosom, a bosom so large that it hung over the keyboard of her computer, obscuring it. "I hard about all that . . . mess over to Manti . . . and Salt Lake."

"Yeah, well, it's a mess, as you say."

"I hope everything tarns out okay," Marla said, and then she finally stood up and smiled. "I'll tell Seegy you're har."

"Thanks."

In her heavy, high-heeled shoes, Marla walked across the floor and opened Seegmiller's door without knocking, entered, and in a moment reappeared and motioned Bybee inside.

With a nod of his head at the woman, Bybee crossed the floor and, sidling past Marla, his chest brushing her breasts, went inside the other room. He had not been in the sheriff's private office since he had confronted the blubbery Sheriff Little with the horrifying letter written by Brigham Young, but the place looked the same—dark, small, with a wooden desk, venetian blinds on the windows, and an old-style coat rack in the corner, a hat and a gun belt hanging from it. Pushed against one wall was a computer on a small table, and above that hung a broken clock displaying the wrong time. Bybee reflexively checked his own watch.

"Brig," Seegmiller said. He was sitting behind the desk, in his uniform, a newspaper spread out before him, the work day obviously over for him. He stood up and extended his hand. "Good to see you."

"Thanks," Bybee said. He shook the sheriff's hand, then sat down in a wooden chair in front of the desk.

Seegmiller spread his hands out the way a fawning loan officer would. "What can I do for you?"

"A lot," Bybee said. "A helluva lot."

"Wol . . . " Seegmiller looked worried, nervous, and he glanced at his watch, then clasped his hands together and leaned across the desk. "What is it?"

Bybee took a slow, deep breath, then released it and gripped the edge of the desk with both hands, as though he were going to push it back against the other man, crushing him against the wall.

"Seegy, I'm in a world of shit. You probably know about it; hell, everyone in town knows about it; the whole damn state knows about it."

Seegmiller cocked his head, embarrassed, then nodded at the newspaper before him. "Wol, it's been in the papers, and all. On TV."

"Yeah, I know," Bybee said, and he snorted in disgust. "I'm famous. I'm a celebrity."

"Wol . . ."

"Look, Seegy, I'll get right to the point. The governor, the attorney general, a sitting district court judge, and half the people in Utah are ready to flush me down a toilet and into a sewer. And they're going to do it this Friday, in Salt Lake, in a courtroom, all proper and tidy and legal, with every goddamned reporter in the state there."

"Brig, I—"

"It will be a formal sacrifice, Seegy. I mean it. Before they flush me, they're going to strip me down and lay me across an altar and, with everyone watching, just rip my fucking guts out!"

Seegmiller's eyes were wide, and he looked frightened, as if he had just witnessed that bloody act. "Don't talk like that, Brig."

Bybee leaned back and pushed his glasses back in place. "They're going to do it, Seegy. I mean it. They're going to do it unless I do something first."

"Wol, what—" Seegmiller looked confused, and he shook his head, trying to clear it.

"I'm going to New Ammon today."

"New Am'? The plig—"

"Yeah. And I'm going to talk to T. Rampton Crowe. The Big Plig. I'm going to offer him a deal."

Seegmiller squinted at the other man. "Crowe?"

"Yeah."

"Wol, what kind of deal?"

"It's too complicated to explain," Bybee said, and he leaned closer. "But I need your help."

The frightened, worried look returned, and Seegmiller

stared past Bybee's head, thinking. "Brig, New Ammon's a polygamist colony; we just don't mess with them. You know that.
We usually just—"

Bybee held up his hands as though he were fending the
sheriff off, inwardly amazed that despite his bumbling naïveté,
his amateurishness, Seegmiller had indeed quickly learned the
unwritten code of Utah cops: leave the pligs alone.

"I don't want you to go with me," Bybee said. "All I want you
to do is be at the Piute Villa this evening, around six. Just wait
there, stay there for several hours. Vesta will let you in the office, or you can wait in your car, but just be there."

Seegmiller shifted uncomfortably in his chair. "What's
going on, Brig?"

"I've got a . . . plan," Bybee said, and then he smiled. "Hey,
everyone should have a plan, right?"

"Wol—"

"I'm going to offer Crowe something, Seegy. If he accepts,
then he'll drive with me to the Piute Villa this afternoon. I'll try
to time it so that we arrive around six. That's where you come in,
because if this son of a bitch accepts what I'm going to offer—"
He hesitated, staring at Seegmiller's air-foil earlobes, mentally
measuring the man, his probable reaction. "If he accepts,"
Bybee went on, "then he's guilty of aggravated murder. Period."

Seegmiller's mouth slowly opened, then shut again. "Brig,
this sounds—"

"You know what Crowe looks like?"

"Wol, I seen pitchers in the paper and—"

"Good. If you see me drive into the motel with Crowe this
evening, I want you to walk up to him and arrest him for agg'
murder, right there on the spot."

Seegmiller was now genuinely confused, and he seemed to
be suddenly roaming around the inside of his head, trying to remember the brief, perfunctory classes the state made him attend after he was elected, the rudiments of search and seizure
law, fundamentals of arrest, the statutes, the Constitution.

"Brig," he finally said, "I just can't go over to thar and arrest
someone. I need some kind of . . . I dunno—"

"Probable cause?" Bybee said. "Reasonable suspicion?" He pointed at the newspaper. "Listen, Seegy, the press doesn't know the full story—not even half of it. Did you read about the woman that everyone is looking for? The woman that they say killed her sister wife?"

"Yeah."

"Well, her name is Chenoya Whiting, and she came running to me last week, beat to hell, and I hid her, out at Zolene's house in Johnson Canyon."

"Yeah, I know."

"And she told me something, Seegy. She told me a story that will make you want to vomit."

"Wol, what?"

"She told me she saw Crowe drag a man, naked, into a big water tank, take a knife, and castrate him, right there, then cut off his head with a sword. I mean it."

"Holy Mother of God!" Seegmiller said, and he seemed to inflate, his eyes bulging, and drew back away from Bybee, away from the imaginary sword that just came slashing toward him, aiming at his throat.

"Yeah," Bybee said, nodding. "Damned ugly, isn't it? Well, if Crowe shows up with me today at the Piute Villa, then he's made an implied admission of that crime. So that, along with the statement made by Mercy—by Chenoya Whiting—is your probable cause to arrest. I—"

"Brig—"

"—mean it, Seegy. No offense, but I've been at this a helluva lot longer than you. If you see Crowe with me, then you arrest his ass. Simple as that." He paused, then nodded at the coat-rack, at the wood-gripped pistol jutting out from the leather holster—a holster probably made in New Ammon. "And take your gun."

Seegmiller was swimming behind his desk, almost gasping for air, confused, desperate. "God, Brig . . . I've never had to do something like this." He turned and looked at his gun belt hanging from the rack as though it were rotted fruit left drooping on the tree, untouched. "I never war a gun."

"Well, you should, Seegy. You're the sheriff. Now and then you've got to do more than just arrest drunk Indians or write up accident reports. Besides"—Bybee suddenly stopped and laughed, and then pointed at the coatrack again, this time at the sheriff's hat that hung there, an old-fashioned black-billed thing, the kind bus drivers or milkmen used to wear—"it'll be a feather in your cap."

Like a man in a trance, Seegmiller slowly turned again and stared at his hat, as though, magically, a feather might suddenly sprout there—a big, glossy, jaunty thing.

Bybee could see the man wavering, his mind tumbling. "You're the only person in this town who can do it, Seegy."

Seegmiller swiveled back around in his chair, the mechanism squealing, and looked sympathetically at Bybee for a moment, and then looked down, still swimming, still paddling in his own confusion.

"I need your help, Seegy," Bybee said. "I truly do. I need someone with the guts, the . . . *balls*, to help me nail this son of a bitch!"

Seegmiller slowly got to his feet. He turned to the window behind him and pulled the cord, and the blinds opened, letting in slivers of light and color, slicing into the gloom, almost in layers. He stood, his back to Bybee, and stared out at 100 South, at the other houses and offices on the street, as though desperately searching for help there, another man, an instant deputy, someone who could assist him, save him.

But there was only DeRalph Seegmiller, class of '79, FFA vice president, father of three, failed businessman, and now, sheriff of Kane County.

He turned back to face Bybee, his body now erect, his head—stabilized by the earlobes—held high, steady, slightly thrust forward. He looked tired, but determined, noble, his eyes now looking past Bybee, beyond the tiny room, at some dim shape in the future. He was a latter-day Gary Cooper—alone, abandoned, the only lawman left in the town, on the planet—and he looked at the clock on the wall, half expecting it to actually read twelve o'clock, straight up. But it was broken, it had always been broken, forever reading half past ten.

"Okay, Brig," he said. "I'll be thar."

"Good," Bybee said, relieved. "Now I've got one more favor."

"Oh, Brig," Seegmiller said, and his face looked troubled again, his shoulders slumping, the heroism suddenly drained away. "What's that?"

Bybee pointed at the dun-colored computer against one wall, under the broken clock. "That fancy machine tell you if there's any warrants out? If there's been an arrest?"

"Yeah. Most of the time."

"Good, because if this plan's going to work, Mercy—Chenoya Whiting—has still got to be out there somewhere, hiding . . . maybe even dead."

Seegmiller frowned and, taking a deep breath, rose, walked to the computer, and bent over it. "It was Whiting, you say?"

"Yeah," Bybee said. "First name Chenoya—C-H-E-N-O-Y-A—maybe an aka of Mercy."

Seegmiller began expertly tapping at keys, pausing, waiting, then tapping some more and peering into the big monitor as though it were a bathroom window and he a shameless peeping Tom. As he watched the sheriff, Bybee wondered at how, seemingly, everyone in civilized society—even simple, uneducated men like DeRalph Seegmiller—could so effortlessly operate those damnable machines, machines that had always flummoxed him, frustrated him.

"Wol," Seegmiller suddenly announced to the wall, "thar's a warrant all right—aggravated murder." He poked at another key and, with his right hand, jiggled the mouse and clicked a button, then squinted into the screen again. "But no arrest." He straightened and turned around. "She's still out thar . . . somewhar."

Bybee felt a twinge of relief, something deep inside of him giving, relaxing. "Good," he said.

Seegmiller returned to his desk but remained standing and narrowed his eyes. "I'm not shore what you're doing, Brig, not shore how this woman's part of your . . . plan, but what makes you think she's not over to New Am'? That she just didn't run home?"

Bybee nodded, acknowledging the simple flaw in his plan. He had thought about this all day, and he had finally formulated a remedy to all the holes in his thinking, an intellectual stopgap, a cure-all.

"That's just a chance I'm going to take, Seegy."

The sheriff looked genuinely worried. "Wol, that's kind of dangerous, and all."

"I know, but it's just as dangerous not to do anything. At least for me, right now." Bybee walked back to the door and opened it. "Thanks, Seegy. Remember, tonight around six at the motel—wait a few hours. I owe you—"

"Brig," Seegmiller said, "what if you don't show? What if I wait and you or Crowe or no one comes to the motel? What then?"

Bybee stood, his hand on the doorknob. This was one part of his plan he did not like to think about, but it didn't matter, for there was really no viable contingency if he did not come back.

"I don't know, Seegy," Bybee said. "If I don't show, if you don't hear from me, then wait a day or two and then contact whoever you're supposed to and tell them . . . hell, tell them I'm missing. Say I'm somewhere in New Ammon, somewhere in the South Pacific."

Seegmiller's eyes widened. "Oh, Brig . . . God. This sounds crazy!"

"It probably is," Bybee said. He hesitated, then withdrew the folded, handwritten letter to Zolene from his rear pocket. "Do you have an envelope?"

Confused, Seegmiller fumbled through his desk drawer, then finally presented Bybee with an envelope, one with the words Kane County, Office of the Sheriff printed in the upper left-hand corner.

Bybee took it, put the letter inside, then licked the flap and sealed it.

"Here," he said, and he gave the envelope to Seegmiller. "When you get a chance, give this to Zolene, if you don't mind. And then tell her—" He stopped; he had been thinking about her all day, the way her blue eyes always fixed on his, her hair glowing in the sun, whipping around her face . . . and then the last, ugly confrontation where everything went dark. "Just tell her to read it."

Seegmiller stared at the envelope. "Okay, Brig."

With a wave of his hand, Bybee walked back out into the outer room, waved again at Marla, and then ducked through the door and was outside. He set out for the Piute Villa, and in a matter of minutes he was crunching across the gravel lot under the big arrowhead overhead, and then he entered the office tepee.

Vesta was there, sitting behind the counter as though hiding, chewing gum and reading a magazine, and when she heard the bell she stood up and sluggishly moved to the counter. She was Zolene's first cousin, but looked nothing like her; she was a mannish woman in her early twenties, with red, chapped hands and limp hair, brown and cut short.

" 'Lo, Brig," she said.

Her voice was flat, and her eyes focused on Bybee's shoulder rather than his face, as though she were embarrassed, ashamed . . . and maybe she should be. Bybee, from the first week he had hired Vesta, as a favor to Zolene, had suspected the girl of surreptitiously renting tepees to her oversexed Kanab cohorts at half price—cash, with no receipts or records—then splitting the money with the Navajo chambermaid if she would clean the room and remain mum. But considering the low hourly wage he paid, and the girl's grudging, laconic loyalty, it was an exercise of free enterprise that he would tolerate.

"Look, Vesta, I'm going over to . . . Hurricane," Bybee said. "Business. Sheriff Seegmiller will be coming over here this evening . . . on business, too. I want you to let him in, if he wants, and let him wait here for as long as he wants. I'll explain later. Okay?"

As if Bybee had simply asked her to refill the paper cup dispenser or clean the counter, Vesta shrugged and continued to stare at his shoulder. "Shore," she said.

"Good. I'll see you . . . well, I don't know when. Tomorrow, maybe. You keep things going?"

"Shore," Vesta said again.

She began to sit down, but then she pointed a big, raw-looking finger behind her, over her shoulder, at the rear of the office. There, beside the box of broken plaster arms and hands and the severed Indian head, was another cardboard box, and next to it, spread in a tangle across the couch, were several shirts, pants, a bathrobe, and an old flight suit—stained with the various colors of the walls of Lamb's house.

"I went out to Zoley's," Vesta said. "Got your things."

"Thanks," Bybee said, and he wavered there, looking at the box and the clothes the way a man might at a car he has just crashed or a garage he has just burned down, bleakly surveying the wreckage for something to salvage, a souvenir, something to toss into the old wooden cigar box he kept in his closet along with the other detritus of his life: a wedding ring, silver lieutenant's bars, his father's pocket watch, steel pennies, military script from Vietnam, a gold crucifix, a hank of hair from his first dog.

Spooky Floyd had materialized outside the glass door, and he made a soft, sighing sound as Bybee opened the door and pushed him back.

"Hey, Floyd," Bybee said, and he squatted down and stroked the dog's head and patted his bony back. "You hold down the fort, okay?"

The dog's yellow eyes twitched, and then he slouched away to the edge of the graveled yard, as though he may have dimly understood the human's words and was dutifully taking up a sentry's position at the perimeter.

"So long," Bybee said, and then he got into his VW bus and set out for New Ammon.

More than a year before, in July, at the Pioneer Day parade in Kanab, as they sat on the porch of the Pow-Wow souvenir store and watched the frontier-garbed revelers eddy around the town, happy, waving toy guns and shouting, Bybee had promised Zolene he would drive to Arizona to visit her the day after Thanksgiving.

And so he did, appearing at Zolene's house in Tucson exactly four months later, standing on her porch, grinning like a schoolboy and holding out a tub of watery coleslaw and a set of silver earrings from the Pow-Wow. And with her two daughters, April and Meredith, they all sat down to a second Thanksgiving dinner, one with turkey and dressing and sweet potatoes—and the godawful coleslaw—but none of it leftovers from the day before. No, Zolene had insisted on starting everything anew and fresh—the turkey, the trimmings . . . and the relationship.

Bybee had stayed the rest of that weekend at a nearby Tucson motel, and the two picked up where they had left off in Kanab, spending every possible moment with each other and with Zolene's daughters, who, although initially suspicious and aloof, later admitted that they liked—truly liked—the new man in their mother's life.

By the time he reluctantly left that Sunday, they had already made vague but excited plans about both moving to Kanab—she as a ranch owner and he . . . well, he would find something, he had promised her. And then, a few weeks later, when he called to say he had made an offer on the Piute Villa, she had laughed —long and uproariously, almost choking—but not at him, not at the strange, silly motel that had always been a Kanab joke. She laughed because she was happy, deliriously and recklessly so, maybe happier than she had ever been.

As she plowed along the highway through the darkness, heading back toward Kanab after a day of negotiating with bureaucrats and contractors in St. George over water rights and drilling permits and estimates and payment schedules, she thought of that weekend. In fact, it was all she could think of: Brig standing foolishly on her porch like a high school kid on his first date, and she, having waited the entire day, nervous, pacing, inviting him into her house . . . her life.

She drove past the cutoff to New Ammon, past Pipe Springs, and in Fredonia, Arizona, she slowed her pickup and, turning north, crept through the flat, dirty town. A mile out, on the short stretch of highway leading to Kanab, just south of the state line, she saw the Buckskin Tavern.

When she was in high school in Kanab—when she was still a member of the church, but beginning to falter, to question the faith—the Buckskin was a place of adolescent lore and legend. It was only a mile or so away, but was regarded by the cow-town Mormon kids as a reverse Mecca, an unholy, faraway temple at the edge of the world, a sure gateway to hell . . . and one of the first stops they made when they escaped, clambering over the encircling red cliff walls and stumbling through the sage and rabbitbrush and Russian thistle, desperately looking behind them.

It was at the Buckskin that she first tasted alcohol—a sloe gin fizz—and got drunk; it was at the Buckskin, in the parking lot, after a number of sloe gin fizzes, that she first allowed a boy—Kevin Chamberlain, an all-state halfback, and dead four years later in a logging accident on the Kaibab—to touch her, clumsily unbuttoning her blouse and struggling with her bra; it was at the Buckskin that, after her murdered grandfather was buried in the Kanab cemetery, she had sunk into one of the cheap vinyl seats and guzzled beer until she nearly passed out.

She slowed the red truck, turned into the dirt and gravel lot, and then stopped, the engine running, and stared at the statue of a man made of old auto parts standing outside the entrance, a frightening metallic humanoid that gaped back at her, warning her.

"Jeez," she said.

She slammed the truck into gear and spun out of the parking lot and back onto the highway. In a matter of minutes she was back in Kanab. At Lloyd Honey's Texaco she turned east and sped along the highway, the headlights cleaving the darkness as the dashed center stripes whizzed by. At Dishpan, she turned off the pavement, and a half mile down the cratered dirt road, near the old collapsed silo, she stopped the truck and turned off the lights and engine. There was something wrong.

Carefully, as though any sound might suddenly awake the canyon, she opened the door and lowered herself to the ground, then gently eased the door shut. She moved around to the front of the truck and limped several feet away, stopped, and stood in the middle of the road, facing west, toward her house.

The whole of Hell's Bellows was smothered by a gummy darkness, the way it always was, something thick and viscous, soundless, usually comforting. But now it was disturbing; something was amiss, out of place. She could feel it, sense it the way she did when she awoke decades ago in the old ranch-house basement, when she knew—knew with an icy, awful certainty— that her grandmother, in bed in the room above, had just died in her sleep. She could sense it the way she knew her dead grand-father, a year ago, was still present, still lurking in the fields or the old barn, trying to tell her why he had been murdered, by whom . . . and then she had actually seen him standing one night, near the tractor, pointing toward the answer.

And she sensed it the way she had felt the presence of Cassie Lee Lewis that evening years before, and then had turned and actually seen the little girl.

She suddenly felt chilled, and she limped back to her truck, got inside, and started the engine. Slowly she crawled down the remainder of the road, past Doug's house, and skirted the edge of the orchard until she came to Lamb's house. She switched off the engine and, fumbling inside the glove compartment, found a flashlight, hefted it, and got out of the truck.

She turned the flashlight on, and a bright, steady beam burst from it. She limped toward the wooden gate, toward the front of her house, holding the flashlight at her stomach and aiming the silvery cone of light into the blackness. But as she walked toward that cone, the physics seemed to reverse them-selves, and now it was as though she held some magical instru-ment, an ancient, mystical object that gathered in the last, stray remnants of light left in the canyon—left anywhere—and sucked them into the cold thing in her hand, leaving more than just darkness behind.

She saw the figure standing on the porch—mute, unmov-ing, looking out at her like the metal man at the Buckskin—and she screamed and fell backward into the wooden fence, one hand flailing outward to catch herself. The flashlight tumbled from her other hand and blinked out when it hit the ground; dropping to her knees, she groped frantically for it, the thing lost in the darkness, half buried in the thick blanket of twigs and leaves.

She twisted around and faced the figure that still stood on the porch, a vague, ghostlike shape, almost hovering.

"Who are you?" Zolene said. "What do you want?"

But the figure did not move; it did not say a word.

"Who are you?" she said again.

12

THERE are those cracker-barrel philosophers in Utah—usually government retirees in flannel shirts and rubber-soled moccasins—who claim they can spot a polygamist colony a mile away—literally. For at that distance, these self-styled experts explain, you can already see the low, staved-in, odd-angled skyline of a white ghetto: a leaning water tower, crooked light poles, sagging roofs of two-story houses, their plywood bedrooms tacked on as quickly and crudely as the new wives are added on, the whole town lopsided . . . like their lives.

And closer, maybe at a quarter mile, along the sides of the road and nestled in the brush and half covered with sand, lie the burned-out carcasses of old trucks, the rusted humps of refrigerators, tiny pyramids of tires, mounds of debris, all of it scattered across the landscape like flotsam from this communal catastrophe.

But if that is not proof enough, then inside the towns, inside those bare, filthy compounds made of composition board and tarpaper and tin, are the polygamists themselves.

They are hollow-eyed and plain, dressed in simple clothes,

some in pioneer garb, all faith-crazed and spiritually drugged, sleepwalking through a wrongheaded world, a world that does not understand them, but a world that is, to them, simply a stopping-off point on their way to celestial glory. They shuffle along their dusty streets, never smiling or shouting to a friend or shaking their heads over some feeble joke. No, they do none of that; instead they simply stare with those empty eyes, stare out at their bleak town, stare out at the dreadful surroundings that hold them fast, stare toward the heavens they have been promised.

And they stare—*hard*—at the outsider who dares venture in.

It was hot, the sun relentless, when Bybee piloted his green VW bus into the heart of New Ammon. Like most, the colony had a temporary, half-finished look, the whole of it bordered by a low half-circle of mud-colored ridges, the so-called Chocolate Cliffs, the lumpy bastard end of the Grand Staircase. He drove slowly down the town's main street—seamed and gouged, like the road to Lamb's house—looking for anyone, any sign of life, but the streets were silent, eerily deserted, as though the entire population had finally come trudging to Judgment and had bodily vanished into the afterlife—whatever it might be . . . or wherever.

And then he saw the first of them—the children. They were boys, about twelve years old, Bybee estimated, youngsters who looked like miniature old men, all of them dressed in dark pants and long-sleeved white shirts and suspenders, and all with shoes or boots so dark and heavy that it looked as though they had bricks strapped to their feet. There were four of them, these young-old creatures, just standing and staring, not kicking a ball about or playfully wrestling—only staring. Then, as Bybee moved by them, he saw the little girls, three of them standing behind the boys, severe and white and washed-out, with their hair pulled back or braided in tight folds, wearing long dresses that reached to their booted feet.

"Lord," Bybee said.

He slowed at what he guessed was the center of town, a wide intersection of two dirt roads, the whole of it lined by squat buildings, some with faint lettering in their windows: a hardware store, a grocery, an auto repair shop. To the east, about three blocks away, stood the largest of the buildings, a sprawling stuccoed factory with a tin roof, the large sign on it clearly visible: BRETHREN INDUSTRIES LEATHER. It was the economic heart of the colony—the leather factory, where sandals and wallets and belts and holsters were made . . . and purses.

On one corner, next to what was once a service station, was a flat, vacant area, half covered in weedy grass, that had been made into a park, with a few benches and redwood tables set on its perimeter.

Bybee turned and pulled up next to the park, turned off the engine, got down from the bus, and walked to one of the benches. He sat, casually crossing his legs, and stretched his arms out along the back of the sagging bench, a man in slacks and a knit shirt and deck shoes without socks, enjoying the hot sun, soaking up the squalid ambience of the place. He remained there, almost unmoving, his head tilted back and his eyes closed. Around him, the town was silent; there were no sounds of a car or truck motor, no children laughing or dogs barking, no doors slamming or radios playing—only the silence of the abyss.

He had been there, in that position, for about five minutes when, his eyes still closed, he heard someone tramping across the dry stretch of grass, then actually felt the shadow that fell over him, a presence.

"Problems?" a voice said.

Bybee opened his eyes and squinted. Standing over him was a man—thin and bearded, dressed in overalls and a white shirt—who was bent at the waist and peering into his face. The sun was directly behind his head, making him look dark, his features hidden.

"Problems?" the man said again. His voice was deep and phlegmy.

Raising his hand to shield his eyes, Bybee looked at the man, and he could finally make out his dull eyes, his billowing beard.

"No," Bybee said, shaking his head. "Not yet, anyway."

"You visiting?"

For some reason Bybee felt a twinge of irritation at the absurd question. Who in their right mind would ever want to visit this place? But, he had to admit, he was not in his right mind, not anymore.

"Well, yes, I am," Bybee said, waving his hand at the dismal sweep of tin buildings and dirt streets and acres of sand and weeds. "I'm thinking of visiting the botanical gardens. Later, maybe I'll play some golf at the club, then drop by the Lexus dealership."

The man considered this a moment, his eyes narrowed, as he slowly moved his head back and forth, gaining momentum, until he was vigorously shaking it. "We don't have no golf course har." He pointed a thin, dirty finger to the south. "Thar's a casino over to the raservation, though. Pipe Springs."

"I was kidding," Bybee said.

"Wol . . ." The man shrugged. "Thar is, though."

Bybee impatiently shook his head. He had set certain time schedules—with Seegmiller, with himself—and he needed to get to the point quickly.

"I'm looking for Rampton Crowe," Bybee said. "I need to talk to him."

This time the tall, bearded man did not need to ponder the question, and he quickly shook his head. "He's not har."

"Oh, yeah?" Bybee said. "Well, I just bet he is."

"He's not. He's over to Hare-i-kin."

Bybee suddenly hooted, turning his face to the sky, and then shook his head. "Lord, Jesus. Is that in some manual somewhere? Is that taught in all the schools?"

The bearded man did not understand, and he hovered there, squinting, confused.

"Well, as a matter of fact, I'm in Hare-i-kin, too," Bybee said, and then his smile faded and he pushed his glasses up along his nose and leaned closer to the other man. "Look, I really don't have time for this. I know Crowe's here, and I want to see him. It's important."

"He's not har," the man said.

Bybee began to argue, but he had already anticipated this. "Well, then, how about Franklin Pugh? He here?"

"Pugh?"

"Yeah. Franklin. You know where he is?"

The bearded man's face seemed to harden, and he now appraised Bybee in a different way, breathing heavily and audibly through his nose. It was hot, brutally hot, and he reached into a pocket on the side of his overalls and withdrew a stained handkerchief, then wiped the sweat from the upper part of his face.

"Franklin Pugh don't live har no more."

Bybee smiled. "Yeah, no shit. I understand he doesn't live *anywhere* anymore."

"I don't know what you mean."

"I mean the son of a bitch is dead, professor. Murdered, in fact. Am I right?"

Again, the man said nothing, only wheezing through his nose, the thick clump of brown hair at each nostril moving in and out like tiny flaps as his dead eyes examined Bybee's face. Behind him, beyond the wretched town center, the sprawl of New Ammon—the eight-bedroomed, two-tiered hovels, the vast dormitory-like shanties—shimmered in the heat, layers of it undulating upward so that it made everything look watery, sunken in a lifeless sea.

Without saying anything, the thin man turned around, shambled across the dead grass, and disappeared behind the grocery store—or what Bybee assumed was a grocery store; wooden vegetable crates were stacked along one wall, and a plywood board was leaning near the door with various prices per pound scrawled on it.

Bybee sat down and rested his forearms on his knees, genuinely confused by the raging contradictions: the brainless simplicity of the man he had just talked to compared to the evil complicity attributed by the government to every male in the colony. Perhaps everyone had overreacted; perhaps everyone had conjured up demons and monsters and twisted, bloody nightmares where none really existed. But then, Faith was dead—that was certain, her head blown apart—and Mercy was gone, or at least, he presumed she was gone.

"Lord," Bybee said, aloud, and he shook his head, now more muddled than it had ever been, and leaned back into the bench again, waiting.

Several minutes later, he heard the sound of engines, and he looked up to see two dirty pickup trucks—one of them the same blue thing with the white camper shell he had seen in Kanab—rattling down the road from the east, dust roiling around them like a brown fog. They stopped in front of Bybee's bus, and at the same time, as though practiced, choreographed, two bearded men exited each truck and the doors slammed shut in a precise tattoo.

Four abreast, they emerged from the dust and marched toward Bybee like men prepared for a fight—shoulders bunched, heads low, their big hands curled, arms swinging. These men did not look confused like the last hayseed; they looked determined, and were bearing down upon him like a street gang.

"Shit," Bybee whispered.

He got to his feet, wishing that he had brought the baseball bat—or better yet, his jogging shoes, for his instinct now, seeing the men advance, was to turn and sprint across the lot and through town, back to the hills and gullies, knowing his long legs —still in good running shape—could outdistance these thugs.

But he remained rooted there, and braced himself as the four men chuffed up and stopped, dried grass swirling around their feet as they instantly fanned out to form a semicircle around him. They were all bearded, all in jeans or overalls, and all looked as though they had been transported here from another time, rustic and rough-hewn, dirty, the smell of grease and smoke and sweat hovering about them, their hair matted, the teeth yellow and crooked.

One of them stepped forward, and Bybee recognized him as the same plig he had seen hovering across the street from Duke's, in Kanab.

"My name is Griffity," the man said. His face was dark and pitted, with a sheen of sweat. "What's yours?"

"Bybee."

"Well, *Bybee,* just what the hell do you want here?" he said. His voice was steady, even, and there was not a trace of the backwoods Mormon accent.

Bybee knew the name: Griffity. Enoch Griffity. Brother Griffy, as Mercy had called him, the man who had supposedly taken Pugh's severed head and held it up like a soccer trophy while he was paraded around on the shoulders of the other Blood Disciples. Next to Crowe, he was the most depraved of the lot, and Bybee's hand began to shake again. He thrust it into his pocket, and in his knit shirt with the Piute Villa embroidery, it made him look postured, overly casual, snobbish, as though he truly did have a tee time at the posh New Ammon Country Club.

"I want to see Rampton Crowe," Bybee said, his voice low and steady. "I want to talk to him about Franklin Pugh and Roma Ann McCallister . . . and Chenoya Whiting. Especially her, Mercy."

It was as though Bybee had suddenly tossed a stun grenade in their midst; the men froze, their mouths open, gaping at him, and then slowly, as they recovered, their eyes moved to Griffity. But the man said nothing; he continued to stare at Bybee, and then took a step closer to him.

"Who the hell are you?"

"I'm the guy who can keep your lord and master out of prison for a long time," Bybee said. "And I'm the same guy that can send his plig ass there for the rest of his life. Maybe even death row."

"Get the hell out of here!"

"Not till I see Crowe," Bybee said. His heart was hammering so hard that he was sure the others could actually see it pulsing beneath the thin shirt, but he took a slow breath and looked Griffity squarely in the eyes. He had a plan, a script, as ill-conceived as it might be, one brimming with pure invention, lies.

"Look, man," Bybee said. "The state of Utah's about to take this asshole down pretty hard, but not"—he waved his hand at the tumbledown houses, where, he knew, dozens of plural wives crouched, probably peering out shuttered windows at this scene —"not for keeping a damned harem. That's chump change, penny-ante shit. The state's going to pop him for aggravated murder. And that's death penalty stuff. You don't believe me, then I'll leave, and by tomorrow, every cop in southern Utah will be here, all of them with a gun and a warrant. And they'll be looking for you, too—all the Blood Disciples."

Griffity appeared to be dazed, and he looked at Bybee as though he had never seen a creature like him, never heard such strange language, such dangerous threats. He blinked at him and opened his mouth to say something, then suddenly struck Bybee's elbow with the flat of his hand, making him stagger backward against the bench.

"Put your arms out," Griffity said.

Slowly, as though he were displaying himself, Bybee held his arms out parallel to the ground, his right hand quivering so much that it looked palsied, while Griffity roughly patted him down, feeling under his arms, his waist, along his legs. He paused, seemingly satisfied that there were no concealed weapons, and then he viciously thrust his hand up the inside of Bybee's thigh and found his testicles, squeezing them hard.

Bybee yelled; the pain was like a hot poker, searing him, burning into his gut, and he twisted away and seized the man's hand, pushing it away, but two of the other pligs grabbed Bybee's arms, pinning them behind him. With Bybee held helpless, Griffity placed his hand to Bybee's crotch again, this time not trying to crush his testicles, but cradling them now, his fingers relaxed, gently probing, massaging.

"If you're lying to me," Griffity said, and he moved his hand so that just his fingertips now touched the underside of Bybee's testicles, tapping at them, playing, "then I'll cut these things off. I will. Do you understand?"

Bybee's groin and stomach ached, and he felt sick and dizzy, his eyes watering, seeing Franklin Pugh dragged naked and screaming to an old cement water tank and then held on the ground while Griffity's or Crowe's knife carved away at his scrotum and sliced off his penis.

He suddenly realized how foolish he had been, how utterly reckless and stupid and maniacal, to have come strutting in here, cocksure, hoping that all the pligs would gape and melt away like the first mumbling oaf he had encountered. But he was wrong—terribly wrong—and it was too late to back away.

Griffity's hand tightened on Bybee's testicles again. "I said, 'Do you understand?' "

"I understand," Bybee whispered. "Lord, Jesus, man. I understand."

"Good," Griffity said, and he pulled his hand from Bybee's crotch, but the other men kept their grip on Bybee's arms, pulling them back even harder. "Now, let's go see Father." He smiled. "That is what you wanted, isn't it? To see Father?"

But before Bybee could answer, before he could even say a single, frightened word, he was marched, his arms still pinned behind him, across the weedy lot to the blue pickup with the camper shell. There, the rear door of the shell was opened and Bybee, like a sack of grain, was bodily lifted off his feet and thrown inside, and the door was slammed and locked shut.

He had passed out, he knew; he woke up crumpled on the grooved, metal floor of the truck, the heat inside insufferable, radiating like an oven, the aluminum sides and roof of the camper shell actually hot to the touch. He was bathed in sweat, dripping in it, and his head throbbed, the heat so intense that he could only breath in shallow, panicked gulps.

He struggled into a sitting position and looked at his watch, turning it into the dim light that came from the smudged plastic window on the shell door, then wiped the sweat from his eyes and squinted at the watch again. It was four-thirty; he had been locked in the shell for over two hours.

After he had been dumped in the back, they had roared away, bouncing along dirt roads as images of the miserable town flickered in the tiny window like a reel of film projected on a miniature screen, houses and old trucks, a few children, staring . . . each colorless scene appearing, then fading as the swirling dust from the truck obliterated them, and then another bleak picture materializing.

They had driven for several minutes, then stopped, suddenly, and Bybee had heard the truck doors slam, the men's voices, a dog barking, someone laughing . . . and then he had been left alone, pounding on the aluminum sides and pulling on the locked door handle, cursing at the big man who stood outside, his back to the truck. But he had been ignored, and all the while the temperature in the aluminum box rose quickly, hellishly, as though they had parked in the middle of a raging fire . . . and then he had finally and mercifully passed out.

Now, on his hands and knees, he peered out the plastic window, seeing only the enormous back and arms of the plig who was standing guard over him. He was thirsty, his body screaming for water, and the heat seemed to be slowly baking him, his hands and arms first, then his feet, moving up his legs. . . .

There was a noise outside, a voice, a fumbling at the lock, and then the tiny door flew up and open, and Griffity thrust his bearded face into the oven.

"Get out."

Slowly, his arms and legs weak, Bybee crawled like an animal to the opening and, halfway through, lost his grip on the hot metal sides and fell into the dirt at the rear of the truck. Instantly two men had their thick hands on him, dragging him upright and pushing him toward a large, silvery trailer—a mobile home—one of the double-wide behemoths that he always saw being tugged sluggishly down the highways, in halves, like big, sectioned boats. The trailer sat alone in a dusty lot, its sides skirted with bent sheets of aluminum, and old tires had been scattered atop its roof. A set of wooden stairs was jammed against the trailer, under the door, and Bybee was roughly pushed up them, then jerked to a halt while one of the pligs opened the door.

"Inside," Griffity yelled.

Bybee began to step forward, tentatively, and to duck his head in the low doorway, but a hand from behind brutally shoved him, and he burst into the room, his arms released now, and fell heavily to one knee. Before he could recover, the same hands grabbed him under his arms and pulled him upright and then held him fast.

He was in the main room, the living room, of the trailer, but it contained no sofas or plush loungers—only a scattering of gray, folding chairs, perhaps fifteen of them. The four men that had confronted him at the park were all there, and at one end of the room, behind a metal desk, sat another man in a folding chair, his hands clasped together behind his neck. Bybee recognized him at once. It was Crowe.

He was just as the photographs had shown: about forty years old, with a sunburned face and a long narrow beard, like an elongated goatee, brown, that hung down his chest. He was short but well-built, and his tight T-shirt revealed that his arms and chest were heavily muscled, strong, his stomach flat. In front of him, on the metal desk, lay a hunting knife—large and heavy, with a shining blade that curved out from a wooden handle.

"Brigham Bybee," Crowe said. His voice was thin, almost high, with a faint rasp. "The hired gun."

Crowe laughed and turned his head to the side, and as he did, Bybee saw he wore a long brown ponytail that, with the flowing beard, made him appear to have two greasy cataracts of hair gushing out of the front and back of his skull.

He swiveled back to Bybee, his eyes dark, set deep in his red face. "You got a lot of balls coming here, Bybee, running your fucking mouth about murder. What the hell do you want?"

Bybee stood, still dizzy, his head throbbing, and tried to focus on Crowe, confused by the high voice, the mundane locker-room vocabulary, the ordinary look of the exalted man—Father of the Faithful, the One Mighty and Strong, the Seer and Revelator—a man who, sitting in a folding chair in a dreary trailer, looked more like a middle-aged hippie, a deadbeat on welfare. He opened his mouth, but his throat was dry and constricted, and he only made a choking sound.

"Well, c'mon, Bybee," Crowe said, and he picked up the

knife and laid the flat side of the blade on the back of his hand, balancing it there. "I don't have all fucking day." He suddenly flipped his hand, and in an instant the knife twirled and landed in his palm, its point aimed at Bybee. "Either do you."

Bybee still felt off balance; he had expected something else: a darkened sanctuary, perhaps the church itself, and Crowe, dressed like the others in sagging farmer's garb, but somehow distant, elevated, near an altar or propped up in an oversize chair, a throne. And the language; he had always imagined it pontifical, biblical, laden with rustic, homespun homilies, like a tent revivalist, at least that of a street-corner proselytizer.

"Look, you ignorant shit, I don't—"

"I want to make a trade," Bybee finally said.

"A trade?" Crowe grinned at the other men in the room. "You want to trade that piece-of-shit green bus these men say you came here in?"

Some of the men laughed, and Bybee took a deep breath and steadied himself. This was the stumbling block, the chief impediment, the unknown, and he might as well confront it now, early on.

"I have Mercy," he said. "Chenoya. I want to trade her for something."

This time, Crowe did not grin at the others. He fixed Bybee with his eyes and then slowly picked up the knife again and hefted it in his hand. Bybee could feel his entire chest pounding, and he waited, beginning to suspect—to feel—that Mercy was here, in New Ammon, and that his ruse was going to end at this very moment, on this very spot.

"Where is she?" Crowe said.

Bybee felt his legs weaken, his sick, tightened stomach relax, but he kept his head steady. It had succeeded . . . at least, for now. "That's part of the trade," he said.

Crowe stood up and pointed the knife at Bybee. "I swear to fucking God, Bybee, if you've come here to play games and toy with me, I'll cut your throat!" He pointed the knife at Griffity, who stood against a paneled wall. "And that's after Brother Griffy has his fun with you. You understand that?"

"Yes," Bybee said.

Crowe sat down again. "Then talk."

Bybee took another deep breath, cleared his throat, and began. "Mercy came to me a week ago. She was . . . crazy; she had been beaten—by you, she said—and was told by someone here to go to Kanab, to find me."

Crowe instantly looked at the men in the room, searching each face for a hint of who the Judas was among them. "Who?" he said in his high voice. "Who told her to find you?"

"I don't know," Bybee said. "That doesn't matter—at least, to me. But Mercy had . . . a story to tell."

"And what was that?" Crowe said.

"That you caught her sleeping with Franklin Pugh and killed him."

Bybee had expected an outburst, a loud, angry protestation, maybe laughter . . . but the room was silent.

"And," Crowe said, "how did Mercy say I killed him?"

Bybee swallowed, his throat still dry and sore. "You castrated him, then decapitated him, held his head up for everyone to see, then took off his arms and—"

Now the uproar he had earlier expected did come; in fact, it exploded. Everyone, including Crowe, began to laugh, all of it deep-throated and loud, echoing around the metal trailer without end . . . and all of it directed at Bybee. But he stood, unmoving, stared at Crowe, and thought only of Zolene—absurdly, incongruously—as she had come laughing up to him one morning after one of Heber Batt's mares had just taken him galloping madly through the sage at Hell's Bellows, Bybee helpless, yelling, gripping the saddle horn as if it were life itself. It was a simple truism, Zolene had explained, in riding, perhaps in doing anything in this world: don't show your fear—no matter how rampant and crippling it is.

Bybee suddenly grinned at Crowe and shook his head as the chuckling from the others subsided. "That's just what I did," Bybee said. "I laughed my ass off; told her she was crazy."

Crowe was still smiling. "Mercy's crazy, all right."

Bybee's face suddenly hardened, and he leaned toward

Crowe, his fabricated story tumbling out easier now, the day's mental rehearsal paying off. "But she also told that story again, several times, the last time to the attorney general's office, to an investigator named Sorenson. And it was all taken down by a court reporter . . . and then, when she was finished, Mercy raised her right hand, swore it was all true, and signed it."

"What are you saying?" Crowe said. Like Bybee's, his smile had vanished from his face, and he glared at the tall man hovering in front of him.

"I'm saying that this . . . *story* that you and your pals are laughing about—that I laughed about—is now sworn testimony. And whether it's pure bullshit or not, it's going to be used in a trial—your trial—for aggravated murder. That's murder after you torture someone, Mr. Crowe. And for that, in this state, you can get the death penalty."

This time, there was no guffawing from the dirty, long-bearded men in the room, not even any winks or grins. Instead Crowe stared at Bybee, stared at him the way the drab children in town had stared at him—vacant, retreating, almost confused. And Bybee pictured Zolene again, her hair blazing around her face and neck, laughing and lecturing him about horses, about life, about you riding the animal . . . and not letting it ride you.

Bybee saw, then, the wavering in Crowe, the slightest fissure in the façade. "All it takes in this state is the testimony of one witness, just one—even if it *is* bullshit—to convict someone of murder. And"—Bybee paused, knowing that this was the most blatant part of the ruse—"even if there's no dead body. That's the law."

The silence seemed to thicken in the room, the air now heavy, the dank smell of the men rising up and mingling with something Bybee had only smelled on himself—fear. They were allowing him to ride them anywhere he pleased.

"But that's only if that witness testifies, live, in court and in front of a jury," Bybee said. "The piece of paper she signed is no good by itself; it's hearsay. She doesn't testify, the state doesn't have a case."

Crowe picked up the knife again and balanced it as before on the back of his hand. "Where is she, Bybee?"

"Tucked away, safe and sound. That's where the trade comes in. I'll give you Mercy if you give me what I want."

"And just what the hell is that?"

Bybee smiled, more relaxed now. "Your signed confession, under oath, that you have engaged in the practice of polygamy . . . bigamy, plural marriage, whatever you want to call it. The Principle."

"A confession?"

"You bet. A confession. It's good for the soul. We do it just like in the movies. You waive your right to an attorney, your right to remain silent, and you let me take down everything: all the ceremonies—dates, places, the sealing—and the wives, the cohabitation, the children fathered. . . ." Bybee shrugged and held out his hands. "All of it. I have a computer, and I'm pretty good with it. Then you sign it, under oath, we get it notarized—the whole shebang. And unlike the statement Mercy has signed, this one is good by itself, because you're the defendant. You're confessing."

Crowe smiled. "And I'm found guilty and go to jail? What the hell kind—"

"Yeah, you do—for about a year, maybe eighteen months, max—then you're out on parole." Bybee was inventing, speculating; the so-called matrix, the sentencing guidelines, was confusing, almost mystical. "That's a helluva lot better than getting popped for agg' murder, because with that—"

"You're fucking—"

"—you get life without parole. But that's if you're lucky, because more than likely, you'll get the death penalty."

The heavy silence that sat in the tiny room now congealed, miring the men and preventing them from moving, from shuffling or shaking their heads, from even thinking, or feeling. Outside, through a dirty window, Bybee could see what he guessed was the church, its plastic marquee proclaiming, with missing letters: HE WHO BELIEV S IN THEIRWORD SH LL HAVE EVERL STING LIFE. Beneath that, in smaller letters, was an announcement for a Sunday potluck dinner on Thursday, the thirtieth—today.

Crowe continued to balance the knife on the back of his hand, his arm held stiffly before him like a halfhearted salute, his eyes lost, sunken into his skull. He was scared, Bybee could see, genuinely frightened, and despite the earlier laughter, he had not denied the murder itself—not once.

"Anyway," Bybee said, moving closer to the desk, "even with the death penalty, you get some options." He paused, dredging up Kendall's cocky speech at the Piute Villa. "You can either be strapped to a wooden chair and have your heart blown out by a firing squad, or strapped to a gurney and get pumped full of Marvel Mystery Oil."

Crowe slowly lowered his arm and tilted his hand, allowing the knife to clatter to the desk. "You're crazy," he said. "Mercy would never testify against me."

"Oh, no?" Bybee said. "She's been charged with agg' murder herself, for the murder of Faith. You know that. But as soon as she's arrested"—Bybee stopped and made sure Crowe's eyes were focused directly on his—"as soon as she's turned over to the AG's office, tomorrow, then she's going to start bargaining—trading—like a crazy woman. Not only will she testify that you hacked up Pugh, but she will also say that you sent her out to kill Faith, that she was your agent, your hitwoman. That's contract murder—a death-penalty pop, too. They'll come at you from both sides."

"She's crazy," Crowe said. "She's a fucking liar. She lies all the time."

Bybee shrugged. "So what? There's nothing that says liars can't swear to tell the truth. And believe me, Crowe, she's going to say anything to save her own ass." Bybee hesitated, then nodded. "Unless we make a trade. You give me that confession, and I'll give you Mercy, and then . . . hell, I don't care what you do with her after that."

Crowe finally shifted his eyes from Bybee to the other side of the room, to Griffity, and the man simply stared back, unmoving. They were all obviously scared, all swimming in dark, dangerous waters, and Crowe looked at each man in the room, in turn, as though he were taking a silent vote.

Crowe turned to Bybee and cleared his throat. "How do I even know you have Mercy?"

Bybee nodded confidently, reached into his back pocket, and withdrew his wallet. "I asked her for something—anything—that I could show you." Bybee opened the wallet, fished out the slip of paper in Deseret, and placed it on Crowe's desk. "I don't know what this says, but she said *you* would."

Slowly, like a man in a daze, Crowe picked up the piece of paper and held it before his face, squinting. He remained that way for several moments, as though he might be deciphering the old Mormon code symbol by symbol, and then put it aside. He took his knife and balanced it on the back of his hand, again, and then, in a sudden, single motion—his fingers and arm and the blade one whizzing blur—he sent the weapon streaking across the room, where it thudded into the wood paneling, point first. At the same time he angrily gestured toward two men in the room, and they stepped toward Bybee and seized his arms again, pinning them painfully behind his back.

Crowe stood up and pointed his finger at Bybee's face. "You're good, Bybee; I'll have to hand you that. You had me going, you really did." He picked up the scrap of paper from the desk. "But I don't understand this Deseret shit." He swept his hand at the other men. "No one in New Ammon does. Mercy tells everyone that I taught it to her, but that's bullshit. She lies. She pretends to teach it to the kids, but even they can't learn it." He looked at the odd symbols again, then wadded up the paper and threw it on the floor. "You're smart, but I'm smarter."

Bybee began to say something, but one of the men grabbed his hair and violently jerked his head back. Crowe smiled, then pointed out the window at the tiny, tin-roofed church steaming in the late afternoon sun.

"I have a potluck dinner to go to, and then"—again he made a gesture to the men, and they began to drag Bybee toward the door, his head pulled back, his throat exposed—"then Brother Griffity and I will deal with you."

13

I N the late 1950s, Cassie Lee Lewis, the daughter of Wester Lewis, disappeared on her ninth birthday, simply wandering away from the party at her house in Johnson Canyon, only a half mile across the fields from Doug and Myrna Farnsworth.

The sheriff in those days, Wendell Honey, Lloyd's older brother, assembled a ragtag search party and combed the canyon, tramping up and down the gulch, around Dishpan, and then east, through Flood Canyon and even as far north as Johnson Lake, two and a half miles away. But Cassie Lee—or her body—was never found.

About a year later, though, visitors to Johnson Canyon—friends of Wester or of the Farnsworths, or deer poachers near Dishpan, or even Boy Scouts camping at the lake—began to report that they had seen something, someone, a young girl in a white dress, always some distance away, always crying. But she never came near, they said, always vanishing into the cliffs, only to reappear a week or a month or a year later.

And so the stories persisted about Cassie Lee, as those kinds of stories always did in Kanab, as they had decades before about

Crazy Freddy Crystal or Josiah Lamb . . . or the Daughter of Zion. And Zolene, spending half her time in Johnson Canyon working for her grandfather, always scoffed at the stories, sadly shaking her head, knowing it was just a part of the muted mythology in Kanab, the gentle hysteria that seemed always to hover over the little town under the red cliffs.

But one summer evening on the ranch, just at sunset, as she broke open a bale of hay in her grandfather's barn, Zolene saw the little girl. She was standing in the tack room, crying, saddles and bridles hanging around her, her white party dress in tatters. Zolene screamed and stood, frozen, baling twine dangling from her hand, and then the little girl turned and ran from the barn, and Zolene never saw her again.

Now, Zolene truly believed that the little girl had returned.

"Cassie Lee?" she whispered.

The figure was on the porch and crying, and Zolene, still crouched in the dark in the leaves, finally found the flashlight and shook it in her hands until she coaxed it to come on again. She got to her feet, swung the beam of light toward the porch, and there, saw a woman slumped against the door, a man's monstrous sport coat draped over her like a cloak.

"Who—"

"Merciful Christs, help me."

Zolene limped slowly to the cement step, then aimed the light directly in the woman's face, still bruised, the skin around her eye purplish, the blond hair hanging in clumps.

"Who are you?" Zolene said.

Mercy said nothing, but only struggled to her feet and stood in the narrow glare of the flashlight, wiping her nose and her eyes with the back of her hand. The oversize coat opened, and Zolene could see, beneath it, that the woman wore tennis shoes and capri pants and a tank top—her own clothes, the clothes Bybee had given her.

"Jesus," Zolene said.

She quickly swept the light over the woman's body, then

pointed it again in her face, closer now, jabbing it as though the beam of light was something tangible and hard, like a fist.

"You're her."

"Please help me—"

Zolene leaned closer. "You're her, aren't you?"

Mercy sniffed and slowly nodded. "I'm Chenoya Whiting."

At the sound of the name—a name that had glared out from the newspapers, been uttered again and again by reporters on television—the leaden fear that had seized Zolene only moments ago now turned molten as she realized that this woman who stood on her porch, the cohab whore who had slept in her house and was now dressed in her clothes, was also a fugitive, a murderess, sought by every police agency in the state.

"I didn't kill Faith," Mercy said.

Zolene involuntarily began to move backward, shrinking from Mercy, sweeping the light over the woman's coat again, imagining, now, where the gun might be hidden, what other weapons she might be concealing.

"Why are you here?" Zolene said. "How"—she pivoted and swept the beam of the flashlight around the yard, looking for a strange car or truck, but there were none—"did you get here?"

"Please help me," Mercy said.

"Damn you!"

"Please—"

For an instant Zolene considered charging past the woman and racing through the house for the .22 rifle in the cabinet on the back porch, but the front door was locked, as well as the rifle cabinet, and it would take an eternity of fumbling with keys to open each of them . . . and then, she wasn't sure if the rifle was loaded, or that it would even fire after all these years.

Zolene spun around and began limping toward her truck, genuinely frightened, her head throbbing, her entire body weakened with fear. She knew that if this woman had put a bullet in the brain of her sister wife she would do the same to her, to anyone, at any moment, and she had to escape, to find Seegy, maybe find Brig . . .

"Mr. Bybee is in New Am'," Mercy said. She had moved

away from the corner where she had crouched, and now stood at the edge, near the steps.

Zolene stopped and turned back to the woman. "What?"

"Mr. Bybee is in New Ammon . . . right now, and Father's probably . . ."

Zolene limped back to the stairs so that she stood only a few feet away and below Mercy. "Brig's at the polygamist colony?"

"Yes."

"Why?"

Mercy shook her head. "I don't know. I just know that he is."

The fear that had coursed through her was now draining away, replaced by a pounding anger that stiffened her, strengthened her. "Goddammit! What the hell is going on? Why are you here? Why did you come back?" She was sure now that the runaway did not have a weapon, was not an immediate physical threat, but she was, nevertheless *here*—again—standing on her own porch, in her own damned clothes. "I'm going to go get the sheriff—*again*," Zolene said, "unless you tell me what the hell is going on."

Mercy folded her hands under her breasts and moved down one step. "I didn't kill Faith."

"You told me that. But why should anyone—"

"Please," Mercy said, "just . . . listen to me. Please."

Zolene pointed the beam of light in Mercy's face, then, seeing again the bruises, the blackened eye, she felt a flicker of pity for the woman, a sudden softening, and took the light away from her face and pointed it at her feet.

"Tell me what's going on," Zolene said, and she aimed the beam of the flashlight to the side, so that the two of them were barely bathed with a weak, reflected glow.

Mercy stood in that dim light, on the porch, her hands clutched tightly beneath her breasts, and told Zolene all that had happened: the flight to Manti, the loud, cursing argument at the safehouse . . . and then, later, when she was alone, out in the yard, the voice . . . and the sound of the gun . . . and then her climbing over the fence and running, running blindly, hiding, afraid of every sound, every person she saw, until she finally

found a phone, at a market, and called the one person she knew
would help.

Finally, after two days of hiding in motels, she was brought
back to Johnson Canyon, to the house in the orchard that was
the only safe place she knew.

As the batteries of the flashlight began to fail, the light
slowly faded and finally went out just as Mercy finished her
story. In the darkness now, neither woman spoke or moved . . .
until Zolene slowly extended her hand and put it on Mercy's
shoulder, tentatively, barely touching her, as though the woman
was so fragile, so delicate, that even a touch would cause her to
shatter. At the feel of the hand, Mercy lowered her head and
took a step toward the other woman, and Zolene reached out
with both arms and gathered her in.

"Oh, God," Zolene said, and she held Mercy tighter, the two
of them pressing into each other, Mercy beginning to cry again.
"I never really thought that—"

Mercy drew back and shook her head. "It doesn't matter,
now. But Mr. Bybee is in New Am', and he shouldn't be. That's
why . . . my friend is there, why he took me here. He was called
by Father. Something is wrong."

Zolene snapped erect and put her hand to her mouth. She
had been so hypnotized by Mercy, by her story, that she had forgotten what the woman had said only a few minutes before.

"God, Brig—" From her jeans pocket, Zolene pulled out a
jumble of keys, found the right one, and opened the front door.
"C'mon," she said, and she took Mercy by the hand and limped
into the living room with her.

Zolene turned on a light and was instantly on the old-fashioned phone, punching numbers on the false rotary dial, and
then she stood with her back to Mercy and waited. After several
moments she punched in another number, waited, then spoke
quickly, paused, then spoke several more words and hung up.

"Let's go," Zolene said, and she took Mercy's hand again. "I
just talked to my cousin at her house. Brig's gone, but the sheriff's waiting for him at the motel. You're right; something is
wrong . . . very wrong."

Without bothering to turn out the light or lock the door, Zolene led Mercy back out to the porch, down the steps, and along the walkway to her truck. They both got inside the cab, and Zolene started the engine, drove back down the road in reverse, turned around at Doug's house, and then roared away into the darkness.

They bounced along the dirt road, then, on the highway, raced toward Kanab. Within minutes they arrived at the Piute Villa and immediately saw, just as Vesta had reported, the sheriff's blue-and-white patrol car parked to one side, near the picnic table and barbecue pit. The lights of the office tepee were off, but the overhead arrowhead sign glowed red, squealing as it slowly revolved.

Zolene climbed down from the truck and had begun limping toward the patrol car when Seegmiller got out, his head cocked to one side, his face lined and haggard, as though he had just awakened from a nap.

"Hey, Zoley."

Zolene came up to him and stopped. Even in the dim, pulsing light, her hair seemed afire, raging around her face. "Seegy, Brig's in New Ammon," she said, "the polygamist—"

"I know. He said he was going to talk to Crowe, maybe bring him back har."

"Back here? When? What time?"

The sheriff cocked his head, and as he did, he noticed Spooky Floyd, who had slouched from his dog tepee and now sat a few feet away, his head tilted in almost the same way.

"He said at six," Seegmiller said, "then to wait a coupla hours. I guess I just fell asleep."

Zolene twisted her wristwatch into the light of the sign. "God, it's almost ten. Something's—" Zolene suddenly turned and pointed back at her truck. "See that woman in there? In my truck?"

Seegmiller squinted into the red-tinged darkness at the shape in the truck, the long, blond hair and the tentlike coat draped over her. "Yeah."

"That's Chenoya Whiting, Crowe's wife, the plig runaway

everyone in the whole damned state's looking for."

Seegmiller's eyes widened, and he looked helplessly from the woman in the car to Zolene. "Wol . . ."

"She says she didn't kill the other woman, her sister wife . . . and I believe her, Seegy."

"But thar's a warrant out—"

Zolene angrily waved her hand in the air, erasing Seegmiller's words, then nodded toward her truck. "That woman knows Crowe better than anyone, and she says Brig's in trouble—" She stopped and looked down, noticing for the first time the unfamiliar holster and pistol strapped around Seegmiller's pudgy waist. "Why are you wearing a gun? You never wear a gun."

Seegmiller looked worried now, panicked, and he bent his head and looked at the weapon as though he too had just discovered it. "Brig told me to; he said I might need it."

Zolene put one hand to her face, half covering her mouth, and closed her eyes. "Oh, God, something *is* wrong." She suddenly grabbed his arm, just below the KANE COUNTY patch. "You've got to get out there, Seegy, to New Ammon. Brig's gone and done something . . . *stupid*, and now he's in trouble. I know it; I can feel it." She pointed back at her truck. "She knows it, too."

Seegmiller swallowed and ran his chubby hand over his face, then looked at the dog, who hadn't moved. "I dunno, Zoley. It's a polygamist colony; we really don't have much to do over to thar; it's—"

"Seegy!" Zolene had raised her voice, and she took both of his arms in her hands, holding him in front of her like a child. "You're the damned *sheriff!* Someone's in trouble and you've got to *do* something, and do it now!"

Seegmiller stood there with his head cocked and his arms pinned to his side, his hands dangling uselessly at his waist. Finally he righted his head and looked at Zolene, at the blue, frightened eyes that were drilling through his, at the hair, the face that he always saw, sometimes at night, in the dark, the way it was now, swimming in front of him.

"Please," Zolene said, and she released his arms and moved closer to him so that her face was now only inches from his, her breath warm.

"Zoley—"

"You've been my friend ever since I can remember," Zolene said, "and for one reason: you're a decent man, and there's just not too many of those around anymore. I mean it."

Seegmiller blinked into her face. She was so close that he could smell the shampoo in her hair, and mingled with it, her perfume, faint and sweet, all of it now like a drug, making his head light . . . making him crazy.

"Okay, Zoley."

Zolene suddenly bent forward and kissed him on the cheek, her hair falling across his face as she did. "Thank you, Seegy."

As though the lips of his secret princess had finally awakened him, magically transformed him, Seegy straightened and looked knowingly about the graveled yard, peering into the darkness.

"Brig must have taken that . . . bus, that green thing. Crowe will know about this place, then." He pointed his finger at her truck. "So you better get her out of har. You, too."

Zolene nodded. "We'll go to my aunt Orm's."

"Good," Seegmiller said. "Call Vesta and tell her to lock this place up and stay away from it. The tourists can just fend for tharselves. I'm going to go to New Am' the back way." He cocked his head and tried to smile. "I know the back way."

He began to turn toward his car, but he paused, looking hopefully at Zolene as though he might receive another kiss, something to fortify him, to propel him manfully into the gloom.

But Zolene only put her hand on his arm again. "Thank you, Seegy."

With a disappointed nod, Seegmiller began to turn away, but stopped, reached into his rear pocket, and withdrew the envelope Bybee had given him earlier that day.

"I almost forgot," he said, and he handed the envelope to Zolene. "Brig wanted me to give this to you."

With that, he walked back to his car, got inside, and started the engine. As Spooky Floyd dragged himself out of the way, back to his tiny tepee, Seegmiller turned his car around and stopped at the entrance. He had put on his hat, and as he drove slowly out onto Center Street, he smiled at Zolene and touched two fingers to the hat's bill.

Zolene stood and watched him drive off into the night, then opened the envelope and, in the faint light, began reading Bybee's letter. By the time she had finished, she was crying, shaking her head back and forth, and then she angrily wadded the two sheets of paper and threw them to the ground.

"Damn you—"

She glared at her truck, at Mercy sitting inside, cowering against the door, frightened, staring back at her with her confused eyes. For a moment she considered ordering the plig bitch out of her truck, out of her life, casting her adrift in the middle of the night, and the hell with whatever calamity might befall her—she deserved it.

But Zolene slowly bent down and picket up the crumpled letter, stuffed it into her jeans pocket, and limped to the truck. She opened the door, climbed in, and, as she wiped the tears from her face, started the engine.

"Let's go to Aunt Orm's," she said. "It's getting late."

It is said by many, maybe the same cracker-barrel experts on polygamist colonies, that the first and principal mission of Brigham Young and the early Mormon pioneers in the Utah Territory was not to build temples, as so many believe, not even to build houses or barns. No, the first order of business in the Great Basin was to bring water into this freakish, arid land of canyons and cliffs.

And so they did, these refugees, finding every stream and spring and seeps, and tapping them, trapping the precious little trickle of water in an extensive network of cisterns and pipes and, eventually, water storage tanks—large round cement affairs that, by the 1960s, were finally replaced by the spindly-legged metal towers that hover over the landscape now like monstrous spiders.

But still, on some of the hilltops and ridges in Utah, on an occasional high piece of ground, the cement tanks remain, empty, stark, and colorless, hollow monuments to the early industry of the Saints, now used only as crude silos or storage sheds or, in New Ammon, as an arena . . . a killing field.

Bybee had been in the cement tank for over three hours, he guessed. When they had brought him here, the light was just fading, and he had been able to see shards of pinkish sky through the tattered tin roof overhead. Now, he could see nothing except stars and the blackness.

After he had been roughly pushed through a crude opening carved in the cement, the thick wooden door slammed shut and bolted, he had retreated, reflexively, to the far side of the tank. He had slumped against the cold, crumbling wall, his head throbbing, truly disoriented, his brain numbed with the horror of what had just happened . . . what was going to happen.

Finally he had begun to focus his thoughts, to gather himself, and one searing image formed in his brain—as it often had over the years, in nightmares, usually—of the South Vietnamese army officer methodically, casually, a cigarette in his mouth, strolling down a line of captured Vietcong guerillas near Nha Trang, shooting each one, in turn, in the head. And the prisoners, their feet and hands unbound, no other guns trained on them than the tiny pistol of the officer, did not run, did not make one last, desperate, screaming, struggling effort to escape, to stay alive, at least to be shot frantically fighting for their lives. Instead, they tamely waited for the officer's bullet as though they were waiting for him to hand out the mail or pay vouchers.

But Bybee would not so easily submit to his own murder; he would, as the old baseball and boxing cliché had it, go down swinging. Once aroused, once the throbbing fear began pumping through him, he groped around the dirt floor of the tank, searching for anything that he could use as a weapon. He found several fist-size chunks of cement, an empty paint can, wire . . . and finally a piece of lumber, a two-by-four about three feet long, half rotted, but heavy enough, like a baseball bat.

And now he crouched in the darkness, his weapon at his feet, thinking of Brileena, his daughter, and of the grandchild she carried, the grandchild he might never see. And he thought of Helena, his ex-wife, now remarried—sealed—to a good Mormon man, she a good woman herself, too good for Bybee, that was certain.

And he thought of Zolene.

He heard a noise, a thumping against the wooden door of the tank, saw a sliver of stars burst into view across the floor, widening, and then heard a man heavily push through, grunting, his breath loud and labored.

Bybee gripped the wood and silently moved along the wall. He knew his eyes, staring into this gloom for hours, would be better adjusted to the dark than those of the plig thug who had just come in, and that would be his advantage. He would strike before this goon even saw him, even had a chance to say a word.

"Bah-bee?"

Bybee stopped; he was half crouched, the lumber in his hand, and for one absurd second he thought that it was Tom Kendall, affecting one of his many stage personas, the drunken, drawling Texas hick, the way he had done many times, in many bars.

"You here, Bah-bee?"

Suddenly, the sliver of stars—the open door—disappeared and a flashlight clicked on, the lens covered by jeweled fingers, making them look pink and translucent. In the reddish glow, Bybee saw a big, bloated man in a cowboy hat and suspenders.

"You best git the hell outta here," Atherton said. His voice echoed in the tank, and he cleared his throat and spit. "Rampton's fixin' to come. Griffy, too."

Bybee squinted at him, at this caricature in tight slacks and a billowing white shirt. "Who are you?"

"That don't matter," Atherton said. He slowly walked across the dirt-covered floor, his body canted to one side, and came up to Bybee. "There's a back road outta here—due north. Follow it; it'll take you to the hahway, about two mals west of your mo-tel."

Bybee still had the length of wood cocked, lying across his shoulder like a batter on deck, but he relaxed and held it loosely at his waist. He knew—or he thought he knew—who this man might be.

"You helped Mercy," Bybee said. "You told her to find me."

"That's rat."

Atherton moved closer, and in the faint light that he seemed to be squeezing out of the end of the flashlight with his fat fingers, Bybee saw his other hand reach inside his pants pocket and withdraw a gun, a revolver—small, with a wood grip. Instantly, Bybee raised the board in his hands and cocked it.

"Don't worry," Atherton said, and he flipped the gun around in his hand so that he held the short barrel, and pushed it toward Bybee. "Take this," he said. "Mat need it. It's loaded; ready to go."

Bybee stared at the cold metal thing in the man's jeweled hand, something he had sworn he would never touch again, then dropped the piece of wood at his feet and extended his hand toward the gun, but he hesitated, his hand hovering.

"Take it," Atherton said, and he pushed the weapon into Bybee's stomach. "These men'll kill you the same way they killed Fenton and Pugh. That's a fact."

Bybee took the gun, feeling the sick, deadly weight of it, despite its size, and then jammed it into his rear pants pocket. He leaned closer to the other man, so close that he could smell the alcohol, see his dull teeth, the rheumy eyes.

"Crowe killed them?" Bybee said. "Pugh . . . and the other—"

"Yeah, he did, but not the way Mercy probably said." Atherton laughed suddenly, a phlegmy bark that reverberated around the curved cement walls and came back at him. "She tells stories lak she cooks. She overdoes it; puts too much crap into everything."

"How did—"

"Crowe sent a knaf straight into Franklin's heart, lak a bullet. Same with Fenton. They're buried behand the leather factory, on the west sad of the machine shop. You'll be there, too, if you don't get the hell outta here."

Atherton took Bybee's arm in his pudgy hand and tugged him toward the other side of the tank, to the door, and then stopped. He switched off the flashlight and slowly opened the wooden door, pausing to peek outside, then threw it back. Cool, dry air rushed in, and Bybee ducked through the low doorway and stood outside the tank, sucking in lungsful of the clean air. About a half mile away the town of New Ammon slept below them, only a few feeble lights on here and there, the whole of it surrounded, smothered, by black sky and the layering of stars.

Atherton closed the door. "When you git back," he said, "you call Zoley out there in that canyon. She'll—"

"How do you know her?" Bybee said, and he brought his face up to the other man. "And how do you know where she lives?"

"Ah met her just once, went out there. Mercy should be out there now."

Bybee shook his head, the dizziness returning twofold. "Who the hell are you?"

"It don't matter. Ah'm a friend of Mercy's, her best friend, so you listen. She didn't kill Faith; no woman would kill her sister waf. That's a fact."

"She had a gun. She had it in—"

"Lak hell," Atherton said. "But she heard a voice at that house in Manti—a man's voice, she said, and one she won't forgit—jes' before she heard the shot. She ran; she found a phone and called me, and ah came for her." He stopped, and Bybee heard the labored breathing, smelled the miasma of liquor hovering around them in the nighttime air. "Ah would always come for her. Anywhere."

He grabbed Bybee and gently turned him around until he was facing away from New Ammon, staring into the deep sky at the Big Dipper, almost indiscernible because of the storm of stars everywhere in the heavens, crowding it out.

"One more thing," Atherton said, and he brought up a throatful of phlegm and spit it out, then took Bybee's arm, like a clumsy dancer, and twirled him around. "Ah know you got some doin's in Salt Lake tomorrow. If you need some tam, then you tell the Rocket Man—and Darvis Gant—that you know about LeVar Eaton, about—"

"LeVar?"

The image of the Salt Lake criminal defense attorney flashed before Bybee—an oily, stupid man who knew nothing about the law other than how to twist it, manipulate it. But that image was instantly replaced by the picture of Gant, the little angry man clutching his ear, screaming at Bybee at the safehouse.

Bybee leaned forward. "What the hell does Gant have to do with you? With all this?"

In the faint starlight, Bybee saw one of Atherton's hands rise, palm outward, as if he was a witness on the stand, blocking out a patch of stars as though he had just ripped a hole in the heavens.

"Ah work for Darvis," Atherton said. "Ah work for everyone. But you just tell them—Darvis and the judge—that you know about LeVar, and about that shitpot full of money, even the fifty one-hunnert-dollar bills Darvis gave me. That's all you need to say, and those boys'll back away. I guaran-damn-tee it. Things always come full circle." He gently pushed Bybee in the chest, staggering him back a few feet. "That's a fact. Now, go. Git."

Despite the order, Bybee stepped back to the man. "I want to know one thing: who the hell told Gant to be at Manti when I brought Mercy there?"

"Ah dunno," Atherton said, "but it wasn't me. Ah didn't know Mercy was at Manti till she called."

The big cowboy then spit, turned around, and began shambling back down the low hill, leaning painfully to one side, his hand raised in the air, still groping at the firmament.

"Take care of Mercy," he said, more to the heavens than to Bybee.

14

TWO years after he had graduated from Kanab High School, DeRalph Seegmiller, while working at the Moqui Cave just outside town, met a homely, loose-jointed woman from Orderville named Nora Chatterly, and after a torrid courtship, the two were married almost a year later.

But the wedding was an ordinary, pedestrian affair—"above ground," some used to say—that is, they were not sealed for time and all eternity in the secret temple ceremony. A month before the wedding, Bishop Morris Foote had discovered that the two horny Mormon kids had slept together—and not just once, but numerous times, even in the very moon-shadow of the church in Kanab, at the Arrowhead Lodge—and so their temple recommends, something akin to spiritual passports, were rejected.

Despite this disgrace, Bishop Foote did officiate at the hushed, hurried ceremony at the Gazebo, sternly instructing the two crazed lovers that, if they were ever to gain entrance to the temple and, by extension, the celestial kingdom, they must live a life of repentance and forbearance. Thus, they must faithfully tithe and keep their testimony strong, he said, and above all, they must always think of the sanctity of marriage and its obligations in a spiritual, God-like way, regarding the other as a beacon, a lighthouse . . . and not, well, not in that "other way," he said.

As he drove through the night, Seegmiller tried to follow the bishop's advice and envision Nora's face ahead of him, shining, smiling, showing him the correct path, but all he could see was her body—and not as it had been in those frenetic days at the Arrowhead Lodge, but as it was now, as she was now: seven months pregnant with their fourth child, swollen, sweaty, waddling around Kanab with the whole brood in tow.

But there was another face, one of which the bishop would surely disapprove, and he breathed deeply of the still-lingering fragrance of her hair and perfume, his left cheek afire from her touch.

He squinted and tried to concentrate on what was ahead. He had been rattling along the weed-choked ruts in his blue-and-white cruiser for almost half an hour, starting at every rabbit that leaped through the headlights' beam and cringing as the old Plymouth sedan slammed into holes and, at times, almost foundered in the deep sand. But he kept plowing ahead as the embankments on either side of the road grew higher, making him feel that he was now driving along the bottom of a wide ditch . . . which he probably was.

He saw it then; it was a figure, a man—he was sure of it—materializing in the far limits of the headlights' sweep as though it had suddenly arisen from the earth, some primordial creature made of clay and straw, ejected from below. But it just as quickly disappeared, loping, almost gliding, over the embankment and melting into the darkness at the side of the road.

"Oh, God," Seegmiller said.

At the same time, about half a mile away, he saw a burst of light flash at him, then wink out, and a few seconds later it shone again, remaining steady this time, two lights now, aiming directly down the road. . . . He stopped and remained in his car, the police lights crazily blinking above him, red and blue flashing out into the sage, and waited for the other vehicle to approach. But he kept one eye out the side window and in the rearview mirror for the shadowy thing he had seen—or thought he had seen— drifting across the road.

When the headlights were about a hundred feet away, the vehicle, a canvas-topped Jeep, stopped, but the lights remained on, shining directly into Seegmiller's eyes. He saw three men emerge and begin walking toward him, only black silhouettes in the glare of their lights, growing larger as they approached but still dark, with no features.

Seegmiller opened the door, got out of the car, walked to the front of it, and stood, one hand resting uneasily on his hip, the other held up in the air as though he were directing traffic at Big Joe's Junction.

"Evenin'," he yelled, with a loud, forced laugh. "You boys about as lost as me?"

The figures drew closer, their features now slowly taking shape—long beards, the farmers' clothes on two of them—and then they stopped. The one in the middle gestured, and the men flanking him instantly mounted either side of the road, half crawling, like animals, atop the embankments, where they stopped and peered into the darkness.

The man left alone on the road walked even closer, and as he came into Seegmiller's headlights, the sheriff could finally see the pointed beard and ponytail . . . and then the man's face.

"Mr. Crowe?" Seegmiller said. His voice was faint, almost quavering, and he cleared his throat and spoke louder. "Rampton Crowe?"

"Get your goddamned car out of this road."

Seegmiller swallowed and then cocked his head. "I'm Sheriff Seegmiller, Kane County. I'm here on official business."

"So am I," Crowe said. He was still dressed in jeans and a T-shirt, but wore a light jacket that didn't quite conceal the handle of a knife jutting out from his belt. "Now get your fucking car out of here!"

Seegmiller moved to his right so that he was directly in the glare of both sets of headlights, about fifty feet away from Crowe. The other men—one of them Griffity—had come down from the embankments and, after muttering something to Crowe, stood to the side and behind him. For several moments no one moved, and there was no sound except for Seegmiller's heavy, panicked breathing, almost in rhythm with the flashing red-and-blue lights atop his car.

Then, slowly, Crowe withdrew his knife and balanced it on the back of his right hand, and as he did, Seegmiller raised both his arms above his head, palms outward.

"God, look, Mr. Crowe, I just came out har to find Mr. Bybee. I think he might—"

"Shut up!" Crowe yelled, and then he took a step forward and stiffly held out his right arm, the blade of the knife glinting in the lights. "Put your hand on your gun."

Seegmiller squinted into the lights and cocked his head, his hands still upraised. Sweat now covered his face, and it dripped down off his chin. "Look, for God's sakes, Mr. Crowe—"

"Put·your goddamned hand on your gun, you ignorant hick. We're going to play a game."

Seegmiller lowered his arms. "Look," he said, "I don't want no trouble; I'll just move the car, like you—"

Crowe took a step forward. "No. Too late for that; you had your chance. Now, you put your fucking hand on your gun—like I told you—and then, when you feel you're ready . . . you go for it!" He turned his head, displaying the ponytail, and laughed at Griffity. "You . . . draw! Just like in the movies, Sheriff! You like movies?"

Seegmiller shook his head. "Please don't do this. I—"

"Look, Sheriff," Crowe said, smiling and nodding at his extended hand. "All I've got is this old knife, just sitting here, not even in my hand. But you've got that gun."

"Please."

Crowe moved a step closer, his right arm stiff. "Well, you ignorant little shit, it's your only chance, because if you don't go for that gun, I'm going to send this knife into your throat anyway. So all you gotta do is draw and shoot before I grab this thing and throw it. Seems like the odds are in your favor. Guns are faster, right?"

Seegmiller straightened and wiped his wet face with his hand. He tried to speak, to reason with the maniac in front of him, but the words caught in his throat.

"Right?" Crowe said again.

"That's right," a voice said. It came from the dark, from the side of the road, and almost as one, the heads of the four men swiveled toward it. "Guns *are* faster . . . especially guns that are already out and pointed."

Bybee stood atop the embankment, only twenty feet away, his arms extended with Atherton's pistol gripped in both hands, pointed directly at Crowe. Having avoided the quick search by Crowe's goons, he had crept back to the embankment and, out of view, had watched, his head roaring with fear, for a few minutes, crouched behind the weeds, until he was sure that the other pligs carried no weapons—certainly no guns.

"Drop that knife . . . now, Crowe, or I shoot. I mean it."

Crowe and the other pligs stood gaping at the figure atop the embankment, frozen in place in the blinking red-and-blue light. Slowly Crowe turned so that his outstretched hand was aimed at Bybee, a horizontal salute.

Bybee's own hand, his right hand, was shaking almost uncontrollably, but it was steadied by the other, and in the semidarkness, he was sure that the others could not see it.

"I'll pull this trigger," Bybee said, "and put a bullet through your fucking head!"

Slowly Bybee inched down the embankment, looking, in his slacks and knit shirt, like a golfer emerging from the rough—a deep rough—but, rather than clutching a five or four iron, he held the small pistol, still in both hands, still pointed at Crowe's head.

He got to the road and moved within ten feet of Crowe, the roar in his head almost deafening. "Seegy," he said, his eyes still fastened on Crowe's face and knife hand, "take your gun out."

As he was told, Seegmiller fumbled with the strap on the holster, then withdrew his pistol, pointing it at Crowe, then the other men, and back at Crowe.

"Now," Bybee said, moving even closer still to Crowe, his heart hammering, "there are *two* guns." He gestured with his own at Crowe's knife. "You're damn good with that, but not that good. Can't take out two of us. Now drop it, or I put a bullet right between your eyes." To drive this point home, Bybee raised the gun and, sighting behind it, aimed it directly at Crowe's forehead. "And believe me, you plig asshole, I will!"

Slowly, mechanically, like a hypnotized subject, Crowe lowered his hand, allowing the knife to fall into the dirt. He glared at Bybee, then thrust his head forward.

"You're dead, Bybee." In the harsh light, his eyes looked deeper, like blackened pits gouged out in his face. "You are fucking . . . *dead.*"

"That's tough talk," Bybee said, "for someone so stupid that he brought a knife to a gunfight."

"Fuck you," Crowe said.

Bybee bent and retrieved the knife from the dirt and threw it as far into the sage as he could, then gestured with the gun toward the men. "I want all of you to take your clothes off . . . all of them."

The men standing in the lights did nothing, and Bybee raised the gun again with both hands, pointing it in turn at each man. He considered for a moment, as they did in the movies, of firing a warning shot into the air, just to prove how reckless and homicidal—and serious—he was. But he was not sure if the gun would fire—despite Atherton's assurances—or whether he had to disengage a safety first, or cock it, or . . . what? He hated guns; he knew nothing about them.

"Now!" Bybee barked, and he waved the weapon at them. "Take everything off and put it in a pile."

Finally, the men—sullen, glowering at Bybee—began to unbutton and unsnap their clothes—jackets, shirts, overalls, jeans, T-shirts—until they all stood in their underwear, Crowe in tight black briefs, the others in their holy garments, dirty-looking long underwear. At their feet lay the pile of their filthy clothes and boots, a stinking mound of unwashed cloth and worn leather.

"Now, sit!" Bybee said, using the same tone he had once used with Spooky Floyd during an ill-conceived and frustrating campaign to train the mutt, months ago. "Sit!"

Slowly the men sat down in the dirt, knees high, their legs splayed everywhere. When they were settled, not moving, Bybee walked to the Jeep, still keeping his gun pointed at the men on the ground. He knew nothing of guns, but he did know a little about the internal combustion engine—and hot-wiring and hidden, magnetized keys.

"Seegy," he said, "keep your gun on these guys."

Obediently Seegy moved to the group of half-naked men on the ground and pointed his weapon at them, his face still dripping with sweat. Assured that the men were subdued, Bybee found the cowling latches on the Jeep, raised the hood, and thrust his hand inside. He located the distributor cap and, after a minor struggle, finally emerged from the engine compartment with the rotor in his fist. He jammed it into his pocket and walked back to the group of men on the ground. He considered delivering some damning, melodramatic speech to Crowe, something laden with homilies about crime and punishment and right and wrong. But the sight of these greasy, bearded animals—the smell of them— made him sick, and he simply wanted to get away.

"Let's go, Seegy."

With his gun still trained on the men, Bybee scooped up the pile of reeking clothes with one hand, leaving the boots behind, and, moving to Seegmiller's car, deposited them in the rear seat, feeling, as he did, the object of the striptease—two cell phones. He then got into the front passenger side of the car and, in a matter of seconds, Seegmiller had started the engine and was driving crazily in reverse, his neck twisted and his arm spread across the back of the seat as he squinted out the rear window. In front of them, the long-bearded pligs in their underwear still sat on the ground, huddled together like gay pioneers at the beach but shriveling now, the entire, eerie scene shrinking, sliding down a black tube, as Seegmiller raced backward. Finally the road widened in one spot, and the sheriff, after several see-sawing efforts, turned the car around and continued to bump down the road, pointed north . . . toward home.

"Lord Jesus!" Bybee said, and he leaned back in the seat. His hand—his whole body—had stopped trembling, but he felt sick, weakened. For a moment he thought he would have to have Seegmiller stop the car and allow him to hang his head out the window. He still held the gun in his hand, his fingers clenched tight around the grip, and he looked at it, studying it as though he had just found it on the seat, and then suddenly dropped it on the floor.

Next to him, Seegmiller sat, rigid, his face wet, but not just with sweat; he was crying, and tears coursed down his cheeks as he tried to wipe them away with his stubby hand.

"Oh, God, Brig."

"Take it easy," Bybee said, and he put his hand on Seeg-miller's shoulder. "We're okay. Let's just get back home."

In silence they drove on, both listening to the slapping of the brush on the undercarriage, watching rabbits dart everywhere, and once, on a low rise, they saw three coyotes skulking in the fringes of the car's headlights, dirty and dangerous, four-legged versions of what they had just left crouched in the road.

After several minutes Seegmiller turned and looked at Bybee. He had stopped crying, but his eyes were red, wretched, rinsed out with misery.

"I'm not cut out for this, Brig. I'm not. It's like every other . . . *damned* thing I do. I just—" He stopped; his voice cracked, and his eyes were wet again. "I'm going to resign."

Bybee twisted violently in the seat and pointed his finger at the sheriff. "No, you're not. You're a good cop, Seegy. More than you know. You went out looking for me in the middle of the night. A lot of cops wouldn't do that."

"But I was scared, Brig. God, I was *so* scared."

"So was I. Probably more than you. There's not a soul in the world that wouldn't have been."

Seegmiller seemed relieved, and he looked appreciatively at Bybee. "Wol . . ."

"You're a good cop," Bybee said again, "and I need your help . . . one more time."

Seegmiller remained silent for several moments, his eyes worried. "Now what?" he whispered.

"Crowe murdered two pligs, and I know where they're buried."

"Oh, God," Seegmiller said, and he closed his eyes, realizing that his lawman's life had become an endless loop, repeating itself over and over.

Hurriedly, while they bounced along in the darkness, Bybee told the sheriff everything that had happened in New Ammon, including what Atherton had told him and the precise location of the bodies.

When he had finished, Bybee leaned closer to Seegmiller. "Tomorrow," he said, "get down to a judge in St. George, swear out an affidavit, and get a search warrant. Then, call the highway patrol and get some help. Go out to New Ammon with enough cars and guns and manpower—and shovels—to get the job done."

Seegmiller suddenly turned and gaped at Bybee. "Are you talking about a . . . raid? Raiding a polygamist colony?"

"You can call it that," Bybee said, "but this is not a raid to bust pligs for keeping a trailer full of wives. This is to bust Crowe for murder. Simple."

The sheriff squinted at the road ahead, widening somewhat now as they drew closer to the highway. "All right," he said, and then, emboldened by his newfound authority, he turned to Bybee. "Brig, Zolene and . . . that wife, Crowe's wife. Thar both over to Orma Frost's house. It's safer. I thought you should know."

Bybee nodded; while he had stumbled down the road from New Ammon, his head had swum with thoughts of both of them, of Mercy at Lamb's house, and Zolene finding her, doing the right thing.

"Good," Bybee said.

"You should go thar, too," the sheriff said, and he smiled at Bybee. "To Orma's. You should."

"Okay."

Bybee considered finding one of the cell phones in the heap of stinking clothes in the rear and calling Orma Frost's house—of calling Zolene—but it was too late, and he didn't know the woman's number. Besides, he had never been able to master one of the gadgets; like everything else today, they were electronic Rubik's cubes—maddening and virtually unsolvable.

They lapsed into silence again, and Seegmiller fought to keep Nora's drawn, sad-eyed, wifely face in front of him, but he failed; the other face constantly drifted before his eyes.

"Brig," he finally said. "Will you do *me* a favor, now?"

"Name it."

"Don't tell Zoley—Zolene—that I was scared back thar. Okay?"

Bybee smiled and nodded. "Okay."

Kanab, Utah, is one of the few communities left in the Western Hemisphere that still enjoys predawn milk delivery, and half the homes in town have, near the front or side door, a white wooden box with SHUMWAY DAIRY stenciled on the side. And half of those homes keep their door keys there, making the job of any would-be burglar in Kanab very simple, very neat.

After Seegmiller left him off at Orma Frost's home—an old, sandstone house built beneath the twenty-foot white *K* on the eastern cliffs—Bybee found the key in the white box and quietly let himself in the woman's front door.

He had been in Zolene's aunt's house many times, usually on bright, warm Sunday afternoons for the woman's standard pot-roast-and-potato dinner and endless games of canasta, but now it was dark and cold and silent. He walked as softly as he could to the old couch in the living room and, finding a woolen throw on a chair, took off his sand-filled shoes, stretched out, and covered himself.

His head, his entire body, still thrummed with the terror of the last twelve hours, as though he had become electrified, a numbing, low-voltage current coursing through him . . . but he could feel himself cooling, sinking.

He needed the sleep that was overtaking him, but he fought to keep himself awake, his eyes open, for just a few more moments so he could piece together what he had to do tomorrow, arranging it in his clouded mind—who he had to see and talk to in Kanab, in Manti . . . and finally in Salt Lake. He had a plan, another plan.

In the dining room the grandfather clock began grinding out the Westminster tune, echoing through the house. He lay, fighting sleep, struggling to hear the end of it, but he closed his eyes and was asleep before the old chimes finished clanging.

He awoke; he was not sure if he had been asleep for just a few minutes, a few hours . . . a few years. It was still dark, and for a moment he thought he was in Lamb's house; the wood floors creaked, and hovering over him was the smell of her, the same smell.

He floated, half awake now, and then tried to sit up, but a hand upon his face gently pushed him back down.

"Be quiet."

Then her lips were on his—familiar but still strange, foreign—and then she slowly lowered her body atop him, and he could feel her breasts, her nipples, the sweet softness of her, all of her, through the filmy nightgown, her warm skin . . . and her hair . . . red, even in the dark.

"Zolene."

"I've missed you," she whispered.

He pressed into her, kissing her, and then one hand instinctively went to her breasts, wedging it between their bodies so he could cup one of them, while the other fluttered along her spine, down to her waist, her buttocks, and farther, the thick ridge of the scar. He pulled her closer and tried to twist her around, under him, and at the same time began struggling with the nightgown, trying to pull it up and over her, almost ripping it.

"No," she said, and she kissed him again. "Aunt Orm will

hear." She kissed his ear and kept her lips there. "Later," she whispered. "Later . . . and a lot."

Through one window, the K on the dark cliff glowed at them, luminescent, and they lay on the sofa, breathing together in a soft, rhythmic unison, their faces pressed against each other, listening for any stirrings in the rest of the house, listening to one another's silence.

He had begun to fall asleep again, her warm body pressed down upon him, when he took her face with both hands and held it before him.

"I need—" he said, but she kissed him before he could finish.

"What?" she said, and she kissed him again, long and hard, then ran her lips along the side of his face, nuzzling him, biting at him. "What do you need, babe?"

"You," he said, and he stroked her long hair and ran his fingers along her cheeks, her nose. "And your truck. Tomorrow."

Zolene remained still, breathing slowly, then put her lips next to his ear again. "Jeez, Brig, you're *so* damned romantic."

15

MOST lawyers, once released from the law school refugee camps, are ferociously eager to display to an ignorant world their talents and knowledge—as minimal as they might be. And they do this, generally, in a courtroom—a theater, really—where they can, like any thespian, proclaim and damn and wheedle and insist and, in the end, simply pray.

But there is, most experienced lawyers know, a better way to win their case—or at least successfully compromise it—without the public scrutiny and the galling histrionics and, most of all, without the outright calamity of the runaway, riderless jury or the crooked judge. It is the pretrial negotiation, the settlement, whether in a civil or criminal case, where the de rigueur prohibitions of trial—hearsay, tainted evidence, speculation, gentle threats and mild extortion, even fabrication—are all welcome, even required.

So after thirty years as both victor and victim in countless trials, from fist-pumping success to head-shaking failure, Bybee had finally learned the true, zealously guarded secret of practicing law: keep the law out of it.

✦

He left Orma Frost's house at six o'clock, just as the Shumway Dairy milkman—these days no longer in a white uniform and billed cap, but in jeans and a BYU sweatshirt—was tramping up the walkway with a plastic basket full of plastic bottles. Bybee, still in the same clothes, returned the milkman's indifferent nod, realizing that he must see, almost every morning, disheveled Kanab men furtively creeping away from houses in the lurid half-light of dawn.

Zolene's truck started with a roar, and in a matter of minutes he was on Center Street and pulling up in front of the Trail's End. The café was not yet open for business, but the kitchen staff was there, the place already steaming and smoking amid the clangor of kettles and the shouting of red-eyed cooks. The morning shift supervisor, Fawn Brimhall, saw him waving and pounding at the front door and let him in. After Bybee explained what he needed, they repaired to a small office in the rear. Fawn opened a file drawer and, from a wad of records in an envelope, finally found what Bybee sought: his computerized receipt for the Rancher's DeLuxe breakfast he had left untouched several days before.

After noting the one critical piece of printed information on the receipt, Bybee thanked her, asked her to safeguard the document, then left the café and hurried back to Zolene's truck. He drove through town, slowed at the Piute Villa to see, as Seegmiller had advised him, that the place was closed and empty, Vesta gone and the No Vacancy sign on, then accelerated and drove out of town.

In the weak light, the Vermilion Cliffs were dark and purplish, streaked with gold, but farther north along the highway the sun finally spilled over the towering White Cliffs and came flooding into the valley, glinting off the thrusting rocks in Zion Park and awakening everything, coloring it all, giving it new life.

But Bybee was not aware of the scenery. He drove on, pushing the red pickup through the Grand Staircase, through the Dixie and Fishlake forests, through Junction and Joseph and

Salina, until, at Sterling, he saw the twin towers of the Manti temple atop the green hill, like an odd, double-shafted light-house.

In Manti, he slowed, and as he expected, he saw Poetry Bob where he last saw him, where he always was, dressed like a male nurse or an orderly, stiffly holding his sign out as his leather bag—probably made in New Ammon—drooped at his side.

Bybee found an empty space at the curb, parked, and then loped across the street to the white-clothed poet, talking as he did, waving his hand, then nodding, then violently shaking his head. To anyone standing nearby out of earshot, it would have seemed as if Bybee, rather than simply purchasing a single poem, was negotiating for the rights to an entire anthology.

Eventually, however, Bybee clapped the white-clad man on the shoulder, then pulled out his wallet, produced a bill, and bought a sheaf of poems that Poetry Bob slowly fished out of his leather bag, expressionless.

From there, the poems scattered across the front seat of the truck, Bybee drove down Main Street, turned on East 200 North, and, groaning uphill, stopped in front of LaWanda Fae Covington's purple-bricked house, where he jumped from the truck and nearly sprinted to the front porch. He banged on the door, and after a moment or two it opened—but only slightly— as the big woman kept Bybee on the porch, glowering at him through the narrow opening. But she answered the one question he needed answered, and he thanked her, or more precisely, thanked the blank slab of the door that was quickly and firmly closed in his face.

Wheeling the big truck around in the street, Bybee raced back to Main Street, turned left, and easily found the Manti Police Headquarters—a simple, unimposing brick building on West 400 South that had every conceivable governmental flag fluttering in front. Again, he nearly ran inside and, after some arguing, was finally able to obtain a copy of the police report on the murder of Roma Ann McCallister—Faith.

At last, armed with all the simple, but devastating, information he needed—all except the answer to one question—Bybee once again pointed the red truck northward and sped toward the Scott M. Matheson Courthouse in Salt Lake City.

Judge Rukamann sat, swathed in his dirty, pleated robe, the cigarette held daintily between his thumb and forefinger. The smoke curled upward into the darkness of his chambers as he sat there, poised, slowly reading the document that lay in front of him.

Finally, he finished and looked up at the man who had thrown the papers on his desk only minutes before, and the man blinked furiously back at him.

"Those are the questions you're to ask," Gant said. He was dressed in a dark gray, double-breasted suit with a red tie. "Each and every goddamned one of them. Especially those for Bybee."

At the mention of the lawyer's name, as though it were the secret word for the day, a metallic voice burst from the speaker phone on the judge's desk.

"Judge," the voice said, "Brig Bybee is here. He wants to see you. Says it's important."

The ash on Rukamann's cigarette fell, splattering on his robe, and he looked helplessly at Gant, his eyebrows raised.

Gant smiled, and as the judge began to speak, the governor's assistant suddenly stood up and leaned across the desk so that his mouth was only a foot from the telephone.

"Send the asshole in," he yelled.

Rukamann instantly jabbed a finger at the instrument, disconnecting it, but he was too late. He glared at Gant, then punched the button again and spoke in a low, soft voice.

"Go ahead," he said. "Send him in."

A few seconds later, the door opened and light flooded into the room, bringing Bybee with it the same way it brought everyone—squinting into the eerie darkness and the smoke.

Bybee stopped in the middle of the room and spread his arms to the side. "The asshole has arrived," he said, and then he looked at Gant, who sat, half twisted in his chair. "In fact, all the assholes have arrived. Why am I not surprised you're here, *Darvis?*"

The judge cleared his throat and began to speak, but Gant waved him quiet, then blinked at Bybee's wrinkled clothes, his unshaven face, the hair that was uncombed and wild.

"Looking sharp, as always," Gant said. "Don't the homeless shelters tell you how to dress up these days?"

Bybee took a step closer to the man, then struck a theatrical pose, scratching his head. "You mean, the governor's little lynchings are formal affairs?"

"Fuck you, Bybee," Gant said. "You're pathetic."

Bybee moved closer so that he stood, now, in front of the judge's desk and next to Gant. "Yeah, you're right. I am pathetic. About as pathetic these days as LeVar Eaton."

Gant and Rukamann froze in their chairs, the judge holding the cigarette up and above his head as though his entire body were suspended from that one point. Suddenly Gant jerked, his body twisting, a victim of an angry, ghostly hand.

Rukamann cleared his throat. "What are you talking about?" He tried to keep his voice low and even, but it was tinged with panic. "Don't follow."

Bybee drew himself up, hooked his thumbs into invisible suspenders, and leaned to one side, as if his body were bent, crippled. He had been thinking all morning about what Atherton had told him, about the money and Eaton, but he wasn't sure how it all fit into place, how to approach it, so he would simply improvise and hope for the best.

"Well, y'all," Bybee said, his tongue jammed into the side of his mouth, his voice slow and drawling, "ah know about ol' LeVar, about that shitpot full o' money." He turned and stooped over Gant, the pose and the false accent gone. "And I know, you little sawed-off piece of shit, about the fifty one-hundred-dollar bills."

Again, Gant and the judge were frozen in place, the only movement in the chambers coming from the smoke twisting up from the burning cigarette. Outside, in the other office, the secretary could be heard, chatting loudly with someone, then laughing.

And beyond her, in the courtroom, Bybee knew, all of the

other witnesses—Cynthia Hassert and Ordoñez and Sorenson and others—all waited, surrounded in the gallery by the drooling media, anxious to see firsthand a sacrifice, a gutting of another human being . . . of him.

"What do you want?" Rukamann finally said.

"Two things," Bybee said, inwardly shocked at how Atherton's words had worked. "First, Judge, you need to call off the governor's little lynch mob." He waved his hand toward the far wall, toward the courtroom. "Cancel this phony show-cause hearing or—"

"You arrogant shit!" Gant said. He stood up and pointed his finger at Bybee's face. "What gives you the fucking right to come in here—"

Bybee knocked the finger out of his face. "Sit down, Gant!" he said, and he reached out and, with both hands, gripped the smaller man at his elbows and seated him, firmly, like a child. "I don't have a right, but you set the rules, you greasy little turd, so I'm playing by them. See how *you* like it!"

It looked for a moment as if Gant would stand up again, but Rukamann waved his cigarette like a wand. "What do you want?" he said again.

Bybee turned back to the judge. "Cancel the hearing; call everything off."

Rukamann nodded, and then looked steadily at Gant. "All right."

Gant jerked sideways in his chair. "I'm going to have your fucking head—"

"And tell everyone sitting out there to go home," Bybee said, "except Cynthia Hassert. Ask her to come here, into your chambers. I need to talk to her"—he pointed at Gant, squirming in his chair—"and him. Alone."

It took several seconds for the judge to realize that he was being ordered out of his own chambers and sent on an errand, but he finally stubbed out the cigarette in the ashtray already heaped with butts, then rose. Gray ash fell from his robe as he moved from behind his desk, and he silently walked across the darkened office, the robe billowing out behind him like a cape.

He opened the door, and a wedge of light from the outer room struck Gant squarely in his blinking, angry eyes.

Bybee was not sure why, every time he was in Salt Lake City, he was drawn to Memory Grove. Certainly it was not because of the wretched war relics—the artillery pieces and the tanks, the hardware of destruction. No, it was something more; perhaps it was the feeling that something was amiss, that something in Memory Grove had been forgotten—himself, maybe, his own name on the innumerable lists of names of the war dead.

So he always prowled through Memory Grove and parks like it, reading those lists—some chiseled out of marble, others in raised metal letters—always carefully inspecting them, knowing that there had been a mistake, that the name "Brigham B. Bybee" had been submitted years before, but for some reason— an oversight, an error, some cosmic carelessness—had been left off.

He stood before a life-size bronze frieze of World War II soldiers—six of them, all helmeted, all with rifles slung across shoulders or hanging from their hands—and listened. He heard the sound of the motorcycle, and seconds later it appeared at the lower end of the park, near the street.

Kendall spurred the Yamaha between cement pylons designed to keep motor vehicles out of the park and guided the machine up the asphalted path, slowing, his left hand now raised in greeting. When he was a few feet from Bybee, he stopped, shut off the engine, and with an expert, practiced swing of his foot, dropped the side stand and let the machine lean.

Quickly he dismounted, pulled off his helmet and gloves, and laid them on the vinyl seat that, Bybee could see, was split and cracked, the foam rubber spilling out of it like yellow entrails.

"Brig," Kendall said. As always, he wore his leather coat and, under it, a white shirt and purple bow tie, and he stopped and posed—the inveterate thespian—and swept his arm in a circle, grinning. "Why the hell here?"

"Why the hell not?" Bybee said. "As good a place as any."

"For what?" Kendall said. He walked up to Bybee and extended his hand, but Bybee did not shake it. Kendall's weathered face grew serious, and he squinted at the other man. "What's this all about? You sounded weird on the phone."

"Sorry."

Kendall suddenly noticed Bybee's appearance, and he wrinkled his nose. "And you *look* weird. Christ Jesus, you were going to go like *that* to the Rocket Man's hearing?"

"If I had to . . . yes."

"Well, you're damned lucky he called it off. What in the hell is—"

"You killed Faith," Bybee said.

Kendall had been unzipping his jacket, struggling with it, but he stopped and gaped at Bybee. "What?"

"You heard me; you killed Faith."

Slowly, in silence, Kendall finished unzipping his jacket, took it off, and tossed it over his arm. Even in the bright sun, his face was dark, as though he stood in a shadow, and he leaned forward, his eyes narrowed.

"I don't like your new brand of humor, Brig."

"It's not humor. Far from it."

"Then you just better watch what you say."

"Or what?" Bybee said. "Or you'll take a gun and stick it in my ear and blow my brains out?"

Kendall took a step closer to Bybee so that their faces were only inches apart. "You're drunk, aren't you?" he said, and he laughed and tried to slap his friend on the arm, but Bybee dodged his hand. "See, Brig, I told you this sobriety shit wouldn't last."

"I'm not drunk," Bybee said, "but I wish to God I were. I just talked to Cynthia and Gant, in Rukamann's chambers."

"Cynthia . . . Hassert?"

"Yeah. She told me that she gave you specific orders, in

writing, a memo, not to bring Mercy to Manti—orders that you were supposed to relay to me."

Kendall shook his head and smiled. "I hope this is one of your dumb jokes."

"It's not," Bybee said. He could feel his hand begin to tremble, and he slid it into his front pocket. "Cynthia also told me how bad you wanted to prosecute Crowe. In fact, you wanted that case so bad that you threw a fucking tantrum in her office when she appointed me—not you—as special prosecutor."

Kendall frowned and held his hands out, palms upward. "She's a bitch, Brig, you know that," Kendall said, his resonant voice deeper now, slowing. "Christ Jesus, why don't you just tell me what the hell—"

"You were getting ready to go down the toilet unless you got that big pop. So when you heard that Crowe had cut off someone's head, it was *you* that had the orgasm, not Cynthia. You've always known that I hated the death penalty, so that was your big chance. If I opted out, then Cynthia would have to let you take the case."

Kendall made his eyes wide and spoke, sotto voce, to an unseen spectator. "The man has been watching *way* too much TV."

"I don't own a TV," Bybee said, "but I've been doing criminal law way too much, and I can spot a motive. You wanted me off the case and you on, so you told me it was clear to take Mercy to the safehouse—when it wasn't."

"I hope you're—"

"Then you called Gant and told him Mercy and I were on our way to Manti. He just told me that."

Kendall began putting on his jacket, slowly pushing his skinny arms through the sleeves. Behind him, on the street, a cement mixer rumbled by, its metal chute chattering, swinging dangerously from side to side.

"You know, Brig, this isn't funny anymore, so if you're through with the fun and games, then I've got to go."

"I'm not through, Tom. See, up till then, you'd done a pretty good job. You made sure that I disobeyed orders from the governor and Cynthia, and you got Gant screaming for my head. But that's where things went sour. When I decided that I'd stay on and prosecute Crowe and seek the big pop for myself, you lost it." He pointed a finger in the man's dark face. "You panicked."

Kendall finished zipping up his jacket, all the way to his wrinkled neck, so that he looked like an overdressed child, lost in the park. "Is that so?"

"Yeah," Bybee said. "You knew that Cynthia liked me, and I just might have convinced her that what Mercy was telling me was the truth . . . and that she would keep me on and fight for me with Gant and the governor." Bybee leaned forward and looked into Kendall's frightened face. "You panicked."

"Fuck you."

"You had to make sure I was an asshole, so you killed Faith to make it look as if, in addition to everything else, I had brought a contract killer right into a safehouse so she could gun down her target."

"Which is just what she did. The plig bitch was carrying a gun, Brig. Christ Jesus, get real!"

"I am. Mercy was wearing some pretty tight-fitting clothes that day; a gun would have been obvious. And—"

"The purse, Brig. You told me—"

"I talked to LaWanda Fae this morning. She checks all the women that come in—for drugs, mainly. Mercy didn't have a gun in her purse."

Kendall, stiff in his leather coat, turned his back on Bybee and looked out across Memory Grove at the rusted machines and crumbling monuments that poked up out of the weeds. Bybee watched him, waiting, feeling the horror that was gathering inside him, a black, deadening of his soul. Thirty years of facing clients and their extravagant egos, their angry claims or tearful denials, their dreadful explanations of why they were sitting or standing before a criminal lawyer, had taught him one thing. The truly innocent somehow proclaimed that innocence, in one way or another: they screamed or pounded on tables or, as Owen Parks had done in the Kanab jail a year ago, just lowered their heads and cried.

But in the last few minutes his friend had done none of that, not once, not even in a frightened, conspiratorial whisper.

Kendall suddenly turned back to Bybee and smiled. "You can't prove shit," he said.

The sickness now rose to Bybee's throat, and he swallowed it back. "Maybe not, but I know that the Manti police didn't issue their initial report on Faith's murder until nine-sixteen A.M. So no one, not the press, not anyone, knew anything until that time."

"So?"

"So, I ordered breakfast that same morning in Kanab at nine-thirty-three, and a minute later Sheriff Seegmiller came in with a message from you that said Faith had been murdered."

"So? I called you after the police called me."

"No, you didn't. Seegmiller told me you had been trying for about an hour to find me, which meant you were calling around eight-thirty, a good half-hour, maybe forty-five minutes, before the public—or you—should have known anything."

Kendall shook his head and smiled. "This is pretty weak shit, circumstantial shit. Anyway, the sheriff could be wrong, the report wrong."

"Maybe, but Poetry Bob, that street freak in Manti, said he saw you leave that day, right after I did. Then you came back, at night, on your motorcycle."

Kendall snorted again. "You told me to take care of Mercy; to keep Gant away from her. That's what I was doing. I wanted to make sure that the little turd wasn't still hanging around. I wanted—" Kendall suddenly stopped and swiped at the air, just in front of Bybee's face. "You know, Brig," he said, his voice low, with the theatrical buzz, "you would never have made it as a prosecutor. All you have is bullshit speculation and circumstantial evidence and some half-baked motive. A *real* prosecutor wouldn't play detective games like this. A real prosecutor would find the little cohab bitch that shot her whore sister wife. That's where you should start . . . you little Boy Scout! So in the meantime, leave me the fuck alone!"

Kendall pivoted on his heel, walked back to his motorcycle,

angrily jammed the helmet over his head, and stuffed his gloves into his coat pocket. He sat, his bony hands draped in front of him on the gas tank, as though his wrists were broken.

Bybee slowly walked over to the motorcycle and placed one hand atop the chromed tachometer. "I *have* found Mercy," he said. "And I know that she heard a voice—a man's voice—inside LaWanda Fae's house just before she heard a shot."

Kendall froze, and his eyes dropped to Bybee's hand resting on the tachometer, and then, with the back of his own hand, he knocked it away. "Keep your goddamned—"

"You have a distinctive voice, Tom, and you know a prosecutor—a *real* prosecutor—can make you say the Pledge of Allegiance or recite a poem at trial . . . anything, if he wants. It's not Fifth Amendment stuff. Mercy will identify your voice . . . identify you."

Kendall slowly reached up with his thin hand and dropped the helmet's shield so that Bybee could not see his face, leaving him to stare into the curved, mirrored plastic, seeing nothing but a distorted image of himself.

"Everything's so easy for you, isn't it, Brig?" Kendall said, but his voice behind the shield was muffled, nearly inaudible.

Bybee stepped away from the motorcycle as Kendall turned a key and pressed a button. The engine came to life, filling the quiet park with its growling, and in an instant Kendall had spun the machine around and was racing away down the narrow walkway.

Bybee watched him leave, watched until the big green helmet disappeared in the late-afternoon shade of the old houses just south of the park, and then he turned away and stared at the frieze of soldiers on the memorial, dead men who were marching toward him, demanding an answer that he could never give them.

16

IT was Doc Lundquist, M.D., a full-fledged "people doctor," and not Doc Durkee, D.V.M., the town's veterinarian, who had suggested to Bybee that Spooky Floyd's depression—and that was the word he had used, *depression*—could be relieved by basic exercise. Moping around a motel parking lot day after day, said Lundquist, who had brought half of Kanab's population into this world, would just not do. The poor creature needed aerobic conditioning, the doctor insisted; he needed to get out and walk, to trot, to chase rabbits or tease cows or to lope crazily through the canyons. Quite simply, the doctor said, the dog needed to go on a hike.

So that is what he did. Two days after the highway patrol had found the wreckage of the motorcycle and Kendall's nearly decapitated body near it, and one day after the Manti police secured fingerprints from the corpse and matched them to those found in Faith's bedroom, Bybee and Zolene and Mercy all went on a hike. In boots and jeans and T-shirts and ball caps—Mercy's outfit new, just purchased at Duke's—they set out from Lamb's house in the morning and tramped up the sunlit Flood

Canyon toward Johnson Lake. Behind them, poor, silent Spooky Floyd drearily slouched along, his head low, his tail nearly dragging through the rust-colored sand.

The group had to stop several times to allow Zolene to rest her leg, but eventually they reached the small, secluded lake, a peaceful place two and a half miles away, surrounded by white-and-red cliffs, and there, at the water's edge, under a tree, they tucked into the sandwiches and potato chips and sodas they had brought.

But Spooky Floyd, despite the doctor's theory, seemed as spiritless as ever, and he watched them from a distance, half hidden in the marshy weeds, muddy and tired . . . and still confused.

Hours later, with Spooky Floyd sprawled at their feet, spent, the three of them sat on the porch at Lamb's house, covered in pink dust, glasses of iced tea in their fists. They looked out toward Wester Lewis's house, across the fields of rich alfalfa where Heber Batt and the Batt boys were standing or bending in the bright sun, tinkering with their rusty Farm-All tractor.

They sat silently in the old metal chairs, Bybee between the two women, listening to the birds chatter in the orchard, soaking up the canyon's calm, the soothing beauty of it . . . its timelessness.

"What time is it?" Zolene said. She wore a yellow T-shirt that read PIUTE VILLA across the front, and a zippered nylon pouch was still strapped to her waist.

Bybee looked at his watch. "Almost three," he said. "He should be here in a few minutes."

Bybee turned and looked at Mercy, at her new clothes, the blue T-shirt with the five-ringed Olympic logo stretched out along her bosom. Her face had almost healed, but her eyes still looked sore, tired—lost—and the film of dust from the hike seemed to accent the tiny wrinkles at their edges, making her look much older than she was. At her feet, near the exhausted dog, the leather purse that LaWanda Fae had returned leaned against an overnight bag that Zolene had stuffed with clothes and toiletries she had bought for Mercy at Duke's, and draped over it all was the monstrous, oversize sport coat.

"You have everything?" Bybee said, then smiled, embarrassed. Mercy had arrived two weeks ago with nothing, only her purse.

"Yes," she said.

Zolene turned and put her hand on the other woman's arm. "I want you to write to us, Mercy. I mean it. To Brig and me. Tell us how you're doing up there in"—she shook her head, spilling the red hair everywhere—"I forgot the name—"

"Packston," Mercy said, and she smiled. "Don't worry, my mother will make sure I write."

Bybee glanced quickly at Zolene. It had been last night, here, in Lamb's house, that Mercy had cried, confessing that she had lied—lied about many things—blurting out that only her father had passed away, but that her mother, a woman who had desperately been trying to lure her daughter out of New Ammon for years, was still alive . . . and still waiting.

Zolene gripped Mercy's arm. "Well, you take care of yourself."

"I will."

They sat in silence for a while, hearing the stubborn tractor finally come to life in the fields, the engine popping, and over it, a faint cheer from the Batt boys.

Mercy sipped at her tea, then turned her head. "Mr. Bybee, what's going to happen to . . . Father?"

"You mean to Crowe?" Bybee said. He stared steadily into her face. "To Rampton Crowe?"

Mercy swallowed and nodded her head. "Yes, to . . . . Rampton."

Over the past few days, as everyone had collected themselves, as the chaos drained away and their respective worlds were slowly being set aright, they had only briefly, and delicately, talked of Crowe and New Ammon. But she had to know the truth about him, the truth about everything.

"He's in jail, Mercy," Bybee said. "Along with Griffity and a few others. Sheriff Seegmiller and the highway patrol found the bodies of Franklin Pugh and Koyle Fenton. Crowe's been charged with murder. He's going to be prosecuted."

Mercy looked helplessly at him. "Are you the one that's going to—"

"No," Bybee said, and he emphatically shook his head. "I'm through being a prosecutor." He smiled at Zolene. "It was a bad idea to begin with."

"Is Rampton going to prison?"

Bybee glanced uneasily at Zolene. "Yes. For a long time. The rest of his life, probably."

Mercy bowed her head, and her lips began to tremble. "Oh, Merciful Christs."

"Mercy," Bybee said, and he put his hand on hers. "There aren't really two—"

But he stopped; she would not understand, and at any rate, perhaps there *were* two Christs, maybe two dozen, maybe thousands of them . . . or maybe no Christ at all.

"He's coming," Mercy said.

She pointed, and they all looked out across the bright fields, near Dishpan, at the plume of pink dust behind a truck that was speeding down the road.

Mercy watched the truck, then stared at Spooky Floyd. "Mr. Bybee," she said. "What about the other . . . wives? My sister wives?"

"They'll be okay," Bybee said. "The state will probably help them out a little, get them . . ." He shook his head. "I really don't know; it's up to them, really. But they'll be okay. I feel it."

"I guess things are going to be a lot different in New Am'," Mercy said. "After all this, I mean."

"Probably not," Bybee said. "Things haven't changed around here for a hundred and fifty years, so there's no reason they're going to change now. The Principle might be here to stay, Mercy. Nothing can touch it."

"Well," she said, "I guess the Principle is—"

She stopped, and Bybee and Zolene waited, waited to hear a plural wife finally denounce the practice of polygamy, to condemn the perversion and sickness that had haunted her life and others, driving them into the shadows.

"—is the way of the world," Mercy finished.

Bybee began to say something, but he heard the growl of an engine on the far side of the orchard, sending the birds squawking out of the apple trees. In a few seconds Atherton's dented truck appeared, and out the side window, his pudgy, jeweled hand was waving in the air.

Almost as one, the three of them set aside their iced tea and stood up, and even Spooky Floyd, recognizing that some momentous human event was occurring, struggled upright onto his haunches.

Mercy leaned over and lightly kissed Bybee on the cheek. "Good-bye," she said, and then she turned and hugged Zolene and drew back. "Good-bye," she said again. "And thank you. Both of you."

Atherton had stopped his truck, but his fleshy hand was still jutting out the window, upraised. Mercy waved back at him and began to pick up her bag and purse and the big coat, but she stopped when she saw Spooky Floyd staring at her. She dropped her things and reached down and lightly patted the dog on the head.

"And good-bye to you, too," she said.

At her touch, Spooky Floyd's tail, forever limp, forever a sad symbol of his mysterious life, began to twitch, and after a moment it actually wagged, thumping against the porch floor. Then he raised his muzzle, strained, his eyes bulging . . . and he barked—a single, hoarse yelp out into the canyon.

"Jeez," Zolene said.

They all laughed, and Spooky Floyd, as though he finally understood it all, barked again, louder now.

REFLECTIONS

OF A JACOBITE

LOUIS AUCHINCLOSS

Reflections
of a Jacobite

1 9 6 1

The Riverside Press Cambridge

HOUGHTON MIFFLIN COMPANY
BOSTON

For Father and Mother

on their golden wedding anniversary

April 19, 1961

with all my love and gratitude and admiration

Acknowledgments

"Edith Wharton and Her New Yorks" and "Proust's Picture of Society" have previously appeared in *Partisan Review.*

"The Novel of Manners Today: Marquand and O'Hara" and "A Reader's Guide to the Fiction of Henry James" first appeared in *The Nation.*

Foreword

I HAVE CALLED myself a Jacobite because so much of my lifetime's reading has been over the shoulder of Henry James. To follow the opinions scattered through his criticism, his letters, his memoirs, even his travel pieces, is to be conducted through the literature of his time, English, American, French and Russian, by a kindly guide of infinitely good manners, who is also infinitely discerning, tasteful and conscientious. It does not really matter whether one always agrees with him, whether, for example, one finds the Russian novels "fluid pudding" or Robert Louis Stevenson the first English writer of the nineties. All that matters is the prolonged opportunity to consider the fiction of his contemporaries through the clear eyes of a master novelist to whom the art of constructing stories was always a desperately serious one. James's long life, to a degree rare even among creative writers, was dedicated to and saturated in literature, from that early day in Washington Square, when a huge, benevolent Thackeray, calling on his father, had boomed down: "Come here, little boy, and show me your extraordinary jacket!" to the time, almost seventy years later, when Edith Wharton sent him *Swann's Way*, and he knew at once that they had turned a page in the history of the novel.

I do not profess in this little book to study James as a critic, or even, except briefly, as a novelist. It is rather that he provides me with my starting point and my common denominator. If it were not presumptuous, I would call him my master of ceremonies. Of the authors whom I discuss, he was a close friend of Edith Wharton and Paul Bourget, a good friend of Daudet and Meredith, a familiar acquaintance of Trollope and George Eliot, and, as a child, had been called "Buttons" by Thackeray himself. It is not clear that he ever knew Proust, though Lucien Daudet remembered a lunch in Paris where both were present. I have added a few authors unknown to James, but wherever possible, I have left it to the master to make my introductions.

I want to offer my thanks to Leon Edel, the unquestioned authority on James's life and letters, and indeed on all of the master's work, for his kind help in supplying me with information and suggestions. I am but an acolyte at the altar where he is high priest.

LOUIS AUCHINCLOSS

Contents

REFLECTIONS

OF A JACOBITE

Early Reading and Alphonse Daudet

F OR A PERSON who has derived so much of his pleasure in life reading novels, I came to it surprisingly late. It was not until my war service in the Navy that I began to read fiction in any quantity with no aim but that of enjoying it. It was escapism, of course, the sheerest escapism, but who but a Churchill would not be an escapist in wartime? As I look back on those long years in the Atlantic and Pacific, the oceans seem linked in my mind by the isthmus of the Victorian novel. I associate the atolls of Ulithi and Eniwetok with Barsetshire and Mrs. Proudie and the amphibious-training base at Camp Bradford, Virginia, with *The Spoils of Poynton*. Nothing else stood by me so well in that time of spasmodic anxiety and prolonged boredom.

It was not, of course, that I began to read in the war, but that I began to enjoy reading. At boarding school I considered myself very literary indeed, but I cannot recall much actual pleasure from books. I read for marks. So serious a business was not to be confused with anything as trivial as pleasure. I burned to make up in academic pre-eminence what I lacked in athletic prowess and popularity, and I looked on books as mere rungs in the ladder of fame, much as a man in the Middle Ages, discouraged with his prospects on the battlefield, might look to a church career for political advancement. The pages of Dickens and Thackeray existed only to be squeezed through the mental grinder that would turn them into grades. My teachers made efforts to improve my standard of values, but what can adults accomplish against the obsessions of a boy? It took a world conflagration to teach me what books were for.

My first glimmering, however, that the reading of fiction might play a nonutilitarian role came before the war, at Yale, in a French course. I do not mean to disparage my English professors, who were all gifted men, but the identification between Shakespeare and the Phi Beta Kappa key was too close to my heart for them to unravel. The French novel, on the other hand, except for *Colomba* and *Le Crime de Sylvestre Bonnard*, was unknown to me until Joseph Seronde's lectures in nineteenth century French literature. Balzac and Stendhal had not been confused with my personal ambition, and I was fascinated to learn how passionately the French public had sided for or against the new trends of the century: romanticism, naturalism, realism. It was my first glimpse of a society where literature was the concern of someone besides teachers and students. I had been brought up to view the world as a more serious affair. I could not imagine my own father or the fathers of any of my friends donning red vests at the opening of *Hernani*. My mother used even to ridicule a college education that consisted so largely of reading novels. It was not that she disapproved of novels — she was and is a voracious reader of them — but she believed that they were intended to provide diversion rather than education. She thought that courses for young men who would have to live in a troubled world should be in science or philosophy or economics. I could and still can understand her point of view. It does seem a bit curious to have to "study" such thrillers as *Jane Eyre* or *Tess of the d'Urbervilles*. But the fact remains that the reading taste established by Joseph Seronde was the most concrete thing that I bore away from Yale and that it has given me more lasting pleasure than I can possibly imagine that I would have received from any course in economics. Yale and French nineteenth century literature will always be bracketed in my mind.

The novel, despite its author's declining reputation, that made the deepest impression on me in sophomore year was *Fromont Jeune et Risler Aîné*. I suppose that no one would rank Daudet today with Flaubert or the Goncourts or Zola, who were in life his friends and admirers. He is among the great casualties of our era, like George Eliot and Howells. But some casualties are caused simply by the growing bulk of our literature. It is impossible to admire every novelist who is admirable. If a writer survives, we keep all of him; we save *The Sacred Fount* with James and *Titus Andronicus* with Shakespeare. We write learned theses in defense of minor works and reprint them with enticing paper covers. But when a writer falls from grace, we tend to pitch all his books after him, except in rare cases like *Cranford* or *Lorna Doone*. It seems a pity that the best of Daudet should be less read than the least of Stendhal.

Fromont came to me at a good time, for I was reacting against an overdose of Dickens. Daudet is a softer, mellower Dickens; there is less smell of grease paint, less glare of footlights. His characters are never so exaggerated, for they are not creatures of fantasy but faithful reproductions of persons whom Daudet saw or knew. I imagine that every eccentric whom Dickens observed suggested an even greater eccentric to his imagination, while Daudet was content with the limitations of his model. Sometimes too content. He and his literary group made a fetish of accuracy in observed details. In his memoirs he relates that while writing *Fromont* he was warned that Dickens had already "done" a crippled doll dresser in *Our Mutual Friend*. For days he roamed the Marais, climbing stairways to look at signs, until he came upon the notice OISEAUX ET MOUCHES POUR MODES, and knew at once Désirée Delobelle's new trade. Daudet made less effort to conceal his sources of inspiration than any novelist before Thomas Wolfe. "It is sometimes a weakness of mine," he wrote, "to leave to my models their real names, and to persuade myself that were the name transformed, it would take away something from the integrity of the creation." One understands why he had so much trouble with his friends.

Fromont is full of the working life of the faubourgs, the straight smoke of the factories, the call bells, the rumble of vans and the rattle of handcarts, the noise of workmen entering and leaving the mills. Daudet, for all the meticulousness of his research, paints his final picture with the brush of a contemporary impressionist. Yet behind the dust and roar of a mercantile Paris one has a sense of beauty and romance ready to burst out, like tough weeds between the cobblestones. Désirée may never leave her attic room where she models birds and flies for fashionable bonnets, but she has the image of Franz Risler to which she can escape, as the tradesmen escape on Sunday to a countryside of grass and flowers. The novel is richly, unabashedly sentimental, but it was a sentimentality that hit me just right in sophomore year. Perhaps I associated the Marais with the somber ugliness of an industrial New Haven and the bleakness of warehouses and machinery sheds by a grey, wintry Long Island Sound. And perhaps I found Daudet's alleviating sense of romance in the melancholy moodiness of nineteen.

I will admit that I have not found quite the same satisfaction in the other volumes of the *Moeurs Parisiennes*, read in later years. It seems to me that their plots are too rambling, their heroes too crushed by circumstance. And when I last turned back to *Fromont*, I wondered if I would find it like the others, beautiful but damp. I wondered how much of my early enthusiasm had been due to youth, and I remembered Proust's warning never to reread one's old favorites, but simply to finger the old editions and evoke the memories with which they are associated. I decided, however, to take the risk, and I was rewarded. After twenty years I found the old charm still there, and the struggle between the good and wicked forces over the paper factory as entrancing as ever.

The factory, around which the plot revolves, is in the Marais, closely hemmed in by shops and tenements. Near it is the elegant residence and garden of the proprietor. The different social strata of the industry are thus brought into the closest juxtaposition: the factory and house, symbols, respectively, of the production of money and its expenditure, become the center of a staring, envious world that has too much to do with the first and too little with the second. Risler, a good man, has eyes only for the factory where he hopes to obtain a modest success by hard toil, but Sidonie Chèbe sighs yearningly over the house and garden which she plans, at any cost, to make her own. Thus the basic conflict is announced, between those who recognize the true function of industry and those who hanker only for its fruits, between the workers and the parasites. When Risler and Sidonie marry, as they do in the very first chapter, there is a fusion of the two ambitions, the good and the bad.

The good will win out, but it will *just* win out. That is what happens in Daudet. The factory will manage to survive the ultimate exposure and humiliation of Sidonie, but Désirée and Risler will be suicides, and Claire Fromont will know her husband for the sorry creature that he is. The cancer is excised, and the victim will live, but the house of Fromont Jeune and Risler Aîné may expect some rocky months and years to come.

Of course it is a melodramatic tale. Of course it is sentimental. There are passages about Désirée as florid as anything Dickens wrote about Little Nell. But I still find it honest. Claire Fromont may be described as a real and Sidonie as a false pearl, but Claire is by no means the faultless heroine that she might have been, conceived across the Channel. Claire's obsessive concern with her little daughter is one of the reasons for her husband's derelictions, as Risler's obstinate immersion in his business is one for Sidonie's. The good people in Daudet are to blame for their willful blindness; they invite betrayal like those who leave open purses about. Risler, particularly, seems almost to deserve his wretched fate. He forfeits our sympathy by his gullibility until he rises to his magnificent revenge. When he looms up at Sidonie's party and thunders: "Madame Risler!", when he throws her and her jewels at Claire's feet and forces her to crave the pardon of her bitterest enemy, is it splendid drama? Or is it corn?

How can one always tell? When I read, as one so often does, of the "nature of evil" in modern fiction, I wonder if it is a complex or a very simple idea. Sometimes there is a good deal of obfuscating discussion of white whales or the ghosts of governesses and valets, but sometimes, also, the critic seems to find the evil just where one might expect to find it — in selfish, dissipated characters. Might I not then assert that Daudet is interested in the nature of evil? Might it not serve to revive his old popularity? But I doubt it. Daudet tried too hard to please. As James says:

> There is something very hard, very dry, in Flaubert, in Edmond de Goncourt, in the robust Zola; but there is something very soft in Alphonse Daudet. "Benevolent nature," says Zola, "has placed him at the exquisite point where poetry ends and reality begins." This is happily said; Daudet's great characteristic is this mixture of the sense of the real with the sense of the beautiful.

Daudet leads his reader through a wilderness which his prose turns into a garden. He tried to be as good a realist as his friends, the Goncourts, and indeed, much of his subject matter is as unlovely to the eye and nose. The hero of *Jack*, chronically drunk and coughing out his lungs in the boiler room of a ship, or the prostitute in *Sapho*, turning into an unkempt harridan, are as minutely observed as the alcoholic doctor of *Soeur Philomène* or the disintegrating chambermaid of *Germinie Lacerteux*. But Daudet is not so stern about his art; he is not so anxious to show off the accuracy of his note-taking. He did not believe that suffering exists only to be described by writers of the naturalist school. Daudet loved Paris, even the poorest sections of it. He did not have to escape, like the Goncourts, when not engaged in naturalist fiction, into boudoir history of the eighteenth century. He did not need the fantasy life of making inventories of the bric-à-brac of Madame de Pompadour or Madame du Barry. Even Flaubert went from Madame Bovary to the exotic scenes of ancient Carthage. When Daudet needed the picturesque, he brought his *Nabob* to the Paris of his own time. And when he took his readers on excursions to scenes of injustice and suffering, he brought a heart that, however sentimental, had still its core of true feeling. He believed that it was the function of a guide to entertain as well as instruct. But I wonder if modern readers are not more in the mood of the Goncourts. I doubt if they want their wildernesses tampered with. They pay, after all, for the "real thing."

Edith Wharton and Her New Yorks

T HE CORRESPONDENCE, and, no doubt, the conversations between Henry James and Edith Wharton, were carried on in the happy tone of hyperbole. It was the pose of each to appear to grovel obsequiously before the other's superiority. She professed to regard him as the master of her art, the wise, benignant guide and mentor, while he likened her to a golden eagle with a beautiful genius for great globe adventures, at whose side he was nothing but "a poor old croaking barnyard fowl." "I have simply lain stretched," he wrote her, on hearing of a motor trip in Tunisia, "a faithful old veteran slave, upon the door-mat of your palace of adventure." Yet, as is often the case in such relationships, beneath the elaborate encomiums lay a vein of hidden mockery, almost, at times, of smugness. He really thought that she was dissipating her energy and talents, while she never doubted that he was hoarding his. And neither appreciated the other's best work.

She found his later novels "more and more lacking in atmosphere, more and more severed from that thick nourishing human air in which we all live and move." Everything in them had to be fitted into a predestined design, and design, to Edith Wharton, was "one of the least important things in fiction." James, on the other hand, found her at her best when most under his influence, and considered her finest work that mild little tale, *The Reef*, where a group of sensitive, cultivated expatriates in a French château are reduced to quiet desperation by the discovery that one of them has had an affair with the governess. There are passages that read like a parody of James himself:

"I want to say — Owen, you've been admirable all through."

He broke into a laugh in which the odd elder-brotherly note was once more perceptible.

"Admirable," she emphasized. "And so has *she*."

"Oh, and so have you to *her!*" His voice broke down to boyishness.

Yet the master found it all of a "psychological Racinian unity, intensity and gracility." The only thing that he questioned was why the characters, all American, should have elected to have their story carried out in France, and he warned her of the dangers of living abroad, with a wry little touch of humor at his own expense:

> Your only drawback is not having the homeliness and the inevitability and the happy limitation and the affluent poverty, of a Country of your Own (*comme moi, par exemple*)!

It was not the first time that he had sounded this warning. Ten years earlier, in 1902, he had written to her sister-in-law that she should be "tethered in native pastures, even if it reduces her to a backyard in New York." Viewed from the vantage point of today, with all of Mrs. Wharton's later novels before us that James never saw, the danger against which he warned her seems painfully obvious. It is difficult to read those slick satires about an America that she rarely bothered to visit without reflecting that she appeared, at the end, to have lost not only her country but her talent. What is curious, therefore, is that James should have foreseen this so clearly and yet should not have fully appreciated how much in 1902, and even as late as 1912, she still *had* a country, or at least a city, of her own. He may have been too out of touch with New York to appreciate how much she still belonged to it. Her ties, of course, were stronger than his. She had been brought up in the city and had married there. She had experienced its social life, in greater doses than she had wanted. She knew its men and women of property; she knew their history and their origins, their prejudices and ideals, the source of their money and how they spent their summers. This knowledge, of course, was eventually to fade with her continued residence abroad, but the ten years that preceded the first war were actually the years when her American impressions were at their most vivid and when she was doing her strongest work. It was the period of *The House of Mirth* and *The Custom of the Country*, the period when, true to her own vocation, she became the interpreter of certain aspects of New York life that she was uniquely qualified to describe.

The thing that was going on in Mrs. Wharton's New York of this period, and which she chose as the subject of her main study, was the assault upon an old and conservative group by the multitudes enriched, and fabulously enriched, by the business expansion of the preceding decades. The New York of the pre-assault era was the New York that she was later and nostalgically to describe in *The Age of Innocence*, the town of sober brownstone houses with high stoops, of an Academy of Music with shabby red and gold boxes, of long midday lunches with madeira, of husbands who never went "downtown," of a sense of precedence that was military in its strictness. As she tells us in her autobiography, when her grandmother's carriage appeared on Fifth Avenue those of her aunts maintained their proper distance in the rear. To this New York belong such of her characters as Mrs. Peniston, Lawrence Selden, the Peytons, the Dagonets, the Marvells, the van der Luydens. It was a city that was worldly beyond a doubt, but worldly with a sense of order and form, with plenty of leisure time in which art, music and literature could play a moderated role. The people from this world may lack strength of character, but their inertia is coupled with taste and observation, as seen in Lawrence Selden's parents:

> Neither one of the couple cared for money, but their disdain of it took the form of always spending a little more than was prudent. If their house was shabby, it was exquisitely kept; if there were good books on the shelves there were also good dishes on the table. Selden senior had an eye for a picture, his wife an understanding of old lace; and both were so conscious of restraint and discrimination in buying that they never quite knew how it was that the bills mounted up.

The young men practice law in a listless sort of way with much time for dining at clubs and trips to Europe. They have a settled sense of how their lives are to be led and no idea of impending change. The change, if change it really is, comes with the infiltration of the other protagonists of the drama, the Spraggs, the Wellington Brys, the Gormers, Sim Rosedale, the Van Osburghs, the Bryces, people who can spend a thousand dollars to Mrs. Peniston's one. Their assault on the brownstone citadel of old New York and its rapid capitulation provide a study of conflicting and ultimately reconciled types of snobbishness. The reconciliation is not altogether a surprise, for snobs *can* usually be reconciled. The old society may have had a brittle and varnished shell, but it covered a materialism as rampant as that of the richest parvenu. It could only be a matter of time before the new money was made to feel at home. Mrs. Wharton anticipated Proustian distinctions in her analysis of the different layers of the social hierarchy, but it is a dreary picture unrelieved by a Swann or a Charlus. From the top to the bottom of *The House of Mirth*, from Judy Trenor and "Bellomont," down through the pushing Brys and the false bohemianism of Mattie Gormer, to the "vast, gilded" hotel life of Norma Hatch, the entire fabric revolves around money.

Conflict is lost in fusion, which brings us to the deeper drama of *The House of Mirth*, the drama not of rival classes who drown their feud in noisy merger, but of their victims, those poor beings who are weak enough to care for the luxury, but too squeamish to play the game as roughly as it must be played. Lily Bart, of course, is the most famous of these. We see her first at the age of twenty-nine, beautiful, vivid but tired, regaining behind a veil that "purity of tint" that she is beginning to lose "after years of late hours and indefatigable dancing," waiting in Grand Central "in the act of transition between one and another of the country houses that dis-

puted her presence at the close of the Newport season."
But we are soon made aware of the sea of unpaid bills
and small favors in which she precariously floats. Lily
suffers from the paralysis of inertia. It is not that she is
unaware of the void that gapes before her; it is rather
that she has too much delicacy and sensitivity, that she is
too much of a lady to make the kind of marriage that will
save her from the fate of turning gradually from a guest
into a hanger-on. Her father has been of old New York,
but her mother, one gathers, is of more ordinary material, and it has been the latter's greed that has driven
him to make the fortune that he is bound, by the same
web of fate that enmeshes his daughter, to lose. So Lily
is of both worlds; she understands both, and, before she
has done, she has slipped between them and fallen pros-
trate beneath their stamping feet. The pathos of her fall
is that the failure to act which precipitates each stage of
her descent does not come from any superiority of moral
resolution but rather from a refinement of taste, a fas-
tidiousness, of which neither her meticulous aunt, Mrs.
Peniston, nor her coarse admirer, Mr. Rosedale, have the
remotest understanding. Indeed, one feels that Lily Bart,
in all New York, is the lone and solitary lady. Yet with
each slip in the ladder she experiences the coarsening that
comes with the increased sense of the necessity of holding on, and though she can never bring herself to tell
George Dorset of his wife's infidelity, even to win the
town's richest husband and triumph over her most vin-

dictive opponent, she can ultimately face the prospect of marriage with Sim Rosedale as a way of getting the money to pay a debt of honor. And when she does stoop it is too late; even Sim Rosedale won't have her, and Lily takes the final drop to the milliner's shop and ultimately to the overdose of sleeping tablets.

In *The Custom of the Country* Mrs. Wharton is again dealing with the conflict of materialisms, but this time the central study is of a parvenu, Undine Spragg, who cuts her way to the top of the heap. Her victim — for there is always a victim — is a man. Ralph Marvell is self-consciously of "aboriginal New York"; his forebears whose tradition he can never forget have been "small, cautious, middle-class" in their ideals, with "a tranquil disdain for money-getting" and "a passive openness to the finer sensations." But Ralph has just enough curiosity to be interested in "the invaders," as he calls the new rich; with cultivated decadence he finds an essential simplicity in their acquisitiveness. His cousin, Clare, another victim, has married invader Peter Van Degen and learned to repent, "but she repented in the Van Degen diamonds, and the Van Degen motor bore her broken heart from opera to ball." Ralph sees it all clearly, but he is to be different. He is to save the "innocence" of the Spraggs; he is to keep *them* from corruption. He goes down to speedy ruin before Undine, and his suicide is almost a matter of course. The victim, however, is too naïve; one's sympathy is confounded with impatience. It is Undine's book; her victims are incidental. She is the personification of the newcomer, absolutely vulgar and absolutely ruthless. Everything happens to Undine, but nothing affects her. She marries once for money, a second time for family and a third time for money again, only to find in the end that her divorces will keep her from being an ambassadress. And that, of course, is the only thing that she ultimately wants.

The Custom of the Country appeared in 1913, and the next four years Mrs. Wharton devoted entirely to war work. Her main job was with the Red Cross in Paris, but she visited military hospitals at the front and from a cottage garden at Clermont-en-Argonne she witnessed the victorious French assault on the heights of Vauquois. But the "fantastic heights and depths of self-devotion and ardor, of pessimism, triviality and selfishness," as she describes the war years, did little more for her as a writer than they have done, in either war, for many others. Their most important effect was to introduce a note of nostalgia, an escape, as she describes it, to childhood memories of a long-vanished America, to the "mild blur of rosy and white-whiskered gentlemen, of ladies with bare sloping shoulders rising flower-like from voluminous skirts, peeped at from the stair-top while wraps were removed in the hall below." But this was the New York, was it not, that she had found so stuffy and confining, that she had shown in losing battle with the Spraggs and Rosedales and from which she had fled to Europe? It was a New York, was it not, that had been passive, inert, confining, a city that had almost deserved to be eaten up by the new money of the energetic parvenu? Now, however, that it was gone, really gone, she found herself looking about and wondering if she had not gone too far in its condemnation. Much later she was to confess:

> When I was young it used to seem to me that the group in which I grew up was like an empty vessel into which no new wine would ever again be poured. Now I see that one of its uses lay in preserving a few drops of an old vintage too rare to be savored by a youthful palate.

Out of this sense of apology came *The Age of Innocence*. It deals with a New York that is pre-Spragg and pre-Rosedale. Newbold Archer is the young Whartonian of brownstone lineage, the Marvell type, a lawyer, of course, with a leisurely practice and an eye for books and pictures. He marries conventionally, and the story of the book is that he does *not* leave his wife to go off with the Countess Olenska, New York born but emancipated. There is no feeling, however, that Archer has condemned himself and the Countess to an unrewarding life of frustration. The author is absorbed in the beauty of rules and forms even when they stamp out spontaneity. "It was you," the Countess tells Archer, "who made me understand that under the dullness there are things so fine and sensitive and delicate that even those I most

cared for in my other life look cheap in comparison."
This is the climax of the message: that under the thick
glass of convention blooms the fine, fragile flower of
patient suffering and denial. To drop out of society is
as vulgar as to predominate; one must endure and properly smile.

The novel, however, despite its note of calm resignation and sacrifice, is pervaded with a sense of materialism. The presence of "things" clogs even the best of
Mrs. Wharton's writing. The author of *The House of
Mirth* was also the author of *The Decoration of Houses*.
One feels the charm of Ellen Olenska, but one feels it
too much in her taste and possessions: "some small slender
tables of dark wood, a delicate little Greek bronze in the
chimney piece, and a stretch of red damask nailed on the
discolored wallpaper behind a couple of Italian-looking
pictures in old frames." She has "only two" Jacqueminot
roses in a slender vase, and her tea is served "with handle-
less Japanese cups and little covered dishes." She finds a
friend in Philistia; he understands Europe, and their refuge is in the arts, but their talk is filled with references to
private rooms at Delmonico's and "little oyster suppers."
Even in her moment of greatest emotional strain,
when she looks at her watch she looks at a "little gold-
faced watch on an enameled chain." The vigor of the
earlier books is largely gone, but the sense of the world
remains.

It was now that Edith Wharton found herself at the

crossroads. She could have continued in the nostalgic vein of *The Age of Innocence* and tethered herself, in James's phrase, to the native pastures of her early memories. The tendency might have been toward the sentimental, but the result could have had the charm of remembered things. One can see this in the little series known as *Old New York*. But, unfortunately, she chose for her major efforts the contemporary scene, especially the American scene, although it was a decade since she had crossed the Atlantic to revisit her native shores. Older and shriller, she denounced the vulgarity that she was now beginning to find in everything, judging America, the country in her eyes most responsible, by the standards of Riviera expatriates whom she did not even know.

The vulgarity on which she had declared war ended by overwhelming her novels. Taste, the chosen guide of her later years, went back on her. In the final dissolution, as with the Barts and Rosedales, conflict is again lost in merger. The very titles of the later books betray the drop of her standards; they are flat and ugly: *Human Nature, The Mother's Recompense, Twilight Sleep, The Glimpses of the Moon*. The caricature of American life becomes grotesque. The towns are given names like Delos, Aeschylus, Lohengrin or Halleluja, and the characters speak an anglicized dialect full of such terms as "Hang it!", "Chuck it!", "He's a jolly chap" and "A fellow needs . . ." The town slogan of Euphoria in *Hudson*

River Bracketed is "Me for the front row." And the
American face! How it haunts her! It is "as unexpres-
sive as a football"; it might have been made by "a manu-
facturer of sporting goods." Its sameness encompasses
her "with its innocent uniformity." How many of such
faces would it take "to make up a single individuality"?
And, ironically enough, as her indignation mounts her
style loses its old precision and begins to take on the
slickness of a popular magazine story. Compare, for example, these two descriptions of a lady on the threshold
of a European hotel. The first is from *Madame de
Treymes,* written in 1907, one of her Jamesian passages,
but highly polished:

> The mere fact of her having forgotten to draw
> on her gloves as they were descending in the hotel
> lift from his mother's drawing room was, in this
> connection, charged with significance to Durham.
> She was the kind of woman who always presents
> herself to the mind's eye as completely equipped,
> as made of exquisitely cared for and finely related
> details; and that the heat of her parting with his
> family should have left her unconscious that she was
> emerging gloveless into Paris seemed, on the whole,
> to speak hopefully for Durham's future opinion of
> the city. Even now, he could detect a certain con-
> fusion, a desire to draw breath and catch up with
> her life, in the way she dawdled over the last but-

tons in the dimness of the porte-cochère, while her footman, outside, hung on her retarded signal.

The second is from *The Glimpses of the Moon*, fifteen years later:

> But on the threshold a still more familiar figure met her: that of a lady in exaggerated pearls and sables, descending from an exaggerated motor, like the motors in magazine advertisements, the huge arks in which jeweled beauties and slender youths pause to gaze at snow peaks from an Alpine summit.

Specimens of old New York in the novels now become spindly and ridiculous, like Mr. Wyant in *Twilight Sleep* and Mr. Spears in *Hudson River Bracketed*. The Wheaters in *The Children* are meant to be rich New Yorkers traveling in Europe. Their children, of various nationalities, their absurd marital mix-up, their impossible, red-carpeted, be-yachted life, with a movie star ex-wife whose favorite swear word is "Fudge!" and an American-born princess who hopes that the size of families will be regulated by legislation, constitute a grotesque parody of international drifters. Mrs. Wharton has no true insight into their lives; she stands apart like her spokesman, Mrs. Sellars, in disdain, describing the Wheaters only in terms of snobbish and disapproving suppositions.

Eventually there seemed to be no aspect of American

life that did not disgust her. It was not only the vulgar rich; there were also the vulgar intellectuals. This passage from *The Gods Arrive* is meant to represent a conversation between young American writers in Paris:

"Poor old Fynes," another of them took it up, "sounded as if he'd struck a new note because he made his people talk in the vernacular. Nothing else new about *him* — might have worked up his method out of Zola. Probably did."

"Zola — who's he?" somebody yawned.

"Oh, I dunno. The French Thackeray, I guess."

"See here, fellows, who's read Thackeray, anyhow?"

"Nobody since Lytton Strachey, I guess."

"Well, anyway, 'This Globe' is one great big book. Eh, Vance, that the way you see it?"

Vance roused himself and looked at the speaker. "Not the way I see life. Life's continuous!"

"Life continuous — continuous? Why, it's a series of jumps in the dark. That's Mendel's law, anyhow," another budding critic took up the argument.

"Gee! Who's Mendel? Another new novelist?"

The meeting between Mrs. Wharton and Scott Fitzgerald, as described by Arthur Mizener, is symptomatic of her uneasy relationships with the younger generation of writers. She found him crude, and he found her stiff and superior. But behind his sophomoric urge to shock a strait-laced old lady, lurked intense admiration and curiosity. He confessed once, half seriously, to Margaret Chanler that he had three ambitions in life: to write the best and clearest prose of the twentieth century, to remain faithful to Zelda and to become an intimate friend of Mrs. Wharton. Mrs. Chanler's response was the same that her friend Edith might have made: "As to your first ambition, I hope you attain it. As to your second, it is too personal for me to comment on. But as to your third, young man, you'll have to cut down your drinking!"

As with so many who seem proud and stiff, Mrs. Wharton's real trouble lay in shyness. She described it to Adèle Burden as the "dread disease" that had martyrized her in youth. She had finally come to terms with the world of her contemporaries, and it may have seemed too much to have to fight that battle with a new generation. She resented the formlessness of a world that seemed to have repudiated the very formalities that she had once satirized. When *The Mother's Recompense* was misunderstood by critics, she was deeply discouraged by the "densities of comprehension" that surrounded her. She wrote to Mrs. Chanler:

> You will wonder that the priestess of the life of reason should take such things to heart, and I wonder too. I never have minded before, but as my work reaches its close, I feel so sure that it is either

nothing, or far more than they know. And I wonder, a little desolately, which?

In 1937, the year in which she died, Mrs. Wharton was working on a novel that shows a brief, renewed interest in the New York of her childhood from which she drew *The Age of Innocence*. This is the posthumously published fragment, *The Buccaneers*, the unfinished story of three American girls in the seventies who make brilliant English marriages and become the envy of a New York which had scorned them. The book has more life than its immediate predecessors, but on its very opening page we find its author still laying on satire at the expense of America with the now customary trowel. She refers to certain tall white columns on the portico of the Grand Union Hotel in Saratoga which "so often reminded cultured travelers of the Parthenon at Athens (Greece)."

Guy Thwarte in this unfinished tale is the thread that links it with so many of its predecessors. Although English, he is still the Wharton hero, tall and good-looking, a Gibson man, and, to the amazement of his family, though he has a "decent reputation about women" and is a "brilliant point-to-point rider," he "messes about" with poetry and painting. Like the heroes of French classic tragedy the Wharton men keep their action off stage. Guy consents to dip into commerce, but only in foreign climes. He disappears to Brazil for four years and returns a millionaire, but the "dark, rich stormy years of his exile" lie "like a raging channel between himself and his old life." The notes at the end of the book show that he was fated to elope with the Duchess of Tintagel; it was to be the triumph of "love, deep and abiding love." One cannot feel after this any keen regret that the story was never finished. Lily Bart's love for Lawrence Selden is the one hollow note of *The House of Mirth*. Undine Spragg in *The Custom of the Country* is, of course, incapable of love. Love in *The Age of Innocence* is stifled by the characters themselves. Mrs. Wharton at her best was an analyst of the paralysis that attends failure in the market place and of the coarseness that attends success. Hers was not a world where romance was apt to flourish.

The Two Ages of Thackeray

MY WIFE owns a pair of pink vases which came from her great-grandmother's house in Lenox and which are decorated with medallion portraits of those unhappy friends, Marie-Antoinette and Madame de Lamballe. The pink is soft and warm, and the vases are pleasing to contemplate, but one sees at a glance that they are engaged in the hopeless struggle of Victorian porcelain to evoke the elusive charm and grace of the eighteenth century. There is too much ormulu on their sides and covers, too many curves in their design, too much placidity in the features of the doomed princesses. They belong in a cluttered window on Madison Avenue amid gallants with powdered hair leaning over to kiss the hands of ladies stepping out of sedan chairs and cardinals taking snuff and all those other porcelain figures who mince and simper like amateurs in a performance of

The School for Scandal. The nineteenth century, torn between envy and disdain, could never grasp the subtlety of its predecessor. The Widow of Windsor had her qualities, but they were not those of the Pompadour.

Thackeray, like my wife's vases, belonged to the later, but hankered after the earlier age. The eighteenth was always his favorite century. He cultivated its relics, lectured on its humorists and kings, and used it as a setting for a considerable part of his fiction. He was a frequent caller on the ancient Berry sisters, who continued to use the old-fashioned rouge and pearl powder and to garnish their conversation with such oaths as "O Christ!" and "My God!" His novels are spotted with sour references to the false prudishness of his own time and its hampering effect on writers. "Since the author of *Tom Jones* was buried," he declares indignantly in his preface to *Pendennis,* "no writer of fiction among us has been permitted to depict to his utmost power a *Man.*" And in *The Virginians* he delivers this passionate apostrophe to the shade of Richardson:

Oh, my faithful, good old Samuel Richardson! Hath the news yet reached thee in Hades that thy sublime novels are huddled away in corners, and that our daughters may no more read *Clarissa* than *Tom Jones?* I wonder whether a century hence the novels of today will be hidden behind locks and wires and make pretty little maidens blush?

We can only hope that the news has not reached Thackeray in Hades that the novels of *his* day are too tepid for the pretty little maidens of 1960. Richardson might have predicted it, but never Thackeray. For the Victorian age blanketed Europe and America in a fog of fatuity so dense that it was almost impossible for anyone living in it to see his way out. Thackeray may have thought of himself as a denizen of the Age of Reason, but we think of him as a leading and rather characteristic Victorian. How it would have pained him!

Yet how can we imagine the rosy-cheeked Clive Newcome in any century but the nineteenth? Or good Amelia or patient Laura or "that touching and wonderful spectacle of innocence and love and beauty," Helen Pendennis? And doesn't the famous ending of *Esmond*, which is supposed to take place in the early days of George I, belong in spirit to the era of the Brontës?

> And then the tender matron, as beautiful in her autumn, and as pure as virgins in their spring, with blushes of love and "eyes of meek surrender" yielded to my respectful importunity and consented to share my home.

Nobody, of course, was more sentimental than Richardson, but there was a wide difference between the sentimentalities of the two centuries. It is impossible to imagine Amelia Sedley or Laura Pendennis or Rachel Esmond suffering the fate of Clarissa Harlowe. The purity of Thackeray's heroines acts as a sensitive antenna to give them early warning of danger. Laura Pendennis, for example, stirs uneasily in the presence of Lady Clara Newcome long before that unfortunate lady has even contemplated her guilty elopement. She would have smelled out Lovelace's evil intentions at their first meeting.

Where Thackeray, however, is by no means typically Victorian is in his distrust — sometimes it almost seems his dislike — of the ladies whose virtue he extols. When the faithful Dobbin finally wins Amelia, she bores him. He prefers their little daughter to the mother for whom he has waited so long. Rachel Esmond's incessant jealousy proves a trial to both her husbands, and Laura Pendennis, that saint of saints, causes Colonel Newcome's death by insisting on the reunion of Rosey and Clive, which subjects the old man to the withering conversational fire of the Old Campaigner. But Laura, like so many holy persons, never stops to consider the consequences of her good advice. She blindly follows her simple rules and blandly reaps havoc and destruction.

This chink in Thackeray's Victorian armor was promptly detected by Charlotte Brontë who appeared on the London horizon like a tiny, astigmatic avenging angel to herald the dawn of a triumphant moral seriousness. She combined the virtues of her era with its worst faults, and was surely the clumsiest craftsman ever to scale Parnassus. Her plots are melodramatic, her prose purple, her dialogues labored and sententious, her satire embarrassingly obvious and her narrators smug, censorious and sentimental. What is it that redeems *Jane Eyre* and *Villette?* The classic answer is passion, Jane's passion for Rochester and Lucy Snowe's passion for Paul Emanuel. But I submit it is not so. It is the vital if unlovable force of Charlotte Brontë's egocentricity that makes these novels so curiously interesting, as it is Queen Victoria's that fascinates us in her journals and letters. They had much in common, those two sober, dour little women of immense sentimentality, immense dignity and immense self-importance. That they took themselves so seriously induces us to take them with equal seriousness. We are engrossed in the story of Jane Eyre long before Mr. Rochester makes his appearance. The cruelty of Mrs. Reed and the evils of Lowood School are just as interesting as his projected bigamy. The reason that *Shirley* is unreadable is that no character directly represents the author. We are left in the wasteland of Charlotte's writing without the oasis of Charlotte herself.

Miss Brontë had placed Thackeray on a towering pedestal before she ever met him. She had even dedicated the second edition of *Jane Eyre* to him. But like so many Victorians she proved an aggressive disciple. She had to get up on the pedestal with a chisel to try to improve the image. When she came to know her hero, she was shocked to discover that he was an enthusiastic frequenter of the very society that he satirized so sharply.

A less earnest observer could have inferred as much from his style. I know, for example, that the author who describes Mrs. Rawdon Crawley's stylish little supper parties must have enjoyed their counterparts, just as I know that Proust loved dining at the Guermantes' and Ouida would have loved court balls, and just as I know that the woman who conceived that ghastly dinner party which Mr. Rochester gives for Blanche Ingraham must have had a deep and sincere loathing for all forms of social life. Miss Brontë had no use for greys; she liked her blacks to be black and her whites white. She marched in upon Thackeray, as he himself put it, like "an austere little Joan of Arc" to rebuke his easy life and easy morals. He found her amusing, if a bit trying, and liked to exasperate her, as when he introduced her to his mother as "Jane Eyre," despite her clinging to the veil of her pen name. But I have an idea that she stung him more than he cared to admit. "She was angry with her favorites," he says, "if their conduct or conversation fell below her ideal." It is always pleasing to one writer to be the passionate ideal of another. Miss Brontë's approbation, after all, was almost the approbation of their era, and her frowns were almost its frowns. The Victorian in Thackeray must have winced at the scorn of so pure a Victorian. He sent her the galley sheets of *Esmond*, and the first authority on his life and letters, Gordon Ray, believes that her exhortations may have borne fruit in the "nobler tone" of that novel.

As Thackeray grew older, he began to have his doubts about his beloved eighteenth century. True, to the end of his life, he maintained a literary attitude of being pro-Augustan and anti-prude (and Mr. Ray speaks of his fondness for dirty limericks), but one notices the increasing sternness with which he judges his predecessors, both fictional and real. In *The Virginians* Beatrix Esmond, now an old woman, who, for all her wickedness, is given the heavy task of enlivening a dull book, illuminates George Warrington on the history of the Castlewood family, using words "not used by ladies of a later time." "And so much the better on the whole," the author comments. "We mayn't be more virtuous, but it is something to be more decent. Perhaps we are not more pure, but of a surety we are more cleanly." Harry Warrington, in the same novel, is a healthy young man from the colonies who is dazzled by the fuss made over him by the London social world. He drinks and gambles and is seen in the company of a French actress of notorious reputation. Yet when jokes are made about her, Harry is ready to draw his sword. He believes in her virtue, as he believes in every woman's. Even conceding that the Victorian had to make concessions to the contemporary censor, surely he did not have to go this far. Harry and his brother, George, cease to be believable as young blades of their century. They are really ambassadors to the England of George II, not from Virginia, but from the Victorian age, legates across time and not space.

Ultimately, Thackeray turned even on such a former favorite as Fielding. Here is his famous verdict on Tom Jones:

> I can't say that I think Mr. Jones a virtuous character; I can't say but that I think Fielding's evident liking and admiration for Mr. Jones, shows that the great humorist's moral sense was blunted by his life, and that here in Art and Ethics, there is a great error.

On Sterne he is even more severe, and he ends his lecture on the author of *Tristram Shandy* with a tribute to Dickens that would seem to enroll him with such lofty Victorians as Martin Tupper and Lord Tennyson:

> There is not a page in Sterne's writing but has something that were better away, a latent corruption — a hint, as of an impure presence. . . . I think of these past writers and of one who lives amongst us now, and am grateful for the innocent laughter and the sweet and unsullied page which the author of *David Copperfield* gives to my children.

Towards the end of his life we find him, as editor of the *Cornhill Magazine*, rejecting Trollope's *Mrs. General Tallboys* because of allusions to illegitimate children and to a woman not as pure as she should be. Had Miss Brontë been living, she might have at last been satisfied. But if Thackeray, as he grew older, became an increasingly complacent Victorian novelist, he became also the greatest of them. I can forgive the century a great deal of complacency that produced *The Newcomes*. It is less read today than *Vanity Fair* or *Esmond*, but the critics of Thackeray's time thought it his finest work. It is a verdict in which I fully concur, though it is not easy to explain why. The faults of *The Newcomes* loom large when considered together.

Surely the story is told in a loose and rambling fashion. Surely great chunks of it are boring. Does anyone care today about Clive Newcome's opinion of Italian painting? Or about the frolics of those young artists who caper as clumsily as Rudolfo's fellow tenants in the first act of *La Bohème?* Is it Thackeray's portrait of a family that gives the novel its peculiar excellence? Gordon Ray says that when we have finished, we know the Newcomes as no other family in fiction. But I question this. The first Mrs. Newcome is little more than a caricature. Her sons, Brian and Hobson, are lightly sketched, and their wives, Lady Ann and Maria, like Dickens characters, say the same things every time they appear. Lady Ann is always languid, and Maria, like Madame Verdurin in Proust, is always being scornful of the people whom she can't catch for her parties. Of the children of Hobson we learn almost nothing, and of the children of Brian we know only Barnes and Ethel. Of three generations, therefore, we have complete studies only of Colonel Newcome, his son Clive, his nephew Barnes, and his niece Ethel. It should also be noted that Thackeray utterly ignores family characteristics. Barnes and Ethel, although brother and sister, have nothing whatever in common, nor really, except for a similarity about pulling whiskers, do Clive and his father. As a matter of fact, I fail to see that any Newcome resembles any other Newcome.

Wherein, then, is the excellence? Well, of course, Colonel Newcome is a great character. We see him clearly, in all his innocence and foolishness and generosity. And we understand his relationship with Clive. Actually, the "Newcomes" boil down to the Colonel and Clive. If Ethel and Barnes belonged to a different family, I doubt that the book would lose much. I even suggest that the device of linking all the characters by means of a family tree is the author's artifice to create an illusion of unity. It allows him to run out on branches whenever he wishes without incurring the charge of evasiveness. In justice to Galsworthy, who has often been compared unfavorably with Thackeray, the Forsytes seem to me more a family than the Newcomes.

Take the novel, then, as the study of a father who adores, without ever understanding, his only son, and who ultimately destroys himself, and very nearly the son, in a valiant but misguided effort to buy the world and lay it at his boy's feet. Of course, there must be a girl who will be the one thing that the son wants and that the father cannot buy for him, and Ethel fulfills this role to perfection. And, of course, there must be a villain to ruin the old man, and Barnes is a perfect villain. Having reduced the plot to its essentials, suppose we then cut the novel to these four characters and their inter-relationship. What do we lose? Simply half of Thackeray's effect. His art is far more than characterization.

But what is it? What is the "richness" that the critics speak of? Does it consist of his long asides, of his interminable lectures on morality, of his elaborate sketching of minor figures, of his evident anxiety to seize upon any distraction to avoid getting on with his story and to fill out the yellow-backed serials in which his novels appeared? Perhaps. There is some of the charm of a stage rehearsal or of visiting a sculptor in his studio in watching Thackeray at work. He appears to conceal nothing from our eyes, and all around lie the props of his art, beautiful backdrops, half-finished figures, chisels, hammers, odd piles of tarpaulin. But there in the center are his great creations: Becky Sharpe, Major Pendennis and above all, above everything, Colonel Newcome. We can never lose sight of them, nor does he. He is quite aware how good they are, and however much he talks or rants or chisels or hammers, he keeps drawing our attention back to them.

We begin to perceive, then, what it is that makes *The Newcomes* a great book. It is the combination of the sculptured figure and the sculptor. While we admire the finished product we find it agreeable to listen to the au-

thor. His personality surrounds his work without overwhelming it, like Charlotte Brontë's. Thackeray is an
urbane nineteenth century guide and commentator in a
portrait gallery that is for all time. One's guide, after
all, must be of some era, and I would not have Thackeray
in any other. I like him just as he is, the restless in-
habitant of a prudish age, nostalgic, discursive, anecdotal,
sentimental, worldly-wise, now warning us, now making
fun of us, now reproving us. If he is Victorian, he is
charmingly Victorian. One wonders, in the end, if he
did not owe his greatest debt to the era he loved to deplore.

He owed the era one other debt, which I will mention
by way of conclusion, and that is his reputation for
cynicism. His name has become almost synonymous
with cynicism, simply because his works are saturated
with a creed of three basic tenets: (1) that everything
yearned for is apt to be a disappointment when realized;
(2) that London society is full of toadies, and (3) that
the motivation behind acts of apparent altruism is usually
self-interest. The last tenet is best summed up in a passage from *The Newcomes:*

> You are pleased that yesterday, at dinner, you re-
> frained from the dry champagne? My name is
> Worldly Prudence, not Self-denial, and *I* caused
> you to refrain. You are pleased, because you gave a
> guinea to Diddler? I am Laziness, not Generosity,

which inspired you. You hug yourself because you
resisted other temptation? Coward, it was because
you dared not run the risk of wrong. Off with your
peacock's plumage!

Imagine an author of today writing a novel to illus-
trate such tenets! Far from being called a cynic, he
would be lucky not to find himself pilloried as a Polly-
anna. For Thackeray's harshest criticism of humanity is
simply the point where ours commences. His perception
of self-interest in every act is the ABC of modern psychology. The whole machinery of our tax law reflects
the assumption that every man will arrange his affairs to
effect the maximum evasion of imposts. We see a yacht
or a limousine or a large party at a restaurant, and consider ourselves simple realists, not cynics, when we shrug
our shoulders and mutter "Tax deduction" or "Business
expense." That a man should consider his economic welfare before the welfare of his nation is so taken for
granted that we require our foremost citizens to liquidate
their stockholdings before taking cabinet office. In sex,
in family relations, in business, in politics, we calmly accept the brute force of the "id." Only in that curious
Victorian era that seals off its decades from the rest of
history in a kind of hothouse of willful illusion could
Thackeray's gentle comments on the essential monkey in
man have seemed unkind.

Is George Eliot Salvageable?

Jᴀᴍᴇs, in his uncompleted "The Middle Years," describes a visit to George Eliot and G. H. Lewes on a Sunday afternoon in the winter of 1878. He was taken by Mrs. Greville, that "large, elegant, extremely near-sighted and extremely demonstrative lady, whose genius was all for friendship, admiration, declamation and expenditure." The scene is highly comic, for the unhappy young novelist feels how little welcome is either he or his bustling companion in the austere parlor of the "bland, benign" author of *Romola*. The Leweses liked them to have come, but "mainly from a prevision of how they should more devoutly like it" when they departed. The nothingness of the visit is summed up in a single sentence:

It is remarkable, but the occasion yields me no single echo of a remark on the part of any of us —

nothing more than the sense that our great author herself peculiarly suffered from the fury of the elements, and that they had about them rather the minimum of the paraphernalia of reading and writing, not to speak of that of tea, a conceivable feature of the hour, but which was not provided for.

When Lewes conducted the visitors to their carriage, "all sociably, *then* above all conversingly," he suddenly bethought himself of an item forgotten and hurried back into the house to secure a pair of blue-bound volumes that Mrs. Greville, on another occasion, had importunately loaned. As poor James received these from his hand and heard his "Ah those books — take them away, please away, away!" the title of his own precious "last" squinted up at him. Yet there was still a compensating Jamesian thrill, as he drove off with the mortified Mrs. Greville, "in thinking of persons — or at least of a person, for any fact about Lewes was but derivative — engaged in my own pursuit and yet detached, by what I conceived, detached by a pitch of intellectual life, from all that made it actual to myself."

Other observers were less charitable. Charles Eliot Norton, met at the door of the Priory by the accommodating Lewes, expected to see him "take up his fiddle and begin to play." The drawing room, hung with pictures of scenes from *Romola*, "bore witness to the want of delicate artistic feeling or good culture." As for his hostess, the Harvard professor had rarely seen a plainer woman, "dull complexion, dull eye, heavy features." She said "not one memorable thing in three hours," but behaved as "a woman who feels herself to be of mark and is accustomed, as she is, to the adoring flattery of a coterie of not undistinguished admirers."

"Always the goddess on her pedestal," was the sour comment of Eliza Lynn, a friend from obscurer days, "gracious in her condescension — with sweet strains of recognition."

The point of view of these observers ranges from enthusiasm to disgust, but the picture of the mournful priestess and her twittering major-domo remains a constant. The same atmosphere of solemn and faintly bogus self-importance hangs over the novels to repel the modern reader. I suppose it was not George Eliot's fault that her collected editions always contain, as well as those dreary, inevitable illustrations of rustic scenes in the Midlands, the famous portrait by Sir Frederick Burton which perpetuates the heavy features of which Norton spoke. But the trouble with George Eliot is that she *wanted* to look that way.

F. W. H. Myers, the author of *Human Personality and Its Survival of Bodily Death*, gives a description of her that reads like a caricature. Walking in Cambridge on an evening of rainy May, they discussed the words God, Immortality and Duty, and George Eliot pronounced with a terrible earnestness how inconceivable was the first, how unbelievable the second and yet how peremptory and absolute the third.

Never perhaps have sterner accents affirmed the sovereignty of impersonal and unrecompensing Law. I listened, and night fell; her grave, majestic countenance turned towards me like a sibyl's in the gloom; it was as though she withdrew from my grasp, one by one, the two scrolls of promise and left me the third scroll only, awful with inevitable fates. And when we stood at length and parted, amid that columnar circuit of forest trees, beneath the last twilight of starlight skies, I seemed to be gazing, like Titus at Jerusalem, on vacant seats and empty halls — on a sanctuary with no presence to hallow it, and heaven left lonely of a God.

Yet the Victorian public must have liked views of vacant seats and empty halls, for George Eliot was the most popular serious writer of her day. She approached her task with the dedication of one taking an oath of high public office. "Man or woman who publishes writings," she warned the literary world, "inevitably assumes the office of teacher or influencer of the public mind." And supposing man or woman simply strives to be amusing? Supposing his only wish is to entertain? He becomes a distiller of "spiritual gin." The test is summed up:

In endeavoring to estimate a writer one must ask: "Did he animate long-known but neglected truths with new vigour and cast fresh light on their relation to other admitted truths? Did he impregnate any ideas with a fresh store of emotion, and in this way enlarge the area of moral sentiment?"

But even in the heyday of her popularity some readers were beginning to stir resentfully at this conversion of a means of entertainment into a pulpit. Was the novel to be turned into a tract for the expounding of austere doctrine? James, in the same chapter where he records the unhappy visit with Mrs. Greville, notes the rise of this criticism:

It was the fashion among the profane in short either to misdoubt, before George Eliot's canvas, the latter's backing of rich thought, or else to hold that this matter of philosophy . . . thrust itself through to the confounding of the picture. But with that thin criticism I wasn't . . . to have a moment's patience . . . I found the figured, coloured tapestry *always* vivid enough to brave no matter what complication of the stitch.

There is some of the enthusiasm of a generous colleague's final summation in this. Actually, James had not always found the tapestry quite so vivid, as an early review of *Felix Holt* can witness. It may be only sensible in looking at tapestries to concentrate on the figured, colored sections, but to a generation that wonders if there *are* any, one must first learn to avoid the areas of overcomplicated stitch. The question will be whether any of the tapestry is left.

Certainly the desolation that Myers felt in George Eliot's philosophy is the same that pervades her fiction. She was woefully preoccupied with duty. And it was duty, too, with no prospect of reward, or even approval, in this life or in any other, duty with no object other than that of the gradual amelioration of the lot of mankind. As the novels progress, this concept of duty becomes drearier and drearier, until it is ultimately duty for duty's sake, and we turn from it with a shudder of repulsion, as from something deformed.

Dinah Morris in *Adam Bede*, an early heroine, is the last to derive any pleasure out of doing her duty, but her duty is preaching, and who would not rather deliver that evangelical sermon on the village green than have to listen to it? Besides, Dinah has the impersonality of a saint; she loves mankind rather than men, which is why we are not convinced of her passion for Adam. Very likely Dinahs exist — I disagree with those who claim that she is altogether a wooden character — but they are no more interesting to meet than to read about. Maggie Tulliver in *The Mill on the Floss* is more sympathetic, and were it not for her habit of prosy moralizing we might become fond of her. But how much fondness can we feel for a girl who speaks in this fashion to her lover:

> We can only choose whether we will indulge our-
> selves in the present moment, or whether we will
> renounce that, for the sake of obeying the divine
> voice within us — for the sake of being true to all
> the motives that sanctify our lives.

Maggie's choice represents the Eliot sense of duty at its purest. She is not engaged to Philip Wakem, nor is Stephen Guest engaged to Lucy Dean. If she and Stephen marry, no pledge will be broken. On the other hand, Philip and Lucy will have nothing to gain from their renunciation, for the passion between Maggie and Stephen is too intense to allow either to fall back on a loveless match. Maggie is helped in her choice by the fact that the road of inclination is shaded by riches and social position, whereas the road of duty lies under the baking sun of poverty and disgrace. Obviously, then, duty must prevail; it makes for a perfect ending that Maggie will have nothing. As she tells Stephen:

> You feel, as I do, that the real tie lies in the feel-
> ings and expectations we have raised in other minds.
> Else all pledges might be broken, when there was
> no outward penalty. There would be no such thing
> as faithfulness.

And so, because Stephen has given Lucy grounds to expect a proposal, everyone's life must be ruined. Small wonder that George Eliot warned us to take the smallest things in life seriously. It was hardly safe for a young man to go to a party if he was to be bound forever by the "feelings and expectations" that he might raise in other minds. Can young people today, or could they in the last half century, for that matter, have any sympathy with such a theme? Gaillard Lapsley, who was Edith Wharton's literary executor, once told me that he could not imagine young people of my day caring for *The House of Mirth,* where Lily Bart's reputation is ruined simply because she is seen to emerge from the Trenors' house on a night when Mrs. Trenor is out of town. But it seemed to me that what saved the novel for modern readers was that Edith Wharton did not believe in the code under which Lily was condemned, and, indeed, there has been a big enough continuing public for *The House of Mirth* to justify its recent republication. What made George Eliot popular in her own day is precisely what has created her present neglect: she shares with the Victorian public an admiration for what we consider pointless sacrifice.

One of the oddest elements in the odd pastiche that is *Romola* is the anachronism of the Victorian goddess of duty in fifteenth century Florence. When the reader is not being dragged about the streets and piazzas to be exposed to the last drop of local color falling from the sternly wrung and rewrung washrag of George Eliot's research, he is made to sit and swallow great doses of moralizing. It was probably Savonarola who attracted her to this period of Italian history. She concedes that fanaticism may have ultimately carried him too far, but her basic admiration is conveyed through the medium of her heroine. At the burning of the pyramid of vanities on the Piazza della Signoria, on which the Florentines tossed not only their wigs and rouge pots, but their books of pagan authors and works of art, Romola is "conscious of no inward collision with the strict and sombre view of pleasure which tended to repress poetry in the attempt to repress vice." Her life has given her "an affinity for sadness which inevitably made her unjust towards merriment." But it is hardly an injustice that the author expects us to condemn. Romola, like Dinah, is a saint.

But whence her affinity for sadness? It comes, like that of other Eliot heroines, from their Achilles' heel of a violent sensibility. There is something pathetic but rather comic about these strong, noble, high-minded women who take fire at first sight of a handsome man. Surely, they are unreasonable in their bitterness at the ensuing disillusionment. By what right, having selected a mate by purely physical standards, do they expect to find a soul as beautiful as the outward form? Yet Romola has no tolerance of the least fault in her husband. She leaves him, not for his real crimes, of which she is still ignorant, but because he has sold her father's library. She then has a typically Eliot argument on the road with Savonarola. Between two duties, that of tending the poor and sick, and that of returning to her husband, Savonarola easily induces her to choose the second, being the more repugnant to her. There are compensations for Romola in the gratitude and veneration of the destitute about which her creator is surprisingly candid:

> "Bless you, Madonna! bless you!" said the faint chorus, in much the same tone as that in which they had a few minutes before praised and thanked the unseen Madonna. Romola cared a great deal for that music.

I would nominate Felix Holt for the most unlovable hero of Victorian fiction. In his very first words he announces his priggishness. The old minister, Rufus Lyon, explains to his guest, perhaps superfluously, that he uses wax light because his delicately framed daughter dislikes the smell of tallow. In "loud, abrupt tones" Holt replies:

> I heeded not the candle, sir. I thank Heaven I am not a mouse to have a nose that takes note of wax or tallow.

And in loud, abrupt tones he continues throughout the novel to catch everyone up on their slightest utterances until we join heartily with the judge and jury who condemn him to four years' imprisonment for a crime of which he is innocent. The other characters, however, join to get him off, though why they bother I cannot imagine, as in the best Eliot tradition he is perfectly willing to be locked up and has indulged himself in a rude speech to the court which seems designed to secure his conviction.

In *Daniel Deronda* the reader is allowed to enjoy himself for almost a third of the book before the duty figure appears to spoil his fun. But we know all the time that he is coming, for we have had a preparatory glimpse of his disapproving countenance at the gambling hall in the first chapter. Daniel Deronda is less offensive than Felix Holt because he is a silent rather than a noisy bore. But he is still offensive. He exudes disapproval of everybody, including the Jews, until he finds that he is one of them. Mirah regards him as her savior, though he has done little more than put her up at a friend's house, and Gwendolen looks upon him as a touchstone against the evil within herself, though his services consist only of little homilies whispered at dinner parties. But they both know he must be good because he is so gloomy.

If the performance of duty is a cheerless task, however, unlit by the prospect of reward or even of gratitude, there is at least the consolation, in Eliot novels, of considering the hideous fate of the undutiful. There may be no heaven, but there is certainly a hell, and right here on earth. Doom hangs over the characters and manifests itself in omens and sudden prognostications: the noise of a rat suggests the tap of a willow wand on the eve of old Bede's death; Dinah foresees Hetty's miserable destiny, and Mrs. Tulliver has a terror from the beginning that Maggie will get herself "drownded." Life is ready with knives and ropes to wreak its vengeance on the trivial-minded and the selfish. Gwendolen Harleth, Tito Melema and Hetty Sorel pay for their egotism with a ghastly price. Yet the reader cannot but feel that there should be a mitigation of the penalty because they, at least, have tried to entertain him.

The pity of it! That a writer with the power of characterization of a Thackeray, the narrative skill of a Trollope, the satirical eye of a Jane Austen and the descriptive ease of a Scott, should have wrecked her work with a foolish didacticism! Never have greater gifts been less valued by their owner. Imagine the perversity of the woman who could so enthrallingly describe the seduction of Hetty Sorel forcing our attention from that to the homilies of Dinah Morris! Imagine, after having started a story as brilliantly as she did *Felix Holt*, with the proud, bitter, disillusioned Mrs. Transome, ruining it with her prig of a hero! And imagine, after fixing our absorbed gaze on Gwendolen Harleth and her terrible marriage, sticking Daniel Deronda before our eyes! She seems to take a malicious pleasure in ringing down the curtain just when we are beginning to enjoy ourselves. "I turn," she says in *Adam Bede*, "without shrinking, from cloud-borne angels, from prophets, sibyls and heroic warriors, to an old woman bending over her flower pot, or eating her solitary dinner." She wanted her rustic novels to be like Dutch paintings, faithful pictures of a monotonous, homely existence. If that involved a loss of excitement and color, well, that was simply too bad:

> In writing the history of unfashionable families, one is apt to fall into a tone of emphasis which is very far from being the tone of good society, where principles and beliefs are not only of an extremely moderate kind, but are always presupposed, no subjects being eligible but such as can be touched with a light and graceful irony.

And this from a woman who was a mistress of irony! Who could say of Mrs. Glegg that, with a front and back parlor, she had "two points of view from which she could observe the weakness of her fellow-beings," and of Mr. Casaubon that "he determined to abandon himself to the stream of feeling and perhaps was surprised to find what an exceedingly shallow rill it was"! Are not Maggie Tulliver's aunts the literary ancestresses of Dorothy Parker's Mrs. Matson and Mrs. Whittaker?

What, then, is to be done about her? Can one expect the modern reader to work his way through *Adam Bede* for the sake of Hetty Sorel, or *The Mill on the Floss* for the Dodson sisters, or *Daniel Deronda* for Gwendolen and Grandcourt, or *Felix Holt* for Mrs. Transome? Can one even urge him to? I fear not. In poetry and music one can save choice bits from tedious works, but a novel is like a painting and can't be cut up, except for those vast anthologies of prose which one never sees again after freshman year.

Is anything left, then, except *Silas Marner* for high school students? Yes. *Middlemarch* is left. That may not, at first blush, seem much, but to me it is like saying that *Anna Karenina* is left. It is the fashion today for East and West to vie with each other in every field, and in an exhibition of nineteenth century fiction, I would offer *Middlemarch* against anything that the Russians could produce. How did it happen that George Eliot, after two dreary years of work on *Romola*, which she said had turned her into an old woman, and more on *Felix Holt* and much lamentable poetry, should suddenly have produced the greatest English novel of manners of the century? I think I can show that it was simply good luck.

It was a habit of Victorian writers to keep two or three plots running in parallel lines through a single novel, sometimes not tying them together until a melodramatic final chapter. We know that George Eliot sometimes conceived her individual plots quite independently of their future companions or even of the novel where they would ultimately meet. For example, there is evidence that she started work on the story of Dorothea Brooke and Mr. Casaubon long before the Garths or the Vincys or the town of Middlemarch itself had occurred to her. When she matched up her plots into novels, she was careful to give each entertaining one a sober and moralizing counterpart; we pay for Arthur Donnithorne with the Bede brothers and for Aunt Glegg and Aunt Pullet with Maggie. But in putting *Romola* together she forgot the entertainment, and in *Middlemarch*, by a happy fortune, she forgot the sermon. I like to speculate that one could create another *Middlemarch* out of existing Eliot fiction simply by a judicious use of scissors and paste. I would lift Hetty Sorel and Arthur out of *Adam Bede* and fit them into *Daniel Deronda* in the vacant spaces left by the excision of the hero and his plans for a Jewish state. They would thus provide an admirable contrast to Gwendolen and Grandcourt, illustrating the dangers of too little and of too much calculation in love. Arthur might even marry Gwendolen in the end. And I would bring Mrs. Transome over from *Felix Holt* to act as Grandcourt's mother and the Dodson sisters from *The Mill on the Floss* to be Hetty's aunts. The fascinating thing is how little one would violate any of George Eliot's conceptions. Her tragedy as a writer is that she never learned the simple lesson that an entertainer must entertain.

Dorothea Brooke, in *Middlemarch*, has all the nobility of soul of Maggie or Romola, but she is saved from being a bore by being a goose. I know of nothing better in English fiction than her deliberate, pathetic, perverted and entirely understandable impulse to throw herself away on the dried-up old scholar, Casaubon, and nothing better than his utter failure to appreciate either her character or her self-sacrifice. Critics of George Eliot's time were inclined to deplore Dorothea's passion for Ladislaw, as they were inclined to deplore Maggie's for Stephen Guest. They felt that such heroines should look higher. But what they failed to perceive was that Dorothea is never going to be ready for love until she has first realized the desperate folly of her marriage, and that then she will be ready to adore the first young man who looks kindly at her. There is a marvellous psychological moment when Dorothea, hearing that Mr. Casaubon has expressly provided in his will that a marriage to Ladislaw will cut off her income, feels a sudden rush of warmth towards the young man so prohibited to her. For until that moment nobody, including herself, has dared to articulate even the possibility of a romantic relationship between them. It is Casaubon's testamentary trick that, ironically enough, brings them together.

The situation of Rosamond Vincy and Lydgate is only a fraction less interesting: the helplessness of a brilliant man in the hands of a determined, mediocre woman. But Mary Garth is responsible for a slight drop in our attention because she has been so unfortunate as to incur the approbation of the author. As Gerald

Bullett points out, the chief thing an Eliot character has to fear is the unqualified moral approval of his creator. In Mary's first appearance, and later, in her father's, we feel the gathering of the grey clouds of that unmistakable Eliot dullness, but, happily, their role in the story is limited, and neither can do a "Deronda" to it.

Another habit of Victorian novelists, besides the weaving of multiple plots, was a "what happened after" piece by way of conclusion. The last chapter of *Middlemarch* has more to say in this respect than many others because it offers us a glimpse of Rosamond Vincy without which our understanding of her would not be complete. We learn that Lydgate dies at fifty, and that she marries an elderly and wealthy physician who took kindly to her four children. "She made a very pretty show with her daughters, driving out in her carriage, and often spoke of her happiness as 'a reward.'" Lydgate has rightly called her the basil plant that feeds on the brains of murdered men. To me there is a greater enlargement of the "area of moral sentiment" in this picture of the triumph of a stubborn female mediocrity over male genius and imagination than in all of Gwendolen Harleth's frantic soul searching in snatched moments at parties with the embarrassed and cliché-loving Deronda. But I doubt if George Eliot would have agreed with me. She had a fatal fondness for underscoring her points.

The Little Duke and the Great King

I AM ALWAYS a bit surprised, whenever I turn back to the memoirs of the Duc de Saint-Simon, at the classic judgment of the French court as a shrine of artificiality and hypocrisy. Every beginner of French history knows the quotation from Taine's courtier: "A genuine sentiment is so rare that, when I leave Versailles, I sometimes stand still in the street to see a dog gnaw a bone." I can see, of course, that life in a crowded palace may have had some of the artificiality of life in a zoo, but that does not have to mean that the courtiers, any more than the animals, *behaved* artificially in it. And as for hypocrisy, would that Saint-Simon had more of it to describe! Except for the fawning over Louis XIV, some of which was perfectly sincere (the king, after all, *was* the state), the people in the memoirs behave with a brutal frankness and a doglike rapacity that is appalling to behold.

Was somebody dying? The talk was only of who would succeed to his offices. To shed a tear was to be accused of the grossest insincerity. Family relationships that we regard as the most vital things in life acted as little or no brake to the march of self-interest. Parents and children regarded each other with a detachment, the example of which was set by their sovereign, who, when the Duchesse de Bourgogne suffered a miscarriage, simply observed:

Has she not a son already? And if he died, is not the Duc de Berri of an age to marry and have children? What do I care which of them succeeds me? Are they not equally my grandchildren? Since she was to have a miscarriage, thank God it is over! I shall no longer be bothered and hampered in everything I want to do by the remonstrances of doctors and matrons.

I am quite aware of Madame de Sévigné and her idolatry of her daughter, but her death is recorded early in the memoirs. Her era was pre-Versailles. Madame de Grignan, whose filial coolness can be read between the lines of her mother's impassioned letters, was more of Saint-Simon's age. Self-indulgence was carried into everything, from love to personal habits. Dogs, surely, could hardly have yielded with more freedom to sexual impulses than the denizens of Versailles, and their lack of inhibition in other matters was commented on with disgust by foreign observers. We even read of one lady who left a "filthy trail" behind her when she got up from the dinner table. The young people occupied their leisure time with hazing and practical jokes such as the following:

> Another time, also at Marly, there had been a heavy fall of snow, and it was freezing hard. The Duchesse de Bourgogne and her suite armed themselves with a quantity of snowballs, slipped quietly into the bedroom of the Princesse d'Harcourt, drew back her curtains suddenly, and overwhelmed her with a shower of snowballs. The sight of this dirty creature in bed, suddenly awakened, dishevelled, shrieking at the top of her voice and wriggling like an eel, amused them for nearly half an hour; but it was almost enough to kill her.

Yet it was this same Duchesse de Bourgogne who "tried to make everybody love her, even the most insignificant and apparently useless people"! One wonders if the impromptu royal visit with the snowballs was intended as a means of access to the heart of Madame d'Harcourt. After only a few chapters of Saint-Simon I find myself giving prayerful thanks that we have outgrown the "naturalness" of the French court. Who would not prefer a little harmless hypocrisy?

But is it true? Were they that bad? It seems quite possible. Take several thousand persons and squash them into a palace so densely that the greatest duke may have only three small, smelly rooms, and you create a kind of gilded Dotheboys Hall, where adults will regress into a ferocious childhood. The men will fight for honors as schoolboys for medals. They will have nothing to think about but their own position vis-a-vis the others, and how can that be indicated except by tags? I shall keep reverting to the analogy of the school, because it seems to me the key to the puzzle of Versailles. It was a school, except there were no diplomas. Louis XIV did not allow anyone to graduate.

Saint-Simon is the perfect guide to the era because his philosophy is almost a parody of the prevailing philosophy. He believed that all history could be boiled down to the simple question of precedence. A good man was one who knew his rung on the ladder and remained perched on it. A great man was one who saw to it that everyone else remained perched on theirs. A bad man was one who tried to climb to a higher rung, and a weak man was one who allowed a bad man to climb over him. Any movement on the ladder, up or down, tended to shake the civilized order. At times Saint-Simon carries it so far that he seems more of a caricaturist than a historian. All of France, all of Europe, is lit up against the ludicrous backdrop of the social ladder. Coaches clash in narrow streets because their owners refuse to yield the right of way; duchesses scuffle and elbow each other for position at the king's table. Foreign princes are entertained out of doors, even in inclement weather, to avoid questions as to the order of passing into a house, and hosts, feigning illness, are carried into dining rooms in litters, to sup lying down, that it may not be said that they have made way for guests of honor. Behind every human act or omission to act the sharp eye of the memoirist detects the eternal question of rank.

He may, of course, have exaggerated. He had a widespread reputation in his own day for disputatiousness in questions of etiquette which he blandly assumed to be a mark of the world's esteem. And we can see in his own self-portrait the jealous eye, the explosive temper and the shrill boldness of the man who is quick to find a personal slight in the least inadvertence. But we learn about disease by the study of desperate cases, and Saint-Simon is an example of how sick the nobility was. In his private audiences with the king we observe the relationship of the squirrel and the mountain. The former can crack a nut, the nut of his perpetual grievances, but it is about all he can do. Perhaps Louis XIV managed to contain his patience by reminding himself that giving ear to the complaints of his courtiers was part of his system. To keep an eye on his squirrels, he had to keep them at court. And so long as he kept an eye on them, they could never become anything but squirrels.

Louis XIV was the perfect monarch — according to the system which he himself had devised. It was to serve as a model to the crowned heads of Europe for the next

century, and one of its numerous faults was that its
founder was the only person capable of living up to it.
It provided, in brief, that the king should be the splendid
living symbol of the state every minute of his waking
hours, that he should perform every function, including
his bodily ones, in public, that he should comport himself at all times with stately good manners and majestic
mien, that he should have no intimates even in his family
(his morganatic wife complained that he had "no conversation"), that he should permit no liberties and that
his court, his palaces, his very gardens should be magnificent extensions of himself, always on parade, always
in full dress, both in times of prosperity and in days of
darkest depression. To accomplish this end, the sovereign had to have an implacable will power, a complete
absence of humor and a robust constitution. Louis XIV
qualified in all three respects. In addition, having succeeded his father at the age of four, he could not remember a time when he had not been king. But he remembered vividly and bitterly the civil wars of his
minority and their hideous affront to his dignity, and
his simple, implacable, lifelong revenge was the slow
emasculation of the peerage, enmeshed in the endless
ceremonial of the Versailles court. What an assuage-
ment it must have been to the persistent anxiety engendered in his childhood by impudent *frondeurs* to
look out over that sea of bowing heads to fountains and
canals that carried his glory to the horizon!

Yet it was a backbreaking job. Later monarchs, exhausted by his system, created Petits Trianons to get away from it. Louis XIV never got away. When he went to Marly or Fontainebleau he took as much of his court with him as those smaller residences would contain. And he always had to know who was at court and who was away and who had died and who wanted what. He could not afford to despise the subjects of the petty disputes that sterilized the power of his dukes. He might keep the peers out of his cabinet, but he had to be careful to compensate them with illusory honors. He had, in short, to play a part, straight-faced, in the tricky game that he had conceived. Saint-Simon never quite understood this. He saw clearly enough that the king was intent on debasing the peerage, but he could not imagine why a sovereign so disposed should ever defend the rights of his nobles. For example, when Madame de Torcy, the wife of a cabinet minister, took the seat of the Duchesse de Duras at the royal supper, the king, to Saint-Simon's astonishment, was irate, and delivered a public lecture on the high rank of dukes, describing it as first in the state and assuring his listeners that he could find no higher honor to bestow on his own family. Anyone, he concluded grandly, refusing honors to a duke was refusing them to *him*. "Those were his very words!" exclaims the gratified Saint-Simon. But it is perfectly evident to us that if the Torcys were to be given the actual political power while the Durases had to be content with seats at the supper table, the full weight of royal authority was needed to sustain the illusion that these seats had any value. The royal game worked, and as we shall see, Saint-Simon himself became a typical victim.

The first recorded conversation between the memoirist and the king occurred in 1693. The young officer had to thank his commander-in-chief for the appointment of a cavalry regiment, and Majesty responded "most obligingly." Saint-Simon was then eighteen and his sovereign fifty-four. He was to remain within the latter's daily sight at court, with infrequent intermissions, for the ensuing twenty-two years. Yet in all that time he was granted only three private audiences. The balance of the relationship between king and courtier was made up of nods, bows, smiles, occasional gracious words and occasional (terrible to relate) long, icy stares. Louis XIV, like a god, was sparing of his personal contacts.

On the death of his father in the same year, Saint-Simon obtained royal assent to the renewal of the family offices. At the *coucher* he approached the bed and related (probably in too great detail) the story of the paternal last moments. The king, who knew how to "season his graces," admonished the new duke to be sensible and to behave properly and promised in return that he would look out for him. It was a good enough start, but Saint-Simon pushed his luck. His first request was for a transfer to another regiment so that he would not have to serve under the Duc de Luxembourg with whom he was already engaged in a lawsuit. He not only wrote to the king about it; he followed him to mass and thence to his carriage. Louis XIV observed the hovering figure, and turned back to assure him: "I have your letter, and I shall remember." Immediately afterwards Saint-Simon received his transfer, but I wonder if he had not already etched his portrait on the royal memory as a litigious young man who took himself and his dignity a good deal too seriously.

If he had not, he surely did at their next recorded talk. By then he was married to a daughter of the Maréchal de Lorges, a discreet, virtuous, strong-minded young woman who in her quiet way watched over her husband's rank as carefully as he did himself. There was always trouble with the House of Lorraine (the Guises) who claimed the status of foreign princes, although really only peers of France, and Madame de Saint-Simon reported to her husband that a slight misunderstanding about places at table had been blown up to the king as a deliberate usurpation on her part. Saint-Simon, boiling over, approached the king at the *coucher* after he had undressed and was standing by the fireplace to bid good night to those excluded from the *petit coucher*. Louis XIV leaned gravely down to give ear to his excited subject, staring quietly while the latter expostulated on the whole misunderstanding "without omitting a single circumstance." At the end he was graciously moved to reply: "That's quite all right, sir. I realize there's nothing in it." Saint-Simon retired before the royal nod and smile, but, suddenly exploding again, he hurried back to assure the king that every word he had told him was the absolute truth. Majesty accorded him another polite dismissal. Always the wise headmaster, Louis XIV never minimized or pooh-poohed the quarrels among his boys. But he had his own opinion of them.

Saint-Simon, unhappily for himself, was soon to prove more than simply importunate. He became downright irritating. Discouraged by lack of promotion, he resigned his commission. Louis XIV liked to keep his young nobles in the army; it was the only way that he could get any use out of them. "Here is another deserter!" he exclaimed peevishly when he read the duke's letter. That night at the *coucher*, he named Saint-Simon to hold the candlestick, as if nothing had happened, but it was the last time that he did so. For the next three years he not only excluded Saint-Simon from the coveted weekends at Marly; he refused to speak to him in public or even so much as look at him. It is interesting to note that Madame de Saint-Simon continued to be included in the royal suppers. She was evidently a young woman who knew how to play her cards.

Still worse, however, was to come. The episode of the alms bag finally brought down on Saint-Simon's unsuspecting head the first overt expression of the terrible royal wrath. Once again it was the Lorraines who started it. On certain days when the king went to mass it was the custom for a lady of the court, named by the Duchesse de Bourgogne, to hand around the alms bag. Princesses of the blood were exempt from the duty, and the ladies of Lorraine, always on the lookout for an opportunity to identify themselves with royalty, began to evade it on various specious excuses. The duchesses, alerted by the watchful Saint-Simon, promptly began to evade it also, and when word of this came to the king, he really blew up. He was heard to exclaim that ever since Saint-Simon had quit his service he had done nothing but "study questions of rank and precedence and dispute with people about them," that he was the origin of all this trouble and that it might be a good idea to send him away where he could cause no more. When this terrifying threat was reported to Saint-Simon, he knew that he was in the direst straits. He consulted the chancellor and was advised to seek the extreme remedy of a private audience (his former talks with the king had been in public). "It was no light thing," he relates, "for a young man so thoroughly out of favor to go up to the king and ask abruptly for an interview," but he plucked up his courage and went to await the king's passage to his private room after dinner. He then asked permission to follow him, and the king, without a word, led him to a window embrasure where he listened in angry silence while Saint-Simon rattled on about the outrageous presumptions of the Lorraines and his own exemplary conduct. Louis XIV cared very little for anyone's precedence but his own. At last he cut through the expostulations to the central point of discipline:

"But," interrupted the king, in the same haughty and angry manner, "you have been making speeches." "No, Sir," I said, "I have made none." "What, you have not been talking?" and he was going on in a loud voice, when I ventured to interrupt him in my turn, and, raising my voice above his: "No, Sir," I said, "I have made no speeches; if I had I would confess it to your Majesty, just as I have confessed what caused my wife to avoid making the collection, and prevented other Duchesses from doing so. But I beg you most earnestly, Sire, to believe that if I had thought for a moment that it was your Majesty's wish, I would have made the collection myself in a dish, like a village sexton."

That was the note to strike! Louis XIV was immediately mollified:

The king then assumed an air of kindness and familiarity, and told me several times, in a thoroughly gracious tone, that that was the right way to think and speak, with other polite speeches of the sort.

Saint-Simon explains that such accounts are the best way to learn about a monarch "so difficult to approach and so terrifying even to his intimates." The audience appears to have salvaged his position at court, and the following year, when he had an operation on his arm, the king "overwhelmed me with kindnesses." In 1706, when there was a question of an embassy to Rome, it was even reported to Saint-Simon that the king was going to appoint him, having observed that he was "young but capable," but nothing came of it.

Only two years later, however, we find him in trouble again. It was reported to the king that he had made a bet that the town of Lille, then invested by the allies under Marlborough, would fall before the French could raise the siege, and he suffered a second period of disgrace. Imagining himself, as usual, the victim of numerous cabals, he again sought a private audience, but this time the king, knowing what he was in for, tried to ward it off. "What does he want to tell me?" he protested impatiently to the Maréchal de Villars. "It's all nothing. Oh, true, I've had a couple of minor complaints about him, but nothing to amount to anything. Tell him to *relax!*" But Saint-Simon was determined on his audience, and of course, he got it. Was it not the right of every schoolboy? He found the king alone, sitting at his counsel table "as was his habit when he wished to converse with someone at his ease and leisure." Whatever else he may have anticipated from the interview, Louis XIV knew that it was not going to be brief.

Saint-Simon began very foolishly. He complained about his exclusion from the Marly weekends. It was an impertinence, of course, for a courtier to assume that the sovereign even noticed him enough to exclude him. The king retorted stiffly that such things meant nothing at all. Saint-Simon then begged permission to "unburden his heart" about all the ways in which he had been misrepresented to the king. But Louis XIV cared nothing for all that. He reverted to his role of headmaster:

> Here the king interrupted: "But you know, sir, you are given to talking and finding fault; that is why people say things against you." I replied that I tried hard to avoid speaking evil of any one; as for speaking evil of His Majesty, I would die first (looking at him ardently as I spoke, straight in the face); as to other people, I said that, though I was very careful, it was very hard at times not to speak my mind naturally. "But," said the king, "you talk about everything, especially about public affairs when they are not prosperous, with bitterness and —." Here, observing that he spoke more kindly, I interrupted him in my turn. I told him that I spoke very little about public affairs, and then very cautiously; but it was true that sometimes, irritated by our misfortunes, I had expressed myself rather strongly.

Saint-Simon then proceeded to tell the poor king in detail the whole background (including the military situation) of his bet about Lille. He went on from here to a good many other matters, describing complaints, actual or imagined, against himself, and giving exhaustive explanations and defenses. He even seized the occasion to review the old episode of the alms bag and to get in some more gibes at the House of Lorraine. The king was reduced to what one imagines to have been a stupefied silence. But it was far better to bore the king than to anger him. Louis XIV did not really mind being bored. What he wanted was submission, and when he had that, he could be very gracious:

"That only shows," said the king, in a really fatherly manner, "what sort of a reputation you have in the world, and you must admit that, to a certain extent, you deserve it. If you had never been mixed up in any of these affairs, or, at any rate, if you had not taken sides so warmly and shown yourself so touchy about questions of precedence, people would not say such things. That shows you also how careful you must be in your conduct, so as to let this impression of you fade away, and not give people any pretext for talking about you."

The little duke almost broke down before this sudden beneficence of his liege lord. It is all very well for us to smile today, but we were not brought up in a society where the monarch and the nation were synonymous.

Saint-Simon was highly critical of Louis XIV, but, like so many of his contemporaries, he had a deep need to reverence him:

> I then went on to speak of my long absence, caused by my grief at thinking that I had incurred his displeasure; and I took the opportunity to go beyond the ordinary terms of respect to express my affectionate attachment to his person, which I did with a sort of frank familiarity; for I perceived, from his looks and manner, and the way in which he spoke, that I might safely venture on it. My remarks were received with a cordiality which astonished me, and I felt satisfied that I had regained his good opinion. Seeing that I had no more to say, he rose from the table; I begged him to remember me if there were any vacant quarters in the *château*, so that I might be able to pay my court to him more assiduously. He replied that there were none vacant at present; and, bowing slightly, with a smiling and gracious air, he went into his further rooms.

This is the climax of Saint-Simon's loyalty to the crown. The critical peer, so conscious of ducal rights and prerogatives, was now humbly begging for a suite of those tiny, ill-ventilated rooms for which the greatest names in the land happily deserted their ancestral acres. But his loyalty was soon to be put to a heavy test, for the old king was engaged in the touchy business of promoting his bastards to royal rank.

Succession to the French crown was governed by the Salic law; only males descended in the male line from a king were qualified to reign. The sons and grandsons of a king were known as sons and grandsons of France, more remote descendants as princes of the blood. Royal bastards had no status whatever unless made peers by the king; normally, they could never hope to be princes. Louis XIV had four such bastards by Madame de Montespan, two sons and two daughters, who were constantly begging him for advancement, aided and abetted by their father's morganatic wife, Madame de Maintenon, formerly their governess. It had proved impossible to ally the daughters suitably abroad (William of Orange had incurred the lasting resentment of the king by refusing the offer of one of them with a crude retort), but they had been duly married off to subservient princes of the blood at home. By thus forcing his daughters into the royal family, the king hoped to ease the way for the ultimate inclusion of their brothers, the Duc du Maine and the Comte de Toulouse. In the meantime the latter occupied a sort of limbo between the peers and the princes. To Saint-Simon, who watched their gradual encroachment with passionate jealousy, it represented a threat to the very existence of orderly society. For once, he had the court with him. To place a bastard in line to the throne, even at the bottom of a considerable list of legitimate heirs, was deeply shocking to everybody. As Saint-Simon points out, if the sovereign could add a bastard to the royal family, could he not place him *ahead* of the royal family? What was to stop him, then, from naming his own successor? And in that event what happened to the principle of lineal succession on which both feudal *and* monarchical society were based? Louis XIV had finally gone too far.

But he knew it. He was old and weary of the importunities of Madame de Maintenon and Maine. He warned them that these new honors would not survive his death. He recognized that his entire court was bound to be with Saint-Simon. After all, like himself, they owed everything to birth. To have resented their attitude would have been idle. All he could do was to placate them by promoting his sons as gradually as possible in the time that remained to him and by obtaining the grudging approval of his court for each step. The sanction of so famous a stickler for precedent as Saint-Simon would be of especial help. The great monarch at last had need of the little duke, and the royal system was again invoked to bring him into line. Saint-Simon found these days that he was always included on the weekends at Marly.

Of course, he had to pay for it. When the king ordained that the children of the Duc du Maine should enjoy the same rank and honors as their father and let it be known that he wished the court to congratulate his son, Saint-Simon was on the spot. As he says: "I had only lately made my peace with the king, and he had warned me to be very careful in all matters affecting my dignity." The entire court was congratulating Maine; to have held off would have meant ruin. He resolved at last to "drain the cup to the dregs," and called upon Monsieur du Maine when the crowd in the latter's apartments was at its maximum, made his hurried bow and slipped away without a word. But nothing at Versailles escaped the royal eye. His visit was immediately reported to the king who was much pleased and remarked that "since *that* man approved of what had been done, there could be no great objection to it." Poor Saint-Simon had been used to make orthodox what he deemed the greatest heresy. It was what happened to dukes at Versailles.

Worse was to come. The Duc de Berri, son of "Monseigneur," the dauphin, had married a daughter of the Duc d'Orléans, and the question arose of the appointment of her lady of honor. Madame de Saint-Simon was rumored to be the king's choice because she was a person of irreproachable virtue (rare at court) and because she was not associated with any cabal. Saint-Simon, when sounded out by the Duc d'Orléans, placed his objections tactfully on the ground that it was a position of the second place (the Duchesse de Berri was ranked by the Duchesse de Bourgogne), but it is fairly evident that his real objection was that the Duchesse de Berri's mother, the Duchesse d'Orléans, was a royal bastard. The royal will, however, could be blunt. "Would you refuse it?" the Duc d'Orléans demanded. Saint-Simon had to admit that, as a loyal subject, he would, of course, obey the express commands of his sovereign. The next he heard of the matter was the appointment itself.

On his way back the king called to me in the Gallery, and told me to follow him into his room, as he wished to speak to me. He advanced to a little table against the wall, at some distance from the other persons present, on the side nearest the Gallery from which he had entered. There he told me that he had selected Madame de Saint-Simon to be Lady of Honor to the future Duchesse de Berri; that it was a special mark of his esteem for her virtue and merit to entrust to her charge, at the age of thirty-two, a Princess of such tender age and so nearly related to himself; moreover, by bringing me into closer access to himself he intended to show me that he was quite convinced of the sincerity with which I had spoken to him a few months ago.

Saint-Simon made a "moderately low bow" and replied "laconically" that he felt deeply the honor so placed in his wife and himself. He assumed that the king would understand immediately from his manner that he was accepting a degrading job from motives of pure loyalty. But the Saint-Simons of this world can never believe that others do not share their petty standards. I doubt if Louis XIV had any reaction to the "laconic" quality of the verbose little duke's reply other than a faint surprise and relief. Certainly there was no apology in his next remark: "But you must keep your tongue in order." Saint-Simon, however, replied "boldly" that he *had* kept it in order and would continue to do so in the future. By this he meant the king to infer that he had not been publicly complaining about the humiliation of his wife's expected appointment! Louis XIV simply smiled, "with a more satisfied expression," and turned to announce the appointment to the rest of the company.

But the nadir was reached in the final year of the old king's reign when the bastards were at last officially raised to the rank of princes of the blood with rights of succession to the crown. Death had played havoc with the king's direct heirs; only a delicate great-grandson, a nephew and one great-nephew stood between the princes of the house of Condé and the throne. As the latter were but remotely related to Louis XIV, having to trace their line all the way back to Saint Louis to find a royal progenitor, a conflict could be foreseen between them and the bastards, who were at least the natural children of a sovereign. Here was despotism, in Saint-Simon's eyes, worse than Peter the Great's. But what did he do about it? Just what Peter the Great's subjects would have done. Accompanying the whole court, whose cringing servility he did not scruple to excoriate, he went to the apartments of the Duc du Maine to congratulate him *"very sincerely"!*

The phrase, however, is not sarcastic; he explains that what he had really resented about the bastards was their intermediate rank between the royal family and the peerage. If they were merged with royalty, the peerage moved back up to its traditional second place. But he does not for a moment convince us that this was the real reason that he bowed to Maine. The real reason was that the king had "fixed his eyes steadily on him" during the supper that had preceded the congratulatory visit. Victory was again with the monarch, but it was his last.

The wise but misguided old sovereign was correct in his warning to his bastard sons that their new-found honors would not survive his death. By will he attempted to give Maine supervision of the young king during his minority and a focal seat on the council that was intended to act as a brake to the regent's power. All this was swept away by the Duc d'Orléans as soon as his royal uncle was dead, without so much as a murmur of opposition. And worse retribution was to come. Only three years after the end of the reign, at a Bed of Justice, the bastards were stripped of their princely ranks and privileges and reduced to the grade in the nobility to which their recently created peerages entitled them. Saint-Simon, who, as a friend of the regent's, had been

instrumental in bringing this about, viewed the proceedings of the Bed of Justice in a passage of his memoirs
that reads like a shrill *Nunc Dimittis:*

> I truly felt as though I were going to swoon, for
> my heart seemed to swell within me and could find
> no room in which to expand. I remembered the
> long days and years of servitude, those unhappy
> times when, like a victim, I was dragged to the
> Parlement to witness the triumph of the bastards,
> as they rose by degrees to a pinnacle above our
> heads. Then I thought of this day of law and
> justice, this dreadful retribution which had elevated
> us by the force of recoil. I could rightly congratu-
> late myself that all this had been brought about by
> me. I triumphed, I was avenged, I rejoiced in my
> vengeance. I delighted in the satisfaction of my
> strongest, most eager and most steadfast desires!

But even if the bastards had retained their royal rank,
as matters turned out, they would never have succeeded
to the crown. The direct royal line and the Houses of
Orléans and Condé continued to produce heirs while the
illegitimate branches withered. Maine had two sons but
no grandchildren, while Toulouse had one son whose
heiress became Duchesse d'Orléans. Thus the great fortune of the bastards, which had originated in the will
which Louis XIV had obliged his unhappy cousin, the
Grande Mademoiselle, to make in favor of the Duc du

Maine as the price of her lover's liberty, reverted by natural succession to the royal line from which it had been raped. The flaw in the great king's monarchical system was catharized by time. Only revolution could now destroy it. From the death of Mazarin, when Louis XIV took over the reins of government, to the fall of the Bastille, it lasted one hundred and twenty-eight years. For all its mammoth faults it held France together as no other system of government has done, before or since.

Because he foresaw the pernicious effects of a bureaucratic government centered about an absolute monarch, Saint-Simon is often given more credit for political vaticination than he strictly deserves. We should remember that his own political solution was simply to restore the power of the nobles. It was the purest feudalism, and almost nobody but Saint-Simon, including his fellow peers, really wanted it. He was like a shrill Wall Street Republican in the days of the New Deal, predicting, with some accuracy, the evil consequences of red tape and high taxes, but recommending in their stead a return to the old, discredited system of laisser faire. The government of Louis XIV was at least an effort to cope with contemporary problems, while Saint-Simon, for all his perspicacity, had his eyes fixed on the past. One wonders if his project of restoring the feudal hierarchy would not have summoned a Robespierre from the masses a century before his time.

Meredith Reassailed

Gᴇᴏʀɢᴇ Mᴇʀᴇᴅɪᴛʜ is to me the most constantly disappointing novelist of the last century, for I can never quite bring myself to abandon the hope that somewhere along the sizable shelf of his fiction I may find another *Egoist* or at least another *Diana*. How is it conceivable that the author of two such perfect novels should never, in a long and productive life, have repeated his double success? And so, every few years, I find myself giving him another chance in the presumptuous tribunal of my literary taste. Perhaps in the past I was too young or too hasty. Perhaps it takes maturity to savor a vintage Meredith. I remind myself how many critics used to scoff at the later style of Henry James and how sacrosanct it has since become. Little by little I wax enthusiastic at the prospect of enrolling myself among a gentle elite who will rediscover the subtle beauties of *One of Our Conquerors* and gather to worship at the shrine of a new "old master." Along the stock exchange of literature I seem to hear the cry ring out: "Buy Meredith!"

But my experience is always the same. I make a good enough start with *The Ordeal of Richard Feverel,* though I find I like it less at each reading, tiring of the iteration of the evil effects of Sir Austin's manifestly absurd system of education. And I am mildly diverted by the trials of the snobbish sisters in *Evan Harrington,* though again I sense the cannon in combat with the mosquito. They are early works and well enough, but I am soon ready to push on. Yet it is at just this point, when I feel that my real pleasure must be about to begin, that all pleasure abruptly ceases. I have traversed the field in my search of water, but I hit a rocky beach in a curious little novel, *Rhoda Fleming,* where a handsome farmer foils the villain by the old stratagem of suddenly producing the villain's first wife. It has hardly any of Meredith's characteristics; one is put in mind of Trollope trying to ape Hardy. Then come the confused, episodic Emilia stories, *Sandra Belloni* and *Vittoria,* and a long picaresque novel, *Harry Richmond,* which, located in the history of fiction midway between *Tom Jones* and *Augie March,* causes one to speculate if broadness in matters of sex is not a quality indispensable to that type of tale. Is not a Victorian picaresque novel, to put it more bluntly, something of a contradiction in terms? I

next stub my toe on *Beauchamp's Career,* the dullest and
most difficult yet, but at least it brings me to the water's
edge of the later style, and my hope revives. I just manage to float with *The Tragic Comedians* and *Lord
Ormont and his Aminta,* each founded on a historical in-
cident, though I cannot but wonder what failure of imagination was responsible for Meredith's new method of
selecting *données,* which seems the equivalent of picking
them from a book of opera synopses. *The Amazing
Marriage* is choppier water, and *One of Our Conquerors*
a towering breaker which, no matter how artfully I dive
into it, will always pick me up and fling me back, panting and exhausted, on the sands of my determination.
Not even that strongest of all drives, the ambition (a
relict of school days) to be able to tell the world that I
have read *all* of Meredith, can give me strength enough
to get through it.

Well, the reader may say, so you don't like Meredith.
Is that so worthy of note? Hasn't he, notoriously, always
had his detractors and his admirers? Siegfried Sassoon
says that "when people dislike Meredith it is useless to
argue with them." J. B. Priestley goes further; he suggests that they have dubbed themselves incompetent
readers, adding that one can spot them by their prefer-
ence for *Rhoda Fleming.* But I *do* like Meredith, and I
don't like *Rhoda Fleming!* I would happily rank *The
Egoist* among the ten finest novels in the English tongue.
Is that not enough to take me out of Mr. Priestley's cage

of Philistines? And turning briskly the pages of his and Sassoon's books on the subject, I note with interest, even with a wry satisfaction, that they appear to have the same trouble reading Meredith that I do. Sassoon admits freely that Meredith groaned under the tyranny of the three-volume novel, that much of what he wrote was "rubble and fustian" and that whole chapters of *Harry Richmond* are "labored and without momentum." Both agree that the style of the later novels is absurdly convoluted and pointlessly, perhaps intentionally, obscure. Priestley is the harsher of the two. To him *One of Our Conquerors* is "a charnel house of slain English" and its author, quite simply, "one of the worst narrators in the history of the English novel." He concludes:

> . . . his manner and style, especially in the later novels, refuse to undertake what might be called the donkey-work of narration. He will go miles out of his way, giving us pages of what can only be considered sheer bad writing, in order to avoid making a few plain statements of fact, necessary for the conduct of the narrative.

For all this plain talking, however, both critics remain stubborn admirers of Meredith's fiction. Why? Priestley praises the curious dichotomy that Meredith creates by placing romantic figures against an intellectual background, a procedure which compels the reader to follow the comic spirit with a philosophic eye and which imbues even the scenes of greatest sentiment with the

bitter-sweet flavor of irony. I have no quarrel with this;
I find it, on the contrary, well put. But where I differ
fundamentally with Messrs. Sassoon and Priestley is in
the low value which they ascribe to narrative. To say
that a storyteller cannot tell a story is to me like saying
that a painter cannot paint. I am too much of a Jacobite
to have any patience with a novel that does not hold together as a novel. James may have paid a handsome post-
humous tribute to Meredith ("He did the best things
best") but hear his opinion of *Lord Ormont and his
Aminta:*

> The unspeakable Lord Ormont has roused me to
> critical rage. Not a difficulty met, not a figure pre-
> sented, not a scene constituted — not a dim shadow
> condensing once into audible or visible reality —
> making you hear for an instant the tap of its feet
> on the earth.

I might plead an exception for Lord Ormont's sister,
Lady Charlotte; surely I hear the tap of *her* feet in the
wonderful scenes where she tries to bully her grandson's
tutor. But, like James, I cannot read a novel for the sake
of a few good scenes. The prospect of Lady Charlotte
will not compensate me for her creator's failure to interest me in his basic theme: why an old man should refuse
to acknowledge his beautiful young wife before the
world. By the time I come to the answer, I have lost interest — largely because Meredith seems to have lost his.
And by like token I cannot feel rewarded by the beauti-

ful descriptions of Alpine scenery in *The Amazing Marriage* when I don't care about the marriage itself. It seems to me that scenery must be secondary, unless it constitutes an integral part of the action. And, worse still, once dullness has set in, I can no longer properly respond to a passage of good writing, which, extracted from the context, might well delight me. It's as if, in a boring play, one of the characters should suddenly recite the "Ode to a Nightingale."

Yet so low does Priestley hold the virtue of storytelling that he does not hesitate to judge *all* of Meredith's work as wanting in it. "Regarded as a narrative," he states flatly, "every novel that Meredith wrote is not merely faulty but downright bad, even perverse in its badness." Now this, I submit, is simply not the case. In fact, my whole thesis is just that *Diana of the Crossways* and *The Egoist* are superlative narratives, elaborately conceived and carefully organized, and for that very reason constitute the only frames in which I can still admire the genius of Meredith with any continuing pleasure. And I would argue further that the reason the other novels, with the exception of *Richard Feverel*, have lost their modern audience is that they are poor narratives or barely narratives at all.

Diana, it is true, has often been criticized as a story. Why does Diana marry Warwick, in the first place? And why does she ruin her second chance for happiness by selling to the press a cabinet secret, told her in confidence by the man she loves? But these are not truly questions of narrative, but rather of the author's success in delineating his central character. The problem of the sale of the cabinet secret is the whole *donnée* of the novel. The task which Meredith set for himself was to create a woman of wit, intellect, noble character and integrity who would nevertheless be guilty of such an act. Now it may be that he has not wholly succeeded, for his task, in my opinion, was insuperable, but, unlike the tasks which he set for himself in the later novels, it at least fascinated him. Consequently, Diana fascinates us, and if her creator does not quite convince us of her midnight trip to the editor's office, his failure does not affect our pleasure in the balance of her tale. Everything in the novel is directed toward giving us a heightened sense of her beauty and charm; the very speed of the prose is designed to make us feel the quickness of her wit (much more than the examples of it) and the suddenness of her impulses. The beauty of the English countryside becomes Diana's beauty, as does the beauty of Lord Melbourne's London. Much time is covered and much space traversed, but there is a fine unity of mood utterly lacking in the earlier books. James's statement that Meredith harnessed "winged horses to the heavy car of fiction" applies particularly, perhaps uniquely, to *Diana*.

If *Diana*, then, is a novel of rapid movement and changing scene, *The Egoist* is one of gravely measured tempo and concentrated action. If the heroine of the first is a swallow that needs to soar, the hero of the other is a rooster that can only strut. Meredith fixes our eye firmly upon the latter at the outset by showing us Sir Willoughby in the center of his demesne, in his great hall surrounded by dependent relatives and servitors, the benign and beaming young baronet, the adored of the countryside, the matrimonial catch of catches, who has everything ready for a triumphant journey through life — except a wife to share the ride. Imagine the fluttering hearts of Jane Austen's mothers! All of the major characters, including the heroine, are either Sir Willoughby's house guests or residents on his estate. The terrifying Mrs. Mountstuart Jenkinson alone occupies a position of independence; she is a neighbor, for she must represent the forces of the great outside world which Sir Willoughby, petty despot and bully that he is at heart, knows that he must placate. Meredith has not had to conceive a duke in a castle or even a duchess to quell his hero; all he needs is a neighboring dowager with a sharp eye and a sharp tongue, brisk, rude and very conservative, but on the side of the angels (at least of an angel like Clara) if the angels have only the courage to state their case. She is not infallible; she can be fooled, but Sir Willoughby must work to fool her. She is no maiden aunt. A "rogue in porcelain" is her verdict of Clara, and the phrase is Sir Willoughby's doom, as he dimly but frantically suspects from the very beginning.

Meredith thus announces his theme: why should such a paragon, such a cynosure, have such difficulty finding a

mate? Why should he be jilted, once, twice, *thrice?*
The closely knit working out of the answer against the
bright backdrop of a green park and a soft old mansion
by characters who enunciate with a high clarity of tone
gives to the novel some of the pleasing artificiality of a
perfectly produced English comedy of manners. Indeed,
from the entrance of Clara to the final curtain the dramatic unities are carefully observed. Oh, true, the action
occupies several weeks rather than a day, and the characters go off the estate to dine at Mrs. Mountstuart's and
poor Clara gets as far as the railway station in her desperate effort to escape her fate, but essentially we are
watching one group of persons against one setting at one
point of time. And the advantage of adhering to the
unities is that once the stage has been set and the central
idea exposed, Meredith can let his ideas spill over the setting in any shape he chooses. He can buttonhole us like
Thackeray and lecture us on comedy and wines; he can
take wing into the romantic or he can roll about in what
approaches farce — everything seems only to enrich his
theme and to heighten our enjoyment of it. And as we
progress through the tale the atmosphere seems less and
less artificial in the growingly intensified glare of the
light which is remorselessly held on the unfortunate
Willoughby. It has been said that in actual life he would
have had no difficulty finding a suitable mate. Perhaps it
is Meredith's triumph that makes one doubt this, but
hasn't one seen just such men, men who appear to be
fatally driven to the very women who will not have

them? For it is not simply that Willoughby is an egoist, a pompous ass. He cannot love — one is almost tempted to see his drama as a tragedy of impotence. As the unhappy man writhes and turns in his frantic search for the increasingly elusive spouse, as he is driven at last to face a bleak and loveless marriage in order to have a bride, *any* bride, whose hand he can hold up to the approaching Mrs. Mountstuart, the world incarnate, glimpsed through a window descending from her carriage as he kneels to the obdurate Laetitia, we begin to shudder in our laughter. The picture of the poor, deflated rooster, his comb drooping, groveling before the drabbest hen in the barnyard, can no longer be viewed with complete detachment. As Priestley says, Sir Willoughby has taken on some of the quality of Everyman.

No sooner have I come to this point and put down my pen to reflect on the beauties of *The Egoist* than I feel once more the prick of my old, periodic urge to revisit Meredith. I scan those thirteen novels on the shelf, of which eleven continue to elude me. How could there not be pleasures still in store? Maybe I was prejudiced because I wanted to be clever and write this article. Maybe if I try again, without the vanity of prospective authorship, maybe if I am patient and relaxed, maybe if I am humble, the secret garden will be unlocked. And I find my hand stealing up again toward *Sandra Belloni.* Perhaps this time I will succeed.

Proust's Picture of Society

GORE VIDAL once told me that in reading Proust he was put off by a nagging sense that the narrator was a conjurer with three balls in the air, busily engaged in the triple misrepresentation that he was not a homosexual, not a social climber and not a Jew. Of course, one can answer that Proust, as a novelist, was under no obligation to endow any character, even the "I" who tells his story, with his own characteristics, but he deliberately invites the identification by giving the narrator his own first name. And when we consider George Painter's exhaustive researches (*Proust: The Early Years*) to prove that every character, every episode, even every landscape, has a corresponding model or models drawn from the author's own experience, when we consider further how little point there would be in writing so many volumes to recapture a purely invented past, we must conclude that the whole work, if not, strictly speaking, an autobiography, is at least bathed in a more intimately subjective light than other novels. It seems to me a consequence that to read the book against the background of the author's known predilections and prejudices becomes something more than the usual academic game of scholarship. It becomes a process that brings the picture into clearer focus.

To take up the first of the misrepresentations, it is now, of course, so notorious that Proust was homosexual that the number of his readers who are ignorant of the fact must be relatively small. Certainly, anyone trying to read the story of Marcel as that of a sexually normal male will be faced with some baffling questions. Why, for example, does Marcel fall in love with Albertine only when Doctor Cottard points out to him that, while dancing with another girl, she is rubbing her breasts against those of her partner? And why does Marcel's mother, who is otherwise represented as a woman of the strictest Victorian morality, tolerate the presence of Albertine in her apartment at night? Why is almost every male character in the book, other than the narrator, an actual or reputed homosexual? A perspicacious reader who knew nothing of Proust's personal life would probably recognize in the author (as the author recognizes in Charlus) the tendency of the homosexual to attribute his tastes to others. But what of the other two misrepresentations? Would the same perspicacious reader become aware that the author was half Jewish and a man who had spent much of his life assiduously cultivating a titled, anti-Semitic aristocracy? It seems less likely.

What difference does it make? Not much, surely, in an appreciation of the work as a whole. But it seems to me that there are certain exaggerations in Proust's picture of the social world that stem directly from his confusion of his snobbishness with his love of history and art, and that an analysis of these exaggerations may be of assistance to the reader, who, like myself, has speculated about them.

I note at the outset that the characters of *À la Recherche du Temps Perdu* are constantly referring to Saint-Simon. Marcel's grandfather is as familiar with everything concerning the bourgeoisie of Combray as was Saint-Simon's Prince de Conti with the family tree of the court. Swann, in the torments of his jealousy, emigrates to "those few and distant parts of himself which had remained almost foreign to his love and to his pain," by reading about court life in Saint-Simon. In his first appearance in the novel he refers to Saint-Simon's volume on the mission to Spain. The relationship of Léonie and her maid, Françoise, is described as a counterpart to the relationship between king and courtiers at Versailles, and the perfect manners, the ceremoniousness, the ignorance and the heartlessness of the Duc de Guermantes is contrasted with Saint-Simon's portrait of Louis XIV.

Indeed, the Duke occupies in the novel the same position at the apex of society that the sun king does in the memoirs. Even Albertine loves talking to Marcel about Saint-Simon. But the character, of course, who revels most in the many volumes of the prolific duke is the Baron de Charlus. He is the successor of those great gentlemen in the memoirs who associate with their lackeys because no one else is good enough for them. As an expert in his own genealogy and as a zealous watcher of any usurped privilege, he excels Saint-Simon himself, for he claims precedence for the Guermantes over the House of France. He brings the past into constant, immediate relation with himself ("There are portraits of my uncles, the King of Poland and the King of England, by Mignard") and amuses himself at parties by creating a sort of tableau-vivant out of the memoirs. We see him at Madame Verdurin's, refusing to rise from his chair when his hostess comes over to speak to him, impersonating in his fancy the Maréchal d'Uxelles who was so proud as to remain seated, under a pretense of laziness, before the most distinguished persons at court. It is a game which I suspect that the author himself may have enjoyed playing at Robert de Montesquiou's or at the Comtesse Greffuhle's. And when, at the end of *Le Temps Retrouvé*, Marcel describes the great literary work which he hopes he may be spared long enough to undertake, which is, of course, no other than the one which the reader is then completing, he feels it necessary to state that he has no intention of reproducing the memoirs of Saint-Simon.

Nor is it my intent to imply that he was. That he might have done so, had he chosen, is demonstrated by the brilliant parody of Saint-Simon in *Pastiches et Mélanges*, where he mixes characters from the court of Versailles with his own acquaintances. I do maintain, however, that he dignified and excused his own snobbishness by identifying it with the snobbishness of Saint-Simon and by consciously adopting the role of court historian to a latter-day Versailles. It was a habit of mind and attitude that distorted his over-all picture of society in three respects.

In the first place, his society characters have a hardness, a rudeness and a maliciousness that is more in keeping with a crowded, jealous court than with life in a large modern city. When Madame de Gallardon speaks to her cousin Oriane about Swann, whom she knows to be the latter's dearest friend, she says: "People do say about your M. Swann that he's the sort of man one can't have in the house, is that true?" The author explains this ill-tempered outburst to a woman whose favor the speaker is anxious to cultivate by describing the latter as one of those persons who can never restrain her highest social ambitions "to the immediate and secret satisfaction of saying something disagreeable." Now this is all very well, and one has known plenty of Mesdames de Gallardon, but my trouble comes from the fact that *no-*

body in Proust seems to be able to resist the temptation to say something disagreeable. The air is more the arrogant air of Versailles than that of Paris within the memory of many still living. When the Baron de Charlus' friends come to Madame Verdurin's to hear Morel, their offensiveness is hard to credit. Typical of the comments, Proust tells us, of each duchess within the hearing of their hostess are: "Show me, which is mother Verdurin; do you think I really need speak to her? I do hope, at least, that she won't put my name in the paper tomorrow, nobody would ever speak to me again. What! That woman with the white hair, but she looks quite presentable," or "Tell me, has there ever been a Monsieur Verdurin?" Poor Odette, in her helpless old age, is treated even worse:

> One constantly heard people say: "I don't know if Madame de Forcheville recognizes me, perhaps I ought to be introduced over again." "You can dispense with that" (someone replied at the top of his voice, neither knowing nor caring that Gilberte's mother could hear every word), "you won't get any fun out of it. She's a bit daft."

The characters behave with a heartlessness about illness and death that recalls Saint-Simon's passages on the deaths of Louis XIV's heirs. The Duc de Guermantes refuses to be told of the death of a cousin because he would have to give up a ball; his wife at the same time affects not to credit Swann's news of his own impending demise, and Madame Verdurin, confronted inescapably with the death of her friend, Princess Sherbatoff, pretends always to have disliked her rather than put on a mourning air that might dampen her party. The Verdurins, indeed, have no mercy even on physical disabilities, as is shown by their treatment of Saniette:

> "What's that he says?" shouted Monsieur Verdurin with an air of disgust and fury combined, knitting his brows as though it was all he could do to grasp something unintelligible. "It is impossible to understand what you say, what have you got in your mouth?" he inquired, growing more and more furious, and alluding to Saniette's defective speech. "Poor Saniette, I won't have him made unhappy," said Madame Verdurin in a tone of false pity, so as to leave no one in doubt as to her husband's insolent attention.

It may be argued that Madame Verdurin is not in society at the time, but later she becomes Princesse de Guermantes. One doubts if she had to improve her manners to suit her new position. For hear Monsieur de Charlus, speaking at the Prince de Guermantes' of Madame de Saint-Euverte, whom he knows to be listening:

> "What would prevent me from questioning her about those passionate times is the acuteness of my olfactory organ. I say to myself all at once:

Oh, good Lord, someone has broken the lid of my cesspool, which is simply the marquise opening her mouth to emit some invitation. They tell me the indefatigable old street walker gives 'garden parties.' I should describe them as invitations to explore the sewers. Are you going to wallow there?"

Conceding that Charlus is a bit insane, would not his interlocutor try to silence him, especially as she knows that poor Madame de Saint-Euverte is overhearing all? And would Madame de Saint-Euverte really fawn on the Baron after the humiliation of hearing herself described as a cesspool?

In the second place, I think it questionable if people in society in Proust's day thought and talked quite so obsessively about their social position. The members of the Guermantes family hold forth with amazing pedantry about their own genealogy. Their prototypes may have done so to Proust, but I suspect that he encouraged them. Did they to everyone? At Marcel's first dinner at the Duchesse de Guermantes' the company (though I admit to the Duchesse's disgust) turns happily from gossip to settle down for the major part of the evening to the serious business of pedigree. It is pedigree, too, at its heaviest: "Not in that way at all, she belonged to the branch of the Ducs de la Rochefoucauld, my grandmother came from the Ducs de Doudeauville," but Marcel, like his creator, is entranced and cannot even respond to the questions of the Turkish ambassadress for fear of missing any of the genealogies. To him, a great name keeps in the full light of day the men and women who bear it; one follows the course of their families, through diaries and correspondence, back to the Middle Ages to recapture a past in which "impenetrable night" would cloak the origins of middle class folk. But his aesthetic pleasure is even greater than his historical:

> The Prince d'Agrigente himself, as soon as I heard that his mother had been a Damas, a granddaughter of the Duke of Modena, was delivered, as from an unstable chemical alloy, from the face and speech that prevented one from recognizing him and went to form with Damas and Modena, which themselves were only titles, a combination infinitely more seductive. Each name displaced by the attractions of another, with which I had never suspected it of having any affinity, left the unalterable position which it had occupied in my brain, where familiarity had dulled it, and speeding to join the Mortemarts, the Stuarts or the Bourbons, traced with them branches of the most graceful design and an everchanging color.

Relating a title to the past is simply projecting snobbishness back into history. Proust was as impressed by a dead duke as by a live one. His characters have streams of consciousness that ceaselessly gurgle over the damp pebbles of rank. The young Madame de Cambremer has married her husband in order to be able to refer to her mother-in-law's brother by the family abbreviation: "Mon oncle de Ch'nouville." Madame de Villeparisis speaks with affected amusement but basic veneration of the convent where her great-aunts were abbesses, which excluded the daughters of the King of France because they were descended from the Medici. Her nephew, the Prince de Guermantes, makes a scene at every dinner party when he is not given the seat to which he would have been entitled under Louis XIV. And Charlus, of course, excels them all, speaking of his relatives who are described in Saint-Simon's memoirs as if they were contemporaries: "We took precedence over all foreign princes. The Duc de Bourgogne, having come to us with ushers with raised wands, we obtained the king's authority to have them lowered." Yet in contrast to the Courvoisiers, a related but rival clan, the Guermantes have a reputation of modernity and liberalness! The latter, whom we meet only fleetingly, are the family who are supposed to be the *real* conservatives in questions of precedence and pedigree. I am aware that there were, and still are, persons as obsessed with these questions as Charlus himself, but to postulate a whole society of them seems to approach the field of caricature.

And, finally, Proust's picture of the society of the Faubourg St.-Germain is too lush, too rich. No matter how painstakingly he underlines the dullness, the selfish-

ness, and the fatuity of the Guermantes set, they remain
to the end still invested with much of the glamour in
which his imagination has clothed them. The beauty of
their women, the romance of their titles and palaces, the
splendor of their pedigrees give them a fairy tale quality
which may be intentionally contrasted with the banality
of their conversation and lives, but which nonetheless
lingers in the reader's mind as an attribute somehow
earned and merited by society people. It is illuminating
in this respect to read a fatuous little volume by Princess
Marthe Bibesco entitled *La Duchesse de Guermantes*. In
Proust's portrait of Oriane she professes to recognize the
blond beauty, the ancient lineage and the high style of
her old friend Laure de Chevigné, and she relates an
anecdote about the latter that might indeed have been
taken from *Le Côté de Guermantes*. Laure de Chevigné,
greeting the Grand Duchess Wladimir of Russia, treats
her with a combination of old court courtesy and near
impertinence that recalls the relationship between the
Duchesse de Guermantes and the Princesse de Parme.
Taking in the Grand Duchess' hat and dress in one
sweeping glance, she exclaims: "Possible, in St. Petersburg, or the Hague, or Copenhagen. *Impossible* in Paris.
I take the liberty of escorting Madame to the Rue de la
Paix, to Paquin's or to Worth's. Yes, now, immediately,
at this moment! Gustave! Call Her Imperial Highness'
carriage!" This, admittedly, is pure Oriane, but Princess
Bibesco has not a word to say about the insipidity, the

selfishness or the vanity of the character with whom she is so proud to identify her old and valued friend. Yet it is not possible (however tempting to suppose) that a woman who has written three books on Proust should have failed to finish his novel. Her attitude is simply further evidence of how much of Proust's adoration of the aristocratic way of life seeps through the meshes of his analytical net.

I have been careful to set down these criticisms of Proust's picture of society because I wish to clear the way for a final judgment of undiluted praise. For never, to my knowledge, in fiction or outside of it, has there been so brilliant or so comprehensive a study of the social world. In fact, it stands so above its nearest competitors as to seem in retrospect almost the only picture of society in all of literature. Most people who write about society, whether they be novelists or sociologists or simply gossip columnists, make the basic error of assuming that there must be some consistency in its standards. They take for granted that there are rules which govern the qualifications of those seeking admission, that if one has been gently born or richly born, or if one can play polo or excel at cards, or if one has the gift of pleasing or is a good shot or a good conversationalist, one may tap with confidence at any closed gates. When the rules are seen not to apply, the observer concludes that they once did, but have since broken down. As the cases of nonapplication multiply, he is apt to shrug in frustration and say: "Oh, well, nowadays, it's only a question of money!"

What Proust alone had the patience to piece out is that any society will apply all known standards together or individually, or in any combination needed to include a maverick who happens to please or to exclude an otherwise acceptable person who happens not to. Nor are society people conscious of the least inconsistency in acting so. They keep no records, and they have no written constitution. Why should their rules be defined in any way other than by a list of exceptions to them? Proust understood this with the clarity of one who had succeeded in being accepted. There is a delightful passage in which he describes how the Baron de Charlus never hesitates to reverse himself. If a nobleman with whom he has quarreled happens to come of an ancient family possessed of a recent dukedom, the precedence of the dukedom becomes everything, the family nothing. "The Montesquious are descended from an old family?" he snorts. "What would that prove, supposing that it were proved? They have descended so far that they have reached the fourteenth storey below stairs." If, on the contrary, he has quarreled with a gentleman possessed of an ancient dukedom, but to whom this distinction has come without any length of pedigree, the case is altered, pedigree alone counts. He says of the Duc de Luynes: "I ask you; M. Alberti, who does not emerge from the mire until Louis XIII. What can it matter to us that favoritism at court allowed them to pick up dukedoms to which they have no right?" Small wonder that Madame Verdurin could not fathom the standards by which he selected her guests for Morel's recital.

Only by conceding the arbitrariness of those on top and by intuitively sensing the bonds of congeniality that hold them together can the observer hope to appreciate the different gradations in position. He must also be prepared for the bad memory of society and its habit of judging its own history by the same erroneous standards of its most misguided student. Take, in *Le Côté de Guermantes*, the contrasted positions of Madame Leroi and the Marquise de Villeparisis. Madame Leroi, the daughter of "rich timber people," has learned to copy exactly the colors of the Guermantes and the Courvoisiers and has penetrated so far into the inner citadel that only a knowledgeable minority is even aware of her existence. Madame de Villeparisis, on the other hand, though a member of the Guermantes family and once treated "like a daughter" by Queen Marie Amélie, has fallen from the first rank because of the irregularity of her life. Her parties seem smart enough to the uninitiated, because her family still attend them, as do many famous artists and men of letters, and because the talk is good. Madame de Villeparisis knows how to make her lions roar, while Madame Leroi, in the tradition of the truly fashionable, seats them at the card table. But it nevertheless remains the sad law of the social world that Madame de Villeparisis would gladly leave her lions to roar alone for the opportunity of sitting at the least of those card tables. Only after the death of both women will their fortunes be reversed. Posterity will judge Madame de Villeparisis a great social leader, because of the glittering names strewn through the pages of her memoirs, memoirs that Madame Leroi would never have stooped to write. The children of people who snubbed her will freely accord Madame de Villeparisis in history the social position that she wanted in life. They will never have heard of Madame Leroi.

The rapidly fluctuating nature of society makes it a perfect theme in a book about time. There is no stain so deep that a little time will not wash it out, no position so assured that a little time will not erode it. Marcel's favorite duchess may be "the eighteenth Oriane de Guermantes in succession, without a single mésalliance," but her reputation at the end is that of a déclasseé who hobnobs with actresses, while the niece of Jupien, the tailor, adopted by Charlus, becomes first Mlle. d'Oleron and later Marquise de Cambremer. Would anyone anticipate that Odette, a prostitute married to a friend of the Prince of Wales and the Comte de Paris, would have to await the death of her husband to be accepted by the smart set which dropped him for marrying her? Who but Proust would explain that the Baron de Charlus' reputation for homosexuality in Madame Verdurin's circle, however abundantly merited by his private life, is still undeserved because they have confused him with another Monsieur de Charlus, whose wide reputation for the same vice is unfounded? Or that Swann, who disdained to boast to Marcel's family of his brilliant position at the very summit of society, should in later years become noticeably vulgar in dropping the names of minor bureaucrats whom he has induced to call on his wife? Or that Madame Verdurin who turns all her hatred on Swann for refusing to join in her denunciation of the Duchesse de la Tremouille, whom she does not even know, should later occupy, as Princesse de Guermantes, the first position in the world she has once affected to despise? Society is not aware of changing its standards, for it has no memory except for its own acts of condemnation, and for these only so far as the individual condemned is concerned. Swann can never be forgiven for marrying Odette, but his daughter, who was not even born in wedlock, can become a Guermantes. Society is violently contrary; it hates to be wooed and fears to be despised. Marcel can be invited to the Guermantes' only when he has ceased to care about being invited. Society is kinder and less critical than he has expected, but only with its darlings; society is harder than he has expected, but only with those who fail to conceal their yearning to enter it, although it is to just this yearning that society owes what glamour and reputation it has. One of the reasons that *À la Recherche* is so long a book is that inconsistency, if described at all, must be described in detail.

Most novels that deal with society take on some of the meretricious gaudiness that it is their avowed purpose to deplore. Their authors become guilty of the snobbishness and triviality of which they accuse their characters. Octave Feuillet and Ouida may shake their heads over the empty vanity of the great world, but they revel in describing it. Proust comes closest to escaping the contamination of his subject matter because he does not set society apart from the rest of mankind. To him the differences between class and class are superficial. Snobbishness reigns on all levels, so why does it matter which level one selects to study? Why not, indeed, pick the highest level, particularly if one's own snobbishness is thus gratified? Society in Proust parades before us, having to represent not a segment of mankind, but something closer to mankind itself. It is the very boldness of Proust's assumption that his universe is *the* universe, like the boldness of his assumption that all love is jealousy and all men homosexuals, that gives to his distorted picture a certain universal validity. It is his faith that a sufficiently careful study of each part will reveal the whole, that the analysis of a dinner party can be as illuminating as the analysis of a war. It is his glory that he very nearly convinces us.

Americans in Trollope

THE GROWTH of James's opinion of Trollope, from a partiality of which he was avowedly ashamed to a rather bemused respect, is illustrated by his two descriptions of the prolific British novelist on an Atlantic voyage, one written at the time and one six years later. In a letter to his family in 1876 James relates:

> We had also Anthony Trollope, who wrote novels in his stateroom (he does it literally every morning in his life, no matter where he may be) and played cards with Mrs. Bronson all the evening. He has a gross and repulsive face and manner, but appears *bon enfant* when you talk with him. But he is the dullest Briton of them all.

His essay in 1883, after Trollope's death, in which he reassesses the departed novelist as "one of the most trustworthy, though not one of the most eloquent, of the writers who have helped the heart of man to know itself," strikes a more reverent note:

> He drove his pen as steadily on the tumbling ocean as in Montague Square. Trollope has been accused of being deficient in imagination, but in the face of such a fact as that the charge will scarcely seem just. The power to shut one's eyes, one's ears (to say nothing of another sense) upon the scenery of a pitching Cunarder and open them to the loves and sorrows of Lily Dale or the conjugal embarrassments of Lady Glencora Palliser is certainly a faculty which could take to itself wings.

So far as I know, Trollope has left no recorded version of his own impressions either of the young James or of his early work. Very likely he had none. But if he had, I should doubt if they were very favorable. Trollope would have found James too intellectual, too refined, possibly too American. For he made very little effort to conceal a stout middle class prejudice against Yankees. One is astonished today by James's own evaluation of Trollope's American characters:

> His American portraits (by the way they are several in number), are always friendly; they hit it off more happily than the attempt to depict American character from the European point of view is accustomed to do.

I can only shudder at the thought of what those less happy attempts must have been. For it seems evident to me that Trollope's American portraits, with a single exception, are the least successful of his gallery, a gallery which, taken as a whole, is to me the most glorious of Victorian fiction. It may be that the pen which could delineate with such accuracy and sympathy English squires, English peers, English bishops and English solicitors, was bound to blunt itself in drawing foreign models. Perhaps nobody could be so understanding of xenophobes but one who had a mild case of the same disease.

The Americans in Trollope's novels fall into three divisions of parody. They are unscrupulous adventurers, like Hamilton Fisker and Winifred Hurtle in *The Way We Live Now*, or grotesque, unsexed women who advocate radical causes, like the Vermont suffragette in *Is He Popenjoy?* and the "Republican Browning" in *He Knew He Was Right*, or pompous political windbags, waving the stars and stripes in the disgusted eyes of their English cousins, like the visiting legislator in *The American Senator* and Jonas Spalding in *He Knew He Was Right*. All in all, they are an unlovely crew, united by the common bond of a "strong nasal twang" and their creator's clumsy spite in the selection of their names: Ezekiel Boncassen, Olivia Fleabody, Wallachia Petrie, Elias Gotobed, Jackson Unthank. I suppose, in justice to Trollope, we should remember that the emancipated Yankee female and the boasting Yankee statesmen may have been as fair game for caricature in the eighteen-seventies as the exiled grand duke in the nineteen-twenties and the bearded Freudian in the fifties. One has only to turn the pages of James's *The Bostonians* to see that such types as Dr. Fleabody and Miss Petrie were as irritating to their compatriates as to the British, and the flavor of Senator Gotobed is preserved to this day in the gusty perorations of convention hall oratory. The exuberant self-confidence of a postwar America (resentful, too, of British confederate sympathies) was probably hard for anyone to bear.

But if we can forgive Trollope his caricatures, it is more difficult to forgive him his attempts to be fair. A parody is quite acceptable as a parody. We are amused when Jonas Spalding, who has declaimed in town halls at home that no English aristocrat can be fitting company for a Christian American citizen, takes up his best gloves and umbrella to call on the son of an earl. And we delight in Miss Petrie when she speaks to the same unfortunate nobleman of "that small speck on the earth's broad surface, of which you think so much, and which we call Great Britain," and tells him that all courtiers will be cut down "with the withered grasses and thrown into the oven." We hardly blame him for wondering if he can bring himself to marry the friend of such a woman. But when Trollope begins to make a case for the American who is parodied, when he begins to point out, as he does with Senator Gotobed, that the misguided legislator is not such a bad fellow after all, he tips his hand to reveal that, in his opinion, Gotobed is no parody at all, but a living, breathing American senator. And this, even after a century, I am inclined to resent.

For never was the smugness of the British middle class more evident than in the chapters where Trollope analyzes Senator Gotobed's gullibility about the wicked Goarly, who has poisoned the hounds. The thesis is simple. If you're a British gentleman, and there's a villain about, you can probably smell him out. Your nose, at any rate, will be your best detective. All of the characters in *The American Senator*, except the senator himself, instinctively sense that Goarly has been the culprit. Has he not objected to the hunt crossing his land? In the same way all the characters in *The Duke's Children* immediately know that Major Tifto has driven that nail into Prime Minister's hoof. And, indeed, it ultimately turns out that Goarly *has* been the poisoner and that the bogus major *has* crippled the noble steed. But Senator Gotobed, in his irritating Yankee fashion, insists that it is not fair to condemn a man for a crime because he objects to a hunt, and Trollope leans over backwards to do justice to his point of view. Indeed, he argues, Gotobed may well be right — in principle. Indeed, there may be things wrong in England, possibly very serious things. But what, basically, is the use of principle in crime detection when the good old nostrils of prejudice can pick out the guilty man nine times out of ten? "Goarly is a

surly cuss who hates hunting; therefore Goarly is the culprit" may seem a harsh syllogism to Americans ignorant
of English ways, but if it be an exact one, how is Goarly
hurt?

There is one American character, however, against
whom Trollope had no prejudice. Radiant, gay, cour-
ageous, unconventional yet untouched by all things base,
the Yankee heroine, accompanied by dim, nasal parents
with whom she seems to have no affinity, makes her appearance on the shores of an old, wise, startled Europe in
the later novels of Trollope, as in the early ones of
James. The latter was guardedly generous about the success of his British competitor in a field which he must
have regarded as peculiarly his own:

> The American girl was destined sooner or later to
> make her entrance into British fiction, and Trollope's
> treatment of this complicated being is full of good
> humor and that fatherly indulgence, that almost
> motherly sympathy, which characterizes his attitude
> throughout toward the youthful feminine. He has
> not mastered all the springs of her delicate organism
> nor sounded all the mysteries of her conversation.

Caroline Spalding in *He Knew He Was Right* and
Isabel Boncassen in *The Duke's Children* marry into the
peerage with the author's rather grudging approval, but
that they should receive even the grudging approval of
so firm an admirer of Britain's class system speaks worlds

for the charm of the American girls whom Trollope must have met. Caroline has some of the freshness and pertness of Daisy Miller whom she antedates by a decade. Charles Glascock is immediately intrigued by the easy way in which she mocks him when he asks about New York:

> "You wouldn't like it at all," said Carry; "because you are an aristocrat. I don't mean that it would be your fault."
> "Why should that prevent my liking it — even if I were an aristocrat?"
> "One half of the people would run after you, and the other half would run away from you."

And when she discovers her betrothed kissing Nora Crowley's hand the day before their wedding, she simply observes:

> "Tomorrow, Mr. Glascock, you will, I believe, be at liberty to kiss everybody; but today you should be more discreet."

But if Caroline can laugh at others, she is also capable of taking herself and her Americanism with a desperate seriousness. She is not in the least dazzled by Glascock's rank, but she is very much concerned at the prospect of being snubbed by his family and friends. I believe in her naïve exaggeration of the problems in store and in her proud resolution to break off with her lover, and I am sure that she would have had an ugly, humorless girl friend in whose wisdom she would have had a willful faith, but Wallachia Petrie is so overdrawn that I cannot quite credit Caroline's dependence on her. That, however, is a detail. When Caroline tries to warn Glascock off, she is superbly comic in her earnestness. There are delightful echoes of Wallachia's lectures in her efforts to explain to him the incompatibility of the old and new worlds and the hopelessness of their ever understanding each other.

"You think it is impossible, Miss Spalding?"

"I fear so. We are so terribly tender, and you are always pinching us on our most tender spot. And we never meet you without treading on your gouty toes."

"I don't think my toes are gouty," said he.

"I apologize to your own, individually, Mr. Glascock, but I must assert that nationally you are subject to the gout."

There is certainly no coyness in her attempt to rebuff him. She bears down on Glascock as hard as a woman can bear. When he tells her sharply that he should not like his wife to call him a fool, she advises him to marry an English wife — and be safe. Of course it is the very thing that hooks him, but Caroline never intends it so. As Nora Crowley says, Caroline will look like a peeress and bears her honors grandly, but they will never harden her.

Caroline, however, is only a countess when we take leave of her, and Trollope had greater honors in store for another American girl. Isabel Boncassen, twelve years later, is to be nothing less than premier duchess of England. But if an American is going to earn such a prize, the American must be worthy of it, and to be worthy of it she must be aware of what it is. The trouble with such awareness, at least in novels, is that even the smallest amount may seem too much. The difference between Isabel and Caroline is that Isabel loves the peerage and hopes (in the nicest way) to become a peeress. In true American fashion she announces her ambition in one of her first passages with Lord Silverbridge.

"Do you ever dance with bank clerks?"

"Oh, dear yes. At least I suppose so. I dance with whoever comes up. We haven't got lords in America, you know!"

"You have got gentlemen?"

"Plenty of them — but they are not so easily defined as lords. I do like lords."

"Do you?"

"Oh yes — and ladies — Countesses I mean and women of that sort."

She is stating the literal truth. The remarkable thing about the novel is that Trollope beams his approval on Isabel's ambition and also on that of Francis Tregear who is interested in marrying Lady Mary Palliser only if he can be assured of her money. As a hero (which he is of a subplot) he is probably the most mercenary of Victorian fiction. Now it may be true that the Duke of Omnium's rank is so exalted and his wealth so enormous that it is impossible for his children's suitors not to be affected by the prospect, but what makes the atmosphere of the novel so unpleasant is Trollope's evident feeling that it would be a kind of *lèse-majesté* for any young man or woman *not* to be affected. To love Silverbridge for himself, in other words, might be an act of black republicanism. How could anyone with proper British values fail to appreciate such social altitude?

Trollope himself discloses a veneration for his Duke of Omnium that smacks of the tweeny reading tabloid accounts of royal princesses. The Duke is the most high-minded gentleman in all of England. He can pay £70,000 of his son's gambling debts and regret only the bad company in which the sum was lost. He devotes himself to the driest kind of statistical work and becomes an indispensable Chancellor of the Exchequer and, ultimately, prime minister. But if he had been born in the Massachusetts Bay colony, he could not have enjoyed his money or his rank less. The world for him is all duty, no play. He will not even hunt, which in a lesser Trollope character would be a sign of villainy. Where his philosophy is peculiarly repellent is that he despises all the aspects of ducal existence that we might enjoy: the beautiful possessions, the country life, the great, crowded weekends, the glittering dinners, and to venerate all the

aspects which we dislike: the narrow genealogical snob-
bery and the unceasing sense of personal superiority.
There was "an inner feeling in his bosom as to his own
family, his own name, his own children and his own personal self which was kept altogether apart from his grand
political theories." When the Duke has finally been induced to give his consent to the marriage of his daughter
to a brilliant young member of Parliament and of his son
to the beautiful daughter of a potential American presi-
dential candidate, he simply mutters that his third child
will probably bring home a kitchen maid. Yet this is a
man whom we are intended to like and admire!

Trollope's enthusiasm for the Duke spills over on Lord
Silverbridge. The oldest son and heir of the pompous and
snobbish Omnium is represented as a gullible scatterbrain
whose virtues consist of a boyish candor and extreme
good looks. He is sent down from Oxford; he loses
money to obvious crooks; he changes his political convictions (such as they are) because he dislikes the head
of his party and he shows, from beginning to end, little
understanding of other humans. Yet our American heroine, who, left to herself, has considerable clarity of vision, is made to view Silverbridge through the author's
rose-colored lenses:

> She had never seen anything like him before —
> so glorious in his beauty, so gentle in his manhood,
> so powerful and yet so little imperious, so great in

condition and yet so little confident in his own greatness, so bolstered up with external advantages, and
yet so little apt to trust anything but his own heart
and his own voice.

I fancy, in reading this passage, that I can hear the
American eagle squawk with discontent. Would a sharp-
eyed Yankee like Isabel be quite so subjugated by such a
nincompoop? But as I read on, I think I would rather
have her taken in by his looks — as can happen to even
a clever girl — than by his rank. What am I to think of
Isabel after the following?

> She was glad he was what he was. She counted in
> their full value all his natural advantages. To be an
> English duchess!

Both she and her rival, Lady Mabel Grex, are intent
upon becoming duchesses. The only difference is that
Lady Mabel Grex, with an honesty as rare as it seems
unnecessary, keeps reminding herself that she is not in
love with Silverbridge. Perhaps the rewards in later Trollope go to the wishful thinkers. After all that he has made
me swallow of the glories of a coronet and a bursting
bank account, I gag when presented with Silverbridge's
ideas of life with Isabel:

> He had thoughts of days to come, when every-
> thing would be settled, when he might sit close to
> her and call her pretty names, when he might in

sweet familiarity tell her that she was a little Yankee and a fierce republican, and "chaff" her about the stars and stripes; and then, as he pictured the scene to himself in his imagination, she would lean upon him and would give him back his chaff, and would call him an aristocrat and would laugh at his titles.

I don't believe that Isabel is going to laugh very much at titles which will then be her own. I am very afraid that, unlike Caroline Spalding's, her honors may harden her. Of course, it is true that the decades which followed publication of *The Duke's Children* witnessed dozens of such alliances. One cannot accuse Trollope of exaggeration in assuming a craze for titles among American girls of the era. But one can resent his attributing it to the finest and best of them. Trollope is more denigrating with his compliments than with his sneers. I have very little to say in defense of Senator Gotobed or Wallachia Petrie. But I hate to see Daisy Miller turned into a gold digger.

James and Bourget

J AMES, writing to Charles Eliot Norton in 1892, speaks with great candor of his friend Paul Bourget. "Have you read any of his novels?" he asks. "If you haven't, *don't*." How this would have pained poor Bourget, who in the dedication of *Cruelle Énigme* had publicly praised the other's *rare et subtil talent!* Yet if we apply James's injunction to Bourget's "serious," as opposed to his "society," novels, it will save us much travail. For, indeed, they express a repellent point of view.

Consider the three most celebrated. *Le Disciple* is the fable of a young man, deeply read in determinist philosophy, who, for reasons somehow attributable to his liberal education, plots the seduction, in cold-blooded steps, of the noble girl who loves him. *Un Divorce* is a warning, equally dire, of the results to be anticipated from the severance of the marriage tie. The heroine's first husband may be a vice-ridden monster, she herself an angel of patience and her second spouse a model of civic virtue — it can make no difference. The outcome is disaster for all. And in *L'Étape* the same stern finger points to the dangers of a too rapid changing of one's class. An atheist professor, born of peasant stock, attempts to raise his children in Paris, away from the soil to which they belong. The result? His son becomes a forger and embezzler, his daughter the victim of a licentious aristocrat. It seems astonishing that such dismal extracts, expressing a social philosophy so appalling, should once have been excitedly discussed in French literary circles, but we tend to forget how much of the royalist "ultra" point of view survived in France sixty years ago. Bourget as a young man had been deeply exposed to the forces of reaction by the national humiliation of 1870 and the excesses of the Commune. The tendency so engendered grew steadily through the years to burst into a fine bloom during the Dreyfus trial. Mauriac relates that when Paléologue protested to Bourget that the issue at stake was not the reputation of the military but justice to the accused, the latter retorted contemptuously, *"Je me moque de la justice!"* After that, it is no surprise to learn that throughout a long lifetime, ending in 1935, he should never once have exercised his privilege of voting.

So far, so bad. But there was more to Bourget than just the reactionary. He was, by all accounts, a brilliant and stimulating person of deep cultivation, widely traveled, married to a wife, who, according to Edith Wharton, was "a being so rare, so full of delicate and secret vibrations" that she never knew by what happy accident she had penetrated her "voluntary invisibility." James described her as ministering to her husband like "a little quivering pathetic priestess on a bas-relief." He had his reservations about Bourget, the man, but none about Bourget, the conversationalist. The latter, "one of the very first of all talkers," was his pipe line into intellectual Paris.

More importantly, however, Bourget was not all his life obsessed with the idea of saving France. In his earlier years he was content to be a novelist and to amuse his reader. The books of this period, *Cruelle Énigme, Un Coeur de Femme, Mensonges* and *Un Crime d'Amour* were welcomed by a public sated with the dry monotony of a naturalist literature which had concentrated on the physical appearance of things to the exclusion of everything else. Bourget's deft handling of the psychology of love and jealousy came as a needed relief. I know it is the fashion today to downgrade these novels and to laud the graver note which Bourget struck in *Le Disciple*. There seems to be a feeling among certain critics that a writer ought to be given marks if he turns from duchesses to determinism, if, in their condescending term, he "matures." But the only question to me is: does he make determinism more entertaining? I agree with Louis Bertrand that the early period was Bourget's *jardin secret*.

We start in the Paris world of the upper bourgeoisie, but we rise on the social ladder as the novels progress, and from the upper rungs we view palazzos in Rome and villas on the Riviera. *Une Idylle Tragique* takes us to witness a Mediterranean race between three great steam yachts, an American millionaire's, a Russian grand duke's and an English peer's, on the last of which the Prince of Wales himself is a guest. But if the backgrounds are inclined to be lush, the details are still accurate and colorful, the characters vivid, the dialogue crisp and dramatic. The wealth of psychological detail gives to each story a rigorous, ordered framework, sometimes at the expense of reality, but artificial flowers have their claim to beauty. James, who in warning Norton off the novels had to admit their "remarkable qualities," saw the danger of his friend's excess of anticipatory analysis and of his tendency "to swim in the thick reflective element" in which he set his characters afloat. In his letter about *La Duchesse Bleue* he observes:

> Your love of intellectual daylight, absolutely your pursuit of complexities, is an injury to the patches of ambiguity and the abysses of shadow which really are the clothing — or much of it — of the *effects* that constitute the material of our trade. *Basta!*

Adultery is the central theme of this period of Bourget's work. Statesmen, bankers, titled idlers, fashionable artists and their wives are all engaged, in one way or another, knowingly or unknowingly, in playing the dangerous game. To the conscious players it is a completely absorbing occupation which taxes all their ingenuities. For in a Bourget world the astute psychologist has the advantage of being able to predict his victim's reactions and is thus assured of success if he only acts correctly. It is therefore worth his while to spend weeks or even months stalking his quarry. If he is a man, he may pose elaborately as a reformed roué (*Un Coeur de Femme*), calling on his victim throughout a whole season without once declaring himself in order to establish a solid new reputation. If a woman (*Mensonges*) she may go to equal lengths to appear as a loyal, faithful, misunderstood spouse seeking harmless recreation in picture galleries. But when success has been achieved — and it always is — the same procedure is observed by all characters.

Immediately, the man will rent and redecorate an apartment in a district unfrequented by the lady's acquaintance, with a sitting room so that the bed may not be observed, either before or after. When the lovers meet at parties in the great world, they murmur daytime assignations *chez nous*. The lady will dress, on the morning of a rendezvous, in clothes that are easy to remove without the assistance of her maid and proceed to the rented flat in a cab (never, of course, in her carriage). When the rites of love have been celebrated the couple

will sip a glass of wine before returning to the more ordinary occupations of their day. In this brief interlude
the lady may contemplate her satisfied lover in hazy
rapture, if she happens to love him, or with an acid eye
if her motive is merely to supplement her husband's in-
adequate income, or with a troubled conscience if she
still has religious scruples. It may occur to her that she
takes great risks for fleeting pleasures. It certainly occurs
to the reader. For under the good manners of her polished
world lurks the constant danger of violence. Sooner or
later there will be a confrontation, between husband and
lover, or lover and lover, and she will be disgraced, anath-
ematized and spotted with blood. The end of a Bourget
novel is like Gerôme's painting, *The Duel after the Ball*,
with a dying Pierrot sinking into the arms of his seconds
on an early snowy morning while his victorious opponent, also in costume, stalks off to a waiting fiacre. The
Bourget heroine is a bewildered, defiant, hunted creature
who snatches what pleasure she can in an oriental world
of passionate, unreasonable men, knowing that she will
one day be indicted and terribly punished for infidelities
permissible to their sex but not to hers. What makes one
increasingly uncomfortable is one's suspicion and ultimately one's certainty that the author feels her fate to
be a just one. It is a point of view that may have received its sublimest expression in Shakespeare, but was
not its lowest Jack the Ripper?

James was appalled at the erotic details of these early

novels. He would not allow that they were proper subjects for fiction. In a letter to Bourget about *Mensonges* he argues that the essential character of love-making lends itself more to action than to reflection, that the moment a novelist begins to "splash about" in it intellectually, it becomes unhealthy and unpleasant. He accuses Bourget of consecrating to Madame Moraines "and her underclothing" an imagination worthy of a greater cause. And for the sensitive young hero who attempts suicide when he discovers that his mistress, a married woman, is something less than an angel of purity, James has nothing but *"un coup de pied dans le derrière."* That the world is full of such things is all the more reason for the novelist not to flood us with them.

James may have gone a bit far — at least in the eyes of a world of John O'Hara readers — but it was advice from which Bourget could have profited. For somewhere along the line, as happened with Dumas Fils, his denouncing side got out of hand. A modern John the Baptist, he turned his finger of scorn from Salomé to the world that had produced her. Society, in his later novels, has no more traditions and no more roots. A Jew like Hafner can rob his way to fortune and marry his daughter to a Roman prince. An octoroon can be the wife of a famous painter and move in the highest circles. And the morganatic wife of an Austrian archduke can receive her lover in the stateroom of an American yacht. If international society had taken on the worst features of the nations that composed it, the only hope for a Frenchman was to stay in his home, in his class and in his church. For the aging Bourget, the menace of the future must have seemed less Hitler or Stalin than Elsa Maxwell. Small wonder that his last years were depressed and his tales somber. He had allowed the crank to swallow the novelist.

Now James, on the other hand, though a man of far greater humaneness (he was on Zola's side in the trial), could be a bit of a crank himself. He deplored the absence in American life of such items of "high civilization" as a sovereign, a court, an aristocracy, old country houses, thatched cottages and ivied ruins; he hankered for "the luxuries and splendors of life," for "Old World drawing rooms with duskily moulded ceilings." One almost suspects that he considered the solace of the humble to lie in the contemplation of the elegance of their betters, for if, like Hyacinth Robinson, they were truly conscientious, they could take no part in the damaging of bric-à-brac that so often accompanies sudden upheavals in the social order. James's letters and travel books are spotted with nostalgia for a world of aristocratic order and tradition that must have appealed to Bourget. But a vital distinction exists. James wanted such a world as a painter might want a particular model, because he sought to re-create it. Its function was to supply him with *données* and his to turn them into beautiful tales. As long as he could reproduce and interpret, he had no need to *change* anything. He never had anything as vulgar as an axe to grind.

It is significant to note that despite all the literary chatter of the past twenty years about James as a moralist or philosopher or social commentator, there is not a phrase in all of his published notebooks to indicate that he ever had anything in mind in his writing but to translate little patches of anecdote in terms of his individual aesthetic. I know of no more illuminating study of the artistic process, though a layman's reaction might well be: "It *that* all it is?" The germ of James's initial idea is impossible to predict or explain; it simply comes. A dinner companion may be telling him a story or describing a family problem, and suddenly he knows that it is *his*. He jots it down later and proceeds to dramatize it, shifting the variables about in different combinations. Is it a daughter chained to her mother's sickbed? Can she escape? Does she? If she does, and flies to Europe, what will become of the mother? Is she cured? Does she rise from her chaise longue in hot pursuit? And might the daughter not then return, her eager parent at her heels? Might they not, pursued and pursuer, cross and recross the ocean indefinitely? "The scenic method," he writes, "is my absolute, my imperative, my *only* salvation." As the characters begin to move across the proscenium of his imagination, entering and exiting in different combinations, he communes with his director-intelligence in crooning phrases of passionate invocation:

Ah, things swim before me, *caro mio,* and I only need to sit tight, to keep my place, and fix my eyes, to see them float past me in the current into which I can cast my little net and make my little haul.

Or:

. . . the prospect clears and flushes, and my poor blest old Genius pats me so admirably and lovingly on the back that I turn, I screw round, and bend my lips to passionately, in my gratitude, kiss its hand.

Whatever one's reaction, one has certainly peeked into the mind of an artist at work. It may come as an anticlimax to some. They may prefer the more edifying picture of the author of *L'Étape* approaching his task of saving France. One sees Bourget, with that obsession of French novelists after Balzac to regard their scattered works as a unified *comédie humaine,* grimly considering which aspects of modern degeneration next to treat with his scalpel. The man who in 1885 had written that he and James, in talks about the novel, had finally agreed that all laws pertaining to it boiled down to the need of giving a personal impression of life had long been lost in the reformer and patriot. The older Bourget succeeded only in giving a personal impression of himself.

His nearest return to readable fiction was with *L'Émigré,* in which he drew a vivid and sympathetic portrait of an old marquis, possessed of a great name and chateau, prodigally dispensing his capital to keep up the standards of the *ancien régime* in 1906. The marquis passionately believes in the duty of the aristocracy to close ranks and preserve what is left of the old France for the day when the disillusioned new shall look again to her true leaders. He abhors all modern inventions, from the automobile to the telephone; he regards the officials of the Third Republic as so many Dantons and Marats, and he is prepared to break forever with his only son upon the latter's engagement to a woman whose sole demerit is her middle-class birth. But he also is a generous and trusting friend, a father to his tenants, a princely host, a man of absolute integrity and courage, a comic as well as a tragic character, in short, a magnificent anachronism. We sympathize with him, but never with his creator. It is easier to forgive a Marquis de Claviers-Grandchamp for tracing all the evils of his century to the fall of the Bastille than it is a Paul Bourget. And that is something which a novelist should never forget. Even his own prejudices can be put to work, but they must first be dramatized.

The Novel of Manners Today

MARQUAND AND O'HARA

Hortense Calisher once told me that, as a writer, she envied me my family. It was her idea that the layers and layers of cousins, concentrated in Manhattan and belonging to a tribe that had done business there for a century and a half, should be grist for any novelist's mill. And so it might have been, a hundred years ago, in a world where family meant something broader than parents and children and where nepotism was a fact and not a bogey. But today, where it is considered rather pedantic to emphasize any relationship more distant than that of first cousins, the different branches of a large family have little more in common than what everyone has in common, and what is that for a novelist?

Perhaps I should state that I am not hankering after any good old days. I have no desire to return to a New

York where servants slept in unheated cubicles on the top of drafty brownstones, with an evening off every second week, and where W. A. Croffut, in his public eulogy of the Vanderbilt family, could describe the old Commodore as "puffed with divine greed." But every writer has two points of view about the society in which he lives: that of a citizen and that of an artist. The latter is concerned only with the suitability of society as material for his art. Just as a liberal journalist may secretly rejoice at the rise of a Senator McCarthy because of the opportunity which it affords him to write brilliant and scathing denunciations of demagogues, so will the eye of the novelist of manners light up at the first glimpse of social injustice. For his books must depend for their life blood on contrast and are bound to lose both significance and popularity in a classless society.

Such great social novelists of the last century as Balzac, Dickens and Trollope attempted nothing less than a reproduction of contemporary society. Even Jane Austen, who limited herself to a village, described in *Emma* a goodly portion of it. Yet, however crowded and variegated their novels, the writers of the century share a common denominator of clearly defined class feeling. Usually it is the author's feeling against the class immediately above him in actual life. Those prickly governesses of the Brontë sisters, those impecunious daughters of Jane Austen's country gentlemen, those rural young men in Balzac and Thackeray whose purses are

too small for metropolitan pleasures, those hungry cu-
rates in Trollope, may all glare resentfully up the social
ladder, but they also stare rather condescendingly down
it. One wonders if Victorian fiction could ever have attained its bulk without keeping its nose so firmly buried
in the rich trough of Victorian snobbishness.

It was not, of course, that the social barriers were im-
passable. The whole drama of Victorian fiction is precisely that they *were* passable. Where would its heroes
and heroines be without its Darcys and Lady Catherine
de Bourghs, its Lord Steynes and Dukes of Omnium, to
get around? Can one imagine Jane Eyre or Julian Sorel
or Emma Bovary without an upper class to resent or con-
quer or envy? But passing the barriers was always an
event. If you made a fortune in the City and married a
duke's daughter, everyone knew you were taking a great
step. Travel between the social strata had not become
the clanging escalator that it is today.

There was, however, more than snobbishness at the
base of the nineteenth century novel of manners. There
were all the things that go with snobbishness, or, rather,
that go with the hierarchical society in which snobbishness is bred. There was fierce prejudice (or idealism, de-
pending on the point of view); there was bigotry (or re-
ligiosity) and a passionate concern with the niceties of
deportment and the chastity of women. The fiction of
the era is peopled with fascinating extremists, magnificently logical and magnificently unjust, whose stubborn

obsessions and murderous jealousies result in the most appalling catastrophes. Where would the English plot have been without the violently opposed marriage, or the French without the duel ? Say what one will about sentimentality and prolixity, it was still a pretty good show.

The public, anyway, loved it, and the public still does. It is a commonplace that the psychological novel, or the stream-of-consciousness novel, or the symbolic novel, has never enjoyed even a small fraction of the popularity of the novel of manners. The book clubs today clamor for a big meaty story about some phase of contemporary society, told from varied points of view and filled with graphic detail. Witness the sale of Allen Drury's study of the United States Senate. It is my simple thesis that the failure more generally to produce this kind of novel is not attributable to the decadence or escapism of mid-twentieth century writers, but rather to the increasingly classless nature of our society which does not lend itself to this kind of delineation. I do not mean by this that we are any duller than the Victorians, but simply that the most exciting and significant aspects of our civilization are no longer to be found in the distance and hostility between the social strata.

John P. Marquand engaged in the Balzacian task of drawing a picture of contemporary American society through a series of fictional biographies. We have a good tycoon, a bad tycoon, a general, a news commentator, a trust officer, a successful playwright, a Boston Brahmin of the old type and one of the new. Except for the Brahmins, the subjects are apt to be of middle class New England origin — often from a town called Clyde in Massachusetts — and their past hovers over their heads, even in the days of their triumph, like a miasma. They are never free of the sense of social distinctions bred into them in childhood. Afraid of condescending and afraid of being condescended to, they are haunted by the idea that they have not alighted on just the right rung of the social ladder. Into their make-up goes a strange mixture of ambition and humility, with some of the drive of the parvenu and some of the resignation of an old English servant. When I think of a Marquand novel I am apt to think of two characters, acquainted from boyhood, facing each other awkwardly over the gulf created by the success of one, as in *Women and Thomas Harrow*, when the local boy returns to buy the big house on the fashionable street and employs an old schoolmate to replant the garden.

"Hello, Jack," Tom Harrow said.

"Hello, Tom," Jack Dodd said. "You're looking good."

There must have been some sort of reverse explanation of why he was pleased that Jack Dodd should call him Tom. He could never be wholly at ease with Jack Dodd or with other of his contemporaries there in town, when he could deal with people in any other place in the world adroitly, affably, and without the slightest sense of strain.

It is not a coincidence that the finest novel of a writer so obsessed with the problem of class consciousness should be concerned with the past. The late George Apley's dates are 1866 to 1933, and he is born at the summit of a formidable Boston pyramid of classes which would have provided Trollope with as rich material as Barsetshire. We are shown the warping of Apley's character by the forces of property and position, we see him lose his early struggle for independence and the Irish girl whom he wants to marry, and we see him settle down at last in defeat to a life of bird watching, civic duties and the arid satisfaction of denouncing a new world. Yet for all his flag waving and for all his bitter prejudices, Apley remains a man of courage and a man of heart. His defeat is brought about by a wholly sincere veneration for the opposing forces. To have married Mary Monahan would have cost him the esteem of every human being whom he has been brought up to admire and disqualified him for the position of leadership that he believes it his duty to take up. The defeat of such a man holding to such a creed is not tragic, but it is pathetic, and pathos has a bigger place than tragedy in the study of manners.

H. M. Pulham, Esquire proves that the passing of a single generation has stripped the conflict of its pathos.

Why should Harry Pulham (who might be Apley's son), a war hero, working in an advertising agency in New York, not marry Marvin Miles? His family might have frowned and criticized her dress and speech, but they would have come around soon enough. Such marriages were everyday affairs in the twenties, even in Boston. Pulham himself recognizes the change in the times when he assesses the social opportunities which his friend, Bill King, has passed up:

> Bill would actually have got on very well at Harvard, I think, if he had cared about trying. It was true that he did not have any connections, but if he had gone out for something besides the Dramatic Club, such as the Lampoon, or even the Crimson, and if he had bothered with the people to whom I had introduced him and who usually liked him, he would very possibly have made a Club.

We see what has happened. Bill King doesn't *want* a club, and Marvin Miles doesn't want Pulham. The shoe is now on the other foot. The trouble is that if Marvin doesn't want him, the reader isn't going to want him very much, either, for Marvin is a shrewd girl. Pulham's problem is not, like Apley's, that he is caught in the vise of a social system, but that he is totally lacking in humor and imagination. It is a bit difficult to sympathize with or even to believe in a decorated war hero who is afraid to ask the family butler for an extra glass and so disclose to the world below stairs that the woman he loves wants a drink before dinner.

After *Pulham* Marquand was permanently stuck with the problem of creating heroes who had to be strongly influenced by less and less influential environments and who at the same time would not strike his readers as Casper Milquetoasts. He solved it partially with the gentleman hero of the suburbs, a kind, earnest patient man of an absolute but rather wearisome integrity, a faithful husband and adoring father, who plods through a dull life in a sleepwalking fashion, prodded by a nervous, suspicious wife who has invested her emotional being in local standards of success and is terrified that her house of cards will fall if she allows her husband, even in joke, to question the least of her adopted values. Charles Gray in *Point of No Return* and Bob Tasmin in *B. F.'s Daughter* both fail with their first loves because they don't push hard enough, thus perhaps deserving the fate of being pushed about by their second. A few words uttered or held back might have turned the scales in Tasmin's relationship with Polly Fulton. Yet he moodily blames his ineptitude on his inheritance:

> I've always been a goddam gentleman, and I've always been afraid not to be one. Let's put it on my tombstone. That's my whole obituary.

In the later novels the function of each hero's elaborately described background becomes even fuzzier.

What does that drugstore in Vermont have to do with Melville Goodwin's wanting to be a soldier? And how does Willis Wayde pick up the habit of sentimentalizing his motives and calling everything "lovely" in a bleak Yankee community like Clyde? Marquand seems to be tracing Willis' hunger for success to his family's move into the garden cottage on the great estate of the aristocratic Harcourts, a thoroughly Victorian situation. Bess Harcourt is as haughty as Pip's Estella, and poor Willis achieves his financial goal only to have her fling in his teeth a bitter Victorian epithet: "Get out of my way, Uriah Heep!" The moral seems to be that to such as Willis, the world of the fine old Harcourts, with its traditions of loyalty and integrity, will be forever closed. To such as Willis, yes. But why? Not because of his social ambition or even because of his business ruthlessness, but simply because of his drooling sanctimoniousness. If he had faced Bess Harcourt boldly, like a John O'Hara hero, and flung in *her* teeth that he was closing down the Harcourt mills because they didn't pay, she would have rewarded him as O'Hara ladies reward such heroes. What she really condemns him for (and who wouldn't?) is that he reads the Harvard Classics fifteen minutes a day and boasts about it.

My favorite of the novels, after *The Late George Apley*, is *Point of No Return*, perhaps because it dramatizes just the point that I have been trying to make, that the paralyzing effect of a class-conscious background is largely illusory. Charles Gray can only be liberated from Clyde by returning there and finding that Jessica Lovell is about to save herself from middle-aged spinsterhood by marrying Jackie Mason, who was born further down the social ladder than Charles himself. The poor old past is now revealed to him in all its smallness and sterility, as sad and foolish as Jessica's neurotic, deluded father who once told Charles that money made on the stock market was not the same as inherited money. So Charles goes back to New York and the Stuyvesant Bank, strengthened in the discovery that his youth was dominated by puppets, and finds that the promotion of which he has despaired has been assured him all along, that his rival for the bank vice-presidency has been as illusory as Clyde. His trip has had the effect of a psychoanalysis. But when the function of a character's background is only his misconception of it, the novel of manners has become a psychological novel.

I do not wish the reader to assume that I think we have attained the classless society. I am aware of the plight of Negroes in the South and of the terrible differences that still exist between rich and poor in our large cities. But every sociologist comments on our enormous suburban white-collar population and its habit of classifying the different strata of which it is composed by such artificial standards as number of automobiles or television sets. I do not deny that people can care passionately for such

things or that their caring is a proper subject for a novelist, but it is thinner material than what the Victorian
writers had to deal with. Today snobbishness is more
between groups than classes, more between cliques than
between rich and poor. Surely the resentment aroused
is of a different degree. Surely there is a difference between the feelings of the man who has not been asked
to dinner and those of the man who has been thrown
down the front stairs. What I find out of proportion in
the novels of John O'Hara is the significance which he
attaches to the former.

In the strange, angry world that he describes, the characters behave with a uniform violence, speak with a
uniform crudeness and make no appreciable effort to
control lusts which they regard as ungovernable. The
most casual meeting between a major and minor character will result either in an ugly flare-up or a sexual connection, or both. It is impossible for an O'Hara hero to
order a meal in a restaurant or to take a taxi ride without
having a brusque interchange with the waiter or driver.
Even the characters from whom one might expect some
degree of reticence — the rich dowagers, for example
— will discuss sex on the frankest basis with the first
person to bring the subject up. And in Gibbsville or
Fort Penn the first person to bring it up is the first person
one meets. A great deal is said about each character's
exact social position, perhaps because it is so difficult to
determine it from his habits and conversation. Everyone,

apparently, does *everything*, and everyone knows that everyone else is doing it. But that does not mean that the shibboleths of an older society are dead. Far from it. The code of an earlier culture, though only dimly remembered, is superstitiously venerated. O'Hara's men and women dance around the Victorian traditions of class distinction and sexual restraint like savages around a cross left by murdered missionaries and now adorned with shrunken heads. The hatred of the immigrant who coughed his lungs out in a coal mine is kept alive in the hatred of the rich Irishman who can't get into the Lantenengo Country Club. And although the O'Hara hero knows that sexual liberty is now the rule, he clings to a dusky little hope that the magic of the marriage vow will somehow safeguard his spouse. Thus Robert Millhouser in *Ourselves to Know*, a man versed in the ways of prostitutes, who has married a nymphomaniac half his age with full notice of her vicious propensities, shoots her dead without a qualm when he discovers that she has been unfaithful to him.

From time to time there emerges from the jungle a superman or superwoman, the darling of the author, to dominate the scene, such as Grace Caldwell Tate in *A Rage to Live* and Alfred Eaton in *From the Terrace*. They differ from their contemporaries in that they have a little more of everything — more sex appeal, more brains, more money, more social position. But, above all, they have more defiance. They look the universe in the eye and spit. They are defeated in the end of their chron-icles, but only by accumulated envy; they have not been able to learn that the other beasts in the jungle cannot endure the sight of so many advantages. Grace Tate might have been able to live in Fort Penn with a husband, but as a beautiful widow she is hounded out of town as an unmated lioness is hounded out of the pride by the others of her sex. And Alfred Eaton, for all his brilliant capabilities, is condemned to a life of idleness because he is too plain spoken. The *hubris* of O'Hara's superpeople is not that they have offended the gods. They have of-fended the grubby little people who share their faults but resent their success.

If O'Hara were consciously trying to describe the chaos of a society where each individual flouts the moral code, yet applies it with brutal bigotry to his neighbor, and where the inhabitants of every town play at being masters and serfs like boys and girls in a school play dressed up in wigs and hoops, he might be a more impor-tant novelist than he is. Surely it is a damning picture of the contemporary world. But my complaint is that what he seems to be doing, underneath all the violence and bluster, is to be writing an old-fashioned novel of man-ners where the most important item about any character is the social niche in which he was born. Each hero must start the race of life with a particular ribbon pinned to his lapel, and he will never be able to take it off, whether he be proud of it or ashamed. To O'Hara, in other words, it really seems to matter if he belongs or does not belong to the Lantenengo Country Club.

If background is everything, background must be described in detail, and O'Hara's descriptions amount almost to inventories. A friend of mine, who was brought up in a Pennsylvania town similar to Gibbsville, assures me that these descriptions are remarkably accurate. But I question their significance. When I learn that Mary Eaton's father wore "pince-nez spectacles with small lenses, a blue and white polka dot bow-tie and a Tau Beta Pi key on his watch chain," that his "tan kid oxfords were polished and he had on black silk socks with a thin white stripe," I do not immediately realize that he is half business man, half professor. I can think of too many lawyers and judges and doctors who might be guilty of the same combination. Nor do I really see the difference in Fort Penn between those who say "The Tates" and those who say "Sidney and Grace." Nor do I really believe that Mary Eaton's Rowland blood would make her "automatically acceptable" to anybody. When Grace Tate tells Roger Bannon that it would take her a lifetime to explain the difference between him and the men at the Fort Penn Club, I wonder if at the end of the lifetime he would know. But she teaches him more than she thinks with a single word:

"A lady? What do you know about a lady? Where would you ever learn about a lady? Have

you ever seen one? You contemptible son of a
bitch, you wouldn't know a lady if you saw one."

"Yes, I would. You're a lady, and probably
you're acting like one."

"Oh, balls."

When he takes for his hero a Gibbsville aristocrat of
the old school, O'Hara, like Marquand with George Apley, writes his most successful novel of manners. Joe
Chapin, in *Ten North Frederick,* is a man who has been
brought up with high ideals (though this is largely
blamed on a passionately possessive mother), and he is
unique among O'Hara characters in that he seeks to live
according to his own somewhat fuzzy conception of the
old moral code. He is faithful to his wife, conscientious
and high-minded in the practice of law and active in civic
affairs. The tragic flaw in his character is his irrational
belief that he is destined to become the President of
the United States. Many men have been so obsessed
but few can have suffered from Joe's peculiar delusion
that he could attain his objective by the simple expedient
of attending meetings of bar associations. The other characters are puzzled as to what Joe is up to, and, indeed, it
takes all the genius of Mike Slattery to guess it from the
nature of Joe's activity. When Joe, in his late fifties, finally decides that the time is ripe to throw his hat in the
ring, he offers Mike a hundred thousand dollars for the
nomination of lieutenant-governor. Mike quietly pockets

the money for the party, and Joe is left to drink himself to death. It is difficult to be sympathetic with a man so deluded, and it is not clear that Joe's ideals at the end are any higher than Mike Slattery's, but the contrast between the two men is always interesting. We see Joe against a background of privilege and Mike against its opposite; we see the even greater disparity between their wives; we see Joe fumble, outmaneuvered, and fall into the clutches of his wily and contemptuously pitying opponent, and we learn more about the forces of society that has placed the two in conflict than in a whole volume about polka-dot ties and fraternity pins.

When I turn, on the other hand, to the defeat of Julian English in *Appointment in Samarra*, I can understand it only in terms of a compulsion to suicide. Taken as such, the novel is certainly a powerful description of self-destruction, possibly one of the most powerful ever written. But again I am troubled with the nagging suspicion that this may not be what the author intends. Is Julian meant to be destroyed by himself or by Gibbsville? Does his instinct to antagonize lead him surely to the most dangerous persons, or is their envy of his looks, his breeding, his easy manner and apparent success what makes them hunt him down? Had Julian lived elsewhere than in Gibbsville, that lumberyard of chips on the shoulder, would he have survived? But I suppose such speculations are idle. Julian belongs to Gibbsville, and it is never difficult to find enough hate in Gibbsville with which to destroy oneself. From one end of town to the other the populace fairly throbs with hurt feelings. Al Grecco provides its motto as he drives through Lantenengo Street early Christmas morning and lowers the car window to shout out at the darkened homes:

"Merry Christmas, you stuck-up bastards! Merry Christmas from Al Grecco!"

Perhaps it is the motto of O'Hara himself and of the contemporary novel of manners.

James and the Russian Novelists

JAMES usually spoke of Tolstoy in terms of guarded respect. His attitude was like that of Delacroix, who said to his students as they passed Ingres' Odalisque in the Louvre: *Messieurs, le châpeau dans la main, mais les yeux fixés à terre.* Neither Tolstoy nor Dostoyevsky was very much to his taste, and he regarded their effect on other writers as little short of disastrous. Turgenev, on the other hand, he loved and admired, both as a friend and a writer, but then Turgenev was a sort of Russian Henry James, an expatriate who cultivated the French novelists and was regarded as an equal by Flaubert himself. His concern, like James's, was with the fine details of craftsmanship; he was, in the latter's phrase, the novelist's novelist, "an artistic influence extraordinarily valuable and ineradicably established." Too many of Turgenev's rivals, James complained, "appear to hold us in comparison by violent means, and introduce us in comparison to vulgar things."

Did he mean to include Tolstoy among these rivals? It seems likely. For observe how he contrasts him with Turgenev:

> The perusal of Tolstoy — a wonderful mass of life — is an immense event, a kind of splendid accident, for each of us: his name represents nevertheless no such eternal spell of method, no such quiet irresistibility of presentation, as shines, close to us and lighting our possible steps, in that of his precursor. Tolstoy is a reflector as vast as a natural lake; a monster harnessed to his great subject — all human life! — as an elephant might be harnessed, for purposes of traction, not to a carriage, but to a coach house. His own case is prodigious, but his example for others dire: disciples not elephantine he can only mislead and betray.

The compliment, if one was intended, fades under the words "monster" and "elephant." Later James became more candid. When Hugh Walpole wrote to ask him if he did not feel that Dostoyevsky's "mad jumble that flings things down in a heap" was nearer truth than the "picking and composing" of Stevenson, James seized the occasion to state his credo in organ tones:

> Form alone *takes*, and holds and preserves, substance — saves it from the welter of helpless ver-

biage that we swim in as in a sea of tasteless tepid pudding, and that makes one ashamed of an art capable of such degradations. Tolstoy and Dostoyevsky are fluid pudding, though not tasteless, because the amount of their own minds and souls in solution in the broth gives it savour and flavour, thanks to the strong, rank quality of their genius and their experience. But there are all sorts of things to be said of them, and in particular that we see how great a vice is their lack of composition, their defiance of economy and architecture, directly they are emulated and imitated; *then*, as subjects of emulation, models, they quite give themselves away.

Leon Edel maintains that the now famous term "fluid pudding" has been misunderstood and that James meant so to characterize the novels of the two Russian authors only insofar as they are used as models. But I question this. A fluid pudding is a fluid pudding, whether one eats it or paints it. James evidently considered the process of imitation as a peculiarly revealing one, for it is precisely here, in his opinion, that Tolstoy and Dostoyevsky "quite give themselves away" i.e., expose their essential fluidity. But surely these imitators, whoever they were, failed because they saw only formlessness where there was form, just as so many Jamesian imitators have seen only form where there was substance. If we are to rate novelists by the efforts of those who copy them, James will fare quite as badly as Tolstoy or Dostoyevsky.

A year later James wrote another letter to Walpole in which he dropped the last pretense of admiration for Tolstoy. If his term "fluid pudding" has been misunderstood, surely there is no misunderstanding the following:

> I have been reading over Tolstoy's interminable *Peace and War*, and am struck with the fact that I now protest as much as I admire. He doesn't *do* to read over, and that exactly is the answer to those who idiotically proclaim the impunity of such formless shape, such flopping looseness and such a denial of composition, selection and style. He has a mighty fund of life, but the *waste*, and the ugliness and vice of waste, the vice of a not finer *doing* are sickening. For me he makes "composition" throne, by contrast, in effulgent lustre!

It was unfortunate that Walpole should have been the person to invite James to consider the Russians. For he did it in such a way as to raise the master's ire against a straw man; he must have known perfectly well that to ask a lover of Stevenson to admire a "mad jumble" was like asking the Pope to admire Luther. He wanted a strong reaction, and he got it. James's explosion has provided a perfect text for extremists to fight over through the years. On one side we can line up all who excuse their clumsy craftsmanship by greatness of purpose, their fudged details by the scope of their panorama, those who profess to deal in raw chunks of life salted with "compassion." On the other we can line up those attenuated scribblers who seek with polished phrases to conceal that they have nothing to write about. It is all great fun, and everybody gets very heated, but we must remember that it is only a parlor game. It has nothing to do with literature, and it has nothing to do with art.

For James's impatience with the formlessness that he unfairly attributed to the Russian novelists leads him to make a false distinction between a work of art and a "mass of life." Tolstoy, according to him, is not an artist but a "reflector of life." Tolstoy and Dostoyevsky fail in composition, but are saved by the "strong, rank quality of their genius and their experience." Now this, I submit, is meaningless. Tolstoy could only reflect life through his art. If life is reflected, it is because art succeeds, and if art succeeds, it is because the form is right. Life is only a subject; it cannot rub off onto a book any more than a bowl of fruit can rub off onto a canvas. There is only one process for James as for Tolstoy, and that process is art. There they fail or there they succeed. "Life" will not help either in the least bit.

Because *War and Peace* is a long book and has many characters, it has been said to "sprawl." Yet actually it is unified by the Napoleonic invasion of Russia which directly affects the outward and inner life of every character. It is true that Tolstoy continually shifts the point of view from character to character, but how else could he succeed in re-creating a war? James can confine *The*

Ambassadors to Strether's point of view because Strether's point of view is the subject of the novel, but if he had set himself Tolstoy's job, he would have needed not one, but a hundred pairs of eyes. In any event, I agree with E. M. Forster that the question of the point of view is one more interesting to writers than readers. It was vital to the construction of James's novels, but it is not vital to that of all others.

To me there is "flopping looseness" in *War and Peace* only in Tolstoy's essays on military and historical theory. I find these as intrusive and boring as commercials in a television play, but they are easily skipped, so long as one is careful not to skip with them the chapters dealing with the personalities of the war leaders and the battle scenes, which are of the essence of Tolstoy's scheme. The pictures of Kutuzov at the front and of Napoleon watching the drowning of the overeager cavalry, of the battlefield of Borodino and of the burning of Moscow, give us the historical perspective against which the individuals must be seen. The form of the novel is the same that was used by Margaret Mitchell in *Gone With the Wind:* the principal character, Armageddon, unites the other characters and changes their lives. But form can be obvious and still be form. And is there a better fictional device for a war?

It is fashionable to describe *War and Peace* as a great, crowded canvas, and to think of Tolstoy as daubing at it with broad strokes. But the more I look at it, the more I am astonished (outside of the essay sections) at the amount of meticulous craftsmanship involved. As Max Reinhardt was able to create the illusion of a vast army with a few soldiers, so does Tolstoy create a mighty conflict with a whiff of smoke, a bit of snow and a handful of aristocrats from Russian court society. Think of our own war novelists and how carefully they delineate the assorted backgrounds of the soldiers of a squadron. Think of those flashbacks that show the lieutenant at Groton and the Negro private in an overcrowded Southern school. Imagine Norman Mailer limited in *The Naked and the Dead* to the Lowells and Cabots of Boston! Yet Tolstoy's characters are not only from the same social milieu; they are almost all related to each other. I suppose it is true that the great landlords and serf owners of an absolute monarchy were more representative of their nation than capitalists are of a democracy, but even so, Tolstoy is telling the story of Russia's agony from the viewpoint of a very tiny class of sufferers. What he understands is that if a human being is described completely, his class makes little difference. He becomes a human being on the printed page, and other humans, of whatever class, can recognize themselves in his portrait. The lesson of Tolstoy is precisely how little of life, not how much, the artist needs.

The only moral classifications into which Tolstoy divides his characters are those of serious and nonserious. If one is trivial-minded about the great questions of life, if one is bent on playing games, like Pierre's first wife, one is condemned. But as long as one cares about one's role in the universe, then, regardless of one's ineffectiveness, all is forgiven. Pierre, for example, makes a mess of everything that he touches, his estates, his marriage, even his social career. When war comes, he wanders, a useless civilian, about the battlefield at Borodino like a sleepwalker, concerned only with his own doubts about the purpose of life. He is arrested by the French in Moscow and suffers great hardships, but he still accomplishes nothing. Nobody but himself is helped by his agony. Prince André, on the other hand, looks after his serfs conscientiously, manages his estates economically and is a brilliant officer in the war. Yet there is no feeling in the novel that André is a "better" man than Pierre. They are both serious men and, as such, appreciate and understand each other. That one is effectively and the other ineffectively good is a mere detail. What concern has God with such details?

In *Anna Karenina* I find only Levin's agricultural theories "floppingly loose." They are as irrelevant to the story as the historical asides in *War and Peace*, and much more difficult to skip, being more deeply imbedded in the plot. But a graver fault in the structure of the novel is Tolstoy's failure to prepare us for Anna's adultery. We meet her first as a charming and deeply understanding sister-in-law who, by consummate tact, saves her brother's crumbling marriage, but we pass with a dizzy speed over the year which elapses between her meeting

Vronsky and her succumbing to him. We grasp Anna's character at last — or a good deal of it — but the hole in this part of the book is never quite filled. We never know why such a woman should have married a man like her husband or why, having done so, she should have been unfaithful to him. But aside from being occasionally bored by Levin and occasionally confused by the early Anna, I find no other looseness in the novel. It is like a well-organized English novel of its period: it has two plots, constantly interwoven and always in dramatic contrast, and in the end married love brings happiness and adultery despair. Even James could not have said that it contained the vice of waste.

Tolstoy liked to accomplish a great many obvious as well as a great many subtle things, and he was not afraid of old and well-worn formulas. What he needed for war was a burning capital and what he needed for a drama of love was a married and an unmarried couple. He never hesitated to hammer in his contrasts with heavy strokes. On the side of Kitty and Levin and lawful love are the rolling acres of a well-managed farm, and Moscow, no longer the capital, but still the center of the oldest, truest Russian values. On the side of Anna and Vronsky and illicit passion are the superficial court society of St. Petersburg and a motley pile of borrowed notions from Paris and London. The great columns of the two plots stand up before us, massive, conventional, imposing and trite, but on closer examination we find that the bas-reliefs that gird them have been carved with the greatest delicacy and skill. Whatever assumptions we make as we go along, we will find that we must qualify, until we begin to wonder if the two columns are twins or opposites.

Levin and Kitty, for example, may be depicted as the young couple on whose love we may properly smile, but in contrast to Anna and Vronsky they are frequently ridiculous. Levin is absurdly and irrationally jealous, and his nervousness on the birth of his child seems almost a caricature of the traditionally nervous father. He is violent, rude and ill-tempered, and Kitty is excitable and possessive. It is true that Tolstoy obviously likes Levin and considers his faults as rather lovably Russian, but he is careful at the same time to show us that the other characters consider him a bull in a china shop. Vronsky, on the other hand, leads a St. Petersburg society life of which his creator disapproves to such an extent that it has become traditional to regard him as a shallow gadabout who is unworthy of the passion that he has inspired in Anna. But consider him more closely. Vronsky may be irresponsible in seducing Anna, but after that he behaves with the greatest possible style. He is never unfaithful to her, never deserts her, always tries to spare her pain, does everything he can to legalize their relationship and even attempts suicide when none of his plans for her happiness work out. There are moments in the book when he and Anna seem a couple unjustly condemned by a censorious and hypocritical society, while

Kitty and Levin seem like spoiled youngsters who cannot find happiness in a veritable flood of good fortune.

For Tolstoy is not really condemning Anna, any more than he is praising Kitty. Anna is, indeed, the more high-minded of the two. He is rather proving that for women of their background and position (Levin's brother's mistress is quite happy as such), cohabitation outside of marriage is impossible. Kitty and Anna are both intensely female in their possessiveness. Levin feels, when Kitty wishes to accompany him to his brother's deathbed, that it is intolerable to be so shackled. Yet she comes and is a great help. Within the framework of a happy marriage such matters can always be adjusted. Kitty becomes absorbed in her babies, and Levin can then attend all the agricultural conventions that he wants. But no such adjustment is possible for Anna. She destroys her life with Vronsky by her mad jealousy and her need to be with him every moment. Anna turns into a kind of monster, making scenes over everything, crazed by the thought that her lover should have any life or interest outside the dull and lonely house where she rants at him. Vronsky is a model of patience and restraint, but he is helpless to arrest her insane course of self-destruction. Anna has been idle and restless in St. Petersburg society, but she is utterly shattered when its doors are closed to her but not to him. It is ridiculous; it is pathetic; it is nineteenth century but it is very feminine. Kitty would have been just as bad.

James in the letters to Walpole deals specifically with

Tolstoy, but Dostoyevsky is included at least by implication. Certainly James does nothing to rebut Walpole's
assertion that the author of *Crime and Punishment* created his effects by "flinging things down in heaps." It
is illuminating and also rather pathetic to contrast Walpole's fanciful picture with the actual one of Dostoyevsky, impoverished and epileptic, at work in Dresden on
the manuscript of *The Idiot*. His notebooks show eight
different proposed treatments of the central theme, and
even when he had settled on the outline, the execution
was agonizingly slow. He wrote to the poet Maykov:

> All this time I literally worked day and night in
> spite of my fits. But, alas, I notice with despair that
> for some reason I am not able to work as quickly as
> I did a short while ago. I crawl like a crab, and then
> I begin to count the sheets — three and a half or four
> in a whole month. This is terrible, and I don't know
> what will happen to me.

Surely the confusion that Walpole finds on the surface of the novels results from the magnitude of the author's task rather than from a failure in artistry. For,
as is now commonly recognized, Dostoyevsky wanted to
show man not only in relation to his fellow creatures
but in his relation to God. Most of nineteenth century
fiction was concerned with character; Dostoyevsky was
concerned with soul. His subject required a new dimen-
sion and an immense amount of planning. It seems to me

that even a cursory review of his books shows a love of craftsmanship as deep as that of James himself.

Dostoyevsky uses three principal techniques in the construction of his novels. The first is the dialogue, or general conversation, usually at a social gathering, where the characters argue with each other about themselves, social conditions in Russia, liberalism and religion. The talks are marked by irrelevancies, low comedy, testiness, self-pity and sudden violent fits of temper. Just when the action seems about to take a step forward, someone inevitably enters or changes the subject to arrest it, so that these sections of the novels have some of the static, frustrating quality of Ivy Compton-Burnett's dialogues. But the comedy, or at times farce, is always hilarious; the lies and antics of General Ivolgin and of old Karamazov have a Falstaffian richness. Farce and tragedy stand up boldly side by side in Dostoyevsky; together they make up the dreamlike quality of a mortal existence where we are separated from God.

The author, however, realizes that he cannot tell the whole story by such discussions, and at regular intervals he interrupts, with a firm editorial hand, to move his plot forward or to fill in the biographies of his characters. In these parts he is smooth, sharply analytical and brilliant. The passages in *The Idiot* that describe Madame Yepanchin's concern about her unmarried daughters are as vivid and clever as any of their counterparts in Jane Austen. Sometimes Dostoyevsky uses his editorial hand to tell a seemingly irrelevant story or legend like the famous "Grand Inquisitor" in *The Brothers Karamazov*. Certainly it absorbs us to a point where we forget the very novel of which it is a part. But as soon as we return to Ivan who has related it, we realize that it is the perfect parable of his own agnosticism, and the parable and Ivan are henceforth inseparable in our minds.

Finally, Dostoyevsky uses the method of dramatic, violent scenes that illuminate the dusky landscape with a sudden shocking light. He may use them as preludes, to foreshadow what is going to happen, or as crises, to explain what already has. In *The Brothers Karamazov* the great scene where the father and sons go to the monastery contains in it the germs of everything that happens afterward, whereas the scene in *The Idiot* where Nastasya, at her birthday party, elopes with Rogozhin, gives us the final key to a character who has hitherto baffled us. It is only when we read such a scene that we realize to the full how necessary the previous chapters have been.

What in all of this becomes of James's "point of view"? It is lost, of course. But it was vital for Dostoyevsky, in his psychic probing, to be able to move in and out of the mind of each of his characters, to substitute himself as narrator or as observer, or even to have the characters create other observers by telling stories. In the massive job that he set for himself he needed every trick in the novelist's bag, and he used them all. To have limited him to one would have been like limiting a playwright to the classic unities. Racine was content to contain his action to a single day and place, but what would have become of Shakespeare? I cannot imagine two novels more different than *The Brothers Karamazov* and *The Ambassadors*, nor can I imagine two novels more admirable. It is idle to choose between them, for one always has both.

Crisis in Newport — August, 1857

WITH PREVIOUSLY UNPUBLISHED

EXTRACTS FROM THE DIARY

OF GEORGE TEMPLETON STRONG

F EW INDIVIDUALS appear more frequently in the four million words of the diary of George Templeton Strong, the Pepys of nineteenth century New York, than his cousin "Charley." Charles E. Strong, four years younger than the diarist and a graduate of Amherst, entered the Wall Street law firm of Bidwell & Strong in 1843 when he was nineteen and practiced there until his death fifty-four years later. At that time he was senior partner and the firm had become Strong & Cadwalader (now Cadwalader, Wickersham & Taft). Like any diarist dealing with his daily intimates George never clearly describes Charley, and we have to look back at him from the memoir of a younger partner, Henry W. Taft, written as late as 1938, to see him as a "genial, benevolent, sympathetic, elderly gentleman," who may never have tried a case, but who for generations was the trusted adviser to "many of the wealthiest families of the city." It is not too easy to reconstruct the younger Charley from this, but we learn from the diary that he was a loyal friend and popular man about town, and from an early photograph, that he had wavy blond hair and a small mustache, and could strike a rather dashing pose with a Prince Albert and cane. One suspects that Charley was not without his reserve of charm. Certainly he was a less complicated man than his diarist cousin. George, introspective and nervous, subject to moods of melancholia despite a rather Dickensian sense of humor, was an earnest and sincere Victorian who thought little enough of his age and less of himself, but who was desperately determined to make the best of both. If his prejudices were violent, his instincts were good; he may have disliked the Irish, the English and the South, but he also detested municipal corruption and colonialism, and he abhorred slavery. He had a fondness for reading, an enthusiasm for personalities, a love of music and a passion for recording everyone and everything in the pages of his voluminous diary. Though obviously a competent practitioner, he never cared for the law as Charley did; he did not have the latter's patience for plugging away at the details of wills and deeds. It is easy to imagine that Charley provided a needed balance to his more volatile cousin, a steadying influence at home and in the office. "There are not many people for whose sickness or health I care a great deal," George notes when his cousin is ill, "and Charley is among the more precious of those few."

It is with great excitement, therefore, that George, in 1850, records Charley's engagement, after a feverish courtship, to Eleanor Fearing, charming, popular and rich, the catch, indeed, of the New York and Newport social seasons. George himself had been married only two years before, and he and his wife (Ellen Ruggles) clucked benevolently over the younger couple. "It is delicious to be in the society of so happy a man as Charley," he writes, "so happy and so hopeful and so outrageously in love." When Eleanor and Charley meet at George's, their presence gives his house "a kind of domestic consecration." In fact, he is quite carried away as his mind roams over the world to think of all the other happy couples "in gay capitals and secluded little towns, in stately old ancestral homes and around humble firesides, everywhere, from the long resounding fjords of the North to the bright shores of the Mediterranean." His heart overflows:

How many thousands of capital fellows as happy as Charley, and each with the same sufficient reason, and all with the same blue sky and bright stars looking quietly down on their happiness. Think of the thousands of beautiful girls, too, blonde and brunette of every shade, simple-hearted little rusticities not dressed in the best taste, and radiant, highbred beauties of every degree, whose little hands are trembling and whose little heads are swimming *tonight*, as they think of the mighty event of the last week and of the announcements and congratulations of tomorrow.

Let it not be deduced that George's own bride was any "simple-hearted little rusticity," or that her dresses were not in the best taste. Ellen Strong was a daughter of Samuel B. Ruggles, the financier. It was simply that her husband had an obsession for the diminutive in all affectionate descriptions of the opposite sex. Ellen is "poor little Ellen in her ignorance and simplicity," "my most imprudent little wife," "poor dear good innocent little Ellen," or his "noble little girl." Even her tasks are dwarfed; we see her "busy with her little household arrangements." The fact that her future cousin-in-law, Eleanor, was also of inconsiderable stature was surely an added guarantee of Charley's happiness.

Our first hint that George may have overstated the degree of his cousin's good fortune comes with the wedding itself. Even littleness, apparently, was no proof against nerves.

The ceremony was badly performed by Dewey. Both parties a good deal agitated — a parlour is far more trying to the nerves than a church. Eleanor saved herself from tears and hysterics and so forth only by a strong and visible effort, for she was evidently in great nervousness and excitement and left the room immediately after the ceremony. I was surprised that Charley felt it so strongly, for I well remember how nonchalant I felt when undergoing the same process, and I was much more likely to have been embarrassed than he. But he was infected, I suppose, by the tremors of his pretty little bride and sympathized in the struggle she was making to control herself.

George, until events later to be recorded, is tactful even in the privacy of his diary about any growth of temperament in Charley's wife. Loyal to Charley, he was presumably working under a presumption in her favor. It is long after the wedding before we discover that all his efforts to promote an intimacy between Eleanor and his own innocent little Ellie have failed from the start. Nor do we have any indication, in these first few years, that Eleanor is subjecting her husband to stormy scenes of willfulness. We see instead the Charley Strongs taking their place with apparent decorum in the social world and attending the Academy of Music with their devoted cousins. In 1851 their only child, Kate, "Miss Puss," was born. The law practice increased, and Charley was duly taken into partnership. Yet there are hints, if carefully watched for, that all is not as it might be in Charley's home. A chapter from George William Curtis' *Nile Notes of a Howadji* has a highly upsetting effect on Eleanor during her pregnancy. While George himself admits that some passages were characterized by "a kind of euphuistic obscenity or puppy-lewdness," Eleanor's reaction of falling into a state of indignant excitement "which might have injured her" seems excessive. Nor is it possible to ascribe this entirely to a moral delicacy that might have justified such immoderation, for in 1855 we find George concerned about Eleanor's unbounded enthusiasm for Rachel, that "Jewish sorceress" whose moral repute was such that she had only been asked once "to meet ladies." Yet we learn that Eleanor "goes every night and experiences fevers and nervous flustrations, with ebullient and explosive hysterical tendencies"! It is hardly a consoling augury.

Eleanor Strong, however, was not to be condemned forever to vicarious excitement. In 1856, the year following that of Rachel's visit, a young journalist and ex-Unitarian minister who also composed hymns and was the author of a travel book of perfervid descriptions, *Gan-Eden, or Pictures of Cuba,* arrived in New York to write for the *New York Times.* William Henry Hurlbert (he had changed it from Hurlbut) is described in the *Dictionary of American Biography* as a "brilliant but erratic genius." He graduated from Harvard Divinity School in 1849, but returned to the university in 1852 for a year of law only to abandon this in turn for his final choice of journalism. Certainly his style was more appropriate to the pages of Putnam's Magazine than to the pulpit or bar. The "L'Envoi" to "Gan-Eden" has the following apostrophe to Cuba:

> *Fair Odalisque upon the purple lying,*
> *Luxurious daughter of the south, farewell!*
> *Upon my ear the palm-tree's passionate sighing.*
> *Fades, with the summer sea's voluptuous swell.*

One can imagine that Eleanor Strong, having graduated from a distaste for George William Curtis to a taste for Rachel, might have sighed with the watchers of the north in reading: "I have already spoken of the exceeding beauty of the Cuban nights, and of the golden moon, which pours over the tropical landscape a flood of luxurious splendor, quite unimaginable by those who have but watched her climb the northern skies with a wan face, and with sad steps."

Hurlbert's social success in New York was immediate. He was a facile talker and handsome in a dark mustachioed fashion, and he condescended to the metropolis in a way that nineteenth century New York ladies found agreeable. In his play, *Americans in Paris, or A Game of Dominoes*, he describes their city as "that domestic paradise" and "that Puritanic capital." It is not surprising that George Strong despised him from the very start. His entry for December 6, 1856 reads:

> Hurlbut called here last night to "consult me" about certain matters connected with "the permanent organization of the Republican Party." A

very transparent device, my opinion on any such subject being dear at twopence, and there being no man, woman, or child in the community who thinks it worth more. Mr. Hurlbut simply wants the entrée of this house, which he shan't have till I know more about him. He's very "thick" with sundry of my friends and the place would be convenient. He has a vast social reputation just now, is considered very brilliant and fascinating, is an eminent litterateur in a small way, with political aspirings, has written some respectable little magazine articles for *Putnam* and a readable paper on American Politics in the last *Edinburgh,* and wishes to be considered intimate with the London *Times.* I suspect him of being an unprincipled adventurer, but perhaps I'm wrong.

But, alas, he was not. Only seven months later the diarist plunges us into the center of scandal. It was midsummer of 1857, and George's Ellie had taken the children to Brattleboro while George remained in town to spell Charley at the office. The latter was vacationing with Eleanor in Newport where the "Abbé" Hurlbert, as George sarcastically calls him, was a frequent visitor:

July 31. — Before I was up Charley came to my room just from the Newport boat, the wretched bearer of a lamentable and disgraceful story. Monday afternoon looking for something in his wife's room, he chanced to pick up a letter, and noticed that it was addressed to her in a female hand (Miss E.G.'s to wit) and that the rest of it was in the calligraphy of that treacherous scoundrel, his and her particular friend, the versatile and accomplished Hurlbert. Its recipient had endorsed it on the date of its receipt (that morning) and Charley had himself handed it to her and been told it was from the lady who had written its address and that a book that came with it was one she had promised to send. He read it, and I've read the shameful production. Such a letter as a foolish man would write to his mistress in the first week of concubinage, a letter from which standing alone, anyone would necessarily infer that she who received it had fallen. She came in, admitted that it expressed her actual relations with Hurlbert, denied actual infidelity (which denial I fully credit) and then Charley went to her uncle's cottage (Daniel Butler Fearing) to say that there must be instant and final separation. She was taken by them to their house, and after much discussion with them Charley left for New York.

Hurlbert has been dining with Charley once a week, receiving all manner of hospitality and kindness from him and shewing him studious attention, for near a twelvemonth, and meanwhile has been teaching his wife to lie, and bringing her within a step of adultery. There is more venom in the subtle scoundrel's fluent plausibilities than I gave him credit for. I have always believed that with all her terrible faults, and her entire want of love for her husband, he could trust her anywhere without fear, relying on her constitutional inherent truthfulness of speech and a coldness of temperament. These two safeguards, the sole buttresses of her husband's honor and her own, has this ungrateful disloyal unprincipled adventurer and sophist been able to undermine.

Miss E.G. has not been identified, nor have her friends and co-admirers of Hurlbert, Mrs. P.L. and Mrs. J., soon to appear in the diary. George will have plenty of things to say about this misguided trio, two of whom were apparently related to Eleanor. The time had come for a gathering of the clans, and the ensuing entries show how formidable an opposition could be coalesced in the New York of that day to face an adventurer like Hurlbert. Henry Fearing was the son of Daniel B. Fearing and Eleanor's first cousin. Bob Le Roy, though an alcoholic who eventually died of his failing, was an intimate of all the Strongs. Charles Kuhn had been a sponsor of Hurlbert's, but quickly saw the error of his ways. John Whelten Ehninger and Daniel Messenger were loyal friends of Charley's.

Charley didn't go down town. Wanted me to go to Newport with him. I agreed to do so and spent the morning in much fuss and tribulation — terrible hot day it was — and left on the *Metropolis* at five. Sultry and rueful voyage, a leaden thundercloud dogged us up the

Sound, and soon after we passed Oldfield Light, came down in roaring rain. Got a nap at the Bellevue House and found that Mrs. Charley had been brought back thither by her uncle and was in charge of her cousin Mrs. Allen (who was Miss Mary Watson, most kindly gentle and womanly person she seems). After breakfast drove to Fearing's cottage, leaving Charley at hotel. Took a letter to Fearing and for three hours had it out with him and his sharp Yankee Mrs. Fearing, both protesting and entreating and insisting that separation *must not be*, for the wife's sake. Finally it was settled that Charley should be asked to reconsider. I came off, and concluded to bring him away that evening, for the atmosphere of the place was plainly unwholesome for him. Wrote to Fearing to say so and that Charley for the present adhered to his first decision, but would take time for reflection before acting on it. Walked to the beach; after dinner drove with Charley and Bob Le Roy to *Bateman's* and came off with them both (Ed: returned to New York). Spent most of the night in discussion with Bob, who has some knowledge of the outline of the case, and is rather cynical about it.

Yesterday a day of violent rain. Wrote to Fearing to say that before any action there ought to be some manifesto or statement by the lady of her views of the past, her intentions for the future, her feelings toward her husband. As yet he has had not even a message from her. Indeed she has been confined to her bed, prostrated and hysterical, and he did not see her while at Newport Wednesday. Charles Kuhn taken into confidence, for his own sake.

Today the only new fact is the statement that Hurlbert went to Newport yesterday, which I instantly telegraphed.

I have no doubt there will be an accommodation of this trouble, but it ought to be after a period of suspense and distress that the guilty party will remember, if it ought to be at all. Charley is anxious to shoot the whelp who has done this mischief and treason, but I guess I can prevent a collision, even if the matter become public, so that a row would not be inadmissable as compromising the lady. Poor foolish illregulated girl, muddled with French novels and by a life of idleness (for her husband took every household duty off her hands long ago). I'm indignant with her half the time, or so bitterly sorry for her the other half.

August 1. Saturday evening. Events progress, and my Scandalous Chronicle flourishes. First came Daniel Fearing with a report that Hurlbert was at Newport yesterday and wanted to see the lady — didn't of course — then Hurlbert came to Fearing's house taking a position in their brief interview the reverse of contrite or humble but what precisely Fearing could not make out intelligibly to me. He cleared out at half past two for New York. Fearing reports Mrs. Charley still in bed and much prostrated, very penitent and prepared to make every pledge for the future. Brought a brief note to her husband, dry and cold, but better than I expected. It must be remembered that she's really ill and very weak and that she never has any facility on paper. It may do for a beginning.

Next came a letter of eight pages from the Abbé Hurlbert to *me*, as Charley's friend, inviting an interview and setting forth his views. Either he is insane, or he feels himself in a horribly false position and wants to cover his retreat by bullying. I replied by a dry note, refusing to recognize his *right to be a party to any settlement between Charley and his wife* (!!! incredible as it seems, that is the ground he takes and unless that be acceded to, he has the inconceivable baseness to threaten to blow the whole affair) and telling him I'd be home at eight tonight, if he wanted to say anything that would enable me to be of service to the lady or the gentleman. I don't believe he'll come. Nothing can exceed the audacious assumptions of right to act for Mrs. Charley, to dictate terms as to what licence her husband is to allow her in case of reconciliation, etc. etc., of which his letter is full. Should he come this evening we shall have a precious time.

Later. He didn't come at all. Went with Charley to John Whetten Ehninger's without finding him and waited for him some time in vain. Charley wants to make him a confidant, in view of ulterior measures, a demand for surrender of the letters, and physical force if Hurlbert decline. Think of his holding them, refusing to deliver them to Miss E.G. on the written request of their penitent authoress, and threatening to publish them if his demands be not complied with! And of his talking about "Christian morals and public order" being promoted by his exaggerated and extravagant baseness!

August 2. Sunday night. That man Hurlbert has been twice in this house today. Do not its walls need ceremonial purification? The glass from which some water was given this dog when he was (unless he were shamming) overpowered by agitation, I have smashed. No guest of mine shall run the risk of catching his foul disease. Things look bad and black; the two Fearings and Jack Ehninger have just gone. Charley, poor fellow, has gone to bed; he spends tonight here.

To church this morning (Trinity Chapel). Saw Rev. Hobart, whose advice Charley wanted as to what would be right and what wrong. It was still an open question this morning whether Charley ought to take her back and plain that he ought at least to hold off long enough to give her a stern lesson. Went to 34th St. with Hobart, and put him in possession of all material facts. Ehninger, Henry Fearing and Charley dined here, and after dinner Ehninger and Fearing went off to see Hurlbert. *He* (Ed: Hurlbert) called a few minutes after to state that I was mistaken in my suggestion of yesterday as to the lady's views and wishes; he had received a letter "from Newport yesterday" confirming his opinion on that subject. Farthermore, he was going thither this week. He was very urbane, and I equally so, but put of course the utmost possible formality and repulsion into my manner. Interview was very short. Went as fast as possible after our two friends; found them by great good fortune. Henry Fearing was taken all aback by this new and most alarming phase. He was for very prompt and conclusive action, and I had hard work to get him to temporize a little. They went after him (Ed: Hurlbert) again, having spent a couple of hours here in debate, at the hour he told me he would be at his rooms, but didn't find him, returned chafing and disappointed. Charley went off to see Hobart, and then this traitor came once more and was received in the library Fearing being speaker, we two merely auditors, a condition Fearing insisted on. The man's decision, promptitude and infernal composure and audacity were appalling. He refused to say anything about the letter from Newport unless with Fearing alone. Jack and I withdrew to the dining room. Daniel Fearing came, and after a time his son came down in an agony of rage and sorrow.

It was too true. The poor weak girl had written Friday (the very day she wrote her husband) a lamentable letter to Mrs. P.L. — "Her relatives were giving her no peace" — "He ought to go to Europe" — "We shall meet again soon" — "Should her husband refuse to receive her, her only hope is in *him*."

The woman (Ed: Mrs. P.L.) had given Hurlbert that letter! Are the ladies of New York to turn procuresses?

Has Hurlbert promised that unprincipled daughter of a swindling financier a commission on the fortune of the victim she is helping him to run down?

At first it seemed that all was lost — perhaps it is — but we've rallied a little.

Hurlbert went out of the house soon after, by the door and not through the window, a shameful fact; he was not insulted, but he did hear, thank Heaven, some pretty plain truths conveyed in conventional circumlocution. He seeks a quarrel and an exposure and thinks he can force it by going to Newport. There he supposes reconciliation impossible and that the lady will seek his protection. With her fortune they could live abroad, at least till he was tired of her, and he can always support himself by his wits and his pen. Loss of position here would be a matter of indifference to a mere nomadic adventurer. That is his game, and he's playing it boldly and well, utterly unscrupulous now as to the means he uses. By the blessing of Heaven he shall be defeated, and the lady shall return to her duty.

But alas for her husband — what a home will his be — and how many dreary years he must pass before there can be a germ of returning affection, even if all go smoothly and well, as it hardly can even if this persevering intriguer abandon the siege. And it is yet uncertain whether this *coup de main* will be repulsed, uncertain how the lady will decide.

August 3. Monday night. Another letter to me from

Hurlbert this morning, opening a new abyss of infamy. It contains a quotation from that lady's (Ed: Eleanor's) Newport letter (how her uncle and aunt *"do not know all"* or they wouldn't urge her to go back) which is meant to convey, doubtless, the worst insinuation against her. And of its falsehood no one has any doubt. *She* means that they are ignorant of some fancied wrong or injury by her husband. He means to suggest to her husband that she has *fallen* and thus raise a new barrier to reconciliation, *the caitiff*.

I'm very anxious and unhappy tonight. If this man seek to force his way to the lady's presence he will be *shot down*. And I fear a duel; my only hope is in the strong suspicion he's a coward.

August 4. Tuesday night. Very warm day, ending in a muggy cloudy evening, with rain falling steadily and straight down through the stagnant air. Have been very busy and much worried closing up one or two real estate transactions that I never heard of till the papers were handed me to be delivered or exchanged.

Three or four despatches this morning from Henry Fearing, the last dated 1.15 P.M. The lady is said to have "promised everything" of her own free will. She's at Fearing's cottage.

Hurlbert did not leave town and is not going to Newport. Dan Messenger has had a long talk with him and was to have had another this afternoon. Messenger assumed the position of friend to the lady, exclusively acting in the interests of no other person. By his account he manipulated this unclean and dangerous beast to some good purpose and brought him to pledge himself to stay in town, to admit that an explosion ought to be averted, not encouraged, and that he must "efface himself" and make no claim "to be a party" to any settlement. He is or pretends to be in a high strung intense excitement and sensitiveness, avows a state of Idolatry, highfalutin' reverence (!) and the like. She's his sole inspiration, the only thing he lives for, source of every virtuous and exalted impulse etcetera, a sort of Platonico-erotico Delirium Tremens.

God help poor Charley through these troublesome times and through the weary years that will follow, when the excitement of the crisis is over and he feels only the depression of his dismal home and the dead weight of the unloving wife to whom he's chained. For they will come together again, I think, beyond doubt. They ought to, if only that this beast may not triumph.

August 5. Wednesday night. Thank God, I believe this poor wrongheaded girl is safe, not from guilt only but from scandal. Henry Fearing came here early this morning and I'd a letter from her husband beside. They agree that her course has been better than they'd hoped: entire penitence, deep mortification, something like an expression of *wifely* feeling, and infinite disgust at the baseness of her fluent friend with the moustache. She promises everything and says she'd try to keep her promises, but knows she may fail. So far well. But all impressions on her are evanescent; any new excitement wipes them out. Probably she'll forget this particular vagabond within two weeks, but hopes founded on her faculty of self denial, self control, common sense and steadiness of purpose cannot be sanguine. She gave Henry Fearing a letter authorizing him to demand of that ornament to society (Ed: Hurlbert) her late correspondence, all letters in his possession; this Fearing gave to Messenger, and Messenger took it to the Abbé's. The Abbé has been sustaining his valuable existence for some days past (Ed: several words erased) and cigars exclusively. His nerves are naturally shaky. He spent an hour stamping about the room, in a semi-maudlin semi-hysterical state, tearing his hair, gnashing his teeth, rolling his fine eyes and knocking his intellectual nob against the wall, like an exasperated bluebottle fly, and finally fell down in a species of caniption fit and foamed at the mouth, and lay for some time in rigors and coma. Messenger stood still and called in no help, the man being in a phrenetic condition and liable to make indiscreet disclosures if he came to. Messenger thought it best to permit the Destinies to have their own way, and let the man die "dacently" without disgracing himself any more. But he picked himself up at last and the upshot was an agonized consent to surrender the letters tomorrow.

It's really pitiful to think that the little brimstone (Ed: Eleanor) who has caused all this mess and given this featherbrained poetaster these spasms and paroxysms, don't in truth care two pence for him, has encouraged his devotion, because it gratified her vanity and gave her a new excitement, and wouldn't sacrifice one atom of social status, or risk losing an invitation to one "nice party" for the sake of all the accomplished Hurlberts between South Carolina and Cape Cod.

August 6. Thursday. Telegraph informs me that affairs are in so satisfactory a condition at Newport that my unhappy friend (Ed: Charley) there wants to get back to Wall Street.

Among the absurdest scenes ever acted on the surface of this planet, by the by, must have been his (Ed: Hurlbert's) last interview with that goodnatured phlegmatic lump of sound practical common sense, Daniel Messenger. An able editor, accomplished scholar and most fascinating member of polite society going about on all fours, raving and roaring, stopping now and then to *bite* another man's fat legs, tenderly apostrophizing [him] sometimes as "his own dearest Eleanor," sometimes adjuring him (as Mrs. J.) to go to his said dearest and tell her to come and put herself under his protection, and sometimes whispering to him (as his dearest's husband) chokily and grimly that he intended to "cut his heart out" at the first convenient opportunity, is a spectacle seldom vouchsafed to admirers of the ridiculous. It's very refreshing besides to find something to laugh at in the performance of so desperately efficient an agent of mischief.

August 17. Monday evening. Letters from Charley during my absence. He's unhappy and despondent about the future, no wonder. I can see that the impression made by even this most narrow escape, on the person whose caprices and fancies are to determine so much of his future, is half-obliterated already. What has he ever done that this calamity should visit him? What have I ever done, that my lot should be so different?

One of the silly sentimental women who have been officiating as bawds in this transaction, without sense enough to be aware of their function, has written a delicious letter of congratulation to the lady (Ed: Eleanor) on the amicable adjustment of her troubles, full of eulogy on her husband's nobleness and generosity, just what she would have expected of one whom she has always upheld as among the most admirable of men!! She must be among the shallowest and most sneaking of women.

August 20. Thursday. Wonderful that the Hurlbert transaction has been kept so close, for at least thirty people know of it. Some leakage is absolutely inevitable.

Charley came to town Tuesday reporting everything at Newport *couleur de rose*, contrition and good resolutions, and the horizon far clearer and the prospect of fair weather more hopeful than any time for the last five years. But he's not sanguine about the future and has no right to be so.

The position of these three women (Mrs. J., Mrs. P.L., Miss E.G.) has changed. They are now furious with our poor little friend because she didn't run away from her husband after all. "She is not the woman they took her to be, and they're satisfied now that she's incapable of true affection." Really it's like the wrath of one of the Mercer Street aristocracy when a new recruit has failed to keep an appointment and offended a customer.

I'm horribly tired of the whole botheration and trust it will soon be over.

August 21. Friday night. Letter from great Hurlbert this morning, amounting to very little, and winding up with a well turned expression of pleasure that the imbroglio is settled to everybody's satisfaction. He has evidently made up his mind that it's best for him to let it be finished up and forgotten with all convenient speed. All I hear of him leads me to believe that his moral vision is organically defective, like the retina in color blindness. His miserable habit of taking counsel of women in all his scrapes, instead of advising with men, makes the consequences of this infirmity worse. He has beyond question a strange uncanny snakey power of fascinating silly females, and winning them to reverent unquestioning faith in his infallibility and goodness. They endorse his suggestions and strengthen his convictions. No stronger proof of his power over them can be found than this case presents. Not to speak of his principal victim, or of two of the three ladies whom he puts forward as his allies and advisers, the third in that blessed Pas de seduction (Miss G. to wit) has always passed for

a sensible good hearted old maid, pious after the Unitarian
fashion, abundant in good works, *virtuous* at least, yet
she is perfectly ignorant that she has been the cat'spaw
of a scoundrel and sympathizes deeply with him in his
heroic sorrow that he as principal and she as doorkeeper
failed to corrupt her kinswoman and dearest friend.

Charley has been here this evening and I've adminis-
tered to him a strong dose of counsel. He had proposed
that Miss G. above referred to be not absolutely cut off
from his acquaintance. I tell him that decency and
prudence and the inherent fitness of things require that
she never darken his doors again.

There remained only the dry matters of dropping all
intercourse with Mrs. J., Mrs. P.L. and Miss E.G. and of
liquidating the remnants of Hurlbert's social reputation.
Charley, however, to his cousin's dismay, continued to
show an "inexcusable and almost criminal" weakness
about cutting his wife off from Miss G.'s society, and
the friends had to be reassembled to bolster his faltering
will. A letter was opportunely produced in which the
abandoned Miss G., clearly devoid of all instincts on
which rested "the whole nature of pure women," actually purported to justify Hurlbert's conduct! George,
after reading the letter, had to go out in the bright moonlight and sea breeze to walk it off. Yet even then Charley
begged that his wife be allowed to retain a formal acquaintance! Daniel Messenger, who was evidently the

peacemaker of the group, brought up the suggestion that Miss G. might have been under a misapprehension as to Eleanor's relationship with Hurlbert, that she might have innocently supposed it to be only the exchange of "literary and aesthetic raptures." It was agreed that Miss G. be given one more chance and confronted with the famous letter that had precipitated the whole crisis. If after reading *that*, she did not forever repudiate Hurlbert, they would know how to deal with her. George, still skeptical, nonetheless agreed to act as their ambassador.

I thought that it would do no manner of good, but it was settled I should call on her, and she honored me with an invitation to do so this evening. I was reluctant to shew her this letter, which compromises so deeply the person to whom it was sent and concluded to ask two preliminary questions before shewing it. The questions were: 1. Did you suppose the relations of these parties to be amatory or merely those of warm friendship? 2. If you see evidence that they were of the former type, will you repudiate your friend Hurlbert? I did not get beyond No. 1. The harridan said with the utmost frankness and simplicity that she knew their correspondence was "ardent and passionate." Whereupon I expressed my regret at having trespassed on her time and walked away as fast as possible. The Destinies clearly meant her to keep a genteel establishment in Mercer Street.

The fatal letter which I read this evening for the first

time since the day the explosion was announced to me is even worse than my recollections of it. Any woman who receives such a letter, and puts it quietly away, has little left to lose; the inevitable act of adultery is mere matter of form, and in the case of any other woman than this I should infer that her criminality had been formally consummated already. Then comes her damning duplicity in writing to her two *bawds* in New York to tell Hurlbert *she* "did not doubt him or want her letters returned, it was her Uncle and her Aunt who insisted on their surrender," on the very day she was professing herself penitent and asking her husband's forgiveness. She's past hope I fear, only not quite as bad as this Miss E.G. They must be vagaries of nature, abnormal departures from the law of their sex. It cannot be that our women are becoming unwomanly disloyal and impure.

After this even Charley collapsed and meekly agreed to write Miss G. a sixteen page letter drafted by George informing her that a "total non-intercourse" would be established between the two households and comparing her propositions "in the plainest terms polite language would allow with the commonly received notions about adultery and pimping." Before Charley's letter had even been sent, however, the incurable Miss G. threw her last shred of principle to the winds and defiantly wrote Eleanor to urge her to leave her false life and go back to her true love. No walk in the seabreeze could help

George to get over this one. In a wholesome society, he expostulates, such a woman would be "pilloried in the Park or flogged at the cart's tail." If his diary is Dickensian in its rapturous passages, it can suggest *Hamlet* in its invective:

> No harridan of Church Street ever talked braver pathos to a timid recruit. The woman must be diseased in mind; if she be sane, her vicious effrontery is the most appalling crime that has occurred in the decent strata of society within my time. For she has no passion to palliate her profligacy; she is past the hotblooded period of life, when sheer *lust* might be gratified in some morbid way by peering through keyholes at a progressive intrigue, and when an impure woman might itch to be an accessory to the impurity of others. She is not even a fool like her colleague Mrs. L., but is rather intelligent, old, out of health, and performs her filthy function in cold blood and with her eyes open. Unless she be a monomaniac on the subject of the great Hurlbert and all his doings she is something not adequately to be expressed in polite language. Enough of her.

The ostracization of Hurlbert himself proceeded with more despatch. There was no trouble here with Charley. In fact George was even concerned that his cousin might go too far. He had to dissuade him from writing formally to one Charles Kingsley to enquire if the latter had really *advised* Hurlbert to be such a scoundrel. With people who had never endorsed Hurlbert's misconduct, however, Charley was more discreet. He gave a hint of Hurlbert's unworthiness, without descending to particulars, to Lewis Jones who, in George's opinion, was one of "the strongest and finest grained of our young men." Jones reacted promptly. When Hurlbert next called at his house on 16th Street, he was not admitted and received word from Mrs. Jones that she was acting on her husband's instructions. The unrebuffable Hurlbert called again and insisted on seeing the master of the house to find out on what stories the latter had acted. Jones replied icily that he chose to exercise the privilege of selecting his own and his wife's acquaintance.

The unfortunate Hurlbert now found himself up against a small but tightly knit New York. When he wrote a "charming episotelette" to Mrs. Sally Hampton, asking when he might call to present his homages, it was returned by her husband with a brief note declining all further intercourse and warning him that any attempt to renew the acquaintance would be regarded as a personal affront. George Strong, finding himself buttonholed by James W. Otis in pursuit of knowledge of Hurlbert, enlightened him with "the driest facts, using no epithets and withholding names." The indefatigable diarist was not averse to taking advantage of prejudices that had nothing to do with the case. When John

Church Hamilton, son of Alexander, asked his opinion of Hurlbert and, receiving it, intimated that the latter would be excluded thenceforth from the "Palazzo Hamilton," George confides to his diary that what really incensed Hamilton was the *Times'* criticism of his biography of his father, with which Hurlbert, in actual fact, had had nothing to do. But severest of all was George's attitude to a Mr. and Mrs. Beals, who had continued to receive Hurlbert in spite of the ban. Providence seems to have come to his aid in dealing with these recalcitrants for in October following the summer events Mr. Beals not only developed a fatal illness, but his business was ruined. His wife, in the greatest distress, begged to see her friend Eleanor, but George, inexorable, had "to advise Charley to be hardhearted and to refuse his wife permission to enter any house frequented by Hurlbert."

Hurlbert decided to leave New York; one cannot believe that he had much alternative. He moved to England where George notes sourly that he was much lionized. He was back in New York the following year but only for a visit, and he steered clear of all Strongs. Unhappily, however, his departure did little to promote the reconciliation of Charley and Eleanor. As George had noted, the trouble was basically in his cousin's wife. The marriage held together through the war, but shortly afterwards, in the spring of 1866, Eleanor and Miss Puss went abroad to live, and Charley sold the house on 22nd Street and moved into bachelor quarters. Yet even in Paris, George ruefully notes two years later, Eleanor's sensibility continued to lure her down strange paths:

Charley Strong shewed me this morning, rather ruefully, a letter just received from Madame at Paris, announcing her "reconciliation" to the Roman Catholic Church. Just what has long been predicted. The lady is a strange compound of cleverness and foolishness; she is jaded with French novels; she wants a new sensation, and she has been talked over by experts in the art of conversion, French and English priests, flattered and caressed and wound round their fingers. Her letter is well written, however, and she declares she will scrupulously abstain from influencing dear little Pussy. I don't expect she will take much trouble to do so, of her own volition. But her Spiritual Directors will enjoin it on her as a duty, and Pussy will be somehow manoeuvred into Popedom before she knows it. Much as I like the mamma, and fully as I recognize her brightness and her many good points, I cannot help seeing that in this transaction, as in many other grave transactions of her married life, she has behaved like a goose.

Hurlbert left behind him, at least in the Strong circle, a reputation of evil incarnate. The diary does not become more forgiving as the years ensue. In 1864 he is described as a "coprophagous" insect and as late as 1872 as "a gaudily-colored and fetid bug . . . among the basest of mankind." The villain, Densdeth, in the posthumously published novel, *Cecil Dreeme*, by George's friend Theodore Winthrop, who fell at Big Bethel, was supposedly based on Hurlbert. The hero, while waiting to see if the villain will ensnare him, becomes involved in an emotional friendship with a pale young man who, to the reader's relief, turns out in the end to be the heroine disguised in male garb. She, too, is hiding from Densdeth. Why they are all so afraid of Densdeth and how he obtains his hold over them is obscure. He simply radiates wickedness:

> Presently, as I glanced up and down the table, I caught sight of Densdeth's dark, handsome face. He had turned from his companion, and was looking at me. He lifted his black moustache with a slight sneer . . . "What does it mean," thought I, "this man's strange fascination? When his eyes are upon me, I feel something stir in my heart, saying, 'Be Densdeth's! He knows the mystery of life.' I begin to dread him. Will he master my will? What is this potency of his? How has he got this lodgment in my spirit? Is he one of those fabulous personages who only exist while they are preying upon another soul, who are torpid unless they are busy contriving damnation?"

The half-comic note of the villain of melodrama may give us the ultimate clue to poor Hurlbert. He was certainly more ridiculous than sinister. It is hard to imagine wickedness in a man whose art gallery, according to an 1883 auction catalogue, contained such titles as "Halt of Cavaliers," "The First Dancing Lesson," "The Abbess Detected" and "Toilette of the Odalisque." It is easier to see him as vain, flashy, eager to please and appallingly sentimental, with a kind of florid charm and a gift of always putting his foot in things, which might have been forgiven had he not insisted on explaining his good intentions. To the end he explained, and with increasing shrillness. Small wonder that people found him exasperating. He was imprisoned in Richmond during the war as a suspected Union agent, yet, released, he stumped for McClellan on a campaign of peace at any price. He advocated the cause of royalism in France of the eighteen-seventies and fought home rule in Ireland under a Gladstone government. Yet he was always vivid; it is possible even today to read his angry books. And he was successful. From 1876 to 1883 he was editor-in-chief of the New York *World*.

At the age of fifty-seven Hurlbert drastically altered his life. He resigned from the *World*, married (for the first time) a Miss Katherine Parker Tracy, sold his art collection and moved to London. If, however, he was looking for peace and quiet after the stormy years, he was not to find it. For it was in London, the capital of justice, that he encountered the final wrong from a universe that seemed always to have conspired against him.

In 1891 a woman named Gertrude Ellis, describing herself as an actress and living under the name of Gladys Evelyn, sued him for £10,000, alleging that in 1887 he had seduced her under promise of marriage three weeks after their casual meeting as fellow passengers in a London omnibus. She further alleged that Hurlbert had hidden his true identity under the pseudonym of Wilfred Murray and that she had lost track of him until another chance meeting in a London street when she had followed him to his house. At the trial, which stirred up considerable public feeling against Hurlbert, Mrs. Ellis was unable to produce any witness who had seen her with the defendant except one individual who was proved to have been her lover. She did produce, however, a batch of obscene letters allegedly written by Hurlbert which were impounded by the court. Hurlbert won his case, and the verdict was sustained on appeal, but when he attempted to obtain the letters as a basis for criminal proceedings against Mrs. Ellis, he was met with a curt refusal. It was the court's opinion that the plaintiff should not be exposed to prosecution because of a technical inability to prove her case. There was also the fact that the attorney-general wanted the letters as the basis for a possible prosecution of Hurlbert himself. Hurlbert, however, persisted with his demands until Lord Chief Justice Coleridge himself was obliged to explain the position of the court to the House of Lords. He managed to do so in a way that tarnished even further the defendant's good name:

My Lords, I ought to say that of Mr. Hurlbut personally I know nothing whatever. I never saw him, I never met him, I never read a word of his writing, I am absolutely ignorant of him; whether he is entitled to the description which an illustrious American gave of him, namely that he is a man of fathomless and measureless turpitude, or whether he is a person entitled to the eulogiums which have been passed upon him, and the respect, admiration and intimacy, which have been given to him by persons of very high rank in this country, I neither know nor care.

It is impossible not to speculate on the identity of the "illustrious American." Could he have been one of the thirty to whom the now ancient secret of Newport had been divulged? We know enough of Hurlbert, anyway, to be sure that he would not let this pass. The man who had been so eager to defend his position in 1857 was not one to bow even to the House of Lords in 1893. Old and bitter, he pulled himself together for a final outburst of self-vindication which appeared in the form of a privately printed volume of more than 500 pages entitled *England under Coercion: a Record of Private Rights Outraged and of Public Justice Betrayed by Political Malice for Partisan Ends, set forth as in a letter to the Lord Coleridge, Lord Chief Justice of England.* This remarkable document can be read as the final symptom of a galloping persecution mania, or, theoretically at least, as a statement of the true facts. Reading it, one remembers the long distant scene when the author writhed on the floor before Daniel Messenger. From all its strange ramblings, its curious irrelevancies, its venom and its quaint oratory, the argument emerges that a powerful political conspiracy has been hatched to discredit Hurlbert as the author of a book, published years previously, that was unsympathetic to Irish home rule. Gertrude Ellis and her shabby little suit have become a snare set by the highest officers of the British crown for an American who dared to speak his mind!

> I leave you here arraigned, my Lord [he concludes], as the prime cause and author of such a series of outrages and wrongs perpetrated under the prostituted forms of English law upon me . . . Does the great commission which you hold put you beyond the reach of justice and of the laws and leave you free without responsibility to perpetrate and to promote such outrages and such wrongs under the coercion of political schemes and of partisan passion? Do the laws of England leave absolutely without remedy or redress every British subject and every foreign resident within the realm of England who may suffer at your hands and through you such outrages and wrongs?

The year that his defense was published was the last year of Hurlbert's life. He died in Italy with an English warrant still out against him for perjury in connection with the trial. It seems quite possible that in the end he had run into a real injustice. Many of his friends believed so. But we can doubt if George Strong would ever have been convinced that his "gaudily colored" bug was not the guilty party of Evelyn *v.* Hurlbert. We are denied his opinion, however, for the diarist had died long before, in 1875. His cousin, Charley, respected and admired, an eminent leader of the bar, survived his old rival, dying in his house at 16 Fifth Avenue in 1897. Eleanor Strong, despite a diagnosis of "incurable tumors" as early as 1870, lived into this century. The New York Social Register records her death in Florence in 1903.

A Reader's Guide to

the Fiction of Henry James

In APPROACHING the great prolific novelists of the last century, it is usually safe for the uninitiated reader to start at the top, with *Vanity Fair* for Thackeray or *David Copperfield* for Dickens. But nobody should try to begin Henry James with *The Golden Bowl*. And if the beginner should happen to start with *The Awkward Age* and to follow it with *The Sacred Fount*, he might well be conditioned for life to finding nothing but snobbishness and triviality in any of the other works. It is better to face at the outset that there will always be a certain number of people to agree with Theodore Roosevelt's dictum that James's "polished, pointless, uninteresting stories about the upper social classes of England make one blush to think that he was once an American." It is not, however, necessary to turn, instead, as Roosevelt did, to the "fresh, healthy, out-of-doors life" of

Kipling. One can learn, with a little application, to isolate the dross in James, and after that *The Jungle Book* is no substitute. Once the reader has been acclimatized to the different Jamesian styles, once he has felt the intensity of that devotion to his aesthetic ideal, he can be safely exposed even to such dreary minor pieces as *Glasses* or *Fordham Castle*. Who knows? He may even like them. For by that time he will be a Jacobite, and the true Jacobite can delight in any prose of the master.

James himself was once consulted on the order in which he should be read. In 1913 he made two reading lists for Stark Young, "the delightful young man from Texas." But he omitted the short stories (the "little tarts" could wait until after the "beef and potatoes"), and he insisted (contrary to the advice of many of his critics) on being read in the revised edition. Each of his suggested reading lists contains only five titles, the first: *Roderick Hudson, The Portrait of a Lady, The Princess Casamassima, The Wings of the Dove, The Golden Bowl,* and the second: *The American, The Tragic Muse, The Wings of the Dove, The Ambassadors, The Golden Bowl.* Both lists have in common with this piece the goal of bringing the new reader as rapidly as possible to what E. M. Forster calls the "valuable and exquisite sensations" of the final novels. But it seems to me that the recommended steps are too short and that *Roderick Hudson* is an actual stumbling block. That James was not the best judge of his own earlier work is shown by his omission of *Washington Square* and *The Bostonians* from the revised edition. My purpose is to present a somewhat more comprehensive list for the beginner, and with this in mind I have divided James's writing life into five periods: beginnings, 1866–1880; the "Balzac" period, 1880–1890; experiments with the theatre, 1890–1895; the "bad" period, 1895–1901, and the final greatness, 1901–1911.

First (1866–1880). This initial period opens with a great clump of short stories reminiscent in style and treatment of Hawthorne. They are well organized and smoothly written, but they incline at once to the prolix and melodramatic. There is little in them to distinguish James from other young American writers of the period, full of Europe after a first grand tour. The reader, like one of the characters, may feel himself an innocent American, visiting a *pension* on his first trip abroad and speculating on the history of the old lady in black who never speaks to anybody, or of the mysterious professor, or of the guileless ingenue, or of her formidable mother who may have designs on a stout young fellow like himself. For the point of view from which these tales are told is not that of the subtle, shadowy, dedicated, keyhole listener of later periods (*The Sacred Fount*), but of the stalwart Harvard man with a bit more than a gentleman's interest in old churches and pictures — yet very much the gentleman for all that — who likes his pipe and his wine and his club and who occasionally steps out of the role of narrator to direct the action himself. "I drew her arm into mine, and before the envious eyes that watched us from gilded casements we passed through the gallery and left the palace." The James of the second period begins to emerge in *The American* and *The Europeans* and comes out altogether in that exquisite little novel, *Washington Square*, where in the ordered stillness of a mid-Victorian New York a girl's happiness is snuffed out by a father who has the vice of being always right.

Second (1880–1890). This I have called the "Balzac" period. James may have felt in this decade that he had settled on the kind of novel that he would write for the rest of his life: the three-volume Balzacian compendium of diverse characters plotted around a contemporary social problem. To many readers this is his finest period. Surely it is hard to pick and choose among such novels as *The Portrait of a Lady* (the conflict between Americans soiled and Americans unsoiled by a dark, beautiful, ancient Europe); *The Bostonians* (the cause of women's suffrage as an arena for sex antagonism); *The Princess Casamassima* (the danger that world revolution may destroy more than it brings), and *The Tragic Muse* (the question of art as a substitute for a political career). The style of these novels is of a dazzling virtuosity; there are passages in *The Portrait of a Lady* and *The Bostonians* as beautiful as any prose James ever wrote. Had he died in his middle forties instead of seventies, he would still be regarded as a master of American fiction. It must, also, have been a period of happiness; I am sure he had a deep satisfaction in feeling his feet on sure ground and seeing ahead the long straight road of a dozen or more novels dealing with the rich themes of the impact of art and socialism and Americans on an established Victorian social order. There is an exuberance in the very speed with which the novels were written; *The Bostonians* and *The Princess Casamassima* appeared in the same year. Yet none of them attained the success of *Daisy Miller*, and James cared about success. How could he not have? He lived in a society which considered it all-important, and he lacked the substitutes of a profession, a family or a fortune. The inner buoyancy of knowing that he had written such a book as *Portrait of a Lady* was not enough. He turned, like so many others then and now, to the theatre, to try to master its trick and achieve the fame that he craved. Perhaps had he been less sure that it was a trick, he would have succeeded better.

Third (1890–1895). This is the period of dramatic experiment, ending with the famous booing of the author at the opening of *Guy Domville*. James to his dying day insisted that he owed a great debt to the theatre, that out of the wreck of his experiments he saved a sense of the dramatic that was to be invaluable in the construction of the later novels. Knowing how desperately authors hate to think of any writing efforts as wasted, I allow myself to doubt this. The dramatic in James's plays (such as it is) strikes me as having very little to do with the dramatic in the later novels. The only thing remarkable to me about James's plays is that any were produced at all. They read like thin, wordy parodies of his poorest fiction and are pervaded with a repellent heartlessness. The bad writing of a professional is like that of an amateur. Bits and pieces of his personality keep showing like slips under a skirt. One of the reasons we are so apt to feel that we could be friends with great authors is that their expert prose covers the smaller side of their natures. James's plays should be concealed at all cost from the would-be Jacobite. He wrote no novels in this period, but he kept his fictional hand at work with a series of perfect short stories, including "The Death of the Lion" and "Greville Fane," written in a clear, finished style that lacks the verbosity of his first period and the involutions of his last. Perhaps these stories also lack some of the warmth and color of the prose of his *Portrait of a Lady* period; there is a certain thinness of material and a growing preoccupation with the fantastic and supernatural. But if there are less high points in this period, there are no low ones. The beginner may roam at will from "The Lesson of the Master" to "The Altar of the Dead."

Fourth (1895–1901). This is what I call the "bad" period, to be avoided almost entirely until the reader is a converted Jacobite. Biographically it is interesting, for it reveals a James struggling to pull out of the disappointment of his failure as a dramatist and popular novelist and to achieve his own unique medium. But such a struggle was bound to be saturated with the bitterness that had caused it, and some of this bitterness creeps into his work, giving it a peculiar shrillness, even, at times, a silliness. There is a triviality in the themes that no amount of good writing can succeed in making important. Peeping behind the curtain of art at the author's small resentments, we glimpse the diner-out who is obsessed with the decline of manners in London high life, the aesthete who prefers houses and ornaments to people, the prude who is shocked by sex. Of course, all of these attitudes can be found in the earlier and in the later work: Hyacinth Robinson in *The Princess Casamassima* (1886) gives up his plans for world revolution because it might muddy the translucent waters of the aristocratic way of life, the contemplation of which must be the eternal solace of the poor, and *A Round of Visits* (1910) transfers the author's high-pitched anger at London hostesses to those of New York. But it is in this "bad" period that these attitudes seem most, as James himself would put it, to "bristle." It is the period of the damp, crushed spinster heroines, of Fleda Vetch and the telegraph girl of *In the Cage*, who live to observe and observe to live, who can never quite handle the overwhelming, suffocating vulgarity that surrounds them. Like Maisie, they know everything, but their comfort is in renunciation, a renunciation that smacks of a disdain to participate.

Too many Jacobites have tried to explain away the

silliness of this period by reading other things into it. I think it is better to face it directly like the audiences of *The High Bid* (James's dramatization of *Covering End*) who burst into applause, to the dismay of the author, when Captain Yule cried out: "I see something else in the world than the beauty of old show-houses and the glory of old show-families. There are thousands of people in England who can show no houses *at all*, and I don't feel it utterly shameful to share their poor fate!"

The best writing of this period is in *The Spoils of Poynton* which prefigures James's ultimate style, but the masterpiece is "The Turn of the Screw." Perhaps one of the reasons for its success is that James never tells us explicitly of what the "evil" consists. If it is simply that Quilt and Miss Jessel have an affair which has not been concealed from the children, I feel that the author has taken advantage, however skillfully, of my propensity to panic.

Fifth (1902–1911). Quite suddenly we emerge from the timber into the high, golden light of the final period and meet in dazzling succession the three last novels, *The Wings of the Dove*, *The Ambassadors* and *The Golden Bowl*. These have created for James the special niche in the history of literature that was the objective of a lifetime of devoted work. Gone now is the shrill anger at bad manners and sexual irregularity. A benign wisdom pervades the atmosphere. The evil in

The Wings of the Dove is not in the affair between Kate Croy and Merton Densher; it is in their concealment of it from an ailing girl whose money they want. When Densher pounds the streets of a storm-swept Venice while Milly Theale faces a lonely death in her palazzo, we know, as nowhere in the earlier James, the agony of remorse. And in *The Ambassadors* when Strether at last discovers what everyone else has always known, that Chad Newsome is living with Madame de Vionnet, that he is enjoying the common-or-garden love affair with the older married woman that is the conventional oat-sowing of the rich young American before his return to the family business, there is no implication that Chad is "evil." It has simply been Strether's naïveté that has made him see another relationship in the affair. But this very naïveté, stripped of James's earlier bitterness and radiant with a new perception, is what lifts Strether above Chad and his mistress. As E. M. Forster puts it: "The Paris they revealed to him — he could reveal it to them now, if they had eyes to see, for it is something finer than they could ever notice for themselves, and his imagination has more spiritual value than their youth."

The themes of the three great novels are worthy of the prose which develops them. There is nothing trivial in Kate Croy's conspiracy to have her lover inherit Milly's money, or in Maggie Verver's efforts to save her own and her father's marriages. But the greatest theme of all is that of *The Ambassadors:* the self-reeducation of an elderly man who is not afraid to make the count of all that he has missed in life. There is none of the contrived aspect of some of James's fictional *données,* yet the plot is the most neatly balanced of all the novels. W. D. Howells' exhortation to the young man in Whistler's garden to live life to the fullest and not to waste his youth was the seed from which the masterpiece sprang. The subject was right; the style was ready, and *The Ambassadors* was written with a confident speed. To me it is the perfect novel.

The remaining stories, except for "The Jolly Corner," represent a falling off to be expected in old age. The subject matter is trivial again, the style even more elaborate. One senses the aging master, sure now of a small but devoted following who will wait indefinitely for the *mot juste;* we can almost hear the prefatory cough, the chuckle as it is finally produced and dangled before their gleaming eyes. But we must not expect the moon. The master had already given us his best.

Like James himself I would submit two lists to the "delightful young man from Texas" of today. My first I believe to be foolproof, but it is a bit long, involving nine steps and a variety of alternatives:

1. *The American,* or *Washington Square,* or "The Aspern Papers," or *Daisy Miller* and *The Europeans.*

2. *The Portrait of a Lady*
3. *The Bostonians,* or *The Tragic Muse*
4. Any two of the following short stories: "The Lesson of the Master," "The Death of the Lion," "Greville Fane," "The Abasement of the Northmores," "The Real Thing," "The Liar," "The Altar of the Dead."
5. "The Turn of the Screw," or *The Spoils of Poynton*
6. "The Beast in the Jungle," or "The Jolly Corner"
7. *The Ambassadors*
8. *The Wings of the Dove*
9. *The Golden Bowl*

My second is less sure, but it is for those with less time for fiction:

1. *Washington Square*
2. *The Portrait of a Lady*
3. "The Aspern Papers"
4. "The Turn of the Screw"
5. *The Ambassadors*
6. *The Wings of the Dove*

It would be preferable to add some of the short stories to the second list, but time, I know, is precious. One shudders to consider what James, who found his own era too full of noise and distraction, would have thought of ours. Except one should remember that he loved the typewriter and the automobile. He might have loved the jet plane. It is interesting to ponder the fate of Daisy Miller in a Rome only a few hours by air from Schenectady.

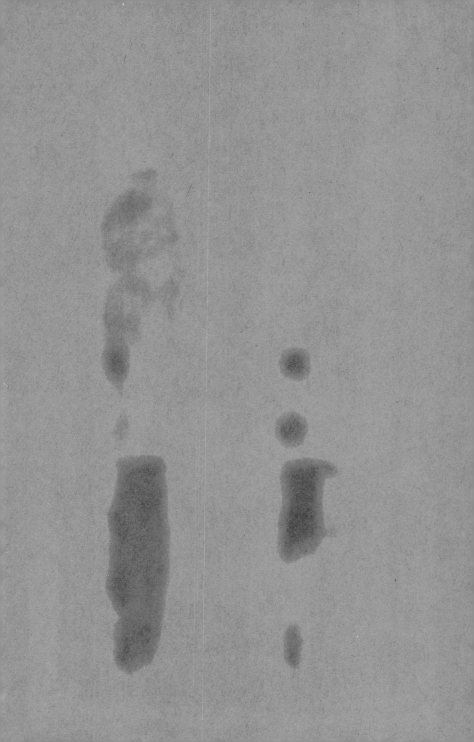